DEATH BY NOIR

DEATH BY NOIR

OLLY SMITH

BASKERVILLE
An imprint of JOHN MURRAY

First published in Great Britain in 2026 by Baskerville
An imprint of John Murray (Publishers)

1

A CIP catalogue record for this title is available from the British Library

Hardback ISBN 9781399829847
Trade Paperback ISBN 9781399829854
ebook ISBN 9781399829861

Typeset in Bembo by Hewer Text UK Ltd, Edinburgh
Printed and bound in Great Britain by Clays Ltd, Elcograf S.p.A.

John Murray policy is to use papers that are natural, renewable and recyclable products and made from wood grown in sustainable forests. The logging and manufacturing processes are expected to conform to the environmental regulations of the country of origin.

Carmelite House
50 Victoria Embankment
London EC4Y 0DZ

www.johnmurraypress.co.uk

John Murray Press, part of Hodder & Stoughton Limited
An Hachette UK company

The authorised representative in the EEA is Hachette Ireland, 8 Castlecourt Centre, Dublin 15, D15 XTP3, Ireland (email: info@hbgi.ie)

My words will soar, O Lord of the Wine Press
And they will not die; I am drinking deep,
Taking the risk, binding my bow with vine shoots.

Horace, *Odes* 3.25, translation Harry Eyres

For Rachel

Preface

Lewes is a place where much of my life has been based. In case you're not familiar with this quintessentially English county town, it's pronounced *Lewis* rather than *Loos* and is fiercely proud of its independent spirit. In this book most of the places mentioned are real with a few notable exceptions: there is no ancient apothecary that I'm aware of on Priory Street and the site of the Bottle Bank wine shop is entirely fictitious. The vineyard at Dandelion Hill also only exists in the pages of this book, though in my mind it is situated just beyond the old racecourse outside Lewes on the way to the trigonometry point of Black Cap, which lies on an ancient path that I've walked for years with my dog Busby. I should additionally make it clear that, winemakers excepted, none of the characters in this story have any basis in fact and all the bonfire societies found in these pages are entirely fictional.

Every single wine mentioned in this book (with the exception of those made at Dandelion Hill) are bottles that have inspired me made by winemakers whose skills I have adored for many years. Here's to them, to you and the wonder of wine.

Olly Smith, March 2025

Old Sussex Words

a monkey's birthday	when the sun is shining and it is also raining
avised	certain
bannicking	beating
bruff	rough
flittermouse	bat
gummut	lout
We wunt be druv	We will not be driven; the unofficial motto of Sussex, reflecting a strong sense of self-belief
maunder	grumble
mizmaze	confusion
moil	trouble
mucked-up	in a mess
nidget	insect
picksome	dainty
poppling	bubbling
rafty	hard to manage
runagate	good for nothing
sarment	sermon
Snuffy	nickname for a grumpy person
twitten	passageway between streets, buildings and courtyards

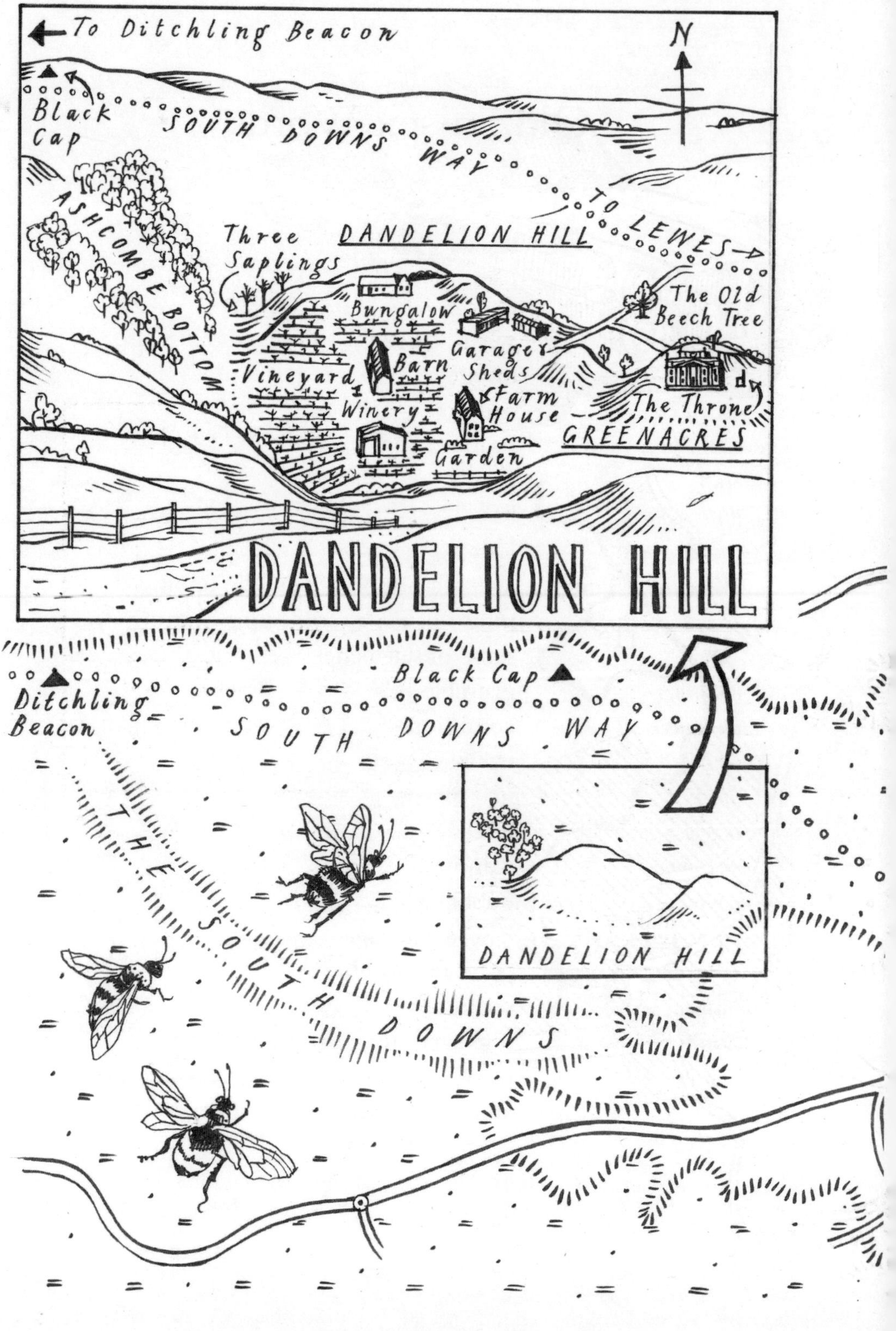
To Ditchling Beacon
N
Black Cap
SOUTH DOWNS WAY
TO LEWES
ASHCOMBE BOTTOM
Three Saplings
DANDELION HILL
Bungalow
The Old Beech Tree
Garage
Sheds
Barn
Vineyard
Winery
Farm House
The Throne
GREENACRES
Garden
DANDELION HILL
Black Cap
Ditchling Beacon
SOUTH DOWNS WAY
THE SOUTH DOWNS
DANDELION HILL

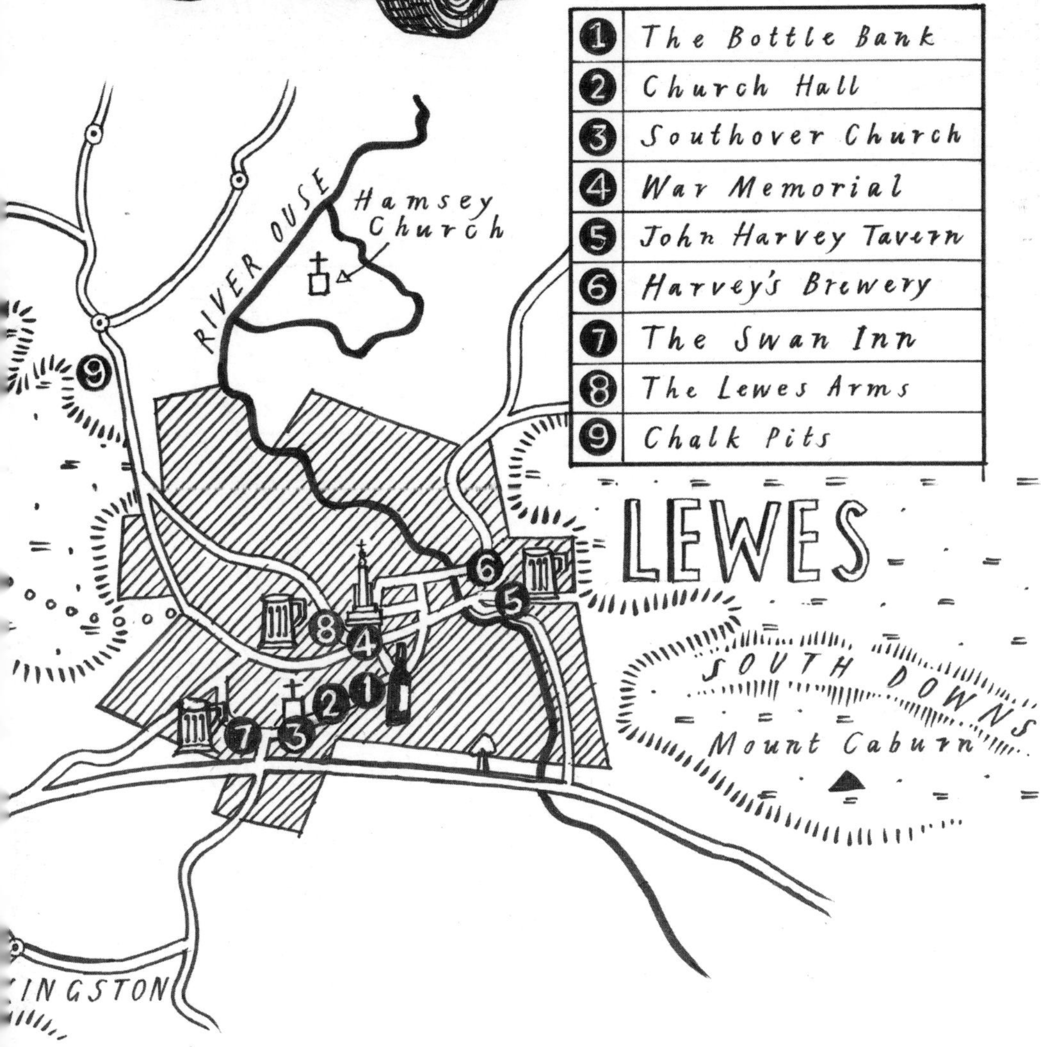
1 The Bottle Bank
2 Church Hall
3 Southover Church
4 War Memorial
5 John Harvey Tavern
6 Harvey's Brewery
7 The Swan Inn
8 The Lewes Arms
9 Chalk Pits
LEWES
RIVER OUSE
Hamsey Church
SOUTH DOWNS
Mount Caburn
INGSTON

1

Under the green scoops and chalk pits of England's South Downs, the little town of Lewes folds into the softness of an ancient Sussex landscape. A living pocket of mysteries surrounded by local vineyards, the flint terraces and cosy pubs are not as they seem. On November 5th, some weeks from now, Bonfire Night will blow this place apart. The townsfolk will take to the streets in a nighttime parade of masked costumes, burning crosses and giant effigies detonated beneath fireworks loud enough to make the Greenwich Meridian tremble towards London. Each bonfire society's darkest secret is the hidden location of their cache of explosives and huge statues tucked behind barn doors and farm gates across the local hills. Lewesians take great pride in who knows what. And some know a great deal more than others.

From an open window above the Victorian stained-glass door of the Bottle Bank wine shop, the jovial sound of humming is cascading into Priory Street below. Rooks are squabbling over the roof and on the doorstep, a bottle of white wine with no label is glimmering in a dewy late summer sunbeam. The sound of a handclap sends the rooks on the roof scattering as Barclay Flint stares delightedly at himself in his shaving mirror. 'The Library of Libations,' he murmurs, rolling the words around his palate as a connoisseur would revel in a glass of rare champagne. The last creamy ridge of soap from the morning shave is resting on his neck like ermine round a kingly robe. Barclay is proud of his smooth, radiant and stout demeanour. Although in his mid-fifties, he likes to think of his appearance as 'youthful poet' and tells himself that a purple paisley silk dressing gown is very similar to a glass of wine – all about the detail. Wiping the last foam from his neck, he briskly pom-poms his way to the door of his bijou flat, his robe billowing in his wake. 'Minty!' he sings out, before realising that Minty is already halfway down the hall stairs wrapped in her large vibrant-green cardigan. Minty slowly turns and addresses him.

'Nineteen fifty-two it was when I left Antigua; did I know where I was coming?'

'It would be rude of me to presume.'

'This riddle of a place. The thing I learnt quick? When someone such as Barclay Flint starts singing before breakfast time, trouble's coming.'

'Do you know, Minty, I could swear you look five years younger this morning.'

'Hold your smooth talking; spit it out, man.'

'New name for the shop: the Library of Libations.'

Minty takes a breath and tightens her grip on a bag of bird seed.

'The pigeons need feeding, you've had a sherry for breakfast and the shop's already got a perfectly decent name.'

Stomping down the stairs, Barclay calls after her: 'I only had one glass. Manzanilla. And it was as cool and crisp as a salty snowball!'

Downstairs, Minty opens the Bottle Bank's elegant Victorian stained-glass front door and retrieves the unlabelled bottle of white wine from the doorstep. Carefully placing it inside on the counter strewn with empty wine bottles and a nearly finished jigsaw of Eric Ravilious' *Wilmington Giant*, she shakes her head at the mess. Wrapping her scarf around her neck, Minty Jarvis steps out in search of advice to give and feathered friends to nourish.

As lights flicker on in the shop with a glimmering twinkle, Barclay's breaking wave of hair frames his head like a halo of possibilities. Perfectly unkempt, this buoyant soul always strives to give the air of someone about to bob up through the very sky of the best mood possible. As he proudly surveys the regiments of bottles on the shelves, Barclay delights in the reflection of his own merry ways; enchanted by puzzles, unmoved by trends and a prodigious scribbler of notes meticulously tied around the neck of each bottle. He takes deep pride in these enticing descriptions, and this morning he's over in the South African section casually reading aloud from his own handwriting, '"A peach rolling down a sunbeam" . . . Ah, wine! You are truly my muse.'

Spotting the blank bottle of white wine on the counter, Barclay's brow momentarily flutters with quizzical consideration. *Hello stranger*, he thinks before munching on a pre-breakfast biscuit and turning his gaze to the unfinished jigsaw. His right hand connecting with the record player next to the till, he barely looks at the needle as music's answer to slow-motion giggling crackles across the shop; Bert Kaempfert's 'Bye Bye Blues' is one of Barclay's favourite tunes to solve puzzles to.

Pinot, a keen-eyed Border collie with a heart set permanently on where the next snack is coming from, bounds through the door.

'Morning salutations my dearest friend,' croons Barclay as he tosses the last nibble of his biscuit over to Pinot, who snaffles it faster than even she could comprehend. 'Aah, she does love me, we understand one another, don't we, Pinot?'

'She understands that you always feed her,' corrects Pearl Finch, clocking into her managerial shift.

In her mid-twenties, Pearl's been working with Barclay for several years and in Barclay's eyes is a Hollywood starlet bathed in the glow of resigned idealism. Pearl, on the other hand, sees Barclay as a fantasist pretending to be real. Though she admits a cool respect for Barclay's knowledge, Pearl rarely acknowledges even to herself that she deeply admires his determination to match the perfect bottle of wine with every person who enters the Bottle Bank.

'I only feed her my very best thoughts,' insists Barclay.

'Whatevs,' snorts Pearl, straightening her broadly striped yellow and black woolly jumper, which resembles a recalcitrant bee that's been stretched through a hoover. 'Made a new sign for the counter,' she says, holding up a tiny protest placard that says USE LESS PAPER. 'And I'm adding the weight of every bottle to the tasting notes today; don't be buying heavy bottles, Barclay. You know what it means for the carbon footprint.'

'With you all the way, Pearl.' Barclay attempts a good-natured salute, but it peters out as a stroke of an eyebrow while he recoils under Pearl's unmoved stare. Getting to work at once, Pearl starts stacking the bottles from the counter into the recycling bin and writing bottle weights on the labels of Barclay's specially curated Hot Bottle section on the shelf behind the counter.

'"Inky as a hippo dipped in Shakespeare"? What does that even mean?' asks Pearl, exasperatedly reading from one of Barclay's handwritten labels.

'Oh, you know, thick-skinned, powerful, complex . . . it's decent, that Cabernet, and from Moldova – how boundless is wine, Pearl, Moldova!' says Barclay putting the last piece of his jigsaw in place. '*Ta-daaa*. Right, on to matters of great importance, this mystery sample. Who's it from?'

'Not seen it, this one?' Pearl points to the unlabelled bottle of white wine from the shop's front step.

'That's the badger, no note, no label and perhaps . . .'

'. . . Laced with poison?' jokes Pearl.

'Nonsense, perhaps this season's first fruit though, looks paler than a moonbeam through a gooseberry,' remarks Barclay as he uncorks and pours two tidy glasses. 'Hmm, lime-gold flecks swirling like liquid jewellery around the glass . . .' Inhaling deeply, his eyes widen sharply. 'Lychees on a pogo stick!' he exclaims before taking a large swig from his glass.

Pearl rolls her eyes as Barclay considers the mouthful. A wave of silence moves through the shop as though his entire being is the portal through which wine becomes alive while the man himself disappears.

Barclay stares at Pearl. She sighs. 'So come on, Barclay, what does the self-proclaimed GOAT of wine tasting make of this mystery bottle?'

Barclay looks up at her with a half-smile, taking a shallow breath before clutching his heart, staggering three paces to his left, falling to his knees, his eyes pleading as his body slumps to the floor with the jigsaw pieces tumbling after him and Pinot giving his cheek a concerned lick.

Pearl lets the silence soak a while. 'Ha ha, yes, very funny, Barclay. You clown, up you get,' she says, sniffing her glass before glancing at it mistrustfully and placing it back on the counter. Standing over Barclay, she peers at his twitching feet, concern mounting, before crouching over him, panic rising.

At that moment county moth recorder and delivery driver for the Bottle Bank, thirty-year-old Teddy Olsen, trips over the doorstep of the wine shop, nearly sending his laptop and book bundle flying before regaining his lanky balance and announcing, 'Ten points to me, for not falling over, further ten points for arriving exactly on time for a Barclay breakfast.'

He notices Barclay prone on the floor as the record plays the final phrase of 'Bye Bye Blues'. 'Alright, Pearl, you killed the boss?'

2

Dandelion Hill is England's most secluded vineyard. A couple of miles from Lewes, hidden from view in a valley ringed by the burly shoulders of three high ridges in the South Downs, its principal visitors are the wildlife drawn to the cover crops of clover, extensive tree planting throughout the vineyard and lack of all chemical sprays.

People rarely visit, unless by strict appointment with Victor Crawshaw, a human volcano under whose long stewardship it became regenerative several years ago. Approaching his eighties, Victor has lived in deep Downland countryside his entire life and is one of the last survivors whose speech is still dotted with old Sussex words. He misses the days when the ancient sayings were more commonplace – when *doddlish* meant 'infirm', *boffle* was a mistake or cock-up, and *mizmaze* was used instead of 'confusion'. In addition, Victor's mental tombola of hot-headed opinions has always made life tricky for his grown-up children, Tabitha and Harold, who live in a state of semi-cordial armistice on opposite sides of the farm – Tabitha in the main house with her father, Harold in a drab 1950s bungalow.

As Tabitha likes to remind her dad, '. . . feuds with local landowners, rows with restaurateurs, too many business partners called uncle something . . .'

'I veto people,' Victor would retort.

In the eyes of Tabitha and Harold, all Victor delights in these days is watching his runner ducks on patrol for slugs and spending his evenings hoping for the first residents to appear in his bat boxes. Where once his skill at creating wine had brought him tantalising pleasure, as the years hunted him down so he'd grown resentful of one too many harvests blighted by frost, battered by hail or smothered with grey rot.

But this year Victor's last hope remains a faint glimmer; to create a wine so sublime that with one sip it could convert the mood of a morgue into the glorious abandon of a Roman bacchanalia. Alchemy for the mind, as he thought of it. Or maybe a last hurrah.

Tabitha and Harold have been alarmed by the slow-down in wine production since the farm became more of a rewilding hobby for their imposing father; in fact, the one thing Tabitha and Harold can agree on is their mutual concern for the diminishing state of the family finances. If they are unable to repay the bank's latest loan by next March, the farm will be repossessed. Victor's insouciance regarding this predicament is gnawing at them both.

Relentlessly pitching their own visions for how the farm should best survive, each one is utterly convinced that the other is wrong. With stalemate rubbing everyone up the wrong way, wildfires have been smouldering through the Crawshaw family mood. And while no one really knows how to quell these latent blazes, one of the few things that distracts the awkward clan from their mutual disdain is the old barn steadily filling with paraphernalia for Priory Bonfire Society's parade on November 5th – the clandestine amassing of explosives the one last thread holding them together.

Shuffling out of a dark crack between the imposing winery doors and leaning on his stick, Victor Crawshaw squints up accusingly at the sky. Tabitha strides towards him across the dusty yard; Victor feels his momentary surge of hope smothered.

What have I done to deserve these children? he asks himself. They are always chattering about finances, entirely missing the point of life beyond people, filling the steady silence of nature with prattle; Victor feels exhausted by the very thought. *Ducks*, he thinks. *Why can't people be more like ducks?*

Tabitha hasn't uttered a word yet, but she knows her father is in no mood for a genial chat.

'Looks like the rain might hold off, Dad,' suggests Tabitha in as neutral a tone as she can muster.

'It's a monkey's birthday, pissing down by noon,' barks Victor as he tries to build up speed on his stick and stride past. At his age, however, acceleration has faded with a sense of inevitable surrender, so he turns and faces Tabitha, barely disguising his sigh of glowering disdain.

'I want to talk to you about my idea for the wedding venue, Dad – I'm totally convinced it can save the farm. I've run the numbers and—' Before Tabitha can finish, Victor raises his hand and gestures over her shoulder.

'Old Snuffy's at it again.'

High on the Downs behind the farm, on the boundary where Dandelion Hill gives way to neighbouring property, Maurice Le Brocq stands with the casual aggression of a veteran general considering whether to invade. Robed in a dark waxed cotton cape, his lean frame of seventy-odd years is powerful and somehow taunting in its cocky alertness.

A sly grin moves over his face as he peers through his binoculars down at Victor seething outside the winery. Murmuring to himself, Maurice turns away and continues his walk up the hill. 'Only a matter of time, dear Victor, before you pop like one of your wet corks, and then . . .'

Down the hill, Victor growls, 'Gummut only does it to boil my bladder. Look at him, trespassing right over my furlong.'

Tabitha rolls her eyes at her father's use of the old Sussex word for lout and prepares herself for yet another rant about the transgressions of Maurice Le Brocq. Meanwhile, inside the winery at Dandelion Hill, the fermenting vats of freshly harvested Pinot Noir are just starting to bubble. The skins of the grapes rise to the surface in a magenta lattice of foaming tissue. Fermentation does not care about family feuds, about border disputes or long-held grudges. It moves forward with its own inevitability.

Outside the winery, Harold in a worn Barbour jacket is stalking over to his father and sister, like an uptight giraffe after years of square-bashing in the army.

Tabitha can barely contain her frustration as Harold's lips purse and he starts ejecting sentences from his face like strips of rag.

'Father, we know that there's a market in people carking it, happens every day, the country's running out of graveyard sites, and that exposed slope up the hill towards Le Brocq's place is about as much use for vines as a ball of chalk, but utterly ripe for a natural burial ground, think how regenerative it would be, the trees, pollinators—'

'Mourners,' interrupts Tabitha.

'Oh Foxtrot Oscar, would you . . .' Harold scowls at her.

Victor discerns the first surge of real pleasure he's felt all day. Somehow when his children fight, it distracts them from pitching him their relentless ideas for making money and he can slip away undetected to poke around one of the ponds for signs of life. He reflects for a moment, with gratitude, that a certain Barclay Flint persuaded him to lead Dandelion Hill into rewilding and regeneration. Victor muses that Barclay is one of the few people he can still tolerate in small doses, tentatively united by their mutual love of wine. He must give Barclay a call.

From the top of the hill, Maurice Le Brocq peers down one last time at the squabbling family below before he smirks and strides back towards his own grounds, satisfied by the knowledge that Dandelion Hill is falling further into ruin.

Soon, he believes, it will all be his.

3

Pearl is peering into Barclay's eyes when she detects a spark of life. Just then, Barclay sits bolt upright with a large intake of breath breaking into a broad grin.

'It's as though someone drew a chalk wand across a tropical garland and somehow made it into wine. Good to be back!'

'Barclay! This behaviour is not OK!' Pearl glowers.

Barclay leaps to his feet, retrieving spilt jigsaw pieces from all corners. Pearl leans in, demanding an explanation.

'Barclay, you just fricking collapsed, what even was that?'

'It's as though so much power passed through my circuits all at once, the whole system shut down,' says Barclay, reverently. 'That wine is truly something else; I shall require a stiff breakfast and several laps of the shop before I even begin to start collating my notes. The riddle of what bottle it could be is made even more succulent by the mystery of who dared send it – and I, Barclay Flint, will solve both these peculiar conundrums before this day is done.'

A sunbeam caught in the shop's front window illuminates Barclay, as if anointing him with cosmic powers.

'But first – and this really is critical – I will design the ultimate nibble to pair with this anonymous wine of mystery and might. To the kitchen!' he roars, followed by Pinot trotting behind, optimistic at the sound of 'nibble'.

Pearl exchanges glances with Teddy before shaking her head and slowly following Barclay into the shop's kitchenette.

Teddy shrugs. 'Guess it's breakfast time, then.' And he shuffles after them, uneasy about where else this day might lead.

And, not for the first time in his life, Teddy Olsen is quite right to feel afraid of things to come. Life explodes. Teddy sees it every year on Bonfire Night in Lewes. November 5th is a clockwork eruption of secrets. For weeks in advance the town is shrouded with the furtive preparations of every bonfire society; to Teddy, it feels as though the place is having an affair with itself, and he never quite knows who to trust. Crafting secret effigies, making crosses to burn, threading time into costumes of elaborate conception, the societies lurk behind every closed door and shuttered window, silently prepping in the low autumn light. With fierce competition over accuracy and detail, troupes of Vikings, soldiers from the English Civil War, Tudors, Ladies and Lords as well as Victorians are all preparing for their procession amid the building sparks of popping firecrackers and a scene of showering sinister red confetti. *It's a wonder*, reflects Teddy, *that there's not been a death in so very long*.

But for most townsfolk of old Lewes, no matter how calmly the slow-flowing River Ouse glides through the rounded crests of the South Downs, allegiance to a bonfire society is a torrent that runs more fiercely than any religion. Looming larger than your favourite sports team, reaching more deeply than the family you are born into, allegiance to your bonfire society holds you to account more strictly than a bailiff on the day of debt collection.

There are seven Lewesian bonfire societies: Coombe, Pells, Grange, Wallands, Cleve, Malling and Teddy's beloved Priory. The one thing they all share is a cultish passion for setting fire to giant effigies every year on November 5th. For Teddy, the costumed procession of combined societies is a flaming

English Mardi Gras that makes something of a radiant contrast from his day job distributing wine for the Bottle Bank. And it's the closest that Teddy – the first to admit he's not the most rowdy – has ever come to attending an actual festival. Teddy is swelling with pride at taking over as delivery driver for the Priory Bonfire Society this year. While it isn't quite the full promotion to effigy building he was hoping for, it all feels one step closer. With the sound of exploding 'rookies' (Teddy loves telling visitors it's what the locals call bangers) peppering the ancient streets on Bonfire Night, Teddy adores the historic atmosphere of the torch-lit parade. Leaving behind electricity, traffic and his daily routine, the procession flirts with the fringes of legality, the police reduced to watching and praying that the whole town doesn't ignite in a fire-fuelled rampage.

Bonfire Night is enjoyed by the considerable crowds stuffed into the streets of Lewes as the biggest party of the year. But to Teddy, the parade makes him proud to be an independent-minded Lewesian basing his life in principled consideration. At heart, Teddy knows there are grave and serious matters of safety to consider when blowing things up. He remembers the first time he drove his fellow Priory Bonfire crew joking and laughing on the rickety road to Dandelion Hill in the Bottle Bank delivery van, he was preoccupied with an inexplicable feeling of dread about the build-up to this year's parade.

'Left here. Cheer up, Olsen, moth got your tongue?' jousted Elsie Sharpe, the thick-set most senior member of the crew. Shrugging off the laugh from the cohort cramped into the van, Teddy focused on the road.

'Ever bother any of you that we blow people up?' he ventured.

'You got a stone in your head?' shot back one of the crew from the back.

'Blowing stuff up is what it means to be Priory, Teddy – and they're not people anyway. Go right down this lane,' Sharpe said with a dismissive frown.

'Yeah, just dummies,' echoed a voice.

'Our dummy's a total diva this year . . .' goaded Sharpe to the crew.

Teddy perked up, itching to know the identity of this year's effigy.

'Who? A billionaire? No, wait, an Avenger?' Teddy asked. The van fell silent.

'What have the ruddy Avengers got to do with divas?' mocked Sharpe, giving Teddy a playful smack over the head.

'Last few movies are total pants, since Iron Man died the whole thing's collapsed – I wrote a sequel with AI bringing Tony Stark back to life through a temporal portal . . .'

'Park over there, Time Lord,' scorned Elsie.

'Temporal portal,' mimicked another voice.

'Ah, forget it, I'll stick to moths,' exhaled Teddy as the van pulled up outside the barn. The crew leapt out, wearing matching navy-and-white diamond check guernseys with matching navy beanie hats. Teddy opened the van doors and they began lugging their cache of fireworks over to the barn. Elsie's expression was a landslide of concern.

'Mind your step and remember, Teddy, Crawshaw hates everyone, especially young 'uns, so get in, get out, right?'

'I'm not that young,' protested Teddy.

'How come he lets us stash here?'

'Guess blowing people up's his thing.'

'But not actual people.'

'Course not actual people!'

As their voices faded trudging over to the barn carrying their stash of fireworks, Victor Crawshaw stared out from the dark winery window, his face set like concrete as the visitors sent a flock of runner ducks scattering beneath their advancing feet. Once he'd seen it, Teddy never forgot that face, framed by darkness with blighted eyes and the sneer of an addled dragon.

4

In Lewes, the golden light of autumn is glinting off the flint-fronted houses of Friar's Walk as Minty Jarvis, wrapped in her green cardigan, wends her way down towards Cliffe High Street clutching a dainty bag of bird seed. She quietly acknowledges to herself that she'll have to stop feeding the birds soon, times are harder than they've ever been and, as her late friend Sandra used to say when times were hard, *ends not met is a no-middle-riddle.* Minty looks around at local faces weaving their way through the chill of the morning. The town is humming with groups in different-coloured guernseys as the bonfire societies shake their tins raising funds for their parade on November 5th. She remembers back in the day when stopping and chatting was the hallmark of life on this street. These days, it's all bustle, hustle, gone. As Minty makes her way onto the bridge, Harvey's Brewery looks majestic over the river behind her and she quietly acknowledges Lewes Cathedral, as the locals call it. The pigeons seem to know Minty and gather at her feet as she takes her seat at her favourite bench.

'Lovely to see you, darlings. Looking so gorgeous, all greens and purples shining so bright. Hey, no squabbling! If you share it there'll be just enough to go round . . .'

As Minty starts carefully scattering small handfuls of seed to make her bag last as long as possible, a colourful octogenarian jogger huffs up the street and, with a few deep intakes of breath, pauses in front of Minty, sending her beloved pigeons flapping up into the sky. Bedecked in an orange jogging top and neon pink shorts, Tom Hurst tunes into Minty's disapproving stare and breaks into a joyful grin.

'Was I being clumsy? Scared away your birds, didn't I?' he beams.

'You noticed,' Minty replies, apparently unimpressed yet discreetly drawn by the brightness of his jogging kit.

'Anyway, they're not my birds,' continues Minty, warming to the subject, 'they're as free as me, and as colourful as your . . . Well, what exactly is it that you're wearing?'

'Sports garb? A dash of joy? I'm Tom, hello, Tom Hurst, desperately trying not to give up jogging and indeed not running into the free pigeons of Sussex.' He smiles as the pigeons begin to return. Minty considers him for a second and gestures to the bench.

'Rest your bones?'

'Love to, what are you feeding these lucky birds?' asks Tom.

'Any seed I can get my hands on, prices are through the roof.'

'Yes, I suppose even our feathered friends are feeling the pinch.'

'Makes them squabble,' agrees Minty, casting a few more grains to the grateful pigeons, one of whom ventures bravely onto the bench.

'Don't mind that one, it's Sandra. Well, I call her Sandra, in fact I call all the friendliest ones Sandra after my late friend.'

'Sandra?'

'Sandra, yes. Or Sandy, she was the best of us, died years ago now, she adored feeding all the birds.'

'She sounds completely wonderful.' Tom dips his hand gently into the bird food and offers his palm of seeds to Sandra. Minty stares at him, struck that there's something alluring about this person, like a burst of warmth on an autumnal evening.

‘My name’s Minty Jarvis. First thing you should know about me – and I’m saying this thinking that I’m not quite as old as you are – I love dancing.’

‘Do you know dancing is the one thing that terrifies me even more than jogging.’

‘I see calypso in those bones. Come to my class, Tom. Church Hall on St James Street, here, I’ll give you a flyer.’ Minty rummages in her bag.

‘I’m a very terrible dancer, Minty.’

‘Tom Hurst, I’ve just seen you jogging perfectly well. And if you’re dancing is half as good then I believe you’ve got the moves like Jagger. Ah. I see Sandra’s taken a shine to you.’ Sandra is sitting on Tom’s leg, eating out of his hand. Minty locks eyes with him. ‘It’s nice to know you, Tom Hurst.’

‘Nice to know you too, Minty Jarvis. But I really cannot dance, unless I am quite squiffy.’

‘Moves like Jagger,’ chuckles Minty.

‘Like Sandra,’ corrects Tom. ‘How about we start with a nice gentle walk around town and take dancing from there?’

‘Sandra, what do you reckon?’ asks Minty. The pigeon seems to nod with a bob of its head as the empty bag of seed returns to Minty’s cardigan pocket and she gets up from the bench, gently taking Tom’s arm.

Across town, Barclay is struck by the alluring scent of his glass of Domaine Georges Vernay Coteau de Vernon Condrieu and writes a neck tag for the bottle: ‘Peaches rolling down a sunbeam’.

5

Maurice Le Brocq is attempting to relax in his library. Dressed head to toe in dark leather and tight tweed, his body is one long sinew on perpetual alert, and although he is telling himself to concentrate on reading his well-thumbed book (*Pheasant Shooting* by David Hudson), his mind is straining. Perched on the crest of the Sussex Downs, his commanding home feels like an extension of this forceful expression. He'd first been attracted to Greenacres by the brickwork, which reminded him of the Tower of London. Le Brocq's home does indeed have the aura of a fortress ringed by endless rolling hills, which, to him, suggests a ship sailing the high seas of influence and power. To almost everyone else, the house looks like a prison. England has many beautiful country estates. Greenacres is not one of them.

Inside, the atmosphere is as taut as a cheese wire ready to splice every moment into fractional doubt. Maurice likes keeping his housekeeper on her toes with his unpredictability, although she's long rumbled him as predominantly a creature of habit. He enjoys boasting that he thinks of his staff as family, yet it's important to note that Maurice loathes his family. The bold incumbent who's been housekeeping at Greenacres for more than two decades is Mrs McRae, a stout Scottish executor of tasks with the gumption of a galleon. Mrs McRae is in contemplative humour this morning as she dusts down the fireplace in the grand hall; she's feeling fortunate to have been in the same employment for so long. Times are tough out there and much as her own indomitable spirit fuels her days, she can't help wondering what made Maurice Le Brocq so determined to live his life with the rigidity of a human icicle. His work overseeing sheep farming across his land seems to hold no fascination for him. She's baffled as to why the odd night gambling over backgammon seems to grip his attention more succinctly. And most of all, Mrs McRae muses over his constant attentiveness to shooting pheasants. Maurice lives for the shooting season and can't get enough of feathers falling from the sky. And though Mrs McRae herself is partial to the taste of pheasant, fondly recalling the flavour of it from her youth on Scotland's west coast near Ullapool, why Mr Le Brocq insists on it every night for his winter dinners is quite beyond her.

Maurice Le Brocq is staring out of the window, the book resting in his lap as he taps his foot impatiently. The rain is sluicing down the narrow gothic windowpanes of his library. Maurice grimly reflects that the weather today is doing its very best impersonation of a car wash. And he bears a grudge for that.

'No shooting today,' he murmurs aloud before calling out for Mrs McRae, who bustles in after a surprisingly brief interlude, her black and white uniform giving the formidable impression of a giant chessboard.

'Mrs McRae, since the weather is murdering my mood and washing out scent trails, my rain cape and boots shall be required for a visit down the valley.'

Down the valley was never a good omen. Mrs McRae lost count years ago of the run-ins her boss has had with Victor Crawshaw on his Dandelion Hill vineyard. To Mrs McRae it is as plain as day that the feud between them is entirely self-propelled, each one incapable of giving up hostilities, and while lulls occur over the summer months when Victor immerses himself in wildlife and Le Brocq sulks in his library unable to shoot until October 1st, eruptions are never far away.

'Quite right, Mr Le Brocq. Would you like a sandwich before you'll be away?' she asks quietly.

'I think not. Best to conduct business on an empty stomach. Keeps the appetite sharp,' says Le Brocq, his slit of a mouth widening into a sour smile. Even after all this time, Mrs McRae finds his spartan facial expressions discomforting.

A short walk down the valley, Victor Crawshaw is hunched over the kitchen table, his head in his large hands. His face is reddened, whether from rage or flushed from the large glass of red wine that sits next to a bottle on the table, Tabitha isn't sure. Being Victor's daughter is hard, as Tabitha likes to remind herself far too often. Today, her dad is in no mood for small talk.

'Fed the ducks, Dad, they're all loving this rain,' she ventures. Victor grunts from behind his hands. He is dreaming of a world without people, where wildlife rules by its own instincts and whether peaceful, violent or mundane, it would at least be honest. With a sigh, he lifts the glass to his lips before squinting out through the kitchen window and spying Le Brocq streaking at speed over the yard towards the kitchen door. Victor exhales deeply.

'Old Snuffy approaches.'

Tabitha opens the door and offers her best impression of a smile to Le Brocq, who doesn't return the kindness.

'Maurice, come in, please.'

As Le Brocq sweeps in, Victor has to hand it to him; for a man well into his senior years, he has the swiftness of a stick insect with a discreet dynamo tucked into its belt. Maurice sits down at the table. A ginger farm cat jumps onto his knee. Maurice's tension reveals that he loathes cats about as much as people who don't shoot.

'No need for tea, I'll come straight to it, I'm sure you have things you'd rather be doing,' he says, staring pointedly at Victor's half-finished bottle of wine.

'Maurice Le Brocq. Delivering another of your sarments?' growls Victor, deadpan, all too familiar with his neighbour's self-interested sermons.

'We don't need to like one another to benefit from a common aim, Crawshaw. And my proposal will, I think, suit your aims for the zoo you seem hell-bent on building.' Le Brocq shoves the cat off his knee.

'I'm scratching along well enough, Maurice, giving my land back to what's natural.'

Le Brocq takes a breath.

'I think I will take that tea, my dear. Black, bag in. Just let it stew.'

Tabitha rolls her eyes and fills the kettle, plonking it on the Aga with just the right amount of attitude to ramp up the air with a further ratchet of tension.

'Victor, I have a proposal for you. This winery of yours is falling into ruin. What you call rewilding, I call a crisis. And I am here, as your neighbour, to offer my help.'

'And a fine help you've been since you took on the big house.' Victor rolls back into his chair, taking a large swig of wine.

'I propose to write you a cheque, here and now, to take possession of Dandelion Hill, giving you the funds to take on your wildlife activities wherever you choose, a project you can marshal from scratch in the surety of knowing you have the cash in the bank to do it and succeed.'

Tabitha is focused, her eyes searching between Le Brocq and her father for the faintest sign of a tell. The stand-off that ensues makes the quick-fire duels she used to see in cowboy films as a young girl seem as cosy as two dozing dormice. The air between these two denizens of the Sussex Downs is almost visibly glimmering with static, the cumulation of years of rivalry, petty put-downs and uncomfortable encounters.

Only the rain breaks the silence as the rising breath of the kettle sends up a vertical fringe of softly coiling steam. Le Brocq's tongue moves between his lips, a snake in a dusty burrow. Tabitha notices his right hand moving almost imperceptibly towards his inside pocket, a detective drawing a sidearm in slow motion. He plucks out a pristine chequebook and smooths it open on the table, holding Victor's gaze.

'Shall we play with numbers?' suggests Le Brocq.

Victor's slouch slowly rolls as he contemplates Le Brocq's audacity. He nods towards the ginger cat

'I'll let Queen Elizabeth decide.'

'Queen Elizabeth?'

'Her name's Elizabeth, behaves like a queen. And by the looks of her, she's noways jumping into your lap for that deal.' The cat rubs herself around Tabitha's feet. 'Some-one-time I'll admit selling's crossed my mind. But look, Dandelion Hill's a lot different to *Grand Acres* now, isn't it?'

'Greenacres has its charm, with each season hosting more shoots, but this place would serve as my shooting lodge. With a few renovations, of course. Shall we say two and a half million? On the generous side, but we wouldn't want to see you out of . . . bottle. Would we?'

'Hunting?' Victor stares.

'Shooting, yes, accommodation and refreshments, that sort of thing.'

'My winery, a shooting lodge?'

'For pheasants in the main. Of course, out of season, from February until October, the gamekeeper would be housed here to build up stocks while you set up your creature retreat somewhere more . . .'

'More what now?'

'You know, old chap, distant. You want out, I want you out, let's conclude our business and depart in peace.'

'Mr Le Brocq, I'm avised of one thing.'

The kettle whistles, and Tabitha raises her eyebrows as she drops the teabag in a mug and places it in front of Le Brocq.

'I'd sooner sell this place to you than take a bannicking from my own daughter,' says Victor. Le Brocq stares him down before gathering himself to his full height, unfurling like the wing of a bat.

'I see.'

'Well, try seeing the door and use it now, would you?' Victor knocks back the rest of his glass and gestures to the door for Le Brocq to leave. Thanking Tabitha for the tea, Le Brocq nods curtly to Victor before vanishing into the rain, the sound of his footsteps retreating across the windy yard.

'That snake,' Victor bellows from his seat at the kitchen table, getting into his stride.

'Don't let him get to you, Dad. It might not be the worst thing in the world to consider an offer, maybe not today but who knows, you could push him to a tidy sum, deep pockets there,' suggests Tabitha.

'I'd rather choke on a flittermouse. Never, none, nothing and no way will I ever be selling Dandelion Hill to that greedy fox.'

Victor picks up his phone and starts to dial.

'Hello, yes, my name's Crawshaw, Victor Crawshaw up at Dandelion Hill, I want wildflower seed, sacks of wildflower seed . . . for a meadow . . . Well how much have you got?'

Tabitha is making a quizzical face.

'I'll be sowing that gummet's freshly ploughed field with flowers. Next summer, no wheat for Le Brocq, he'll have my meadow instead, all bees and butterflies with forage for all and . . . Yes, it's Crawshaw, C, R, A, W . . .'

The wind is picking up and the rain is hammering at the kitchen windows, spattering out like steel roses in the fading light.

Maurice Le Brocq arrives leering through the doorway at Greenacres handing his cape to Mrs McRae.

'How was your meeting with Mr Crawshaw, sir?'

'I wish he was dead, Mrs McRae. Bring a pot of strong hot tea to the library.'

6

Organising a wine tasting, Barclay reflects as he dusts off a record behind the Bottle Bank's counter, *is rather like planning a wedding*. He's carefully considering the details of decor, music and seating arrangements, which all contribute to the overall feeling on the day. As the joyful sound of the Dell-Vikings' 'Come Go With Me' jostles around the wine shop, Barclay slowly dances his way over a few pieces of jigsaw before turning his hand to the shop's diary. The diary is a battered hardback book which lives on the counter listing deliveries, stock and the odd doodle of Pinot from Barclay's own hand. His well-upholstered finger traces through the days as he casually snacks on a Ritz cracker. Teddy carries a case of wine from the front door to the storage room out the back.

'We're getting through a ton of Malbec, Barclay, we one hundred per cent need to order another pallet.'

'Aah, the season of steaks and stews is upon us, dear Teddy. I'll compile a list of the beefiest reds to fortify the good people of Lewes against the deluge of drips which the season insists on thrusting upon us . . . Zinfandel, Tannat, St Chinian, Priorat, the lavender metronome of Crozes-Hermitage and a cohort of Australian Shiraz will see us through, never fear. More pressing than that, of course, is the monthly tasting. Pearl! Time to plan our line-up!'

Pearl takes a break from setting up the shop window display and Pinot rouses from her slumbers next to a case of Grand Puy-Lacoste 2016, a classic red from a fine Bordeaux vintage which means nothing to a snoozing sheepdog and all the world to Barclay's never-ending quest for *silky red splendour.*

'Any theme you want to chase? Weather's trash this week, something upbeat might get people hyped,' Pearl says, straightening her denim jacket and stretching from crouching down.

'Counterintuition, I love it. How about rich whites, the feeling of autumn's glow in the mellow memory of the ripest summer majesty?' Barclay suggests.

'Bold whites, love those vibes, Barclay. Even a sparkling Pét Nat?'

'Your obsession with Pétillant Naturel wines is duly noted and we shall find a celebration soon enough to deploy their raw sparkling charms.'

'Drop a white port in at the end?'

'Better yet, a welcome drink of white port and tonic garnished with a wedge of orange, the most invigorating aperitif yet bafflingly it never catches on.'

'Kind of like the climate emergency, heaps of chat, sod all action.'

'On the contrary, your recent one-person protests across Lewes have indubitably got the town's tongues wagging.'

'What, zip-locking the petrol pumps?'

'I was thinking more, when you blocked access to the Cuilfail Tunnel with hay bales. And let's not forget that you did also shut down an entire supermarket by pouring orange paint over the entrance, Pearl.'

'Big deal, there's mad potential for the whole town to be tons more self-sufficient.'

Teddy makes his way across the shop to fetch another case from the van.

'How's the allotment doing, Pearl?' he asks.

'You know, slow, putting it all to bed and sticking in winter veggies. Found a lil' toad the other day, all cosy for winter, so I put it back in the ground.'

'A living seed, Pearl. Life gets everywhere,' croons Barclay as Teddy pops out to the delivery van.

'It's all we've got, Barclay, that and the planet.'

'How right you are. We float through space riding a giant seed, pollination popping around us no matter the moment, and the perfect companion to life's mysterious flow is, of course, wine. So, for our tasting, we shall kick off with a white port and tonic, then we'll need at least four prime whites with all the weight and grace of peaches dipped in bullion. Let's work backwards. We culminate in a Condrieu, all apricots and cream; penultimately, perhaps a South African Chenin Blanc blend . . .'

'Palladius?' suggests Pearl.

'Palladius is a marvellous choice. Eben Sadie hosted a tasting with me here once, you know, before your time, capital winemaker, loves a glass of scrumptiousness almost as much as I do. Second place . . . an aged Assyrtiko from Santorini perhaps? Have we any left of Hari Hatzidakis' final vintage of Mylos?'

'The 2017? Wait up . . . only got two bottles left.'

'Perfection. Then let us kick off the tasting with some liquid dancing. Neudorf Home Block Moutere Chardonnay from magnum, it'll have them all singing like nightingales hooked up to the National Grid.'

Pearl looks up from scribbling down the line-up of wines. She nods, impressed, and meets Barclay's twinkly grin.

'We're going to have a ball,' says Barclay as he plucks a cold bottle of Hoffmann & Rathbone Blanc de Blancs from the fridge. 'Time to celebrate, only the best of course – and the perfect opportunity to pin down once and for all the perfect snack with an English sparkler!'

'Cheese straws, total winner,' suggests Pearl as she makes her way back into the window display, gently stepping over Pinot.

'True, but I have one better that's been rattling around my noodle like a frozen pea in a ding-dong bell – herring roes gently fried in butter served on pillowy toasted sourdough with a graceful scattering of freshly chopped parsley.'

Teddy, carrying another case of wine through the shop, is not impressed.

'That's like a one out of ten snack situation, the only thing fish eggs are good for is making more fish.'

'And yet paired with a glass of English fizz, Teddy, they form the very peak of Gastronomy Mountain. I shall prepare you this nibble of dreams at once; Pearl, mind the shop.'

Pearl gives him a wave of assent from the shop window as she precariously balances a giant bottle of wine on a stack of empty wooden wine cases. Teddy hops over to give her a hand.

'I had an idea for you, about the allotment, why don't we do some filming for your socials? I've watched a fascinating bunch of tutorials on YouTube about how to edit and put shots together – if we upload quality content directly onto your feed, you'll have apex impact, get people sharing your passion for the greener life.'

'Aww, thanks, Teddy. That's so sweet of you. Didn't know you were into filming?'

'Perfect for cataloguing moths, photos are hit and miss, filming lets me choose still shots from the whole reel, I've got some crazy lenses for my phone we can play with.'

'I don't want it to look like a fairground mirror, Teddy.'

'You'd look great in any mirror,' he says unguardedly, before realising he's blushing and retreating with a few stutters back to unloading the van. Pearl watches him quizzically as he walks into the van door.

7

Several days later Tom is decked in fluorescent fitness kit, all orange and neon pink. He's helping Minty climb over a stile in her long warm coat, which, he has just noticed, is the same shade as the plumage of pigeons. Purples, greys, magentas and greens seem to radiate from the very fabric. After a recent rainfall the curved Sussex Downs are as sleek as giant broad beans rolling over the horizon.

Tom is pointing out various landmarks to Minty along the footpath where he loves to jog. At his age, he insists, jogging is more of a plod, but he loves the way the fresh air makes him feel, inside and out. Over there is his favourite tree, an oak nearly perfectly symmetrical, with a large branch on one side listing where the prevailing wind has tried for decades to tip it back into the rolling ground. That lopsided tree is how he sometimes feels about being in his eighties: mainly upright with a slight risk of being toppled by gravity's dogged persistence. Minty, breathless, is enthralled by the wide-open space around them, telling Tom that she's lived in Lewes for seventy years 'but it's been too long since I've climbed these hills'. When she was young she used to come up on the Downs, playing with her friends in the abandoned chalk pits near Black Cap. She loved those long hot days surrounded by the scent of wild marjoram and the irrepressible chatter of skylarks singing up above. And today she feels a streak of youthful joy fluttering in her heart.

A solitary swallow passes just above their eyeline, heading out towards the English Channel. 'A late traveller to warmer shores,' remarks Tom as he and Minty consider the beauty of the creatures that come and go with the winds of the seasons. Strolling gently on in their dreamy state, they haven't yet noticed the inky shape moving towards them from a high line of scrubby gorse. As it approaches, the figure starts moving at pace and seems to have something crooked over its arm – could it be a thin stiff coat? Or a shotgun. Maurice Le Brocq's dark cape is catching the wind in a manner which suggests his mood is, at best, torrid. Tom gives him a cheery wave.

'This is private property, what's your business?' barks Le Brocq.

'Oh, I'm deeply sorry, I was just telling Minty here that I've always loved jogging this way, we're just taking a breath of air together, such a lovely day for it. Are you local?' Tom brims with limitless liveliness.

'My property is not some sort of recreation ground, off back the way you came and be sure to leave no damage or this conversation will escalate to aggravated trespass. Now, for my records . . .' Le Brocq struggles with his phone as he tries to take a photo of the trespassers for his collection. He inadvertently takes a selfie and curses. Minty offers to help, grabbing his phone. She takes a beaming selfie next to Maurice Le Brocq. In the photograph, Le Brocq looks as though he's just swallowed a beehive.

'If you want a selfie, you just have to ask, Mr . . .?' smiles Minty.

'Want one with me too?' asks Tom innocently. Le Brocq scowls, still unable to get his phone off selfie mode. He turns and takes a photograph of the top of his head with a blurry image of Tom waving merrily in the background.

'Come on, Minty, let's head down the hill and leave Mr Selfie here to play with his pop gun.' Waving playfully, Tom and Minty stroll amiably away as Le Brocq seethes, peering after them with his binoculars until they round the hill.

Minty is delighted that Tom's mood has not been weighed down by a single molecule of Le Brocq's weighty behaviour. As reflected in his exuberant choice of sports attire, Tom just doesn't seem to acknowledge the maze of rules which cut invisibly across the old English ways. Rather like the last migrating swallow, Tom's course is always set for sunnier climes, and Minty adores this most of all about her new friend. Tom, meanwhile, is pointing down the valley at what seems to be a farmer with some huge bags; he is hurling seed into the air like a youngster playing in the waves at Seaford beach. When Tom tries his luck with a friendly wave, Minty stops him and gently lowers his arm.

'I know him, that's old Victor, Victor Crawshaw, friend of Barclay's, you know Barclay at the shop? The colourful type I was telling you about. For years they'd be away jawing about wine for hours on end, but this one's not such a people person any more.'

Tom nods ruefully as he leads Minty by the hand back towards the path to Lewes. Across the town, smoke from the chimneys is threading up into the sky, grey yarn stretching into the woolly clouds above. Victor Crawshaw pours out the last of his bags and exhales with a satisfied grunt. *That'll learn you, Maurice, enjoy next year's meadow, you maxon,* he thinks, pleased by imagining his neighbour as a steaming heap of manure, before stomping back towards Dandelion Hill with the crows following him like seagulls behind a trawler. In his pocket he feels the sharp edge of his pruning knife and is struck by the dark thought of his papery skin lingering just one nick away from eternal silence. 'Time for the last harvest,' he murmurs.

8

Pearl and Pinot are playing ball by the ruins of Lewes Priory. Pinot has the speed and agility of the wind itself, no angle or distance the ball is thrown in can flummox her. Pearl takes a moment between each toss to check a couple of dating apps on her phone. Holding the ball in one hand, she swipes away a bunch of candidates before her phone pings with a possible match. Pinot is waiting expectantly for the ball to be thrown. Opening the match, Pearl spots Teddy's beaming face, with five pink and green Elephant Hawk-moths perched on the end of his fingers. She reacts as though her phone has momentarily turned into an electric eel, spilling it into the air. Pinot catches the tumbling object in her mouth and gently returns it to Pearl's hand. Pearl recovers herself and throws the ball for Pinot, hastily deleting the app.

A couple of miles away, deep in the South Downs, a bunch of ripe grapes is cradled in a hand weathered by the wind, fingernails worn by hours rootling in the soil, teasing out places for roots to thrive. Red grapes tend to glow from behind a grey haze of nature's own wild yeast, which is rubbed off to a sheen when handled. As this bunch is tossed into an old tin bucket, another bunch is cut by the stem with a swift and expert slice of an old pruning knife. The rain is holding off over Dandelion Hill. Victor always loves harvesting at the last minute, risking his crop being washed out by a late autumn deluge in a bid for optimum ripeness. This year, his judgement is impeccable, he's not seen Pinot Noir of this quality in thirty years, and he considers the old adage that you can't make good wine from bad grapes.

Today, Victor is taking a moment to marvel at these simple clusters of magical berries whose contents will transform into what he believes will be the best Pinot Noir ever made in Sussex, if not the whole of England. Although, to him, wines are not exactly made – they *happen*. With too much intervention they can be *unmade* and lose their identity. He won't let that happen to these grapes harvested from his beloved Runner Duck vineyard. In all his years harvesting from his quaint vineyard and selling his curious bottles, he finally understands that the best vintages occur when he is preoccupied with other things and therefore unable to interfere too much while the yeast feasts on his fruit and in exchange pumps out carbon dioxide and alcohol.

The winery is a place of transformation and one of the rare sites indoors where Victor Crawshaw finds a sense of equanimity. Usually, his solace in this world is the majesty of a single wide horizon, the comforting sound of a runner duck quacking or the audible flight of spring's first bumblebee with all the promise of pollination that it brings. Out in nature the great matrix of connections allows him to feel a deep sense of closeness with something broader than he can speak of in this world. At harvest time, the fruit containing the secrets of the season passes through the winery, drawing him into a dialogue with a wine that's never been made before and will never be made again. It's a moment where possibility and precision meet – and Victor's favourite time of the year quite simply because nobody, not least himself, ever has the faintest clue as to what the outcome might be. Soon after harvest, the winery settles into the rhythms of raising the wine – Victor always uses the French term *élevage* – which gives the sense of nurturing, as you would a child. Or more aptly in Victor's case, a runner duck.

Every year, Victor and the emerging wine flow towards one another in a surreptitious stream as they learn to raise one another. Victor stirring up yeast cells in barrels and, in the case of his beloved red wines, pumping wine over the cap of floating red grapes to flesh out texture and keep the process moving at an even temperature. Sometimes he instinctively chooses to manually 'punch down' the floating cap of skins and pips with his favourite old rake, to liberate sugar from the grapes, boost temperature and encourage more structure in the final wine. He might even decide to do nothing at all, as in this case, such is his confidence in the quality of the fruit. Every decision he makes or chooses not to make, rather like an emerging song in the hands of a great musician, will change the fermentation in myriad ways and encourage the unique character of the finished wine to flourish.

Perhaps the biggest decision of all in the hands of a wine-maker is the simplest: whether or not to add yeast. The yeast that naturally coats the grapes out in the vineyard will bring something to the fermentation, but, as Victor knows well, it's hard to predict exactly what. Adding a cultured yeast – from a packet – can encourage certain themes in the wine, such as aromatics, fruitiness and colour, and operates more like a well-rehearsed spell than an ingredient. Whenever possible, Victor prefers to trust the wild yeast that nature provides, sometimes risking the fermentation getting stuck; for the sake of working with nature, he feels it's worth the risk.

Dandelion Hill's winery is the only place indoors where Victor's sense of trust in his own instincts remains intact. To him, every other building beyond the borders of this realm feels like serving time, where his anxiety rises until he can be free once again outdoors. He defines his decisions by the maximum benefit to all the life he finds, from dragonflies to beetles, starlings to newts. In old age, he now sees all life as one project. Humans are the exception. He finds their obstinacy as objectionable as Maurice Le Brocq's determination to exterminate every pheasant he can aim a gun at.

Carrying the last bucket of grapes over to the winery, Victor empties it into the press where Harold waits to initiate the final crush of the season. The old machinery rumbles to life, pink juice waterfalling in rivulets beneath. Over the noise of the press, Victor leans next to his son who is flushed and horrified by the tiny quantity.

'Dad, there's barely enough here to fill a single tank.'

'Why maunder, Harold? Best fruit I've seen in years, not much of it, but see the quality, true magic.'

'But it won't pay the bills.'

'I'm beyond bills.'

'Wildlife doesn't pay for anything, Dad, if we can't make money from this place we'll have to sell up by springtime, don't you get it?'

'You move on to find your money purse, I'll muddle along fine.'

'No you won't, Dad. Where will you live?'

For a split second Victor could swear he is talking with a runner duck the size of Harold. He shakes his head at his momentary confusion.

'I'm all of a mizmaze.'

Victor makes his way outside, pulling a package from his coat pocket, leaving Harold to watch over the press. Victor fiddles with what looks like a small camera. The sound of an engine distracts him from the gadget in his hand as the Bottle Bank delivery van pulls up and Teddy hops out carrying a large box of fireworks.

'Hi, Mr Crawshaw, it's Teddy from Priory Bonfire Society, just delivering a few more fireworks to store in the barn.'

Victor stares at him blankly. *Looks like a duck. If I don't speak to the duck, the duck won't speak back.*

'What's that you've got? Ah! A motion-activated wildlife camera? That's a top ten piece of kit, Mr Crawshaw. Had one of those growing up, once saw a wild boar, strapped to a tree. I wasn't strapped to a tree, hang on, to be clear the boar wasn't strapped to a tree either, the camera was strapped to a tree.'

Victor takes a step back. *Ducks don't usually talk, why is this one talking?*

Teddy is unsure what to do; he gently puts the fireworks down.

'Everything OK, Mr Crawshaw? Those cameras can be a bit fiddly, do you want a hand setting it up?'

Teddy reaches out to take the wildlife camera and Victor erupts, making a noise Teddy will later recall sounded exactly like a red deer roaring during the autumn rut. Teddy is goggle eyed, rooted to the spot. Victor stares back at Teddy before roaring once again, shocking Teddy into action. He grabs his box of fireworks and trips along towards the rickety old barn.

'No worries, Mr Crawshaw, I'll just pop these in the barn and be on my way.' Victor's bellowing has piqued Tabitha, who opens the kitchen window and leans out.

'Everything alright, Dad?'

'Leave me be!' Victor yells and he paces to the nearest vine post, hastily strapping his camera up as Tabitha hurls invective from the open kitchen window.

Teddy dumps the fireworks inside the barn and in the dim half-light can see that the Priory crew already have begun building their effigy to burn on Bonfire Night. Hurrying back to the van, he sees Victor securing his camera to a vine post near the winery and quickens his pace as he passes Tabitha shouting from the open kitchen window at her dad. Teddy manages a cheery wave as he gets into the Bottle Bank van and promptly reverses it into a tree. As fast as he can turn it, he yanks the van into gear and pulls away as Harold exits the winery and joins his sister in a tirade against their father. Victor strolls steadily away from the winery and the noise of his children, towards the relative quiet of the vineyard.

'Happy families,' Teddy mutters as the scene grows smaller in his rearview mirror, and he wonders what he'll tell Barclay about the tree-grazed bumper. In the winery, Harold Crawshaw starts dialling on his phone and leaving a message. 'Mike, I'm in the mire, Dad's started behaving like a total weapon. You were right about coming home. Can't help thinking it'll all be simpler when he's gone. Mad times. What am I even saying? Just buzz me when you get this.'

9

Victor Crawshaw loathes surprises. Up on the ridge above Dandelion Hill, a line of silhouetted guns are waiting on their pegs. He is staring in silence at their shadowy outline, his ears slowly turning scarlet with rage. He is holding his pruning knife open in his hand, gripping it with intent. Each of the guns is dressed in green wellingtons, tweed breeks, a green jacket and cap, and has a facial expression that's caught between desperation and delight. *If shooting animals is your idea of fun,* Victor Crawshaw says to himself, *reckon you'll no-ways mind me chasing y'all out the Downs by my knife.* Victor feels in his bones that while he spins ever further away from the orbit of society, something is fermenting deep within him. His worry for the decline in the population of wild creatures, from bumblebees to starlings, has tipped him into an ever more lonely place and one which has left him grasping for strands of joy wherever he can find them. Which is the precise opposite of staring in red-eared horror at a line of beaters frightening pheasants into the sky, to be blasted by Maurice Le Brocq's line-up of guns.

While some pay for the privilege of attending a shoot at Greenacres, today Maurice has invited a few local bigwigs from the League of Rural Affairs for a jolly. This explains why he is dressed in his smartest Purdey shooting cape, which gives him a bolstered stature rather like a mummified lamppost boosted by a long sarcophagus. Victor turns his back on the shoot, pockets his pruning knife and begins hitching a trailer-load of spent grape skins, gleaming like a mountain of pink pumice, to the back of his ancient Little Grey Fergie tractor. As he starts the engine he pulls out his mobile phone and jabs at it, his old weathered fingers rapping the battered screen to dial Barclay Flint.

Just over the line of the Downs in Lewes, around six minutes for a sparrow to fly, Pearl and Teddy are choosing the best angle to film on her allotment at Paddock Road. The day is a graceful steel-skied autumn blazer and the chill in the air contrasts with the hotness inside Teddy's head as he wrestles with the lens he's trying to attach to his phone. Teddy is a great fan of repurposing, upcycling and learning new skills. The only drawback with this enthusiasm for the world of tech is his tendency to make life a little more complicated than it needs to be. As he struggles to jam the lens onto his phone, Teddy is beginning to realise that he probably spent too much time staying up late last night watching YouTube videos about how to direct social media content. But to make Pearl happy, he knows in his heart there are very few lengths to which he won't go.

'Got it, OK, let's go for a test shot, if you stand over there, I'll shoot from this angle, just say anything,' directs Teddy.

As Pearl begins a halting monologue about the virtue of growing your own food, she attempts to extol the benefits to pollinators as well as one's own health: 'Growing your own veggies is a recipe for celebrating everything that's . . . for things that live . . .' As she finally hits her stride, a funeral cortège starts slowly pulling along Paddock Road in the back of shot and a solitary raven settles on a wall cawing loudly behind her. Teddy looks up with a frown and suggests they try filming from the other direction, with Paddock Field in the background. Pearl's delivery is flowing more freely as her confidence settles, and she realises with a deep breath that all she has to say is what really matters to her and the content will look after itself. Teddy is lining up his shot, checking the notes he made on his phone.

'AI says keep the pace quick, start with a big hook and don't linger on one shot for too long, so you keep ploughing on and I'll pan around you. Remember, people scroll fast so give it plenty of movement, Pearl. I want to see arms, legs, head, just keep it all jumping, OK, and action!'

Pearl, momentarily thrown by the direction, starts leaping about with a sheet of cardboard, diving to the ground to show how she's pursuing a 'no-dig' style of planting by covering the weeds. 'It's all about giving nature a sec to bed in . . .' Behind her a teenage couple are making out with gusto on a bench. Teddy stops the shot to change the angle once again.

'Teddy, I'm overdoing the jumping around, feels like I'm getting lost in the chaos and the message is a mess.'

'It's all good, Pearl, eighty-five per cent of people watch social media with the sound off so I'll stick a bunch of colourful subtitles on and trust me, the more you move the more clicks you'll get, it's going to be mega, remember, just ask people to comment, it's all about engagement, maybe try a line with a hook, you know, do a Barclay, say weird stuff . . .'

'You got all this from AI?'

'Everything, even my favourite recipe for meatballs in tomato sauce, which is pretty much all I cook now, you pad out the mix with breadcrumbs soaked in milk and—'

Pearl cuts him off with a look.

'Yep, back to filming,' nods Teddy.

A man in paint-stained overalls walking his Alsatian passes by the allotments and recognises Pearl. 'Oi! You the one who shut down the tunnel the other week with them hay bales? Made me late for my own wedding, you tosser!'

Pearl waves at him politely before gesticulating less politely when his back is turned. 'Thanks for being a climate hero,' she calls after him.

'Tosser!' he replies without turning around.

'Back to filming?' asks Teddy.

'Get on with it.'

Teddy jumps to it and starts shooting very close up to Pearl, who pushes him away; he trips backwards, landing in a raised bed. The footage from his camera shows Pearl looming over him, unimpressed, looking like an angry giant. 'Let's call it a wrap for today . . .'

10

Barclay wraps himself in his loose-fitting charcoal herringbone Daks woollen overcoat as he fumbles in his pockets for the keys to the Duke. Parked just along Priory Street is a 1970 Rover P5B coupé in silver birch with the contrasting roof in burnt grey. DUK 922J has been Barclay's pride and joy since he inherited it from his late father. His only rule when behind the wheel of the Duke is that the music of Jimmy Cliff must always be playing. Partly it's the only CD in the car, but also because Jimmy's sound is altogether suffused into the jolly vibe of every button, leather finishing and carved wooden trim, which rather makes Barclay feel like he's gliding around Sussex on a floating sofa.

The key turns in the ignition and the old Buick engine rumbles to life, the sound of a giant budgerigar trilling in slow motion. *One does not drive the Duke, one chauffeurs oneself*, Barclay remembers his dear old dad saying on the first day he rode in the passenger seat as a young boy, his feet barely touching the floor. In those days the sound of Jimmy Cliff made Barclay feel like anything was possible. These days the crucial difference is that he knows everything is possible. The grey clouds over Lewes look as though they might buckle under the weight of their own darkness and the last rays of silver sunlight scurry beneath them to take refuge over the horizon. A distant flash of lightning catches the Duke's rear-view mirror as Barclay adjusts it and careens off towards the

Downs, leaving the town's fading lights twinkling like a lost harbour in his wake.

The road up to Dandelion Hill veers off the main road to the port of Newhaven and leads steeply up into the South Downs, a wild realm ruled by the song of skylarks whose billowing flights are impersonated throughout the summer months by their human paragliding counterparts. Flicking the Duke's headlights to full beam, Barclay is all too aware of the Downs' tendency to make things appear larger than they are. He still swears he once saw a cow the size of a double-decker bus on a walk to Ditchling Beacon. Tricks of the light, topography, squinting; all are perfectly plausible explanations. But Barclay has no doubt that he saw a giant cow, which is why he turned back hastily for the refuge of the Duke's plush interior at a dignified trot that summery day. Running over the top of the Downs and rolling down towards Victor's vineyards, Barclay can see Maurice Le Brocq and a group of friends grouped around a massive pile of mauve grape skins blocking his driveway, with a line of cars unable to leave his premises. Le Brocq's face matches the inclement weather as the first spots of rain start bashing on the Duke's rounded windshield. Barclay gives Le Brocq a tentative wave as he rolls along the lane towards Dandelion Hill as the last of the daylight gives way. Le Brocq does not wave back, his face a murderous mask.

Pulling up beside the open door of the winery, Barclay heaves himself up and out of the Duke. He gives his old ride a trusty pat before making his way inside towards the glimmer of steel fermentation tanks and the scent of woody old barrels.

'Victor, I see your feud with Le Brocq continues unabated,' croons Barclay warmly as he approaches Victor, who looks up from filling a jug and stares blankly.

'It's Barclay, what's in the jug?'

'Runner Duck vineyard. Open your nose-holes.'

Barclay takes a deep inhalation of the jug, and as he does so his hair vibrates from the roots to the tips. 'By the beard of Bacchus, dear Victor, this is your magnum opus!'

'Enough fancy talk. Along of its purity, no punch down, pump over, not even yeast, I'll add nought but nature to this ferment.'

'Who'd have imagined you, the tinkerer turned non-interventionalist, the world turns like a spinning penny,' Barclay remarks.

'I'm set upon turning invisible,' Victor smiles faintly as he pours from the jug and proffers Barclay a glass of purple youthful red. Barclay carefully sips, swooshes and spits the fermenting wine judiciously into a grate. His eyes dart to Victor's. Victor waits expectantly.

'Life! Vivacity. Liquid shooting stars.'

'Always such oration with you, Barclay, if shooting stars be summer fruit then I'm agreeable. Picksome is it not?'

'Its daintiness is indeed its power, Victor, boosting energy from root to fruit, from glass to heart!' Barclay flexes himself like a superhero imbued with limitless power. A micro-moth flits between them.

'Another owlet, they come for the light,' whispers Victor conspiratorially. 'Rafty times for the nidgets, that much I know.'

'And you do also know that you dumped a ton of spent grapes on Le Brocq's drive?' Barclay cajoles gently. Victor peers from beneath the lids of his eyes, a naughty schoolboy looking up from a smouldering pile of leaves.

'Balderdash.'

'I saw that maroon mountain of grape skins with my own eyes, Victor.'

'Saw my ducks and all, did you?'

'Must have missed them.'

'My little babies, I'm bringing the vineyard back to nature, all for the wild, those grown trees, innocent weeds, creatures great or small. Folks should quit the stage, Barclay, nature needs her turn.'

Barclay looks across at Victor. He's always been garrulous. But this time he's playing straight. It strikes Barclay that Victor's bid to enhance other lives seems to have convinced him of the lack of value of his own. For the first time, Barclay is deeply concerned about old Victor Crawshaw.

Victor slowly pulls something out of his pocket. For a split second Barclay wonders if the old man is about to draw a blade. Instead, a small smooth black stone is in the outstretched palm he proffers Barclay. The merest tremble is detectable in Victor's hand as Barclay takes the small misshapen egg of a pebble.

'Pocket stone for you. From my Runner Duck vineyard. Little bit of my terroir. Keep this close, leave moil aside and always remember miracles start small.'

'You need it more than me, old friend, here.' Barclay tries to give it back, but Victor's hands are held together in a pointed gesture of prayer.

'Guard it in your pocket,' Victor says with a wink.

As Barclay tucks the pebble away, he is intrigued by a sudden scent that catches his nostrils. He turns like a terrier catching the faint whiff of a burrow with warm prey hiding inside, follows his nostrils towards a tiny stainless steel tank and points to it. '"Lychees on a pogo stick". That bottle of fragrant white left at the shop, it was you?'

'You were all so mucked up, took you far too long of an age. First of its kind in Sussex, that wine, England for that matter. Traminette's the grape, got the only plantings, I have.'

'It's a completely magical wine, Victor.'

'More to come, my old hands want work to do. God willing.'

'And I salute your dear old hands! It's completely gorgeous wine, Victor. Scented as summertime and heady as a perfume counter in full bloom.'

Victor surveys Barclay. Barclay feels as though he's looking at a late self-portrait of Rembrandt, all shadows and layers of light over a weathered lonely complexion.

'Always been partial to you, Barclay, the only soul who truly grasps my ways.'

Victor shuffles deeper into the winery and off towards the darkness with a gentle beckon; Barclay pauses and reflects on the life of Victor Crawshaw. So many relationships built through wine, now as faded as a favourite T-shirt whose holiday memories have all but come out in the wash.

'Victor, there's plenty more harvests to come, old friend. You'll make more wine, I'm sure of it.'

Victor turns. 'We'll see, won't we, Barclay. We wunt be druv.'

He disappears around a tank, and Barclay reflects on the man's stubborn determination to do things his way. From his first visit to Dandelion Hill as a teenager, Barclay remembers being struck by the eccentricity of Victor Crawshaw playing an old accordion in the barrel hall to his silently maturing barrels of wine. Barclay wonders about Victor's music being absorbed into those wines as he replays the haunting melody in his mind. Time seeping into wine. Some bottles never end. Queen Elizabeth the ginger cat weaves her way around a barrel as Barclay follows Victor into the darkness, neither one of them yet knowing that this is the last time they will ever meet.

The forecast on the radio is warm for the night as Teddy drives the Bottle Bank van through the golden dusk towards

Dandelion Hill in the hope of a late autumn moth haul. Parking up the lane outside the farm, he is alone as he carries his moth trap over the Downs towards his favourite spot in Ashcombe Bottom. Some people dance, others go for a pint, Teddy finds a sense of deep satisfaction through identifying as many moths as he possibly can. To Teddy, their beauty, fragility and endless variation are as wide and wild as the flavours of Barclay's beloved world of wine – and yet where wine is mainstream, moths remain in darkness, not so much shunned as invisible to almost everybody else. If Teddy was prime minister there'd be a compulsory course on moths for every school kid, to show how integral they are to the natural ecosystem. But for now he's happy to keep his records and contribute to the noble lineage of county moth recorders in Sussex that's existed down the years. How he wished his predecessors could all be brought back to life for one weekend of moth study together, sharing and comparing data. But for now he's hoping for a Merveille du Jour in the trap when he opens it up tomorrow. Seldom found in high numbers, his luck will have to be in – to see its green wings trembling in his trap would be even better than that Christmas where his dear Granny Alice bought him his first magnifying glass. The excitement in Teddy flares as the wind in the woods dies down and the air grows curiously still. This will be the last trap of the season before the winter takes hold.

11

Harold is stalking across the yard at Dandelion Hill with a shovel over his shoulder while the dawn breaks over a silvery heavy dew. A little way off, Teddy Olsen slams the door of the Bottle Bank van. Harold watches the van pull away and immediately spots that the winery door has been left open all night with the lights on. He approaches and calls for his father. *Dad never leaves the lights on*, he thinks to himself. Two wine glasses and a jug have been left on a barrel. He calls out. The echo of his voice bounces off the stainless steel tanks as he turns towards the exit and narrowly avoids tripping over Queen Elizabeth the ginger cat streaking out from behind a barrel. Where could his father be? He powers through the rows of vines outside glistening red and gold, their scent turning to a first hint of mulch which will only increase as autumn and winter dissolve the leaves away from thick, cracked trunks.

The cat sits on the doorstep of the winery staring after Harold as he threads into the misty morning, a solitary upright strand. To Queen Elizabeth it almost looks like one of the vines has uprooted itself to stalk through the morning in search of a better place to set down roots. Harold's knees click as he makes steady headway up the hill towards his test burial site. He's going through the calculations in his mind and muttering as he walks: '. . . graves only need be three feet deep, biodegradable coffins or shrouds, wildflowers sown on top, it's perfect for Dad's rewilding operation, how often will mourners really come? Once a year? And the dead are silent. Money in the bank and a quiet profit building as people breathe their last. It's the perfect system to monetise the farm . . .'

As he approaches the open grave, his face falls, horrified. He drops his shovel and slowly approaches the lip of the pit. Staring down inside, his furious reflection shimmers back at him: it's partially filled with water and two runner ducks are merrily swimming, bobbing and preening.

Tabitha in her dressing gown is still a touch bleary from the rain which kept her awake last night. She's listening to BBC Radio 3, her hands wrapped around a steaming mug of hot tea as she considers her breakfast, dropping two pieces of bread into the toaster which begins ticking as she turns the dial to start it off. Smoke quickly rises, and she hastily switches it off as the kitchen starts to fill with the acrid smell. Unplugging it, she retrieves a rogue charred crust with a wooden spoon and opens a window as Harold piles in, his eyes hot and burning in a wild fury.

'Which muppet filled my grave up with water?'

'Someone's in a good mood.'

'Was it you? That pit was empty yesterday, a perfectly executed test burial site that's now home to Dad's ruddy ducks. Did he do it?'

'Harold, it's been pissing down. Perhaps you dug your grave in clay?'

'Rubbish, there's no clay; chalk chalk chalk over that side, perfectly drained. Someone interfered,' he says, peeling off his damp jacket, the steam slowly rising from his shoulders.

'Interfered? With what, Harold? I don't want the dead around our family home. Desperately sad people day in day out, have you even thought about the legal side of bringing …' She hesitates. 'Bodies up to the farm. Actual dead people, Harold, this isn't some military mission, this is our literal home. I don't want it, not one bit.'

'I'm glad it's not your call.'

'Dad's never going to have it.'

'If it makes money and gives wildlife a boost, then why wouldn't he take a shufty at it?'

'Because he hates people, Harold. And may I remind you that if you think you're going to be the face of this burial ground, you'll need to do a shedload of work on your bedside manner because you're about as sympathetic as … as a tractor,' says Tabitha, her voice quavering.

Mrs McRae is shovelling the last of the pink and purple grape skins into a wheelbarrow at the end of the driveway to Greenacres. Dressed in her well-worn Barbour jacket and grey herringbone Harris tweed fedora, she is as stout and formidable as the old beech tree that stands at the entrance to Maurice Le Brocq's fiefdom. The damp air does not deter her from her task, and even Le Brocq notices her ardent form as he drives towards her in his glinting black new model Range Rover. He toots his horn as he passes by and drives down the lane to Dandelion Hill. Inside the car the knuckles of his wiry hands are gripping the steering wheel with the tight determination of a python throttling a mouse.

Stepping down from his car at Dandelion Hill, he appears collected, although his nostrils are flaring in a manner which suggests an eruption is imminent. He can hear the raised voices of Tabitha and Harold from inside the kitchen, locked in a heated argument, and the smell of burnt toast is wafting from the open window. He approaches and yanks the window further open.

'Morning,' says Le Brocq with all the friendliness of a wolf. Tabitha and Harold snap from their hostilities and both shoot Le Brocq the same familial look of hostility.

'If you could fetch your father, I have a matter to discuss. Unless it was either of you dumping a ton of old grapes on my driveway? It's taken Mrs McRae hours yesterday and an early rise today to get it all shifted. I won't stand for it.'

'Nobody's dumped any grapes, Mr Le Brocq,' hisses Tabitha. 'As if we'd do that?'

'I'll do a recce, see if I can find Dad,' says Harold, leaving Tabitha to make her toast while ignoring Le Brocq who lights up a cigarillo at the window, taking the time to survey the property and, in his mind, convert it into his new hunting lodge.

Harold calls upstairs to Victor's bedroom. No reply. He paces up the stairs. The bed hasn't been made, but then Victor hasn't made his bed since their mother died in the 1990s. Downstairs, there's no sign of Victor in the study either. A cursory glance outside at the vineyards yields no sight of him. Harold wends his way to the kitchen window where Le Brocq is stubbing out his cigarillo.

'Dad doesn't seem to be around,' says Harold, trying not to feel concerned for his father's unusual absence.

'If you'd be so good as to let him know that the police have been notified. No doubt their enquiries will lead to his front door. There will be a reckoning. This time your father will pay the price for his recklessness. In full. Good day.'

Harold flicks a V-sign at Le Brocq, who sees it in the reflection of his windscreen and chooses to ignore the gesture. His time for vengeance is coming. And as Maurice Le Brocq knows, vengeance is a debt he prefers to be settled with interest. Harold turns to Tabitha. 'Tabs, when was the last time you saw Dad?'

'He was with Barclay Flint up in the winery, they went in together, they must have been up until late, the light was still on when I went to bed, did you see them?'

'I saw Barclay arrive, well the car pulling up anyway, I was at my desk, didn't see him leave. I haven't seen hide nor hair of Dad since then.'

'Nor me. No answer from his phone?'

'Tried that earlier, just goes to voicemail.'

'Well that's hardly suspicious. He's probably taken himself off . . .'

'Tabitha, when did he last leave the farm?'

'I see.' Tabitha begins to look alarmed. Harold grabs his coat.

'Look, you stay here, I'll take another scout round the farm. Give Barclay a call, would you, see if he can shed any light.'

Barclay is singing along to Jimmy Cliff's 'You Can Get It If You Really Want' as he pilots the Duke through the narrow lanes that trail up through the Downs. A few seagulls are wheeling overhead causing him to remark inwardly, *Must be a storm at sea.* His favourite view in Sussex is the crest of the valley that leads over to Dandelion Hill. No matter the time of year, it always reminds him of opening the first page of a pop-up book.

Growing up, his favourites had always been pop-up books. There's one that he still remembers fondly and occasionally searches for online, fruitlessly thus far. It is a book of magic spells and, even from a young age, Barclay always delighted in the colour of the potions and blends, wondering what flavour they might have as well as dreaming of their effects. A good part of him in childhood was hoping to discover that *wizard* was an actual career path, but since he'd once been described by *Sussex Life* magazine as the 'Wine Wizard', he felt the box had at least been ticked.

It's true that wines feel like different spells to Barclay. In his book of notes he lovingly describes the characteristics of each one. In their more florid moments his notes reveal the extent to which he is able to feel the impact of a wine, such as a recent crisp white Austrian Grüner Veltliner which he describes variously as 'chiselled', 'precise' and 'an apple plucked from a glacier'. Barclay invariably feels as though each bottle is a prism of the place where it was grown, containing all the magic that made that liquid trapped in time so peerlessly specific. Rarely does he take time away from his love of wine. Only in moments of total exhaustion, when he cannot muster a response to the question posed by a glass, will he abstain in favour of something delightfully simple in its familiarity, such as a small iced glass of French pastis. Although he has to be careful, being a fiend for liquorice, one glass leads to another and before you know it he's singing the Marseillaise in his pants.

The Duke crunches along the gravel where the road ends at Dandelion Hill. Ahead of him, Barclay spots Tabitha clearing brambles from the barn. He halloos her as he steps out of the car and, remembering that Victor Crawshaw is currently missing, instantly regrets his jovial tone. He also realises that he was probably playing Jimmy Cliff far too loudly on arrival. If he was wearing a tie, he would be straightening it for a distracting confidence boost as he advances, but since his shirt is as open as his spirit, he settles for clenching and unclenching his fists as he approaches.

'Any sign of Dad?'

'Not a thing, thanks for coming, Harold's out searching the farm again. It's really odd, I can't fathom why Dad would just wander off.'

'At his age, who knows. Perhaps he's chasing one of his ducks?'

Tabitha shakes her head. 'I've checked the local taxis, no one picked him up and the cars are all here. It's a bit of a mystery, Barclay.'

'Well he does have a rare tendency for unpredictability. I remember once we were at a tasting together, some bigwig was over from Italy and pontificating about the reds he was showing us when your dad piped up, "You do know that your wine smells like maxon, don't you?" Had to pretend that instead of "manure", *maxon* was an old Sussex term for "tobacco". Your father was not happy. My point is, the old boy hasn't lost the ability to surprise us. Give it time, he'll show up.'

Tabitha rounds on Barclay, 'I don't want him to surprise us, Barclay, I'm desperately worried . . .' Tears welling up, Barclay steps forward and gives her a hug. He takes her hands.

'You should be wearing gloves, Tabitha, these brambles are as sharp as the devil's own horns.' Barclay rummages in his pockets and hands her his pair of leather driving gloves. 'Look, I'll ring round the wineries locally, see if anyone's spotted him in a tasting room or poking around their vineyards. He'll turn up, we'll find him.'

Across the farm, Harold Crawshaw is stalking in full military mode, squaring off each piece of terrain before meticulously moving to the next. His phone rings.

'My old mucker, you're a hard man to track down. Mike, I'll get right to it, Dad's gone AWOL, yes, bit of a Charlie Foxtrot to be honest. It's possible, but an extra pair of eyes would be . . . Sounds elusive, when will you know? Still beasting you, are they? With any luck he'll have turned up by then, but look, stay in touch. Yep, will do, thanks, Mike.'

Scanning the horizon as he ends the call, Harold turns back towards the farm where he sees the Duke parked next to the winery. His face screws into a ball as he advances with the intensity of a terrier on the scent of a rat. Before he reaches the yard, the Duke starts reversing away, the sound of Jimmy Cliff bursting into life far too loudly for the circumstances. Inside, Barclay is singing along, his finger tapping the broad, elegant steering wheel and his nostrils revelling in the familiar scent of old wood and vintage leather. His mind is wandering to his earliest memory of the Duke when his father took him to Seaford beach and he tasted raspberry ripple ice cream for the very first time. He can still feel the glare of the peacock-blue sky, the flash of cold as the ice cream met his lips and the sweet creamy flavour laced with sweet bright raspberry trails. It was the first time he associated the cadence of flavour impacted by temperature, and every time he pours a wine today he will use the index finger of his left hand to gauge the bottle temperature. Some use a thermometer; Barclay is a human thermostat. Eight to ten degrees C for white wine is as familiar to his finger as that curious sensation rising now in his stomach.

It's not indigestion. He shuffles uneasily in the driving seat. He is worried for old Victor Crawshaw. And Barclay's instincts, like his childhood appreciation of raspberry ripple ice cream, leave an indelible mark.

12

The winery at Dandelion Hill is calm. In the old days during harvest, the air was filled with the fragrant scent of grapes as the bunches and berries got sorted good from bad, toppling into the machinery that crushed them before being pressed into cool juice transforming into the magic of wine. Entering this place filled with memories of his father, Harold Crawshaw is poking his head around the door.

The scent of wooden barrels fills the air and while most wineries have a meticulous laboratory to analyse every detail, save for a few test tubes, cones and thermometers, Victor's tiny 'kit corner' is little more than a few jugs and tasting glasses. Harold finds his dad's phone charging and as he runs his eye over the basic kit on display, is reminded that where wine is concerned, his dad always relies on his own sense of taste over statistics and numbers. As Harold grew up, his father's curt way of tasting through the tank and barrels taught him one lesson well: 'Harold, only two types of wine: good or bruff.' The familiar scents of the winery are at once a gateway to memories of childhood and a reminder that when adulthood finally arrived, he pointedly chose not to step into his father's winemaking shoes. While army life served Harold well enough, since returning to the farm he feels the gap in his knowledge of wine as keenly as the distance that's been growing between him and his father.

★

Picking up a tasting glass, Harold turns the tap on the first tank of wine for a sample. Swirling his glass, he gives it a sniff before tasting and spitting onto the gravel floor. 'Good,' he muses. He passes to the second tank and tries turning the tap. The wine does not flow as easily and when he gives it a sniff, something is off. *Bruff.* The lack of flow in the tasting tap vexes him as he tries turning it on and off.

'Clogged,' he mutters, climbing the steps to the steel mesh walkway running along the tops of the tanks. The sound of his boots echoes around the silence of the winery. Reaching the top of the clogged tank, he kneels down and flips open the lid.

He recoils at the sourness of the emanating funky scent. If Barclay Flint was appraising its colour, he'd describe the fruit as being 'dark as a mulberry down a coalmine'. But the aromas are far more devilish. Peering down into the black floating grape skins, Harold grabs the rake which has been left up on the gantry and gives them a poke. Something heavy is sitting beneath the surface. A clump of grape skins? Whatever it is, it's blocking the tap below and will need breaking down.

Harold gives a heave with his rake and the face of Victor Crawshaw rolls up from under the floating cap of puce grape skins, his lifeless lips stained the same colour as the wine. Harold lets out a gasp as he falls on his haunches, dropping the rake into the tank as his father's body slides back under the surface.

Calling the police, comforting his sister and fighting back the memory of his dad's swollen purple body tumbles into the next twenty minutes as Harold's world blurs with the sun beginning to roll lower in the sky. As the light begins failing over Dandelion Hill, Detective Inspector Nuria Alpert arrives on the scene. Wearing an impeccably smart black suit, her athletic demeanour glides out of her navy Skoda Yeti ignoring the mud and puddles of Dandelion Hill that instantly stick to her polished black boots. From the passenger seat, hawk-eyed youthful Detective Constable Oscar Keane emerges in a navy slim-fit nylon suit, his fat knotted grey tie and crumpled blue shirt giving him the air of a school leaver stuffed into an outgrown uniform. Tabitha instantly judges Keane to be too young to be useful as the police walk towards the winery door where she's fighting back sobs. DI Alpert identifies herself and DC Keane to Harold inside, who guides them up the gantry. 'And you found him at what time?' DI Alpert asks.

'Twenty, thirty minutes ago, I called directly, soon as I found him.' Harold is pallid but focused as he reopens the tank and the soaked clothes of his father's back gleam in the winery's fluorescent light. Oscar Keane's eyes light up; it's his first time seeing a body on an actual case. Nuria begins making calls on her phone, simultaneously taking in every detail of the scene with calm fluidity and practised expertise. As Keane pulls out his notebook, he drops it tumbling towards the wine tank with the body of Victor Crawshaw before Nuria nimbly grabs it with her left hand, thrusting it back into Oscar's chest and eyeing him sternly. This clearly isn't the first time she's prevented her young detective constable's eagerness from disturbing a potential crime scene, and her look reprimands him with silent composure. Nuria Alpert moves with the speed and grace of a falcon as she begins surveying from the floor to the roof, hungry for clues.

Harold helps Tabitha across the yard wrapped in a tartan shawl, her face blotchy, her eyes red and her tremors revealing a state of deep shock. Arriving police are carrying spotlights into the winery; a photographer bustles past as a cordon is set up around the perimeter. Blue lights are flashing in the yard as Maurice Le Brocq in green wellingtons and a dinner jacket strides through the scene demanding to know what all the disruption is about. Harold ushers Tabitha into the house and rounds on Le Brocq, who weathers Harold's tirade with cold insouciance. Dabbing his mouth with a handkerchief, his cool demeanour on hearing the news that a body has been found riles Harold to the point of apoplexy.

From inside the winery, Nuria Alpert notes raised voices and follows the source of the noise outside. With sharp interest, she watches Harold bellowing at Le Brocq, who remains unmoved. 'You'll forgive me,' Le Brocq begins, 'but I really must get back to my guests. I'd appreciate it if you could encourage the police not to block my driveway, carriages are in half an hour.' Swinging around, he sets off at pace back towards Mrs McRae, who is waiting to escort him home with a brolly. As DC Keane emerges from the winery, he stands next to Nuria and swigs coffee from his thermos, instantly spilling it down his tie. As he dabs with his fingers, Nuria Alpert's incisive gaze moves between Harold shouting from outside the house and Le Brocq departing into the night. Her appetite for information is piqued as an instinct for tracing the cold roots of conflict ripples like mercury through her veins.

13

Next morning, in their cramped office, Nuria Alpert and Oscar Keane face one another across shared desk space. Nuria's side is impeccably kept, a regimented grid of order with a gleaming laptop surrounded by meticulously neat filing boxes and a pristine gym bag. On the other side of the desk, DC Keane's space is a mess of crumpled paper, old cups of tea and a collection of Post-it notes stuck around a bulky desktop computer. As she sips from her reusable water bottle, Nuria is perfectly still, thinking deeply. As she inwardly surveys the scene back in the winery at Dandelion Hill, she is troubled by her instincts. Contemplating the discovery of Victor Crawshaw's body, seeing him sluiced out of the bottom of the wine tank onto the black body bag, the red juice, pips and skins appearing magenta and black, it strikes her that it was almost as if he was being born again, from blood-red wine.

Her gaze fixes on Oscar devouring his morning bacon bap liberally glossed with tomato ketchup; he seems entirely oblivious to the sounds he is making. 'You know they say someone's desk lets you see right into their brain?' she asks Keane.

'Yeah, well, brains don't feed themselves, want a bite?' Keane proffers his bap across the desk and a drip of ketchup falls right on the dividing line.

Nuria grabs a napkin and dabs it clean. 'No, thank you, I work better when I'm hungry. So, Victor Crawshaw,' she holds up a file, 'what do we know?'

Oscar takes a hard swallow and thinks for a moment.

'Well, he's definitely dead,' he says, as though revealing the secret of time itself.

'Yes. How and why is he dead, Oscar?'

'Fell in?'

'Actually not bad, one of the most common winery fatalities is caused by workers inhaling carbon dioxide from fermentation tanks – they fall in unconscious and drown.'

'Drowning in wine, not the worst way to go.' Oscar licks his fingers finishing his bap.

'Unless you're teetotal.' Nuria points at herself; Oscar nods sagely as though Nuria has just told him she has seconds to live. He can't help but imagine tucking into a large cold pint of cider. 'And besides, Oscar, until the coroner's report is in, we can't assume anything at this point, there are some crazy characters about.'

'Yeah. What did you make of the son? Bit uptight?' he asks, burying the crisp bubbly taste of his favourite Crowman Sussex Cider deep in his thoughts.

'Harold Crawshaw seems a cool hand, army background, ticks all the boxes for staying calm in a crisis.'

'Or, psycho in the making; if I'd just found my dad dunked in wine, I'd be rattled out of my bones.'

'Lost his cool with the neighbour . . .' She checks her notes. 'Maurice Le Brocq.'

'Now that guy's a pillock.'

'What makes you say that?'

'More pissed off about driveway access than a body turning up at the neighbours. Red flag pillock alarm.'

'Maybe he's in shock?'

'I'm the one who's shocked, shocked at king of the pillocks.' Oscar pulls open a can of Dr Pepper, which sprays towards Nuria in a dark sticky gust. 'Sorry, did I get you?'

Nuria shakes her head, focusing on her notes. 'What about the Priory Bonfire lot?'

'The ones stuffing the barn with bangers? Might have seen something. Weird lot those bonfire societies, all cults, witchcraft types, once had a girlfriend, one of the Coombe lot, obsessed with crystals, never got it, how can lumps of rock do anything? Am I right?'

'Perhaps she wasn't throwing them hard enough at your head?'

'Nice. The son, was it Barry?'

'Harold,' corrects Nuria.

'Harold, that's it, said something about one of them Coombe lot being up there loads, a moth man or something . . .'

'Teddy Olsen, works at the Bottle Bank. Harold said he saw Olsen driving away the same morning he found Victor.'

'Got an ID?'

Nuria flips her laptop around to show Oscar Teddy's dating profile with the photo of him with five pink and green Elephant Hawk-moths perched on the end of his fingers.

'Eww, insects,' says Oscar. 'That is so *Silence of the Lambs*.'

'Bottle Bank?' suggests Nuria rising to her feet and crisply closing her laptop with a snap.

'Bottle Bank,' agrees Oscar draining the last of his Dr Pepper and getting up from his chair with a semi-silent belch.

The Bottle Bank is curiously quiet. From the street outside, the shop seems dimmer than usual, as though operating on a depleted battery. The colourful fairy lights in the window display have not been switched on and outside, on the pavement, two rooks are squabbling over a snail hiding deep in its shell. Inside, Pearl is polishing the counter around Barclay's unfinished jigsaw. Pinot is curled up in her bed, following

Pearl's movements attentively with keen eyes. She licks her lips, sensing tension laden with uncharacteristic melancholy. Teddy is in the kitchen watching the kettle boil. Upstairs, Minty is knocking gently on the door to Barclay's flat.

Inside, Barclay is pensive, the red wine he is drinking expanding through his senses as he tastes not just the flavours but its deeper secrets too. The coolness of the year gives tension, zip and energy to the structure of the wine, taut as a Victorian suspension bridge, yet yielding just enough to sway and move with silken grace. The grape itself, in this case Syrah from France's Rhône valley, oozes with the depth of a black olive enhanced by a fragrant spell cast by a breath of lavender. Alain Graillot's Crozes-Hermitage is a classic that's proudly stood on the shelves of the Bottle Bank for a decade and more. As it is such a benchmark, Barclay often overlooks opening a bottle since there's such a constellation of new wines in perpetual orbit around his mind, tugging at the firmament for a moment to shine. Yet now he sips it, he's reminded of why wine is the deep well from which his life so seamlessly springs. Like the textures, colours and brushstrokes of a favourite painting, each is laced with the clues of its origin, which coalesce into a sense of meaning as it permeates every molecule of Barclay's body; the wine and the person are entwined as one, held in mutual flow, each describing the other in a silent matrix of exchanged code.

Barclay revives himself from the trance-like state of tasting his first sip of Graillot's 2023 Crozes-Hermitage and immediately remembers that Victor Crawshaw is dead. *Not only have we lost one of England's most talented wine growers*, he muses. *With the passing of Victor Crawshaw, we risk forgetting what it means to make wine.* Minty knocks loudly on his door.

'Barclay, d'you want to talk? My love? I'm very sorry about

the news of poor Mr Crawshaw, we're all here for you. Whenever you're ready.' She hesitates before deciding not to knock again and turns off down the hall. Barclay's door opens a crack behind her. She turns to see him mustering the faintest of smiles through a face that looks as though a pale rain has washed it clean of sleep. 'Thanks, Minty,' he says gently. 'I'll pop down in a moment, just gathering myself, glad you're here.' He reaches out his hand through the crack in the door. Minty holds it in both of hers and meets his gaze with a tender smile.

'I'm going to take one of my stews up to Dandelion Hill, did you want me to give them any message?'

Barclay thinks before gently shaking his head. 'I'll go up myself, possibly tonight, once the effects of this whole . . . pomegranate spice grenade of a situation have at least begun to settle. I just can't believe it, Minty.'

'Poor Tabitha and Harold must be beside themselves. I'll leave you to your thoughts, Barclay – you ring me if you need anything at all, alright?'

She turns as Barclay's door shuts behind her. Fetching an ovenproof dish covered with foil from her flat, she carefully carries it downstairs and nods goodbye to Pearl. Minty steps out into the road where Tom is parked waiting by the open passenger door of his old navy Peugeot 105. He settles Minty in and helps her with her belt before getting into the driver's seat and giving her hand a squeeze.

'All set?' he says, before driving slowly away.

Queen Elizabeth is wrapping herself around the legs of the kitchen table beneath Tabitha, who is sat wrapped in a large rug, holding a cold mug of tea with both hands. She's not sure how long she's been sitting there, but Harold is keeping an eye out as he finishes washing up and slowly putting the plates away. Through the kitchen window, the police cordon around the winery is flapping in the wind. Harold lowers his head with a shake. Tabitha's vacant stare draws into a little more focus as she takes a deeper breath. 'What was he doing?' she whispers hoarsely. Harold talks half a look over his shoulder as the cat jumps onto Tabitha's knee.

'Who can say? It's a damn mystery,' he answers. The memory of his father's upturned wine-soaked face rolling back under a mottle of purple grape skins flashes into his mind. He shakes it off. 'I just hope it was quick.'

Tabitha bursts into sobs.

High on the hill in the drawing room at Greenacres, Maurice Le Brocq peers down through his old telescope at Dandelion Hill. He can obliquely see Tabitha's shoulder shuddering at the kitchen table and the cat bobbing in and out of view. He stands upright and drums his fingers on the optical tube. A small navy car is weaving its way down towards the intersection of his driveway and the lane leading to the vineyard. He glides over the scene, following the car with the practised aim of a marksman leading his target. Focusing his scope on the car pulling up, Le Brocq watches Tom open the door for Minty. She steps out carefully carrying a foil-covered dish. As he edges along the scene, Le Brocq spots Harold standing in the yard at Dandelion Hill staring fiercely up at him.

The crackle of a log spitting in the fireplace splits the air, sending embers showering into the fireguard. Le Brocq stares at his quarry down in the valley, unmoved by the sharpness of the sound. As the scent of burning oak reaches his nostrils, a dark mood uncurls through his body down his slender limbs to the taut skin around the tips of his cold fingers. He senses Mrs McRae entering the room behind him. Without looking around, he stares out through the window at the blue-black clouds rolling in from the coast. From Mrs McRae's vantage point in the doorway, he seems elongated, a spider hanging from a dark branch.

'Mrs McRae, just for once you could anticipate my luncheon requirements. But since that ship has sailed, I shall take the usual.'

He turns towards her, his yellowing teeth set like a stubborn cliff unwilling to yield to the power of the sea. Unmoved, Mrs McRae bustles to the kitchen where she's already laid him a tray with a warm bowl of hearty pheasant stew.

Barclay is deeply absorbed in his jigsaw puzzle of Wilmington Church as the sound of 'Stranger on the Shore' by Acker Bilk & His Strings coasts gently around the Bottle Bank. His fingers are drumming on the counter with steady solemnity to the music and his glass of Crozes-Hermitage is perched within comforting reach. The door tinkles and Barclay's gaze slowly rises as the scene soaks into focus. DI Alpert moves with a purposeful smile towards him, her black trouser suit barely creasing with each stride. DC Keane is immediately distracted by a large Balthazar bottle of red Rioja, the equivalent of sixteen bottles in one. DI Alpert flashes her identification.

'Hello there, I'm Detective Inspector Nuria Alpert and this is . . .' She notices Keane admiring the large bottle of red wine and reading the tag tied around its neck.

He smiles at her, gesturing to the bottle, 'Ever seen one this big?'

Nuria imperceptibly shakes her head and continues, 'This is Detective Constable Oscar Keane.'

'Care for a taste?'

'Mr . . .?'

'Flint, I am Barclay Flint, proprietor of this wine haven, my pleasure.' As Barclay moves to pour another glass, Nuria waves him off with a curt gesture of refusal.

'I'll pass, thank you. We're here to see Teddy Olsen, he about?'

'D'you do wine tastings, then?' asks Keane.

'I do indeed, impromptu or more formally once a month and you're both most welcome to attend. There's a sheet to sign up somewhere around here . . .' As Barclay aimlessly shuffles a few papers on the desk, DI Alpert moves closer.

'We're fine, thanks. Is Mr Olsen around?'

'Due back any moment from his round of deliveries, now where's that infernal sheet?'

'I'm sure you've heard about the tragedy up at Dandelion Hill?'

'A devastation. Victor was the last of the old Sussex guard. What's dear Teddy done to pique your arousal?'

'We'd just like to ask him a few questions.'

'When's this next wine tasting, then?' asks DC Keane, approaching the counter. 'I don't know nothing about wine.'

'I'd be delighted to show you the ropes next Thursday. Ah, Teddy!'

Teddy steps through the door and advances hesitantly as the police introduce themselves. His mind spins into a vortex as he's quizzed about his multiple visits to Dandelion Hill. Anxiously moving from foot to foot, he feels embarrassed by his self-consciousness and can't help wondering if the police are noticing his fidgeting. Seeing Teddy struggling with his words, Barclay steps up.

'Teddy's a loyal member of Priory Bonfire Society, the secret effigy they're building is nearing completion inside that barn, isn't that correct, Teddy? All will become clear on November

5th when its identity will be revealed. Either of you planning to be in town on Bonfire Night?' asks Barclay good-naturedly.

'I'm down, love Lewes Bonfire, totally *Wicker Man*,' enthuses Oscar Keane.

'Mr Olsen, can I ask for your whereabouts two nights ago?' asks DI Alpert.

'Two nights ago, um . . .'

'Up at Dandelion Hill, perhaps? We've had reports you've been up there a great deal.'

'That's true, I've been up there delivering fireworks, Priory's stash is up there, I use the delivery van, Barclay lets me, don't you, Barclay?'

Barclay nods calmly.

'Any interactions with the deceased?'

'Mr Crawshaw? No, not so much, I mean I tried to help him with some wildlife stuff the other day but he was being tetchy so . . .'

'So?'

'He was always tetchy, to be honest, so I just left him to it.'

'And two nights ago, where did you say you were?'

'He didn't say,' Barclay points out. Nuria's gaze is frosty.

'Please go on, Mr Olsen.'

'Pretty sure I'd have been moth trapping up at Ashcombe Bottom.'

'Anyone with you?'

'Not that time, no, but I got some awesome photos, hang on . . .' Teddy pulls his laptop out of his rucksack; it's been taped up from various knocks. He switches it on with a few gentle taps of coercion.

Barclay sips at his glass of red, keeping a close eye as he notices DI Alpert observing Teddy's every move with increasing scrutiny.

Teddy scrolls through some images before proudly showing them a photograph of a strikingly elegant white moth with blocks of dark orange and black decoration. 'Crimson Speckled. Find of the year, super rare moth, sporadic migrant, I was full house lucky that night – it was warmer than normal, less than two hundred of these recorded in the last hundred years. Probably came from North Africa and ended up in my moth trap at Ashcombe Bottom, I waited all night. What are the chances?'

'Yes, what are the chances,' murmurs Alpert.

DC Keane leans in and, with Teddy's permission, examines the image and file on the computer.

'He's good for it, date, time and . . . that Bottom, all checks out.'

'Ashcombe Bottom, moth trapping, Crimson Speckled,' nods Teddy.

Nuria Alpert takes a long last look at the image of the rare moth before giving Teddy a final cursory glance. 'Moth trapping. Well I never. I think that's all we'll be needing for now, thank you for your time.'

She is already out the door while Oscar is still signing up for the next wine tasting on Barclay's crumpled sheet. Catching her look of disapproval as she reaches the car outside, he hurries out to join her, bidding an awkward goodbye to Teddy and Barclay.

Teddy is unnerved. 'Whoa, what was that all about, moth trapping's suddenly a crime?'

'Most peculiar.'

'What happened to Mr Crawshaw was an accident, right?'

'Indeed it seems so, yes, a rather grizzly accident, sad to say, dear Teddy.'

'So why did those two want to know about my Crimson Speckled?'

'I've no doubt they're merely attending to their dottings and crossings.' Barclay takes a long slow sip on his glass of wine, somehow it doesn't taste quite as scented as the previous sip. *Curiously bitter finish*, he remarks inwardly.

Driving away, Nuria shoots Oscar a stern look. 'Oscar, when we're working can you at least get a grip of yourself, what were you doing signing up for the wine tasting?'

'I'm interested in learning the stuff about them wines.'

'On police time, not OK. Your time, fine.'

'I didn't know you were the wine police too.'

Nuria answers an incoming call on speakerphone. 'DI Alpert, who am I speaking with?'

'Harold Crawshaw.'

'Mr Crawshaw, how can I help, sir?'

'Last night. You said if anything occurred to me . . .'

'Go on.'

'Our neighbour up here, Maurice Le Brocq. He and Dad were always at one another, dog and cat, been going on for years. Lately things took a rather hot turn, their feuding seemed to ramp up to a new peak. I can't say I know the reason, but matters turned . . . hostile . . . shall we say. He's been peering through his telescope down at the farm. Thought you should know about it.'

Nuria's eyes are alight. Oscar Keane is holding both his thumbs up at her as though posing for a photograph backstage with his favourite band.

14

Mrs McRae is polishing the component parts of a dismantled shotgun. Spread over white linen on the table in the hall, they look rather as though a giant metal beetle has discarded its limbs before curling up for a legless snooze. The cloth in her hand is clean and dry, and comforting to the touch as it glides over the metal and skims the grain of the wood. The atmosphere of Greenacres envelopes her like a sterile old shroud. The house is coated with the dark sheen of an abandoned hotel with everything kept in readiness should a guest ever choose to return. Even the plants saluting silently from their pots seem darker and more polished than their living counterparts outside. The very brickwork seems to be packed with mournful whispers; the memory of a party, children singing, the sweeping of an old brush.

The room in the house that she truly adores is her snug attic bedroom. It's a refuge for her modest collection of detective books and the leggy geranium she's kept alive for more than nine years, which is always reaching for the narrow skylight. The view from Mrs McRae's rooftop window looks down over Dandelion Hill and, before she tucks herself into bed every night, she loves to stand on tiptoe peering down and dreaming of one day living there herself, free at last from the sterility of Maurice Le Brocq.

*

As she silently works her thoughts drift back to childhood. She recalls the strange sight of her great-uncle Leo wheeling himself around the rambling house of Kirkwell in his large Victorian perambulator. Uncle Leo had seemed positively ancient at the time, but on reflection she guesses he must have been in his forties at the latest. Polio had robbed him of the ability to walk, which, to her young eyes at the time, gave him the air of one who seemed to have lived for a thousand years.

She loved to hear Uncle Leo's stories of stalking on the moors, and it gave him solace too, recalling memories of his body moving freely through the Scottish Highlands under the wide billowing skies of his beloved Assynt. With Rascal the old terrier on his knee, Uncle Leo gave off the feeling of guidance, guardianship and steadfast aplomb. The first time she walked through the door at Greenacres, the impression of the place had reminded her somewhat of her great-uncle's imposing home. But only for a fleeting moment. As soon as Maurice Le Brocq began his line of questioning, she knew from her very first interview that life in his service would be one of direct instructions under strictly professional tension.

The sound of the grinding old doorbell rattles along the hall and at almost precisely the same moment Mrs McRae is up and rushing towards the dimly lit entrance hall. It's as though the doorbell rings inside Mrs McRae herself a split second before ringing in the house, such is her communion with the bones of the place. Even though Mr Le Brocq's manner is rarefied and often remote, Mrs McRae relishes knowing exactly where she stands in every footstep of her life. If she sat down to create an equation for the ratio of happiness in her days, her mathematics would confirm that, for her at this time, certainty is worth the tax in sublimation. And some day soon, she may yet have the freedom to live elsewhere, perhaps Dandelion Hill, running the shooting lodge for Maurice Le Brocq. Her hand touches the front door and the faces in the doorway are two that she can easily read. This is no social call; to her eyes, the impractical town clothes worn by DI Alpert and DC Keane are clearly no match for the onslaught of late autumn in the countryside.

As she shows them to the library, she muses with some alarm about what the police could possibly want. With such comings and goings at Greenacres, Mrs McRae puts her best foot forward, somewhat discombobulated by this disturbance to her daily routine. Nuria clocks the dismantled shotgun in the hall as Oscar edges into the library, his eyes casting about with the abandon and wonder of someone stumbling upon the northern lights in the lavatories of a pub. Oscar is already beginning to rummage, awed by so many leatherbound tomes, while Nuria is taking in the whole staid scene, evidently laid out by the mind of a meticulous creature of habit. Maurice Le Brocq prowls into the room and takes up his seat behind the great desk.

'I trust Mrs McRae offered you tea? I usually take mine later, perhaps in this instance, though, I will take a cup a little earlier.'

'She did, tea is on the way, Mr Le Brocq. Apologies for turning up unannounced, my name's Detective Inspector Alpert and this is Detective Constable Keane. We're piecing together the last few days before the sad loss of your neighbour, Mr Victor Crawshaw.'

'The old toad.'

'You weren't close, then?'

'The thorn in my side finally breaks free. No, we were

cordial at best but it's no secret the deceased and I lacked a certain repartee.'

'That a posh word for party?' asks Oscar.

'He means they didn't hit it off,' corrects Nuria, eliciting a nod from Maurice.

'From the very beginning there was always something he required or didn't desire or insisted I'd taken from him, the man was a prig whose only interest was in starting a safari park for weeds, wastrels and bad wildlife. Still, what happened is, I suppose, for his family at least, one could say, a setback.'

'His death is a setback?' Nuria's curiosity is piqued.

'A setback, yes. All the paperwork, red tape, ruddy ridiculous these days. On the other hand, perhaps those children will finally see sense and rid themselves of the whole farce of a vineyard. It's a millstone, the whole farm's fallen into rack and ruin.'

'Seemed an alright spot to me,' Oscar shrugs as he fumbles with a book.

'The last time you saw Mr Crawshaw would have been . . .?' asks Nuria as Mrs McRae delivers two cups of tea on a tray.

'The day before he died. Mrs McRae, I shall also take tea, the usual. Or possibly the day itself, I'd have to check my diary. Seeing him these past weeks seemed an almost daily occurrence. Regrettable ones all, I'm afraid to say.'

'Things between you were getting worse?'

'Low as the Dead Sea. He dumped a load of grape skins on my driveway earlier this week. It took Mrs McRae two days to shovel us free. Not wishing to sound callous but it feels as though this valley's trespasses have finally been forgiven. Certainly, my breathing has never felt quite so free.'

Nuria sizes up Le Brocq, who realises how his last sentence sounded. 'You don't suspect foul play, I presume? The man clearly fell into his wine and drowned,' he says.

'We're keeping an open mind.'

'Well, of course I never wished any physical harm on the man, certainly we didn't like one another but, well, my words may have sounded ... Well, to be clear, he and I were ... Look, plenty of people loathed the old toad, it's not just me.'

Oscar holds up a book on Sussex bonfire societies. 'Can I borrow this?'

'No,' replies Le Brocq. Oscar nods and replaces the book on the shelf.

'Where were you on the night of Mr Crawshaw's death, sir?' asks Nuria.

'Here. Where else would I be? I'm sure Mrs McRae will be able to corroborate,' says Le Brocq indignantly. Oscar knocks over a small porcelain pheasant, which he awkwardly catches and replaces on a shelf, eliciting a scowl from Le Brocq.

'Mr Le Brocq, we've taken up enough of your time, I'll leave you my card, if anything occurs to you, my phone is always on.'

'Thank you, Detective Inspector Alpert. I shall keep this card and advise if ...'

Mrs McRae enters with a cup of tea, glancing furtively at Nuria and Oscar as she approaches Le Brocq. Le Brocq stares at her, dropping his sentence like wet rope from a drifting ship. 'I shall take my tea at the usual time after all, Mrs McRae.'

Mrs McRae changes course in the manner of a steadfast tanker, diverting in a wide berth around the detectives towards the door, followed by DI Alpert and DC Keane. Maurice Le Brocq is left stewing in his dry skin surrounded by books that he realises he has never even thought to read. Ruminating darkly on the last time he saw Victor Crawshaw alive, Maurice Le Brocq stares into the hearth and feels the fire of anger rising inside his throat.

15

Pearl, in her favourite psychedelic jumpsuit, is carefully jotting down notes on the line-up of wine bottles she's placed on the counter for the monthly wine tasting. Teddy is trying to show her some footage on his phone.

'Teddy, it looks like a monkey did that filming.'

'Haven't finished editing yet but it'll be fast-paced, *bam bam bam!*, engaging, quickfire, people will love you, you'll have so many hits, Pearl, this is going to be so big, like bigger than "Money For Nothing".'

'What's Money For Nothing?'

'Dire Straits, one of the biggest bands of the eighties.'

'Twenty years before I was born, mate.'

'More than ten years before I was but Mark Knopfler's still the greatest guitar player of all time. "Romeo and Juliet"? "Sultans of Swing"? Nothing?'

Pearl shrugs, reaching past Teddy for more wine bottles.

'Move please, Mr Guitar Facts. All I want is for nature to shine, and if the allotment can flex for climate awareness, great, but Teddy that clip makes me look like I'm glitching. What are my arms even doing?'

'It'll make sense in the edit.' Teddy spots Barclay across the room, deeply engaged in swirling a glass of red wine and giving it a sniff before murmuring, 'A cranberry comet . . .'

'Think he's OK?' asks Teddy. Pearl shoots Teddy a look.

'After Crawshaw? Er, no. But I'm telling you, that content makes about as much sense as a cranberry comet.' Teddy misunderstands, thinking she's finally into his directing.

'See? It's going to be ace.'

Pearl stares at Teddy for a moment before widening her eyes and turning back to the bottles lined up on the counter.

'I am a wine detective,' whispers Barclay Flint to his reflection in the shop window. 'Solving wine crime wherever I find it,' he adds with a toss of his head and a flourish of his pink tartan jacket. Exhaling deeply, his confidence building as he admires his smooth, rounded cheeks, he begins twinkling a little more brightly, a star basking in his own firmament. 'Marvellous,' he confides in himself before running a hand through his mop of rampaging hair and turning back to face the shop, shaking off feelings of dread at Victor Crawshaw's untimely demise.

Barclay's adoration of hosting a wine tasting is only surpassed by the feeling that breaks across his body during a second glass of wine, which he describes curiously as 'liberation', 'excelsior' and 'supposing'. The theme of today's session, which he is about to present (Rich White Wine), requires little preparation. He knows the selected wines inside out, and while discombobulated by Victor's death, he knows that engaging with people will help keep him mentally afloat.

He thinks of his tasting groups as hives. From his days keeping bees, he knows that every hive has a different collective character and the moment you lift off the lid, the mood is obvious. A gentle buzz, harmoniousness and easy handling. Or roaring, shrieking squadrons of attacking stinging insects. The latter is less simple to deal with and requires the diligence and wisdom accumulated through years of handling both bees –

and wine tasters for that matter. Sometimes, a heckle from an awkward know-all can be a blessing from the gods, material with which to turn the crowd onto wine and away from snobbery. The worst mood is when there's a sense of ennui, a tiredness verging on boredom which Barclay alas remembers only too well from his German lessons at school with Mr Whistler. He later discovered a deep passion for learning languages, German among them, and concluded that a dull tutor, the same as a corked wine, is a travesty against the topic.

The assembling wine tasters are a mixed bag as they make their way into the shop and settle in for the session. A couple of retirees, a group of three exuberant students preloading before a drinking session, a pair of suited professionals feeling like life's true meaning has eluded them and one rucksack-carrying tourist who Barclay inwardly describes as a modern-day Viking with an air of perpetual Glastonbury.

Sitting in the second row, the Viking is studying the wines with a deep frown and looks up occasionally to stare at Barclay as a cat might stare at an injured bird while deciding how long to toy with its life before crunching its body into a paste of splintery goo. From behind the counter, Pearl is squeezing between the chairs and tables to pour everyone the first glass of wine while Teddy is struggling with a bottle and corkscrew on the counter. Teddy plucks out half a cork and peers down at the bottle of wine with embarrassed panic; he grabs the attention of Pearl who, well versed in the art of saving a bottle of wine, pushes the cork back into the bottle before decanting it and beginning to serve the customers with impressive speed and élan.

Barclay is taking all of this in from his vantage point in the corner of the shop. He marks out the Viking as a possible troublemaker, the students will doubtless be great fun, and the rest, he divines silently, will be as malleable as hot honeyed porridge. Teddy is wrestling with the cork of yet another bottle and he notices that Pearl has served the opening two wines; almost time to swing into action. Pinot trots over with an expectant air. 'My friend. What's in the magic pocket?' Barclay asks her. Pinot's nose moves to his right-hand jacket pocket. Barclay nods with a chuckle and delivers a gravy bone, which the dog snaffles at the speed of a blackbird's blink. *Showtime*, Barclay tells himself, striding to the centre of the room, the ringmaster, magician, impresario and show-off that he is so delighted to be.

'People of Lewes, welcome to the room of dreams!' he kicks off, and, right on cue, Teddy drops the needle on the vinyl for Bing Crosby and the Andrews Sisters' 'Life Is So Peculiar' to begin proceedings.

Barclay moves around the shop like a teddy bear on roller skates, performing what can only be described as one of his famous 'wiggle dances'. The Viking is unimpressed. As Pearl passes in front of him, her eyes meet his for the first time; for Pearl, it feels as electrifying as Greta Thunberg speaking about climate change on the steps of a courthouse. Pearl Finch is falling through the Viking's eyes and deep into the place that nobody quite knows until they find it.

Teddy looks up from the counter to spot the Viking and Pearl locked in a loaded gaze. He pulls a cork out so hard he inadvertently flings the corkscrew away behind his head, and it smashes into a row of bottles behind.

Neudorf's opening Chardonnay served from magnum is a revelation to the crowd. In answer to Barclay's question, 'How many of you are ABC people, Anything But Chardonnay?', at least two-thirds of the room raise their hands. But this New

Zealand Chardonnay has changed all that with its plush zing and thrilling freshness, 'a solid gold peach of a wine' as Barclay puts it. The mood is bubbling along beautifully, the Viking is alternating between staring at Pearl and checking his phone while Teddy is doing his best to make sure he and not Pearl serves wine to this Scandinavian interloper, to keep them as far apart as possible. He has that same feeling of inevitability that he gets when waiting to cross a busy road just as a motorbike swings round a corner that would flatten him if he stepped out, an ant beneath the fist of an ape.

Barclay is charming the students, and the professionals and even the retirees are warming to his theme.

'And now, I will show you how to decipher a wine without even tasting it. And believe you me, these skills are not just fit for identifying a wine – in life, these tips and tricks give you what I like to call the "Marple advantage". Observation is only half the battle, intuition and logic are the missing parts that open the gates to a land where theories give way to solutions, pleasure and facts. Swirl your glasses, please. Perfect, well done, that poor wine has been cooped up in the bottle for far too long, it wants to stretch out and express itself, the more you swirl the higher you're turning up the volume on those aromas. What's the character that you smell? Fruity? In this case the aroma of salt with a whisker of spicy smoke is overwhelming. There's only one place in the world that produces such a savoury aroma, think of it like a giant green olive hurled from the core of an icy volcano – you're quite right, an excellent guess, it is from the Greek island of Santorini which headlines the local Assyrtiko grape. By merely smelling this wine, we've identified the place and the grape, and since this is even more intense and tantalising than Frankie Goes To Hollywood at the height of their

Pleasuredome era, the producer must be a great one – and since there's a decent amount of savoury depth and textural lavishness when we sip it, we can deduce that it doesn't have the fruit and freshness of a young wine, no, this is maturing very well indeed. The last vintage of the late great Haridimos Hatzidakis from the legendary Mylos single vineyard and the final jigsaw piece in the puzzle of this wine. No young vineyard would be capable of producing a wine of such complexity, these vines are more than a hundred years old. Nose, tongue, eyes, all capable of solving any mystery. And when you cease swirling, behold how slowly the tears trickle down the side of your glass. We can decode therefore that the alcohol level is reasonably rich, hovering around the fourteen per cent mark I would say – a wine with a lower level of alcohol would trickle back down the glass far more quickly.'

To the sound of applause, Barclay sees himself momentarily on stage at the Albert Hall, a full house in rapturous applause as he thanks his conductor and orchestra at the end of belting out one of his favourite arias. And he's back in the room.

It is empty now, save for Teddy clearing away the chairs. Only Pearl remains with the Viking, deep in conversation over the counter, sharing a glass and heatedly discussing the climate emergency with equal parts gusto, indignance and enthusiasm for their mutual love of protesting. Teddy advances at speed, sending chairs tripping behind him; he takes the two glasses and to Pearl's consternation declares 'Closing time.'

Barclay interjects. 'We're open for another hour, Teddy.'

'Right, well I have to leave, so closing time for me, full marks on the tasting, Barclay. I'm Teddy, I work with Pearl, we, er, work together.'

'Hey, Eddy. Good to know you, man, I'm Axel. So your name's Pearl, huh, like the sea diamonds, that's what my grandmother used to call them when we used to swim and pick them off the rocks of Norway, the flowers by that seaside were so beautiful that sometimes I wondered if it was my heart stopping from their beauty or the coldness of the ocean, you know. Crazy times.'

Barclay is still savouring his reverie, murmuring his thanks to his imaginary Albert Hall audience. 'Right, Teddy. What's the only thing to drink after a wine tasting?'

'A pint of Harvey's Best.'

'Exactly, come on lad, I'm buying.'

'But I'm locking up . . .'

'Pearl, you OK to lock up?' asks Barclay. Barely taking her eyes off Axel, Pearl waves in assent, deep in close conversation.

'Pearl?' calls Teddy.

'My round,' calls out Barclay, leading the way to the door. Teddy falteringly follows, looking back over his shoulder.

'We're going, then . . . we're almost gone now, Pearl? Now we have gone, bye, bye, then . . . bye.'

Two seconds after the door tinkles shut, Pearl waves at them both through the window while Axel proffers a cool salute. Only Pinot's gaze follows Teddy and Barclay through the shop window as they head out in search of England's finest pint.

16

The following morning Harold shoos the runner ducks out of his way, carrying a heavy spade over his shoulder and marching across the yard towards the bare downland beyond the barn at Dandelion Hill. Underfoot, the ground is firm after a light frost and the air has the stillness of a held breath. Tabitha is at the doorway of the barn as Harold passes. She's dressed in dungarees, her hair tied back and a tape measure stretching from one hand to the other. Over the entrance to the winery, the tape of the police cordon has begun breaking away and flaps in the air like the land-locked tail of a crash-landed kite. Tabitha watches her brother pass in silence, runner ducks pouring from either side of his purposeful stride in flapping feathery waves. Harold is muttering under his breath, a heavy frown set deep across his brow, which is being further pinned down by his tight-fitting flat cap.

Up on the hill he makes quick work of digging, swift into his rhythm as angular rocks of chalk fly up over his shoulder, momentarily vanishing against the low cloudy sky before tumbling back in a growing pile on the grass. Physical exercise, for Harold, is the equivalent of plainsong in a monastery. It soothes and fills the space in which he finds himself, the task masking the chatter of thoughts pipping through his nervous system like Morse code down webs of copper wire. His research into natural graves suggests that several thousand pounds can be made from a hole just a few feet deep with the deceased's remains boosting microbial activity in the soil. 'We're really just composting bodies' he used to say when trying to convince his late father of the merits to his plan. The dead have never bothered Harold. He's seen enough pain during his days soldiering to know that the body is capable of tremendous regeneration. He keeps asking himself how on earth he'd failed to convince his father of the dead giving their life force back to the ecosystem as well as yielding an honest living to the landowner. Harold's spade hits a bony lump of chalk and he begins chipping away harder and harder as his fruitless conversations with his father rise and swirl in his head like a menacing spell.

The voice of Harold's internal monologue snaps shut as he realises that Tabitha is standing over him.

'I think you've killed it, Hal.'

'Huh? Oh, tough as concrete this stuff. Sorry, Tabs, I was miles away.'

'What's the hole for?'

Harold squints up at her, framed by grey and white clouds.

'Well, I thought . . . Dad.'

'What, here?'

'Why not? Overlooks the vineyard. We can keep an eye on him.'

'What about badgers digging around?'

'Foxes more likely, fencing will sort that, I'm sure he'd approve.'

'He wouldn't have wanted a churchyard, I suppose.'

'And it's the perfect dry run for my burial ground . . .'

'You can't seriously be using Dad as a test case for making money?'

'It's a perfectly logical solution to the needs of the farm and it also happens to give Dad a place to rest in exactly the spot where he would most want to be.'

'And what about the funeral? Are you planning to have it in the barn with guests sitting on explosives overlooked by that creepy statue of . . . Who is it, anyway?'

'I have no idea, I think it's a witch.'

'Well, it's not as simple as you digging a hole and dropping Dad in it, Hal. The coroner's not released his body and lord knows when that'll all get sorted, and we haven't ever discussed this whole burying Dad at home idea. What if I have a thought? What if my idea is for Dad to be cremated, say, or scatter his ashes at sea?'

'He hated the sea.'

'I know he hated the sea, but alright a lake.'

'Fish food? No way.'

'Fine, but I might want Dad in a particular place that means something to me, I honestly don't know how I feel about having him here in the garden.'

Harold steps out of his shallow pit and gently holds Tabitha by the arms.

'Tabs, this is a dreadful situation. Dreadful, OK. We've got to stick together and think about what's best for this farm. We're the only ones who can make this work. You're all I've got. And like it or not, I'm all you've got.'

Tabitha meets his eyes with her gaze. Her brother's sincerity deflates the tension in her shoulders and they drop.

'Fine, let's see about putting Dad here. Who do we even need to ask?'

'Leave it to me, I'll sort the permissions. What's going on with the barn?'

'Someday it's going to make a lucky bride very happy, I can feel it,' she says.

Harold tries to smile. Although he disagrees with the colossal investment of capital required to convert the barn into Tabitha's wedding venue, he holds back, a tactical retreat for another day of battle.

Seagulls wheel overhead as the siblings look down at the tidy white hole in the chalky soil on their family farm, a final place to rest for their late father. Not far off, the runner ducks are keeping a watchful eye out for worms from the newly turned soil.

Nuria Alpert is typing into her computer while Oscar Keane leans back in his chair throwing scrunched-up paper balls towards the bin. His throw goes wide.

'You're busy,' says Nuria.

'I'm thinking. The man Crawshaw fell into the wine right, let's say he drowned. Either way right, that Le Brocq's got some bad juju, I'm telling you.'

'You think he had something to do with it?'

'Definitely not saying he didn't. You heard his words, Nuria, the man had no love for Crawshaw, he was properly glad to see him gone.'

'Yeah, that was strange. But to knock him off over a row between neighbours? That's got to be something massive.'

'Could have been big beef, Nuria. There's weird stuff happens in the country. They're all bored out of their minds. Apart from growing grass to feed the animals, what is there?'

'Bump off the guy next door?' Nuria jokes.

'Honestly, I'd be that frustrated living with nothing to do except look out the window and count books and stuff, I'd go nuts, maybe I'd end up knocking off a neighbour, or even two.'

A uniformed constable pokes her head around the office door.

'Got a Mrs McRae here to see you, says she's from Greenacres, ring any bells?'

Nuria nods. 'Thanks, Debbie, bring her in.'

Nuria and Oscar exchange a glance. Oscar tosses a ball of paper into the air. It bounces off Nuria's computer and into the bin. 'Still counts, that's a goal,' he says as Mrs McRae walks in carrying two jute bags of supermarket shopping.

Taking off her headscarf, she smiles genially at Alpert and Keane. Nuria offers her a seat which she takes and a cup of tea which she politely declines. She's learnt over the years that nobody ever leaves the bag in to stew for long enough and a poor cup of tea is not worth the time it takes to cool. 'I was passing just now and I thought best pay you a wee visit after you'd kindly ventured all the way out to Greenacres.'

'All part of the job, Mrs McRae. How can we help?' says Nuria.

'Well. I know, only too well do I know, how Mr Le Brocq can sometimes seem . . . how to say it? You know. But I've lived with him for several decades now and while he's certainly strict – he'll suffer no fools – the reason I wanted to pay you this wee visit is to assure you that he is not, and never has been, a bad man.'

'Bad man?' asks Oscar.

'A bad man, yes.'

'And how would you describe a bad man?' asks Nuria.

'The thirst of the devil and a scorpion's temper. As for Mr Le Brocq, he is certainly what you might call rarefied and he can be very firm, he surely can be put out on occasion, but he's never done anyone any harm.'

'Unless you're a pheasant,' suggests Oscar.

'Unless you're a pheasant,' agrees Mrs McRae. Nuria offers a good-natured smile.

'So, Mrs McRae. Are you suggesting foul play might have come to Mr Crawshaw from another direction?'

'Och, who's to say, such a terrible tragedy, I just wanted to be clear from my side that Mr Le Brocq has been at home fixated on his new swivelling shooting chair – or the Throne, as he calls it – these past few days. Aye, it's true that he sounded more glad than he should have at poor Mr Crawshaw's passing. But I wanted you to know Mr Le Brocq is . . .'

'Not a bad man,' Nuria suggests to a nod from Mrs McRae, who is struck by a thought and rummages in one of her bags.

'Exactly so. Brought you some shortbread.'

Oscar is thrilled and immediately starts unwrapping and crunching away; Nuria patiently swallows her instant disapproval as Mrs McRae smiles delightedly at them both from behind her shopping bags.

Later that night Barclay is pacing the Bottle Bank with a glass of red wine, his last before bed. He's a little tipsy and the melancholy of Victor's passing is catching up with his mood.

'What precisely was Victor's game, poking around in that infernal tank? One lungful of carbon dioxide can knock you out cold; tumble in, under the wine you go.'

He peers around the shop for a response. Only Pinot looks up at him. 'Pinot, sometimes I feel my words are as lost as crystals in an avalanche. Who even cares a solitary jot for what I have to say about Victor, wine or anything else for that matter? I'm a foghorn with no ships to save from the reefs of this world. Yet there is one thing of which I am certain: this '09 Pichon-Baron is as dense as a pencil in the grip of a black fruit fever dream. Fever. Yes, wine fever, the Vino Disco, perhaps that shall be the new name for the store!'

With Barclay in full flow, Pinot settles back down understanding that there'll be no snack for another long while; at least until Barclay settles down from compiling his new list of names for the shop. 'The Amethyst Ocean, Planet Plum, Liquid Loot . . .'

17

Early the next day Minty Jarvis presses 'stop' on her portable stereo, which is making a sound like woozy birdsong. She ejects the cassette and carefully tightens the spool with a pencil. In faded handwriting, the cassette label reads BEST OF ARROW with a bow and arrow drawn across it. Carefully placing it back into the cassette deck, she presses the button marked 'play' with a loud clunk and immediately sways to the music.

Music to Minty is as encouraging as sunlight to a seedling. Southover Hall is empty but for some tiny chairs from the local nursery school stacked around the entrance. While the scene may look forlorn, in her heart, Minty Jarvis is in bloom, moving with the grace of her years, muscle memory of her time touring as a backing dancer flowing through her body with joyful freedom. Barclay has often suggested he ghost-writes her biography to capture her kaleidoscopic tale in all its beauty, including her brief uncredited stint singing backing vocals for David Bowie on his Isolar tour. Minty's body is her language, effortlessly melding with the sounds around her, vanishing into the beat.

From the outside the pale brown pebbledash hall tucked away on St James Street might seem careworn but for the faint sound of calypso music from within. There's a sunny yellow poster on a small A-frame pavement sign which is flapping perilously in the rising wind. Distinctly homemade, it says CALYPSO CLASS

WITH MINTY J, ALL AGES WELCOME. A mother with a toddler, both well wrapped in colourful jumpers and anoraks, together with a chocolate Labrador walk past and read the sign – they can faintly hear the music from within. The dog sniffs the sign and, before it can cock its leg, is tugged away to a walk it doesn't really want to be going on. Inside, Minty moves around the whole floor, oblivious to the grey day outside, bringing the music into herself and slowly dissolving into its joyful tones. Two dads burst in with their daughter who's dressed as a beanstalk. Minty is roused from her reverie and invites them in, excited at the prospect of some pairs of feet to teach.

'Rehearsals for the Southover panto?' asks one of the dads. Minty shakes her head and points to the tatty paper timetable on the noticeboard.

'That's tomorrow my darlings,' she says. The dads exchange glances, each one wondering how the other got the day wrong. The little beanstalk looks up. A dad looks down with a grin. 'Who's for cake?'

'Yay!' calls out the beanstalk. Making their excuses to Minty they back out of the door in search of sticky treats. Minty turns back to the hall and checks her watch. Her shoulders fall. *Calypso's fun*, she thinks, *how can I convince Lewes to have more fun?* The door swings open with a jolt. Minty turns hopefully to see the brown Labrador straining at the leash with the woman and toddler in colourful jumpers straining to keep it under control. 'Sorry!' calls out the woman. 'Archie come here, heel Archie, heel!' Edging back out of the door with an embarrassed glance, they leave Minty to her music. Beginning a few steps, she hears the door swing open once again and turns round with a glare.

'What do you want?' she says in a raised voice that's uncharacteristically emphatic. Tom is standing in the doorway blinking. His neon tracksuit is a splendid shade of fuchsia with white go-faster stripes down the jacket and trousers. He looks like an elderly pioneer of the disco-era training for a seventies California track and field event. Minty beams with the warmth of a thousand stars.

'Um, to learn calypso?' says Tom hopefully.

'Tom! You're here!'

Minty dances over to him, enveloping him in a warm hug of epic breadth. Tom's smiles reach from the front of his head right around his mind, a halo of happiness.

'Of course I'm here,' he whispers, and slowly Minty leads him across the floor with a first few tentative calypso steps.

The delight on Minty's face is matched by Tom's concentration. He chuckles diffidently whenever his steps go awry. If Barclay was watching, he'd almost certainly think that they looked like a cat matched with a pantomime horse in a skating contest, but in themselves, these two are dancing in a mutual space that's too big to be filled by a single human heart.

Across the street from the Bottle Bank, in a parked navy Skoda Yeti four-by-four, DC Oscar Keane and DI Nuria Alpert observe Barclay unlocking the door and leading Pinot inside. Oscar is fiddling with his phone while Nuria's laser-sharp attention is on Barclay's every move. Letting the dog off the lead, Barclay reaches for a dog treat from a jar on the counter and offers one to Pinot before inquisitively sniffing a second one himself. He thinks better of it and tosses the dog treat to Pinot who snaffles it and curls up in her bed.

The lights of the shop are just flicking on as Alpert and Keane make their way over the street and step silently over the threshold. Barclay looks up from his jigsaw. 'Welcome back, browsing or sipping this time?' he asks with good grace.

'Neither today,' replies Nuria. 'We'd like to ask you a few questions concerning the last time you saw Victor Crawshaw.'

'Seems you was the last to see him living,' Oscar continues.

'Was I?' asks Barclay.

'You was,' nods Keane.

'Indeed,' replies Barclay, reaching for a bottle of Tio Pepe En Rama from the fridge. 'Care for a glass? Fino sherry, normally as curiously light and moreish as a green olive plugged into a light bulb socket, but this is En Rama, straight from the cask, richer, more umami, not quite the full savoury cigar but utterly irresistible as a livener of loveliness.'

'No, thank you, Mr Flint,' replies Nuria, who senses that Oscar is about to request a sample and gently rests her hand on his arm. 'We're both fine, thanks. Could you give us an outline of how Mr Crawshaw seemed the last time you saw him.'

'Certainly,' begins Barclay, taking a generous sip from his glass. 'Victor was in a reflective mood, he seemed, well had seemed for some time, as though he was, I believe the common parlance is, "going on a journey".'

'Where was he going?' asks Oscar.

'A figurative journey,' corrects Nuria.

'Exactly so. He was a changed man from the forceful bull I once knew. Withdrawn, troubled, anything to avoid people . . .'

'What did he want with you, then?' asks Oscar.

'It was odd. We'd not been in touch save for the odd wine tasting in a long time. But then out of the blue he phoned, kept mentioning ducks and something about a hunting lodge and sounded deeply agitated. I took it upon myself to soothe his furrowed spirit.'

Nuria watches as Barclay pours himself a second glass of sherry. Oscar starts reading the label.

'So Fino is a type of sherry, then?' he asks.

'One of the lightest, it matures in casks under a blanket of yeast – we call it *flor* – which seals the wine and prevents oxygenation. That's how it stays so golden and light. A dry fortified wine with a briny tang, the faintest echo of sourdough toast about it. And still a bargain, nobody seems to drink the stuff anymore, except me. The last fine wine for a fun price, you might say.'

Oscar sniffs the bottle. 'Oh yeah, green olives.'

Nuria picks up the thread, trying to contain her exasperation with Oscar at luring Barclay away from the last known movements of Victor Crawshaw. 'What was Victor like when you met him that night, his mood?' she presses.

'He seemed more withdrawn than I've known him. He was in the winery and we tasted some samples together, he was particularly proud of his Pinot Noir from the Runner Duck vineyard, he planned to do absolutely nothing to it, the fruit was as vivid and striking as a rainbow in a snow globe, but when his mind turned to his children, the agitation, you see.'

'With one another?' asks Nuria.

'They were in a triumvirate tailspin. Thing is, I never expected Victor to tell me this, but it did strike me as odd at the time. He said he was planning to change his will to name me, of all people, sole inheritor of Dandelion Hill.'

'Any reason you didn't share this information with us earlier?' Nuria asks casually, meeting Keane's glance with an air of cool caution.

'Honestly, I thought he was joking so I put it completely out of my mind. Now that he's gone, I must say it has rather been rattling around my noodle. A cork in a tumble dryer, if you see what I mean. So there, out it popped.'

Pinot yawns with a stretch as Nuria Alpert gathers her thoughts and draws them into pure focus. 'Did you have any reason to think Crawshaw might be in danger?'

'From himself, perhaps. But when I left him, he certainly seemed equanimous.'

'Why do they serve it cold, the Fino?' asks Oscar.

'Jerez is a hot place and southern Spain can sizzle. The temperature meets the wine's style to succinctly deliver maximum quench. Although if you really want to feel doused by Fino, you need to make a Rebujito, the world's simplest cocktail: a shot of Fino sherry over ice with a few sprigs of fresh mint topped up with Sprite, 7Up, lemonade, whatever you've got to hand. I drink it by the jug when I'm over there and curiously it never seems to get anyone tipsy, least of all me, which is both an upside and a downside.' Barclay drains his glass and tops it up.

'Reb-oo-hee-toe' says Oscar Keane, rolling the cocktail's name over his tongue; he can almost taste the Andalusian sunlight dripping from Barclay's mind and wonders if it's similar to the wild freedom he once felt as a teenager in Benidorm.

'One thing's for sure, no British fridge should be without a bottle of ice cold Fino. With that simple little stopper sealing the bottle, it's the quickest way to get liquid splendour into your glass at the end of a long hard day. Toss in a nibble of cheese or a fresh prawn and instant enlightenment ensues.'

'How long did you know Victor Crawshaw, Mr Flint?' asks Nuria.

'Since I was a child. My late father used to take me up there to visit him. I suppose he must have been in his twenties or thirties when I first met him, I remember him planting his vines up there, all by hand, but he always seemed ancient to me. He was always moody – and stubborn – that's for sure.'

'And did he have many enemies?'

'You might as well ask whether champagne has many bubbles. Victor was a living hothouse of fiery feuds. I always imagined that retreating up to the middle of the Downs would ensure a quiet life, a settled mind, but somehow Victor managed to fall out with everyone from his neighbours to the National Trust.'

'But never you?'

'Curiously not.'

'Why was that, would you say?'

'I suppose our mutual love of wine. We rarely strayed from the subject.'

'Were you the son he never had, then?' asks Oscar.

'Well of course he did have a son, Harold, who I imagine he loved very much, so no, I wouldn't say that.'

'You *imagine* he loved his son?' presses Nuria, her instincts zeroing in on Barclay's choice of words.

'Victor was someone who kept his cards close to his chest when it came to emotions.'

'But not with his inheritance, I mean he offered you the farm.'

'Well he joked about it . . .'

'Doesn't sound that funny,' Oscar chimes in.

'I don't imagine his children would find it amusing, do you?' asks Nuria.

'Well, as I said, it was silliness really, perhaps my tumble dryer of a brain has spat out a dud cork.'

'Oh no, I think it's very much the right cork. We just need to work out if it was sealing anything else up in that noodle of yours, right, DC Keane?'

There's a silence as Nuria's gaze tracks the shop to find that Oscar has wandered off to the sherry section and is reading the label on another bottle.

'What's PX, then?'

'Pedro Ximenez, the sweetest sherry, imagine a galaxy of figs and dates squeezed through a black hole; stunning to sip with Christmas pudding, lethally lovely with a square of dark chocolate and life-changingly good when poured over vanilla ice cream.' Pinot perks up at the sound of ice cream while Nuria moves over to lead Oscar away from the bottles.

'Thanks for now, Mr Flint. If any other corks pop out of that tumble dryer of yours, I've left my card on the counter for you.'

'My salutations to you both – and I hope to see you at the next wine tasting, Detective Constable Keane.' Before Keane can reply, Nuria Alpert shoves him through the door and out onto the street. As the doors to their car clank shut, Nuria takes a breath. Before she starts, Oscar begins apologising.

'I know, sorry, I was just interested in the sherry stuff, he's an interesting dude. Never met anyone who speaks like that. It's like he eats books or something.'

'He is that, I don't doubt it. Tell you what else I don't doubt. The more we dig into Victor Crawshaw's death the more I feel something is very wrong about it.'

'What, boss?'

'Not enough to go on. But I don't think he was alone in that winery the night he died.'

18

Next day, the front page of the *Sussex Express* is dominated by a single headline: 'Death by Noir'. A girl on a BMX picks up a stack of papers from the newsagent's on the high street and cycles around the town making her deliveries. A copy thumps on the doorstep of a terraced house on Sun Street. Wearing her navy-and-white diamond check guernsey and munching on a piece of toast, Elsie Sharpe opens the door and takes the paper inside. A bundle of copies land at the newsagent's outside Lewes Station. DC Oscar Keane is walking to work listening to hip-hop music on a pair of massive headphones with the newspaper tucked under his arm. A rolled-up *Sussex Express* spins and lands on the doorstep of the Bottle Bank. Outside Lewes Prison, one of the guards is reading the front page. Up at Lewes Castle, Nuria Alpert jogs under the ancient barbican arch and narrowly avoids being run down by the papergirl on her BMX sending a flurry of pigeons up into the sky. A pigeon lands next to Minty Jarvis reading the coverage of Victor's death in the paper. She is sitting on her favourite bench on the bridge over the Ouse, the Harvey's Brewery towering behind her. Beside Minty, a bag of bird seed is unopened, and pigeons are hopping enthusiastically around her hoping for a bite to eat. As Minty reads the article she is shaking her head. 'Such a tragedy,' she whispers.

Tom approaches from across the street carrying two takeaway coffees. 'Here you are, Minty, one frothy cappuccino as requested.'

'Here, Tom, these details of Mr Crawshaw's death are just awful. Knocked out by inhaling carbon dioxide, falling into his own wine to be drowned. It's just so tragic.'

'That poor family. What does the coroner's report say?'

Minty reads further down the piece. 'Here we are . . . Post mortem . . . seems it was a terrible accident. Says here that he "fell into the fermenting Pinot Noir unconscious". Nobody would have even heard a thing if he was already unconscious. I cannot believe it, you know, we just saw him on the Downs a few days back.'

'Life can be so cruel.'

'So strange, thank you for the coffee, sweetie.'

A pigeon hops onto Tom's knee.

'Think it's Sandra?' asks Tom.

'Definitely Sandra, you can tell by the beady eye; come on, then, let's give you some food, my darling.'

Minty sets the paper aside and opens her bag of bird seed. The pigeons erupt in a flapping competition to get closest to the bag, flustering Tom and Minty who start flinging handfuls of seed as far away from themselves as they can.

'So where did all this carbon dioxide gas come from?' asks Tom as the pigeons settle down and he senses a moment of calm. Minty picks up the paper.

'From the fermenting wine. The yeast makes alcohol and . . . oh yes, it says here the yeast "releases carbon dioxide as a by-product of fermentation".'

'So he lifts up the lid to the tank, takes a big whiff of CO_2, it knocks him spark out, he tumbles into the wine and drowns, just like that?'

Minty shrugs. 'Guess that's how it happened.'

Nuria Alpert is freshly groomed from her post-run shower and standing over Oscar Keane's desk, smart and ready for work. 'I don't buy it.'

'Coroner says accident.'

'Something's off. A guy who's been making wine all his life, so much experience, just topples into a tank? The weird moth guy, the wordy wine shop owner, that creepy neighbour – there's something here we're not seeing.'

'How come any of them would do him in?'

'I don't know, I'm not even saying it's definitely murder, could be a suicide, all I'm saying is something is off.'

'Nuria, there's not enough to go on, it's done.'

'Maybe. But I reckon Harold Crawshaw might have something to say about it.'

Nuria grabs her keys and speeds out the door. Oscar Keane continues to read the paper. Nuria's face pops round the door. 'Well, come on, then!' Keane slowly folds the paper and follows his boss through the door.

Some way distant, Mrs McRae is out in overalls and wet-weather gear, piling barrow after barrow of cuttings and fallen leaves onto a large autumn bonfire. Down the valley, Tabitha is sobbing in her pyjamas over the kitchen table. She's clutching Queen Elizabeth a little too tightly for the ginger cat's comfort and hasn't touched her breakfast of a boiled egg with soldiers. A cold mug of tea is perched on top of a copy of the *Sussex Express*. Through the window, Dandelion Hill is covered by gusts of blue-grey smoke wafting over the valley from Greenacres. Harold Crawshaw is sitting in his late father's study; heaps of paperwork, wine notes, empty bottles and old maps of vineyards are washed up around the desk, the flotsam of a life devoted to the study of grapes. Picking through a few Post-it notes, he is moving with a certain slowness, almost as though the blood in his veins has mysteriously become twice as heavy overnight.

The doorbell rouses him steadily from his chair and he makes his way to open it. DI Alpert and DC Keane are struggling to avoid inhaling the thick smoke that's drifting down from Greenacres. Harold invites them into the kitchen where Tabitha shoos the cat from her knee and starts dabbing her face with a tissue.

'Apologies for the intrusion, the coroner's report formally closes matters for us so I just wanted to come in person to offer our condolences once again and to let you know my door is always open if there's anything either of you need from us going forward.'

'Yes, we'll both keep doors open, my door is open too,' adds Oscar with misplaced enthusiasm.

'That's appreciated, thank you both,' acknowledges Tabitha, blowing her nose.

'I'd hoped we might find out a little more, to be honest. It seems so strange that Dad was here and now he isn't and all we really know for sure is that somehow he fell . . .' Harold tails off, the memory of his father's body soaked in wine is still too raw for him to fully process.

Nuria jumps in. 'I was a little surprised by the speed of the coroner's verdict but from the standpoint of our enquiries it does bring matters to a close.'

'I rather suppose it does,' replies Harold.

'Although one thing did strike us during our interviews which I thought might be worth sharing. Barclay Flint told us that your father mentioned changing his will the night he went missing. Had he ever mentioned anything like that before?'

'Not to me,' says Harold, reddening. Tabitha shakes her head. 'What did Barclay say, exactly?'

'He suggested that your father was considering passing the estate solely to Mr Flint himself.'

'Did he now!' snorts Harold indignantly. 'Well Mr Flint will find himself severely disappointed, Tabs and I are the sole beneficiaries of Dad's will. Damn thing's missing but the solicitor's confident it'll turn up in his files.'

'Why Barclay is even suggesting such a thing is very off, Dad certainly never mentioned any such idea to me,' says Tabitha.

'Nor me,' agrees Harold. 'And when the will's found it'll set Flint straight in no time.'

'Well, just thought you should know. Sorry for your loss, we'll leave you to it. DC Keane, shall we?'

Oscar Keane is reading from an old map on the wall. 'Odd Bottom . . . where's that, then?'

'Our next valley over, Dad always reckoned it would make a wonderful Gamay vineyard. Now we'll never know,' says Tabitha, tears welling in her eyes.

'Indeed. Thanks for the visit, both of you. We appreciate your care in coming to see us.' Harold shakes hands with DI Alpert and holds out his hand for DC Keane who is still staring at the map.

'Thank you, both,' agrees Tabitha as Harold shows them to the door, a large gust of smoke billowing in as he opens it.

'Blasted Le Brocq. What's he thinking, having a bonfire in these winds? Goodbye, DI Alpert, DC Keane.'

Closing the door behind him, Harold's face settles into a heavy mask.

'Flint,' he hisses, his mouth venting like a volcanic valve.

19

Between the branches of an autumnal oak a plump garden spider is making its way across a wide web dotted with a perfect sheen of dewy droplets. Some metres beneath, a red stag is standing under the orange canopy, which is blazing with silvery sunbeams. Around the trunks of oaks receding into darkness, a group of hinds are peering out into the clearing. With dark eyes glimmering on alert, the stag trots out into the light and begins roaring. Some distance away, tucked into his anorak, Axel is watching the stag through his binoculars. Pearl is next to him, peering towards the stag which is pawing up the ground and digging at the turf with its antlers as another stag approaches at speed. The two clash antlers, heads down, shoving in deadlock as they spin around butting and driving with all their might.

'You cannot beat a good rutting,' says Axel, handing Pearl the binoculars.

'How long's this go on?'

'Until one tires or gives up the fight.'

'Got deer in Denmark?'

'Our largest mammals. Everyone always thinks that deer are Scottish, but no, they are Danish, English of course, Iranian, Moroccan – you can even find them in Peru and New Zealand now. You hear that roar?'

'Sounds like Barclay on the sherry,' she says as the victorious stag lets out a roar, sending his opponent clattering away across the clearing.

Barclay is yawning audibly with a wide bear-like stretch as he sprawls over the counter of the Bottle Bank. 'Palco' by Gilberto Gil is playing on the record deck; it rouses him to a gentle boogaloo movement in his upper body and he twirls steadily, much to Pinot's bemusement. His hands are ebbing and flowing like a conjuror drawing out a spell over his latest jigsaw, a watercolour of Wilmington Church, its squat pointed tower reaching for the sky like a wizard's hat. 'Nearly there, only a handful of pieces to go . . .'

He is in the flow, laying the final pieces out, until it comes to the last gap. A single jigsaw piece is missing from the middle of the church's spire. Barclay carefully peers around the detritus of the counter; old receipts, vinyl records, corks and notes scribbled on a collection of pads are all washing around the surface, a tide of rubble left by his receding thoughts. Looking under the counter, Barclay struggles to find the final piece. He checks his pockets, pulling out a handful of dog treats.

As he hands one to Pinot, he is struck by a sudden thought. *Might I have inadvertently fed the missing jigsaw piece to Pinot?* Pinot looks up at him expectantly. Barclay stares back, considering how to retrieve the missing piece.

In a moment of stillness at Dandelion Hill, Harold is trying unsuccessfully to feed a prawn from his last mouthful of sandwich to Queen Elizabeth. She hisses at him as he finishes his cup of tea and drops the unwanted prawn back onto his plate. The hushed quiet pervading the kitchen reminds Harold of the tension of the two minutes' silence at the Cenotaph in London every year on Armistice Day. As the silence grows, the slightest sound or slightest movement takes on epic proportions. He remembers quite clearly the night his father went missing, Barclay's car was parked outside the winery. The wine merchant's jovial pomposity stirred some rancour within Harold that he is still struggling to digest. He's always felt that Barclay Flint is so full of himself that he might actually burst. But since the loss of his father, something about the wine merchant doesn't sit right. The police revealing his father's plan to change his bequests is sharpening Harold's suspicions and the missing will drills into his thoughts; he tries to picture his father's last movements and sees Barclay looming behind Victor. Then Tabitha comes in with a roll of architect's drawings under her arms.

'Fancy seeing the new plans? Working title is Hope Barn.'

'Not now, Tabs. I can't get wretched Flint out of my thoughts. What was he doing that night with Dad? And what the hell is all this talk about changing the will?'

'It's very off. But I don't think Barclay seems the type to engage in dark deeds. Really, Harold, I think we just have to accept that Dad had a tragic accident. It's very horrid, but there it is.'

'I don't think it's that simple, Tabitha. Dad never even came close to having an accident like that before.'

'What if he'd had a bit to drink?'

'Did you ever once worry for him after a glass?'

'No, not really. But like the coroner said, the gas from the tank knocked him right out, he wouldn't have known a thing.'

'But was Flint still lurking around at this point?'

'Harold, please. Dad's gone. Painful as it is, we have to let him go. All the theorising in the world isn't going to bring him back. We have to sort his funeral and look to the future. Now, let me show you these plans. Look, there's even a wedding fair coming to Lewes and I'm definitely going.'

20

The weathervane on the tower of Southover church is a large shark gently turning as the wind gusts up the Ouse valley with the muddy taint of the tidal river. The story goes that the weathervane proudly commemorates a colossal basking shark washed up in days gone by on Brighton beach – the huge revenue from its precious liver oil was used for medicine, cosmetics and fuel at the time. *Jaws moves in mysterious ways*, reflects Barclay, peering up at it.

He wonders what the last memories of that poor basking shark were on that beach all those years ago. The bleary sight of delighted townsfolk approaching with kitchen knives? Or perhaps a solitary child stumbling across its final breaths at dawn and offering it words of kindness and comfort. The shingle must have felt incredibly painful under its belly, like sprawling supine on a bed of marbles. Did it occur to anyone to attempt to save its life, this vast sea creature that was beached against its will, gasping from its gills?

Poor Victor, he reflects, *suffering the same fate, suffocating and drowning within seconds of opening that tank of lost wine.* He wonders what Victor's last thoughts were and what his own will be when his time comes. *I rather hope it's the satisfaction of completing an epic jigsaw*, he muses as he shuffles behind the slow-moving queue of people steadily filtering into the church.

★

Some funerals are colourful affairs, the so-called celebration of life. Victor left no particular instructions for his, and aside from a few cursory natural details – a few vases with the reds, golds and burnished copper of autumnal vine leaves – there's very little in the church to suggest the setting is at all personal to the late winegrower. Barclay files into the church followed by Pearl with Axel. Teddy is fidgeting nervously behind them. Minty and Tom are close behind, and Barclay finds his nerves are steadied by the sound of Nobuyuki Tsujii's recording of Beethoven's 'Auf dem Hügel sitz ich, spähend'. The sounds transport him to a place of broad rivers flowing under Alpine mountains, the sense of peace that only a deserted lake in the silence of off-season can promote. Stillness from depth, the waters scaly on the surface but mellifluous and mysterious beneath. Beethoven's last words, Barclay recalls, were of sadness that the consignment of Rhineland Riesling from his homeland that arrived moments before his demise was just too late for him to enjoy.

'Schade, schade, zu spät!' whispers Barclay loudly to Axel and Pearl. Axel looks blank as Pearl makes a face at Barclay for speaking too loudly. Barclay nods appreciatively as the Bottle Bank crew settle into their pew. Teddy whispers to Pearl. 'Think Barclay's eulogy will be alright?' he asks.

'Yeah, it'll be fine. As long as he has remembered his notes.'

The service begins with the youthful vicar Macarena Soto, recently arrived from Chile, showing a PowerPoint presentation of the migration of the soul from the body back to the bosom of Christ. Teddy is transfixed by the weirdness of how specific Macarena is being, while Minty and Tom's hands find one another resting on the softness of her large coat wrapped up in her lap. Pearl is laying her head on Axel's shoulder, Pinot tucked between her feet. Barclay is attempting to read the notes for his eulogy and struggling to hold the paper at the correct distance away from his eyes to focus adequately. Harold Crawshaw, disturbed by Barclay's rustling, turns around from the front pew and stares at him with a hot look.

It's only now that Barclay stares ahead and really absorbs the sight of Victor Crawshaw's coffin. It seems somehow smaller than the man, woven from wicker and draped with a few vines around a solitary bottle of red wine in a Burgundy-shaped bottle. From where Barclay is sitting, he's guessing it's Victor's favourite grape, Pinot Noir. *But didn't he drown in Pinot?* wonders Barclay, questioning the poor taste of including the cause of death with the body.

Before he has time to fully disappear down the warren of his own mind, Macarena is calling him up to deliver the eulogy. As Barclay bumbles out of the pew, climbing over his colleagues and ambling up the aisle, Pinot, piqued by the scent of treats from his pocket, breaks out from under the pews and trots after him. A moment of levity ripples through the congregation as Barclay gives Pinot a treat and gestures for her to rejoin Pearl, which, after a few false starts, she finally understands.

All but Harold Crawshaw find this a relief from the tension. Harold's face is set like thunder in aspic as Barclay ascends the pulpit. Tabitha gives Barclay an encouraging smile through dewy eyes and her trembling chin. Barclay fumbles in his pockets and fails to find his notes. Teddy and Pearl exchange an anxious glance.

Barclay clears his throat. 'Victor was quite a guy. Whether you knew him as Mr Crawshaw, the godfather of Sussex wine, Dad, or, for his beloved runner ducks, the seed feeder, the one thing everyone in this temple of . . . Jesus . . . can agree on is that he was strong mustard. It seems we are living in an age where judgement falls like a collective veil of moderation, a veil that muffles, for fear of standing out. I'm speaking about humans. Personalities. And Victor was certainly one of those. A big one. A whopper, you might say.'

Teddy is silently praying while Pearl swallows nervously as Barclay continues.

'The thing I loved most about Victor from the first time I met him as a young boy – I was a young boy, he was a mature man – was that he meant business. If he made a mistake, he might not immediately own up to it, but you can be sure he used that process to build mountains in his mind, and he climbed every single one of them until there was nothing left to conquer. His wines were as ineffable, frustrating and sublime as he was. Sometimes the greatest, other years not so much. But for Victor the truth of the place was all that counted in his wine. He saw himself as a mere scribe faithfully dictating the will of the weather. I learnt more about wine from tasting with Victor Crawshaw than I ever did sitting in classrooms blind-tasting and making notes that nobody would ever read, least of all me. And that's what keeps me interested in wine: Victor's idea that it flowed from a place none of us can see and yet in which we all live. That place is right now. Because that's all we are and all wine is: the captured moment of that season to be opened, poured and enjoyed. So Victor may no longer be pouring us a glass, but he's certainly always going to be "right now" in my heart, and that's the place none of us, not even Victor, can ever escape from. Victor Crawshaw is here to stay and, like the best vintage wines, the memories he leaves will only get better with age.'

Pearl and Teddy exchange hesitant glances, trying to gauge the reaction of the congregation as Barclay descends the pulpit, on the way giving Victor's coffin an affectionate pat causing the wine bottle to wobble which elicits a gasp from the congregation as he passes back to his pew. Macarena is giving her brightest smile as she prepares to give her blessing. A few breaths of approval can be heard, and sighs of relief from the Bottle Bank crew who all know how close that eulogy could have come to Barclay reciting his latest list of new names for the shop. Pearl shudders at the thought and imagines Barclay in full flow at the pulpit: 'The Kingdom of Sip. Wine Eyrie. The Chalice of Mystery . . .' As Macarena's enthusiastic dismissal echoes around the rafters, the congregation begin chatting and moving from their pews. Only Harold Crawshaw remains seated, staring straight ahead, his eyes fixed on his father's coffin. His mistrust of Barclay is seething into a froth of fantastical might.

21

Across Lewes, the chimneys look like piles of books releasing sooty ribbons to join the smouldering sky. The sun is setting, a red lollipop swallowed by the open horizon, and across town, fires are being lit by cold hands in dry hearths. Hot tea is brewing in innumerable pots and the pubs are preparing for the evening rush, serving foaming pints of Harvey's Best Bitter to a steady throng of thirsty locals.

Passing the King's Head on the way back to the Bottle Bank, Barclay Flint is marching at a rolling pace on the way to host Victor's wake. His usual gait is somewhere between a polar bear and a penguin, but after Victor's funeral, Barclay is in a hurry to open his domain and welcome the congregation of guests with a few glasses of 'exquisite filth', as he put it to Pearl earlier that day. Going over his eulogy in his mind, he can't quite decide if he'd managed to remember everything he wanted to say and wishes he'd referred to his notes. Tapping his front pocket, he finds his scribbled speech on crumpled paper and tries to scan it while marching at speed. Deeply absorbed in his own thoughts, he walks straight past the door to the Bottle Bank before stopping, turning and rummaging in his pocket for the key. Down the street he can see the first guests are already steadily moving up Priory Street from Southover church. In the far distance the shark-shaped weathervane abruptly swings in a new direction as a chill wind bites from the north.

*

Tabitha rests her hand on Harold's shoulder inside the church. He's been staring at their father's coffin for what seems to her an awfully long time. He looks up and their eyes meet in heaviness.

'Time to go, Hal,' says Tabitha.

'I'm not going.'

'Why not?'

'Flint. What was that eulogy all about? The man is just . . . off.'

'Look, I asked him to handle the eulogy because neither you nor I are in any fit state. This is all so difficult, it's time to put our best foot forward. Come on, we'll go to the Bottle Bank together.'

Harold rises steadily and stares at his father's coffin, tears brimming in his eyes. Tabitha leads him slowly away down the aisle with a few comforting words as Macarena Soto patiently waits to see them both safely out at the door to the church.

The wind picks up while a bottleneck of people forms on Priory Street waiting to file steadily into the Bottle Bank. Inside, Pinot is wagging her tail and making friends with everyone coming through the door, ever hopeful of bagging a falling canapé. Teddy is handing around a tray of nibbles while trying not to look at Pearl who is circulating deftly while pouring from a magnum bottle of Contino Gran Reserva Rioja 2011. Axel is sat behind the counter playing a game on his smartphone while Barclay steadies himself by taking a large sip of red wine from his favourite Zalto Universal glass. Plucking his notes from his top pocket, he begins urgently tapping his glass to draw the gathering to order. As the crowd settles down from conversation through sedate murmuring and into a hushed silence, Tabitha escorts

Harold through the door with a tinkle of the bell. Barclay hoists himself up onto a chair to begin speaking and holds his speech aloft in triumph.

'My top pocket, it turns out, is the lost and found. The notes for my eulogy were, as with all the greatest deductions, hidden in plain sight. My mind solves things, mainly wine of course, but things that are missing send me over the edge of my own thoughts. Victor's work here in Sussex touched us all for many years and while I may have glossed over a number of ideas written here on this scrap of paper, I can't miss the chance to share something profound with you all here today. What I'm about to reveal will change this place forever.'

Pearl slowly moves towards Teddy, wondering what's about to spring from Barclay's brain.

'My friends. For too long we have been labouring under false pretences. What's in a name ...'

'Here it comes,' whispers Pearl under her breath to Teddy whose eyes are tilting upwards with a surge of anxiety.

'A name that no longer holds any meaning. I know Victor would agree from his heavenly seat at St Peter's saintly wine bar. Henceforth, this shop shall be known no longer as the Bottle Bank but as the Wine Thesaurus.'

Around the shop the silence is palpable as the gathered crowd try to digest why Barclay is taking this opportunity to share this curious idea. He steps down, clearly delighted with himself as Pearl hops up onto the chair and raises a glass. 'But to keep things simple we'll stick with the Bottle Bank for the foreseeable, here's to Victor and to wine!'

'To wine!' The toast echoes around the store and as Barclay frowns he finds himself caught in Harold Crawshaw's heavy stare. Tabitha breaks the ice with small talk as Harold simmers in Barclay's general direction. Bemused, Barclay is shuffling his hands through his pockets as though searching for a secret portal to allow him to escape to a sunlit vineyard. Harold's words are about to boil over and Tabitha falls into an awkward silence.

'So, Flint. I gather you want to inherit Dandelion Hill?' begins Harold.

Barclay looks quizzical. 'Harold?'

'The police told me all about your little chat with my father the night he died. Utterly inappropriate and never going to happen, Tabs and I are the sole inheritors, when the will turns up you'll see. So you can put Dandelion Hill out of your mind for good.'

'I can assure you both that the only designs I have on Dandelion Hill are to continue tasting its wines for as many vintages as I am fortunate enough to live through.'

'Not if I have anything to do with it. You'll be as far away from us and our place as possible.'

Harold's face is sharpened to a dagger-like glare. Barclay's gaze is neutral as he deciphers his predicament and accurately assesses Harold Crawshaw's rage levels at typhoon force. Something inside Barclay shifts. His forehead relaxes as though a spiritual valve has been released from deep within, and he pulls his hand out of his pocket clutching a jigsaw piece.

'Found it. This jigsaw piece has left a hole in Wilmington church's spire for the past several days and it has been driving me wild. Rejoice!'

Tabitha seizes the opportunity for levity and exhales with relief. 'That's marvellous, Barclay. We're going to head off, but thank you for the words in the church, I know Dad would have appreciated your candour.'

'As I always appreciated his,' replies Barclay.

Before Harold can fire another tirade, Tabitha grabs him by the arm and together they move towards the doorway, watched by Pinot, disappointed that they are not spilling treats as they exit. Barclay reverently carries the final piece of his jigsaw over to the counter where he places it in the final gap, completing the spire of Wilmington church. Admiring his handiwork, he notices that Axel is still playing games on his smartphone. Teddy and Pearl are circulating the snacks and wine and over in the corner, by the champagne and sparkling wines, Minty and Tom are smartly turned out, utterly absorbed in one another's close conversation.

Almost sensing that they are being watched, Minty and Tom suddenly share a mutual realisation that on this sombre occasion they are both behaving with the cheerfulness, nerves and excitement of a very promising first date.

22

The next morning Axel's entry to the Bottle Bank tinkles the bell above the door.

'Oh, here for another tasting?' asks Teddy with a hint of bitterness as he tidies up some of the empties from the night before.

'Helping Pearl with knitting today, we are planning a knitting protest, isn't that cool? I have to say your boss Mr Flint's wine knowledge was super enlightening the other day, I love that he made such a connection between what we put into our bodies and what comes out of the ground.'

'He does that. What does, er, a knitting protest involve, exactly?' asks Teddy.

'We're stopping the traffic!' chimes Pearl from the storeroom.

'What, all of it?' asks Teddy.

'Come on, let's knit, babe! I cannot wait to deploy our car-catchers,' says Axel. Teddy hurries across the shop clutching three bottles of wine in each hand and stacking them quickly on the shelves.

'I've always wanted to learn to knit, why don't I give you a hand?' Teddy blurts.

Pearl eyes Teddy suspiciously. 'You realise this protest is for real, Teddy?'

'Well, all I can do is support you, Pearl, nature knows best. Hey, did I say I found a Crimson Speckled in my moth trap on Ashcombe Bottom . . .?'

'Ned, you're a great guy,' Axel grins, handing him a pair of knitting needles and plucking several colourful balls of wool from his rucksack. Pearl snatches the needles back with a smirk.

'We'll be fine. Just restock the shelves, Teddy.'

Several hours later, a trail of wool leads from the Bottle Bank counter out to the storeroom where Pearl and Axel are surrounded by knitting. The room is festooned with balls of wool and colourful scarves of every hue. Stripey, multicoloured, tartan and check, it's as though a woollen volcano has erupted between them. As Teddy squeezes past reams of knitting while picking up boxes of wine to restock the Bottle Bank's shelves, he can't help thinking that Pearl and Axel look like a couple of birds cooing at one another from deep within a knitted psychedelic nest. And, uncharacteristically for Teddy, it makes him feel queasy.

His fondness for Pearl has always been rooted in their shared love of nature and he's surprised at how much he's recently been thinking about her allotment. The way she explained biodynamic gardening to him – planting and harvesting in sync with the phases of the moon – changed his world in a breath. Of course, the moon has power over the oceans and therefore all liquids, he remembers, so the sap in plants must be similarly affected by its waxing and waning. Rather like the ups and downs of a rollercoaster, in tapping into those cycles to move with the natural world rather than against it, we will enable plants to thrive. 'Go with the flow,' as Pearl had put it. To Teddy, Pearl's ideas have almost always made sense. But the swiftness of her devotion to Axel is leaving him with a sense of something odd, the flame of a candle burning without a wick. It seems to Teddy that Axel banging on about his popular climate protests back in Denmark is a little on the boastful side.

'So then the whole city was on our side, it was beautiful, magical, like a revolution with no guns and only love for the same thing,' Axel is saying.

'You?' jokes Teddy.

'I wish, no, it was unity in love for our mother planet.' Axel bows his head and Pearl marvels at his marvellousness. Teddy cuts a path between them through a pile of wool.

'Sorry, can I just squeeze . . . past . . . thanks. How does the knitting work on this protest, then?'

'Neddy . . .' says Axel.

'Teddy . . .'

'Can I just call you Ted? It's better; this is a web. A web for catching cars. Like a spider car-catcher.'

'If you need to catch a car I can always give you a lift . . . to the station, perhaps?'

'No, Ted, the point is exactly that we hate cars. Cars are the big enemy. Even the electric ones. So bad. Don't you get it? We have to stop moving to see where we are.'

'But you came here from Denmark.'

'I walked.'

'Across the North Sea?'

'Haa, you got me, buddy, you got me good. No, that part I sailed.'

'He sailed, all on his own!' Pearl enthuses.

'Of course he did,' says Teddy, not entirely sure what *catching cars* even means, his flustered stomach rising in silent bubbles. Feeling the need for moral guidance on his growing antipathy for Axel, Teddy heads to where Barclay is removing his coat and already sipping sherry behind the counter while listening to John Field's Nocturne No. 2 in C Minor H. 25.

'Not easy listening today, Barclay?'

'John Field, Teddy, is the easiest of listening. His nocturnes cast a spell so uplifting that the spirit flies without the need for borrowed wings – we are this music, Teddy.'

As Teddy listens, it strikes him that Barclay's jovial words are not matching his expression, which is tilting uncharacteristically towards glumness. *Must be his mate Victor's death weighing him down*, he reflects. 'Barclay, have you nailed that whole bottle of sherry?'

Barclay peers at the empty bottle on the counter. 'No, that's from yesterday,' he says, holding up a newly opened bottle of Pastrana single vineyard Manzanilla. 'This stuff is so moreish I'm tasting tomorrow today.' He sniffs the glass. 'Honeysuckle smoke; it's inspiring me, Teddy! Ah! New name for the shop: Valhalla's Vineyard.'

'Are you saying that because Axel's around?'

'Axel? The Dane? By Jove, no, vines and Valhalla just seem to fit with the idea of bottles of the gods. There I go again! Bottles of the Gods! Even better.'

'People like the Bottle Bank.'

'People don't like what they don't know,' suggests Barclay.

'Seriously, what does that even mean?' asks Teddy.

'We like what we think we like, but do we, Teddy? Do we really?' Barclay turns back to his new jigsaw of the Brighton Pavilion.

After a moment of reflection, Teddy ascends the stairs to the flats above Bottle Bank. He knocks gingerly on Minty's door. She flings it open in her apron and welcomes him inside to her realm of golden glowing decorations, an abode so bright Teddy wouldn't be surprised if she'd kidnapped the sun. The sound of Labi Siffre's 'I Got The . . .' further warms the scene.

'Come in, dear Teddy, I'll fetch you a tea, one sugar, am I right?'

'One's perfect, thanks, Minty. Thanks, my brain needs a reboot, software update required, Minty style.'

'I'll just get us a slice of ginger cake, tell me what's ailing you?'

'It's silly really, I just can't get Axel out of my mind.'

'Which one is Axel?'

'The Dane, came to Barclay's tasting and now he and Pearl are like glue.'

'And you like this Dane?'

'What? No – he's incredibly annoying, I just want to hang out with Pearl but Axel's practically moved into the shop.'

'And you're not happy.'

'Not really, but then again it's cool Pearl has a new relationship, I just don't want her to disappear from my life.'

'She'll come around, Teddy, and in the meantime all you need concern yourself with is how best to catch that attention when she swings your way again, which she will.'

'Some sort of present to impress?'

'Less about a gift, think about something you can say with your heart to show her you care.'

'Strong feelings, flex my emotions, thank you, Minty, I get it. OK, cool, I'm going to spend some time on this, I'll find the right system to convey my feelings. Minty, you're the best.'

Minty smiles at him and hands him a slice of freshly baked ginger cake. 'Teddy, there's nothing in life that cannot be solved with a slice of sticky ginger cake. Fireworks for the soul.'

Teddy is struck by the word *fireworks* and remembers he's due another delivery to Priory Bonfire's cache of explosives at Dandelion Hill.

The barn at Dandelion Hill has stood there for centuries, its grey flint walls glimmering against heavy steel skies, autumn's tussle with summer's exit and winter's advance. The months topple into years and, from the point of view of the barn, not a lot has changed. Things come, things go, but each of those stones, laid by unseen hands now long dead, has stayed put and held its guard against the weather, harvests, rivalries, marriages, deaths and living poetry of families born and families passing into memory. Inside the barn the atmosphere is as still as a candle in a crypt. Even on the wettest days there's solace inside this place that has served as a home to countless mice, starlings, solitary bees, house martins, slow-worms and more down the ages. Today, Priory Bonfire Society has made it their nest. Piles of fireworks and cross-shaped torches are piled up at one end. At the other, the effigy for November 5th is at last taking shape, a large looming human shadow that's fixed in the barn, unmoving, silent, a witness to the comings and goings of teams in navy-and-white diamond check guernseys moving in and out like curious bees in an ancient hive.

Outside, the faint pattering of rain is building on the old roof as the latch to the old door lifts and Teddy Olsen pokes his head into the half-light. He's immediately struck by the thought that there must be a good number of moths using the barn to overwinter and heaven knows what other wildlife taking a quiet time of dormancy until the weather relents next spring. Stepping inside, he carefully places his box of fireworks with the rest of the explosives, the faint rustle of birds settling to roost in the rafters making him look up.

What an ancient building! Spitfires would have rolled across the skies above it in the Second World War, this place would have been around when Queen Victoria was on the throne, might even have been around when the Spanish Armada was gathering on the horizon in 1588. Slowly turning around, Teddy feels a huge pair of eyes in the darkness locked onto him – it's almost a sixth sense, perhaps how a rabbit feels when a fox is hurtling towards it, all teeth, fur and fright. With a shudder, Teddy turns his body to face this looming creature in the darkness.

Behind him, Priory's partially completed effigy commands the space – twenty-five feet tall with eyes bulging and arms contorted as though conjuring a kingdom-wide spell. Teddy falls to his knees in horror. He can barely mouth the word as he identifies the person who Priory will this year burn as the focus of their pent-up civic rage.

'Pearl,' moans Teddy, hiding his head in his hands as he backs away and makes a dash for the delivery van in a rising storm.

23

Seagulls are whipping across the sky and being swept out to sea by the gathering storm's deepening gusts. Far below, the Downs are hunkered under the furrowed sky with Dandelion Hill a lonely outcrop. Fading leaves from the vineyard are scattering in the stiffening breeze, leaving dark bare wood behind. Some vineyards look majestic in winter. Barclay always likens them to 'gnarled hands reaching up from the earth ready to grasp the next sunbeam'. Today, the vineyards at Dandelion Hill are looking more like a retreating army of war-torn veterans, bandaged and barely able to stay upright. Up on the side of the hill, Victor Crawshaw's grave is marked by a mound of earth with an oak sapling waiting to be planted in a large pot beside it. Permissions were more forthcoming than Harold might have imagined and he was pleased with Tabitha's agreement to keep their father's remains on the farm, the place he had retreated to and from which he rarely relished departing. Now Victor Crawshaw would never have to leave again.

Trudging towards the grave, a burly man in a dark navy combat jumper with shoulder and elbow patches is carrying a spade. The man's reddening hands are bunched against the cold, resilient, calm and steady. His scalp-cropped hair and bulky build suggest a lifetime of heavy work. He has a face laid with the weathered thickness of living rock and though he is passing through his fifties, Mike Delves moves with impressive fluidity, his weighty frame matched by the cadence of fiercely controlled strength. Down the valley, Harold walks towards his shabby 1950s bungalow tucked at the edge of the vineyard while up on the hill Mike Delves begins digging a hole to plant the tree. Shovelling at speed with rhythmic determination, he is unmoved by the flurry of rain that threatens from above.

Recently returned from his errand to Dandelion Hill, Teddy is frantically pacing around Minty's flat. 'They planned the whole thing, Minty. Pearl has obviously pissed off the whole town with her protests, but I never in a million years thought Priory would make her one of the effigies. No wonder they kept me at arm's length from the build. What am I supposed to do?'

Minty settles back in her chair with a slice of ginger cake. 'Teddy, first we've got to be sure that effigy is definitely Pearl.'

'I saw it with my own eyes. I should have taken a photo. Can't believe they'd do this to me. It's crazy.'

'What have you told our Pearl?'

'Nothing yet. She'd blow her top.'

'She's going to find out sooner or later, on Bonfire Night for sure.'

'If it was me, I'd want to know before.'

'Right then, there you go. You've got to tell our Pearl that her likeness will be dragged through the streets and they're going to ignite it, like it or not. She may see it as a mark of respect.'

'Or Axel might. Then again, he might hate it as much as I do. It's all kicked off since that ruddy Dane arrived. What am I going to do?'

'You'll do the right thing, Teddy. That's all you can do.'

★

Harold's bungalow is well worn inside. Utilitarian rather than cosy, it is a place of function more than comfort. His office is cramped with stacks of old Ordnance Survey maps and books about geology, and a cork board pinned with notes and plans for his proposed natural burial ground hangs from the wall behind his desk. Harold sits down with a mug of tea and flicks on his aging desktop computer. Before he has a chance to open his emails, Mike Delves lets himself in through the front door, damp and hot from his labours. He picks up a jar of pickled onions from the sideboard and joins Harold.

'All done. Just started shedding down,' he says.

'Mike, I appreciate you coming down to help, it may all be in my head but as I said on the phone, something just isn't right about Dad's death.'

'Was he losing it?'

'Stubborn as ever but I refuse to believe he'd top himself, if that's what you mean.' Mike Delves clicks his neck from side to side uneasily.

'Any ideas?' asks Delves.

'Some. Barclay Flint was with Dad in the winery, last person to see him alive and, here, Dad's notebooks are explicit about the tank he was found in. It says here, underlined, "Do not open".' Harold passes a notebook over to Delves, who flexes his knuckles.

'Who'd open it, then?' asks Delves.

'No idea. Flint was with him and, according to the police, Dad was talking about leaving the whole place to him.'

'What's the will say?'

'All comes to me and Tabs, down the middle. Dad's solicitor Moss has "temporarily mislaid" the damn thing but the old boy assures me it hasn't been changed in years.'

Delves crunches on a pickled onion.

'They smell lethal.'

'Stops me thinking about the cigs. So what's in it for this Flint guy?'

'Wants the vineyard for himself, I reckon. And he's not the only one. Christ knows, Dad had enough enemies. Le Brocq over the hill chief among them.'

'The shooter?'

'Hated Dad's guts. I mean, don't get me wrong, Dad loathed him just as much, but he would never physically hurt the old git. The other way round, I'm not so sure. Dad dumped a ton of old grapes on Le Brocq's driveway, didn't go down too well.'

'I can imagine. Why dump the grapes?'

'Le Brocq tried to buy the farm from Dad, said he wanted to turn it into a hunting lodge. Dad was pretty fired up.'

'Interesting. This Le Brocq ever pull anything to, you know . . .'

'Intimidate? Not exactly. I mean he's incredibly entitled and thinks he's Lord of the Manor, always strutting around trying to make the little people bend to his will, but as far as muscle, no, never that far.'

'Who are his lot?'

'No family, just his housekeeper and the Range Rover brigade, anyone who thinks they can secure a bit of social standing by being in his set. Why on earth anyone would want either of those things is beyond me.'

'What do you make of this coroner's report?'

Harold opens an email and scans the content. 'Drowning is the cause, by accident. Reckon he opened the lid to the tank, the build-up of CO_2 in there knocked him spark out and he tumbled in unconscious.'

'And you don't buy it?'

'Look, Dad made wine his whole life long. Not so much as a scratch. He was eccentric, sure, but he was meticulous.

He'd opened tanks of fermenting wine hundreds of times, what made this one any different?'

'More carbon dioxide than normal?'

'I don't see how, no.'

Delves fishes out another pickle while thinking and slowly crunches into an onion with a loud bite.

'You always did love pickled onions.'

'No sugar spike.'

'What did you call them in the field?'

'Face grenades.'

'Ha! It's good to see you, Mike. In touch with the other boys?'

'Whistler I saw, probably five years gone. Not much from Tommy Hadlow, settled in Scotland last I heard. And nothing from Lima in years. Probably cutting his way through a bloodbath same as always.'

'Loved the action, that one. Handy in a scrap.'

'Not as handy as you. Saved my life.'

'You'd have done the same for me, Mike.'

Delves crunches into another pickle. 'Your dad, he seem off the last few days?'

'His feud with Le Brocq was raging. He'd certainly become – what's the word – withdrawn, over the past year or so. Absolutely hated leaving the farm, I mean like a screaming toddler about it. Obsessed with the wildlife, though, treated the runner ducks like his long-lost grandchildren.'

Delves offers the jar of open pickles to Harold.

'Not for me. I mean, who would want to see Dad out of the way?'

Mike Delves shifts uneasily in his chair.

'It doesn't add up. Enough to go on, Mike?'

'Plenty for starters. I'll get the measure of Le Brocq, and I don't like the sound of this Flint. He knows something, I'd bet my boots on it.'

'What's the plan?'

'Stake him out, extract what he's holding back and if need be, apply a bit of friendly pressure. Just a little bit. You know, I do my thing.'

'Yes. Your thing.'

'Never fails. If Le Brocq or Flint had anything to do with what happened to your dad, I'll flush them, catch them and, if need be, gut them.'

'Just one thing. Not a word to Tabby, right?'

As Mike Delves nods and fishes around for another pickle, Harold notices his own fists clenched tightly on the desk. Releasing his fingers, he exhales and purses his lips in a determined reciprocal nod. Delves nods back, expressionless.

24

'Teddy, what is with you?' asks Pearl, flustered as she steps back from a smashed bottle of red on the shop floor.

'My hand's all sweaty.'

'Why's your vibe so off?'

Teddy is hopping from foot to foot surveying the mess he's made. Each time he glimpses Pearl's face he sees a flash of the giant effigy in the barn at Dandelion Hill and it feels like a cattle prod to his soul. He stares down at the mess.

'I'll fetch the mop.'

'Teddy what's making you so salty? Hello, I'm over here!'

Teddy averts his eyes from Pearl as he hurries out the back to hunt for a mop. He's desperately trying to focus on visualising his favourite Buff-tip moth, which looks like a little silver birch twig. If only he could camouflage himself to disappear right now – or better yet, find a way to save Pearl from being burned as an effigy on November 5th. He's rummaging in the store cupboard, pulling out the mop and bucket, when Pearl pokes her head around the door behind him.

'Teddy?' Shocked, Teddy leaps in the air, arms flailing, and brings the contents of the cupboard crashing down around him.

'MG Teddy, what is with you?'

'I'm fine, everything's fine . . .' he stammers, trying to gather up the brooms, J-cloths, detergent and cleaning supplies from the floor and fit them back into the cupboard.

His attempts are about as effective as skiing on pipe-cleaners. Pearl dives in to help and he recoils as he catches another glimpse of her face, which blasts the thought of her effigy right to the front of his mind.

'Hey, relax, come on, let's manifest calm, Teddy. You sort the mess in the shop, I've got this.'

Breathing at speed and puffing his cheeks in and out like a hyperventilating hamster, Teddy grabs the mop and heads back to the shop, desperately trying not to catch a glimpse of Pearl by holding it up to block her obliquely from his view. Pearl shakes her head, wondering what the hell is going on, when she's struck by an idea. Closing the cupboard, she heads into the shop.

'Teddy. Are you jealous. Is this drama about Axel?'

'Axel? Axel? Why would anything be about Axel, I mean, he's Axel!'

'Teddy. I saw you on Lovelink.'

'Lovelink?'

'The dating app.'

'What dating app?'

'The one you're on, Teddy, your profile pinged me. If you're shook about Axel, there's no need, you and me will always be, you know, solid. Oi! Can't you just look at me?'

Teddy swerves his eyeballs elaborately sideways and moves his head to follow before finally focusing on Pearl. 'This has nothing to do with Axel. There's a . . . there's something I have to tell you.'

'All ears, shoot.'

Teddy thinks of the looming effigy and imagines telling Pearl, her indignance, her humiliation, her devastation. He can't bring himself to share the secret. 'You're spot on. I was on Lovelink. I haven't had a date in forever, I never imagined it would match us up, of course I deleted it as soon as I saw we'd been matched.'

'Same!'

'You did?' says Teddy, suddenly a little put out.

'Well, you know, felt a bit weird.'

'Yes, I mean, silly really, totally bonkers actually. And, besides: Axel.'

'It's unreal. We are getting on so great. You get him, right?'

'Not as much as you do,' says Teddy, crunching glass hard with his mop. 'You really like him?'

'Yeah, I really do.'

'In that case I am also fond of him, full marks to Axel.' Teddy grins slightly maniacally as he plunges the mop into the bucket with the force of a pirate ramming wadding into a cannon.

Mike Delves is sitting at Harold Crawshaw's desk, the computer whirring as it resurrects itself from deep slumber. Delves' eyes are slate grey, his pink eyelids rimmed with the redness of someone who routinely doesn't get enough sleep. Shuffling his papers on the desk, he pulls out a black and white photograph of Maurice Le Brocq. A shotgun is broken over Le Brocq's left arm and he is standing in front of Greenacres with all the pride of a magpie that's just devoured a nest of stolen eggs. The computer flickers to life and Delves logs in. On the screen, his most recent windows open, file upon file about Greenacres, Le Brocq's membership of the League of Rural Affairs, charity dinners, shooting parties and his time as a student at Durham University. Delves makes a note on a pad. 'Not Oxbridge'. He sits back in his chair and looks at the assembled dossier on Le Brocq. Taking out his phone, he dials a number. 'Hello, is Mr Le Brocq there? Mike Delves, no he doesn't know me, I'm writing a piece for *County Ways* on the Sussex shooting scene. Thanks . . .' As he waits for Mrs McRae to fetch Le Brocq, he flips open another dossier filled with press cuttings and photographs of Barclay Flint.

At the same time, inside Southover hall in Lewes, three couples are moving across the old parquet floor to the sound of calypso music. The harsh strip lighting fringes their costumes. Minty and Tom are moving gracefully, Tom in one of his trademark tracksuits, this one a burnished orange with yellow go-faster stripes. Minty is guiding him patiently through his steps and forgiving his tendency to freestyle. With the reverence of a meditation instructor, she gently brings him back to the path and they move smilingly around the floor together, their mood as fragrant as jasmine unfurling underneath a tropical sunset. The other two couples are a stark contrast to one another. One young couple are both wearing a lot of leather and awkwardly trying to do their dance steps from memory, while the two senior women dancing together in flowing dresses are as natural and synchronised as though they are each wearing one another's shoes. At the end of the song, Minty claps everyone to bring them around and garner their attention.

'Lovely, just lovely, my darlings. Now I'm going to focus on the turn, step, turn out, step back, hands together. OK, this is the part where you're both strolling along in the sunshine, having a good time and showing everybody just how much love is in your heart . . .' She pauses as the doors swing open and Pearl enters with Axel.

'Yikes, we too late to join?' asks Pearl.

'Pearl, darling, you can come any time. Just make your donation later.' Minty gestures to a bucket near the doorway with a cardboard cut-out of a pigeon and a handmade sign reading BIRD FOOD FUND. 'OK, everybody, this is Pearl and Axel, both of you are beginners, right?'

'I have done a little salsa before but the calypso I admit is completely new to me,' says Axel.

'Then you're in the right place. Pearl, you dance with Tom; Axel, let me show you the basics, my lovely.'

Minty flicks on the music and the dancing begins once again. Pearl can't help but think about Teddy as she dances with Tom. She suspects that there's something more amiss with her friend than he's letting on. And she is beginning to wonder whether it might have something to do with the death of Victor Crawshaw.

25

Construction on Lewes Castle began in the year 1087, just a few years after William the Conqueror sailed the English Channel to invade from France. Originally built from wood, the stone construction followed later. Whenever he strolls beneath the Barbican Gate, Barclay always likes to muse that its flint ramparts have kept watch over the town for the best part of a thousand years. What sights it must have seen: the ancient track crossing the Downs used by the fishwives of yesteryear to carry the catch from the coast to the county town; the A27 bypass opening in 1977; the Battle of Lewes on the 14th of May in the year 1264 when King Henry III sheltered in the castle in retreat from the rebel barons. Time here is as jumbled as the flint bricks laid in place by the hands of builders now long gone and laid to rest in local churchyards some ten centuries ago. Barclay likes to wonder whether the moods of the cumulative lives witnessed by the ramparts on this old station of war have somehow been suffused into the very mortar. Perhaps the deepest memories only stir for an annual instant with the fireworks of November 5th, a distant echo of the battles fought long ago.

Today, Barclay's attention is distracted by the strong breeze which is choosing to use Lewes Castle as its playground, swirling with exuberance around the West Tower Gardens perched high above the town. To Barclay, erecting a gazebo in fine weather is as baffling as teaching a sea lion to ride a bicycle; add a few strong South Downs gusts and he may as well be attempting to build the Great Pyramid of Giza out of toothpicks in a live volcano. Mercifully, Teddy is on hand to take command and, with vast experience of overnight camping while tending to his beloved moth traps, his deft touch soon has an impressive display of wine lined up on a trestle table beneath a perfectly constructed shelter. And, as if to rub salt in the wound, the sun comes out just as the wind dies down.

Today's wedding fair at Lewes Castle is enticing an impressive array of town businesses to ply their wares. Florists, caterers, dress designers, photographers, musicians, chauffeurs, breweries, videographers, cheesemongers, DJs, beauticians, chocolatiers, hairdressers, travel agencies, bakers and the Bottle Bank are all represented in a merry range of displays, each one proudly displaying their livery ready for the visitors to arrive. Tabitha's wedding stall is a delight and draws the eye like a jewel in the beak of a magpie. It is a miniature world of bucolic charm, and a floral display of pinks and whites arching over the display of a scale model of the barn at Dandelion Hill surrounded by idyllic vineyards draws Barclay's attention.

He wanders over, glass in hand, reflecting on how ravishing it all looks. Lavish photography is proudly showing off the summer splendour of the vineyard, with ripe hanging fruit of purple, green and gold surrounding the stall. Barclay raises his glass to her as he surveys the scene, a touch of pride for the world of wine blending with fondness for his memories of this magical English vineyard founded by his late friend Victor.

Tabitha's mood is a welcome shade brighter than Barclay is expecting and she embraces him fondly with a warm hug. Behind them, the shadows of the first visitors are growing.

Wearing a navy parka jacket, well-worn boots and a black beanie hat, Mike Delves is among the first of them. He moves towards Barclay with the insouciant inevitability of a bull drawn to an open gate. Pretending to scroll on his phone and circling out of Tabitha's eyeline, Delves is tuned in to every word of their conversation.

'So, what do you think, Barclay?'

'Dandelion Hill will doubtless make a marvellous wedding venue. And your dad would doubtless be billowing with pride, Tabitha.'

'I'm not sure he ever really billowed at anything, Barclay. Except perhaps the ducks. This finally feels like my time to dream. You know, a little business, making people happy, open up the farm again. Feels like we've had our gates shut for far too long.'

'And what does dear Harold make of such colourful plans?'

'Dead against, hates every bit of it, still working on his own wretched graveyard scheme and the less said about that the better. But it isn't just his story, is it, Barclay? Thankfully, one of us has at least got an idea that will, fingers crossed, begin turning a tidy profit come spring. And save the farm from the clutches of the wretched bank.'

'An admirable ambition, Tabitha Crawshaw.' Her eyes well up and she dabs at them with a tissue.

'Tabitha?'

'Silly really, Dad used to call me Tabitha Crawshaw when he was telling me off . . .'

'I'm so sorry, I've blundered.' Barclay gives her his pressed clean handkerchief and smiles with the warmth of the Mediterranean in June. 'But what exactly was that phrase he used to use that meant scolding?'

'"Dish of tongues", what a good memory you have. Yes, when he was cross he used to say "Tabitha Crawshaw . . .

you'll get a middlin' dish of tongues when your mother comes to hear an't".' The two of them share a moment of levity at Tabitha's impersonation of her father.

'Perhaps I could give you a hand with this wedding caper. I presume you'll be pouring lashings of your own wine but if there are any requirements beyond, I'd be thrilled to curate a list of incomparably romantic wines.'

'You sweetheart, I'd love that, Barclay! We're actually horribly low on stock of our own wines, the opposite of lashings, what with Dad diverting all his attention to rewilding the place. And there's Dad's last wines still fermenting in those tanks, which heaven knows what we'll be doing with. Drain the lot, I suppose.'

'Sacrilege! Those unfinished wines are precious beyond compare and simply must be completed. Symphonies in the making, dear Tabitha. I would be delighted to conclude their composition in the style of your dear late father's own "unmaking", as he'd doubtless put it.'

As Tabitha gladly accepts Barclay's offer, Delves' attention locks onto Barclay. Just as a fox can pounce from a distance of three metres, Delves' whole body is alert and ready to strike. Considering his options, rather than make his move here and now, he silently resolves to pursue his prey with the relentless cool of the iceberg awaiting the *Titanic*. Edging steadily away from Tabitha's colourful stall, Delves starts making his way through a gaggle of hopeful brides, nervous grooms and parents-in-law all scouting the ideal wedding to match both their dreams as well as their budgets.

A few feet away a model dressed in a flowing bridal gown is being posed with the view over the rooftops of Lewes behind her. She is joined by a groom in a kilt and together they smile for promotional photographs. The photographer calls to the bride to throw her bouquet behind her. She angles herself for the best shot before tossing the bouquet high in the air. Eyeballs follow its arc up into the sky where a sudden gust of wind snags and hurls it over the ramparts down to the town below. All eyes stare as a squeal from the bride and the groom's pointing finger show its rogue hurtling trajectory away from the fair.

Far below, Minty Jarvis is making her way down Lewes High Street tucking a dainty paper bag of bird seed into her pocket. A distant cry overhead draws her attention and she looks up just in time to see a bouquet of flowers tumbling towards her. Taking the stance of a dancer in readiness, Minty Jarvis surprises herself by executing the perfect catch. The flowers' fragrance instantly floods her world and by her blissful grin, Minty Jarvis is feeling overwhelmingly blessed. Peering upwards and shading her eyes from the sunlight, she spots a bride waving gleefully down at her over the ramparts.

'Keep them, they're yours!' she shouts.

26

Greenacres is a house whose looming ghastliness commands a moment of stillness from all who make their way up its wide and immaculately raked gravel drive. Passing under the giant beech tree casting deep shade at the entrance, Mike Delves is taking it all in. Taking a final drag, he throws his fat roll-up to the ground and grinds it into the gravel with his right foot. His boots are thickly polished and he's wearing Harold's old Barbour jacket, a stiff white collar crowning over his navy jumper. Pulling a pad and pen from his jacket pocket, he begins his approach to the front door and notices a shifty figure peering from a downstairs window.

Mrs McRae is scrutinising Delves from the window of the drawing room adjacent to the porch and pretends to be dusting around a vase as she scopes out the approaching shadow. She has only felt the soft tremor in the soles of her feet that she is feeling now once before. It was a long time ago when she watched a boy from her class at school, Ivor Hooper, pinching a lollipop from the local shop. She was the only one who had noticed and it plagued her that justice was never served. She still occasionally imagines what Ivor might be up to now. Robber. Banker. Or worse. Every now and again the image of that blue lollipop in its crinkly plastic wrapping disappears into Ivor's pocket and Mrs McRae has to breathe deeply to shake it off. But today she feels exactly as she did when Ivor lifted that lolly. And try as she might, she cannot understand why. Her reverie is interrupted by the rasping of the old grinding doorbell. And she hurries to open the door.

'Good afternoon, sir.'

'That doorbell original?'

'I believe it is, yes. How may I help?'

'Needs oiling. Name's Mike Delves, we spoke on the phone about talking with the boss.'

'Of course, *County Ways*. You're a wee bit early.'

'Better than late.'

'I'll see if Mr Le Brocq is amenable.'

'Fine.' Delves nods curtly as Mrs McRae disappears inside. He starts writing something on his notepad as he stares down the hallway noticing every detail through the door which Mrs McRae has left ajar. The rack of walking sticks. Fading flowers in a vase on the hall table. The faint smell of stale bone broth. He stealthily moves around the edge of the door for a better view, to see Mrs McRae bustling at speed and beckoning him in.

'Follow me, Mr Le Brocq will see you in the library. Will you take a cup of tea?'

'Got coffee?'

'Certainly we do, how do you take your coffee, Mr Delves?'

He notices how unsettled she seems. 'Black's fine. Just the two of you living here?'

'Has been for a while now, aside from the guests who come for the shoots. Right, here we are. I'll fetch your coffee just now. Mr Delves to see you, sir.'

Maurice Le Brocq is standing facing away from the door, hands clasped behind his back. He is hoping that the effect is of one surveying his grand estate from the ramparts of an ancient castle. In the event, Mike Delves takes the chance to scan the whole room as Mrs McRae closes the door. Silently assessing every detail, Delves scans the books: a little too well dusted, haven't been read in years; an ashtray that's never been used; a porcelain bowl painted with the initials M. L. B. and a very threadbare faded gold Steiff teddy bear that's long been forgotten in a corner. Le Brocq's eyes move from side to side, unsure from the silence if his guest is there. He takes a deep nasal inhalation. Delves quietly sits down next to the fireplace and rests his notebook on his lap.

'Good of you to see me.'

Le Brocq masks his involuntary start at the sound of Delves' voice by swinging around and looking towards the doorway. Noticing Delves already seated, he feels instantly irritated and marches to his own seat. 'Make yourself comfortable, Mr Delves. *County Ways*, isn't it?'

'Yeah, they asked me to write about pheasants.'

'So I understand. And how can my little estate be of interest to the readers, I wonder?'

'Lot of them are shooters, not many see it from your side of the business.'

'And how would you describe my side of the business, Mr Delves?'

'Well. You know. Can I call you Maurice?' Le Brocq nods offishly at Delves' pronunciation of 'Maurice' as 'Morris'.

'It's like this, Maurice. They come and have a whale of a day blasting pheasants out of the sky, you do all the work, don't you?'

'I wouldn't call it work, it's more of a hobby for me, a year-round pursuit managing the land, conserving it for the next generation and so forth.'

'She been with you long? McRae?'

Before he has time to answer, Mrs McRae knocks and enters with a coffee, which she places next to Delves on a little table. 'Will there be anything else, Mr Le Brocq?'

'No, thank you, Mrs McRae. Mr Delves, did you have any specific questions?'

Delves continues as Mrs McRae leaves, probing Le Brocq on when he started shooting. Once he starts, Le Brocq's floodgates open as he reveals his childhood love of shooting and passion for sharing it with like-minded individuals.

'Of course it's really about society, shared values and ultimately a reflection of my love for nature.'

'Nature?'

'The sky, the gun and the bird. Shoot much yourself, Mr Delves?'

'Yeah.'

Le Brocq's demeanour changes at once, his slit of a mouth relaxing into more of a hole. 'Pheasants?'

'Rough shooting. Pheasants, rabbits, whatever's around. I'm all about the chase.'

'Twelve gauge?'

'Beretta Silver Pigeon,' says Delves with a nod.

'How delicious. May I call you Mike?'

'Sure, Maurice.'

'Mike, I have something that I think may fascinate readers of *County Ways*, step this way.'

Maurice leads Mike back into the hall and down a side passage where he opens his gun cabinet, plucking out two Purdeys with the practised ease of a barista serving hot espressos. Further down the passage, Le Brocq retrieves a box of cartridges from his ammunition box and leads Delves outside. Delves is intrigued by the spring in Le Brocq's step as the conversation flows with ease around the topic of cherished shooting memories. Rounding the rear corner of Greenacres with a sprawling view over the Downs, Le Brocq points to what looks a bit like a cross between a barber's and a dentist's chair bolted to a square of concrete on a raised hummock of turf. Mrs McRae brings up a sleek black Labrador walking to heel and Delves is about to give it a pat when Le Brocq snaps, 'No touching. Toby isn't a pet, he's a worker. Two simple rules: no affection and never inside the house. Thank you, Mrs McRae.' Toby sits obediently next to Le Brocq's boots.

'I'll clean out the kennel, sir.'

'Do so. Behold, the throne, Mike. Designed it myself for when I can't get about. I'll strap myself in here in my dotage while Mrs McRae swings me through one hundred and eighty degrees and the beaters flush the birds up to my gun. The old-timers love it, already had a couple of bookings just for the throne alone. Never designed it as a money spinner, but it's already paid for itself three times over. Care for a turn?'

Intrigued, Delves takes a seat, reclines a little way and Le Brocq gently swings the chair from side to side before handing Delves a shotgun and offering the cartridges.

'Shall we?' Delves gives the smile of a shark closing in on a baby seal.

As Mike Delves strides away down the driveway of Greenacres, the sound of Maurice Le Brocq shooting in the distance can still be heard. Delves never imagined he'd be able to find common ground with a type like Le Brocq. And yet they'd passed an amiable while together blasting into the sky, including one very satisfying shot that took a duck clean out which fell directly before the throne, 'a life given in homage', as Le Brocq had quipped.

In fact, the only thing Mike Delves is remotely suspicious about when it comes to Maurice Le Brocq is his treatment of his gundog, Toby. Still, the dog made an excellent retriever, didn't miss a single bird. And Le Brocq had seemed genuinely delighted with their haul. Delves pulls his phone from a pocket and dials Harold.

'Went good, bottom line, Le Brocq's not our man. Told me all about the run-ins with your dad while blasting pheasants. Reckon he's going to miss all that scrapping with your old man. No, not a chance. Le Brocq feeds on a fight but he's a straight bat. He's still shooting now, left him to it. Wouldn't want to be his dog, though. His housekeeper, McRae, something shifty there. Got some intel on the other one too, Flint. Yeah, he's got a target on his back. And as Le Brocq'll tell you, I don't miss.'

27

Barclay holds his pint of Harvey's Best Bitter aloft in the John Harvey tavern not far from Lewes' historic brewery. In his mind's eye he briefly sees Excalibur wielded by King Arthur and then remembers it's impossible to spill a sword as a tiny trickle of beer runs down his wrist. Admiring the burnished copper hue of his pint, Barclay's eyes glow like the sun, his expression as rapturous as Michelangelo's first glimpse of the Sistine Chapel.

'Clarity is key, but the living foam above is the halo of truth. The yeast inside the cask gives thousands of tiny bubbles, far smaller than those you'll find in the classiest glass of fine champagne, and if you hold the first sip on your tongue, you'll feel their infinite feathery caress, which is why, for me, Harvey's Best Bitter served from the brewery tap is the drink of the gods.'

Opposite him, a toothless eighty-year-old man with a white wispy beard is staring vacantly at Barclay. Next to him is a woman who is dressed in robes which fall, according to Barclay's categorisation, somewhere between 'immensely stylish' and 'witchcraft'. Between them, Pinot is sat focused on Barclay's every word lest 'treat' should fall among them.

'Nectar! I could swear it,' Barclay continues after taking his first sip, 'that depending on the time of the year, the profile of the hops changes. In summer when last season's hops have all but dried out, rather like the herbs in your store cupboard, the beer takes on a malty prowess, whereas in late autumn with the first harvest of hops, the bitterness is intensified making each sip a sort of foretelling as you feel instantly thirsty for the next . . .'

Barclay and his motley gang are sitting in half a large open barrel converted from the brewery to the pub with a rounded cushioned bench. The pub is thrumming with movement but every now and again, sitting in the opposite barrel, Barclay catches sight of a man nursing a pint of lager whose stare is as unnerving as his reddened blotchy stubby head. In a navy crew-neck jumper with shoulder and elbow patches, the man seems immobile, as though carved from the same wood as the giant barrel that he's sitting in. Mike Delves hates pubs and the small talk they bring. The only upside is the taste of a cold crisp lager, the one drink he'll happily sip year round, as long as it's from a brand he recognises. And in this pub, buying pickles in a packet has made his job of surveillance another notch less onerous.

Barclay finishes his pint in short order, makes his excuses, gives Pinot a treat from his pocket and escorts her out of the pub with the pride of the father of the bride striding down the aisle of a church. Barclay adores his regular constitutional walks with Pinot and Pearl is delighted that her dog is getting the extra exercise. Passing left out of Bear Yard and crossing the River Ouse, they make their way through gatherings of various bonfire societies shaking tins and raising funds for their parades and displays on November 5th. Barclay wonders which poor local bigwig will be marched through the streets as an effigy this year. Pinot stops for a pee and Barclay waits patiently, holding the end of the lead and idly scanning the view. The river is flowing fast. High tide is not far off and its running in at quite a torrent. As he turns back towards the town, Barclay catches sight of a thick-set figure wearing a navy beanie hat who appears to be looking up at one of the old warehouses next to the river. Barclay reaches for his spectacles and recognises the blotchy-headed fellow from the pub. Turning up his collar, he hurries Pinot and they take the shortcut through the woods back towards the Depot Cinema and on towards Priory Street and the safety of the Bottle Bank.

Pearl and Teddy are playing backgammon at the counter. Teddy is twitchy, his ten fingers tapping all at once. All he can think about is Priory Bonfire Society setting fire to Pearl's giant effigy while he screams from a crowd of braying costumed onlookers. Pearl eyes him askance, wondering what her friend could possibly be keeping from her.

'We're playing backgammon, Olsen, not the piano. Chill, would you?'

'Sorry,' says Teddy folding his arms. 'Just, er, thinking of my next move.'

'Better think fast,' says Pearl, taking one of his pieces just as Barclay and Pinot careen through the tinkling doorway. Barclay releases Pinot from the lead as she scampers to her bed while he peers back to the street with the elaborate aplomb of a 1970s spy checking into a hotel room and peering out of the windows for enemy eyeballs.

'Lost something, Barclay?' asks Pearl.

'Hopefully . . . Could have sworn there was a worrisome chap trailing me from the pub.'

'Come off it, you're not exactly 007, Barclay.'

'What did he look like?' asks Teddy.

'Bald and weathered, a snooker cue ball rolled in bad memories.' Barclay turns away from the door and leans on the counter, setting his phone down beside a boxed jigsaw of the white cliffs at Birling Gap.

'Was he wearing a navy parka jacket?'

'Why yes, how did you know?' says Barclay.

'He's coming into the shop,' says Teddy, slowly backing away to the storeroom.

Barclay swings around to see Mike Delves advancing through the shop door. The merry tinkling bell seems to mock the sobriety of the moment. Barclay is momentarily taken aback before regaining his composure and launching with fierce gusto into his usual routine of a welcome that, in this case, is more hot than warm.

'Traveller! Set your care aside and allow me to shine a light on the source of your thirst.' Plucking a bottle of south-western French white from the fridge by the neck, he holds it like a torch as he moves towards Delves who is standing motionless. Barclay notices a packet of gherkins poking out the side pocket of Delves' parka. 'Perfect for a palate that's partial to a pickle. A zinger, sir. Barclay Flint, proprietor of the Bottle Bank, delighted to meet you Mr . . .'

'Mike Delves.'

'Well, Mike Delves, if sharp flavours are your go-to, as they say, may I instead recommend a Gaillac white from south-west France? So sharp every bottle should really come with a scabbard.'

Barclay chortles at his own joke; Delves ignores him and starts browsing the wines near Pinot who curls up a lip and gives a low growl.

'Pinot!' calls Pearl, chastising her.

'It's OK. I like dogs. Even when they don't like me. What's a good lager?'

'Augustiner Lagerbier Hell from Germany, all the purity of a chalice hewn from diamonds dipped over a golden field of barley,' says Barclay.

'Hell? I'll take a case.'

'Admirable, Pearl, would you be so good as to please fetch one from the store for Mr Delves.'

'So this Chablis, any good?' asks Delves.

As Barclay moves up to the shelf and begins rhapsodising on the quality of the wine, Delves slides backwards to the counter and quickly starts meddling with Barclay's unattended phone. As Delves edges back to Barclay, Pearl emerges from the back carrying a case of bottled beer which she sets down on the counter and moves Barclay's phone to one side. Delves tunes back into Barclay's monologue:

'. . . so it's the Kimmeridgian marl, that soil packed with marine life, that dips under the Channel and up underneath these Chardonnay vineyards that gives Chablis its trademark pristine freshness, perfect to pair with all manner of shellfish . . . Tempted?'

'Just the beer, thanks. You were mates with Victor Crawshaw, right?' Barclay stands a little more stiffly as Pearl rings the beers through the till. Teddy is hovering in the darkness of the open door to the storeroom.

'We knew one another well, yes.'

'Saw him the night he died, right?'

'That is indeed correct.'

'Seems odd. You're the last person to see him alive and then: oops.' His card pings on the machine and Pearl gives him a hard stare.

'Barclay's never hurt anyone.'

'I don't doubt that. They say drowning's nice.'

'Tell that to someone who's been waterboarded,' says Teddy moving with nervous defiance into the shop.

'Now now,' cuts in Barclay. 'I'm sure Mr Delves didn't mean to imply anything unsavoury.'

'Oh, I did, Flint. Cheers for the Hell beer.'

Delves shoulders the beer as though it's as light as a tin of tomatoes and disappears down Priory Street. Barclay watches after him before looking at the bottle of Chablis in his hand. He plucks a corkscrew from his top pocket and opens it as Pearl stares agog.

'What was that all about?'

'Yeah,' says Teddy. 'What's that bloke's problem, Barclay?'

'His problem, my dears, is that he has never sampled the delights of Grand Cru Chablis served cool to assuage the peculiarities of baseless accusations'. The cork pops out of the bottle and Barclay sniffs the open neck.

'Aaaah, a blaze of nectarines.'

Pearl shifts uneasily. For once, she doesn't share her boss's demeanour of carefree bonhomie and wonders if his ebullient words are merely a best effort at putting on a brave face.

28

Priory Street, lined with colourful houses, is known by the local school kids as Tutti-Frutti Street. The traffic can snarl up around the narrowness caused by on-street parking which, when a large lorry is attempting to navigate the street, all too often leads to local tempers flaring.

On the site of an ancient apothecary, the Bottle Bank shop front always catches the eye of travelling motorists, most of whom vow to return and pay a visit to the alluring window display of bottles, painted signs and, in the run-up to Bonfire Night, a skilful diorama of the parade and fireworks which gets wheeled out every year.

This year's miniature scene has so many lights it's the Bottle Bank's answer to a Christmas tree. Pearl updated the models last year, adding troupes of colourful figurines marching with their burning crosses behind floats carrying neatly caricatured effigies. There's Pope Paul V, Muammar Gaddafi and Margaret Thatcher all being carted through the streets of Lewes by tiny bonfire societies. Around them are the processions of marchers; the burgundy guernsey with centre chest sage green triangle of Wallands, Coombe's orange with violet lightning bolts, light blue with pink spots of varying sizes for Pells, purple with green Morse code spelling out SOS for Malling, dark green with yellow crescent moons for Cleve, navy-and-white diamond check for Priory and Grange's yellow with a turquoise stripe down the middle.

There's even a miniature of the Bottle Bank with Barclay, Pearl and Teddy handing out bottles of wine from the doorway to a group of bonfire boys pushing a burning tar barrel down the street.

Barclay's huge face looms over the scene, quizzically. 'My face looks as leathery as a wallet on a sunbed. Aaah, Bonfire Night, it's as though Lewes has a birthday and a funeral all at once. Joyful mourning is such a heady combination, perhaps only truly reflected in the tantalising sweet bitterness of a green glass of Chartreuse, perhaps the finest digestif in the entire world.'

Barclay raises his glass of Chartreuse to the scene behind him in the Bottle Bank, raising his eyebrows at the chaotic vista. The Bottle Bank is piled with long knitted scarves of all colours, shapes and sizes, coiled up on chairs, over the counter, draped across the shelves. 'It looks as though the gods of knitting are settling a centuries old tiff in my wine shop. How long will all this darning unravel across my lair?'

Pearl reassures him that their plan to deploy the knitting is imminent.

Axel is rallying to the moment. 'If the traffic won't stop by itself then we will stop it with yarn-bombing.'

He takes the end of a long scarf and drags it out into the street, tying it around the nearest lamppost with all the passion of a virtuoso violinist in peak flow. Pearl joins him with armfuls of woolly scarves and weaves her way between the cars slowly trundling down Priory Street. In just a few moments an impressive amount of knitting is looping across Priory Street between the lampposts, quickly drawing traffic to a standstill in both directions. Teddy carries his attempt at a knitted scarf out of the Bottle Bank and as soon as he grabs an end to tie to a lamppost, it unravels in a heap of yarn at his feet. From inside, Barclay raises his glass of Chartreuse to Teddy and drains it with a smack of his lips. Pearl and Axel are high-fiving in the street as the last of their scarves are tied across the road and they begin reacting with good-natured face-pulling to the first toots of car horns and exasperated gesticulations from frustrated drivers. Teddy is attempting to gather up his wool, chasing it around as it catches in the wind, his awkward gait that of an emu trying to chase a box of escaped chicks.

A lady in a yellow beret steps out of a car and asks Teddy what's going on. Faltering as he gets hopelessly tangled in wool, Teddy explains that it's a climate protest by Axel and Pearl.

'How long will it last?' she asks.

Teddy shrugs and points inside to where Pearl is making a giant fuss of Pinot. He squeezes past Axel in the doorway filming the scene on his smartphone, followed by the woman in a yellow beret.

'Welcome!' booms Barclay.

'I didn't have much of a choice.'

'Ah, the scarves, well, they won't be up for long, will they, Pearl?'

Pearl nods as Barclay continues, just as an irate painter and decorator bursts through the door in his overalls demanding the scarves come down. 'I'm already late for a job, mate, I don't want to be ringing the police but you can't just be blocking roads willy-nilly,' he says angrily, drawing his phone from a pocket.

Before he can finish, Pearl leaps into action, plucking a bottle from the nearest shelf. 'How'd you like to snag a free bottle of wine and have a quick chat about the climate emergency?' At her most charming proffered smile, the man slowly puts down his phone as Axel begins unleashing a barrage of facts and figures about switching off car engines.

A group of angry drivers is gathering at the door. Teddy welcomes them in one by one like an usher at a wedding.

'Here for the climate emergency or would you like some free wine?' Pearl is getting into her stride, handing out bottles of wine and relishing the chance to engage her fellow Lewesians on what everyone can be doing to address the climate crisis.

Barclay wades into the throng and steps onto a chair, a seasoned soap-box speech-maker ready to rally and tame this restless hubbub. 'Now just hold on one hot second, all of you. Pearl here is doing her bit for the climate and I fully support that. In precisely five minutes, she will be taking down her yarn-bomb protest and you will be free to move once again through your day. But free wine? Free wine? This is not something that Barclay Flint can countenance. I demand that you hand those bottles back.'

Feathers are ruffled as bottles are returned to Pearl and Teddy, who replace them on the shelves.

Axel is about to speak when Barclay continues, 'For if you are to be given free wine, it must all be the same wine, and a wine that you can all learn one single fact about. Teddy, open three cases of Soalheiro Alvarinho and hand one bottle to each and every person on the premises and then share the bottles with the traffic jam outside while Pearl dismantles her protest. This Portuguese winery is organic, energy efficient and prides itself on its eco-friendly approach to teasing fruit from the vine. But that is not why I am prepared to give you a bottle. The wine is like surfing a peach slice on a lime wave of citrus splendour, and once you sip it, your day will be brightened immeasurably. I wish you merriment and raise my glass to Pearl and Axel whose moment has made friends of us all. Before I finish, how do you all feel about changing the name of the Bottle Bank to the Drinks Portal?'

Pearl waves him down as bemused silence turns to polite chat. As Barclay steps down, the contented sound of motorists returning to their cars fills the scene, with Pearl and Axel returning the scarves to the shop. Barclay turns to the woman with the yellow beret and hands her a bottle of Jean-Marc Burgaud's Morgon 'Côte du Py' with a smile.

'An extra bottle for you,' he says.

'Ooh, thank you, I will definitely be back, this must be the best wine shop in the whole world.'

'It really is, thank you, Barclay,' says Pearl.

Axel shakes Barclay's hand before kneeling and kissing it with reverence. 'My prince,' he says.

Teddy rolls his eyes. Barclay is tickled.

'Alright, up you get, it's just a few bottles of wine. Now then . . .' He hands Pinot a treat from his pocket. 'What the hell do we do with all this knitting?'

29

Pearl and Axel are grabbing their coffees from the counter at the Patch on Market Street in Lewes – Pearl's cappuccino gleams next to Axel's jet-black Americano. The mood in the cafe is conversational, genial even, as Pearl and Axel join a waving woman who appears to have come from the North Pole wearing layer after layer of practical, warm wet-weather gear more suited to a night under canvas in Norway than a morning coffee meet. She's riffling open a notebook and struggling to find a pen in her extensive network of pockets and zips.

'You must be Pearl and . . .'

'Axel.'

'He's Danish,' enthuses Pearl.

'Axel, that's right. Well, I am Monica, Monica Reeves of the *Sussex Express*, always on the hunt for a good story and yours sounds like a ripper.' Monica peels out a chime of unnervingly high laughter. Axel is bemused, and Pearl shoots him a look to behave.

'Anyway, I would love to write up your protest on Priory Street, the whole town's talking about it, I want to see it from your point of view rather than . . .'

'Rather than what?' asks Pearl.

'Well, you know how people can be, all of a stew about it. Silly, really, I mean, the traffic was only blocked for all of, what, five minutes?'

'More like a quarter of an hour,' Axel corrects. Monica makes a note with a tiny pencil that she finds tucked in her hair.

'And what's fifteen mins when the planet's in crisis?' asks Pearl.

Axel continues, 'We just wanted to ask the people driving all those cars to take a beat, just for accountability, like you guys are bringing nature to a standstill, we want to show you what that feels like, to be stuck for just a few moments, just like we're stuck with your fossil fuels burning down our environment.'

'Yes, very good, so would you describe yourselves as eco-warriors, climate activists . . .?'

'We're just people trying to link up with folks who feel the same! This isn't about us and them, we just want a fair deal for this planet which is, like, our home. We can't keep taking from Mother Nature, that's just not cool.'

'Pearl is exactly correct, this planet is not an endless battery, everything has its limits.'

'And what do you say to the people of Lewes who might feel they reached their limits with their daily lives being inconvenienced by some . . . woolly scarves, is that right?'

'Yarn-bombing,' Pearl announces proudly. 'We spent ages knitting those scarves as a symbol of the changing drama, simple way to stop traffic and start a convo.'

'In Denmark we have a saying, "Ondt er at stötte sig til ludende væg", which means, it is bad to lean against a falling wall.'

'What we're saying is, let's learn to lean against each other,' nods Pearl.

Outside the Patch, two builders are walking past in high-viz overalls. Spotting Pearl and Axel they recognise the yarn-bombers and make their annoyance plain with a series of expletive gestures and loud curses. There's an awkward pause. Monica proffers a professional smile.

'Is that response typical of the people of Lewes?'

'Unfortunately it seems to be,' begins Axel.

'Well, not all of them, no – some peeps actually did seem to get it . . .'

Monica checks her notes. 'Were these the ones who . . . let me see . . . were gifted free wine?'

'Yes but that's not why they—'

'Is it appropriate to sway opinions with what some might say is a bribe?' probes Monica.

'Not exactly a bribe,' says Pearl.

'What would you call it, then?'

'Peace offering,' replies Pearl tentatively. Monica is steeling up. Pearl starts to feel a little rattled.

'What are you planning to put the people of Lewes through next? Actual bombing?'

'Hey, we are strictly non-violent,' Axel interjects. A voice chirps up from a nearby table.

'Not if I have anything to do with it, took me an hour all told to get around that jam, you two are a joke.'

Around the cafe eyes silently turn on Pearl and Axel, who feel the heat and make polite excuses before backing away from Monica and heading to the door.

Monica calls after them, 'Call me if you have any further comment!' As soon as Pearl and Axel are out the door the cafe returns to the sound of bustling conversation and she starts writing feverish notes.

Teddy is poring over photographs of moths on his laptop. Downloading close-up shots from his sturdy Canon 70D camera, he is camped at a small table in a corner of a cafe off Lewes High Street. A little pile of books on nature, some open at the page, rest beneath his hands. Surrounded by plates of bacon sarnies with bubble and squeak, the cafe is the living spirit of the sixties. Teddy sips a steaming mug of builder's tea as he scrutinises a pristine image of a crisp green Merveille du Jour, a handsome moth with mossy grey and black fern-like markings across its wings. To his eye, it has the flair and style of what would be his dream wallpaper in his fantasy nature library. Teddy's gaze is one of elation and gratitude, it's one of his favourite moths to see at this time of the year, the equivalent of Barclay getting overexcited by the annual Beaujolais day on the third Thursday of November when the French release their first young red wine of the season and the Brits rush to get their hands on the very first bottles.

Barclay loves to tell the tale of how he once took part in a race to get the first bottle back to the UK and managed to talk his way onto a private Learjet in the 1990s. He insists the record still stands as the fastest Beaujolais to be poured into British glasses. But depending on how many glasses he's sipped before he tells the story, there are a number of variations to the outcome, one resulting in a two-day bender with Keith Richards through Brighton, the other a trip to Scotland with Lady Diana and a shady military type known only as 'the Colonel'. One thing Teddy is certain of, Barclay had an absolutely brilliant time in the 1990s, and one day he hopes very much that the memoirs will be shared in lurid detail, if only so that he can live vicariously through his boss and experience what 'real fun' is all about.

For now, though, Teddy is proudly surveying his laptop. A five-year-old boy is looking at his screen, unimpressed. 'What's that butterfly doing on the egg box?'

'Well, that's a moth, a bit like a butterfly that flies at nighttime, and I use egg boxes in the moth traps for them to shelter and hang on to.'

'But why?'

'To see them.'

'Why do you want to see them?'

'Because they're beautiful?' suggests Teddy. The boy's expression is flat. 'You don't think that's beautiful? Look at the colours.'

'It looks like leaves.'

'Exactly, so it can hide.'

'But you found it.'

'I did.'

'Not very good at hiding, then, is it?'

The boy's attention is tugged away by the squawk of a younger sibling and he trots back to his table. Teddy raises his eyebrows and exhales as he clicks on the next photograph of a striking elegant white moth with spaced-out blocks of red-orange and black decoration. Reminded of his encounter with a rare Crimson Speckled moth down at Ashcombe Bottom, Teddy lets out an audible gasp of joy. To a non-moth fan, it sounds as though he's recovering from a sudden gripe in his guts; the truth is, the image is so potently delightful for Teddy that it's actively taking his breath away. The pride he feels is a wellspring of boundless thrills as he jumps up and punches the air, spectacularly losing his balance and tumbling backwards.

Outside, Pearl and Axel are walking with Pinot past the window of the cafe. As they pass by, from the corner of her eye Pearl spots a figure inside tipping backwards over a chair, feet flailing in the air sending a laptop tumbling. With an unfriendly glance from a postman who asks if they're the climate protesters, they quicken their pace, hurrying along towards the allotments on Paddock Road.

★

Teddy examines his cracked laptop as he gets up to leave. Wondering how much it'll cost to get fixed, he mutters under his breath, 'Such a loser, Teddy. Even Pearl thinks you're a loser and no wonder she thinks you're a loser, you *are* a loser. A loser with a broken laptop.'

Making his way outside, Teddy kicks a pebble on the street, and it rebounds off a wall onto his shin. Hopping in pain, he clenches his arms and lifts his face to the sky, making a noise that sounds like a gymnast squashed into a matchbox.

Pearl's allotment has the air of an empty nest with scant feathery memories where warmth once revelled in its own good company. Winter is beginning to outplay autumn's late advantage and all along Paddock Road the morning frost is stubbornly clinging to the ivy, gripping its way blindly along the low flint walls. Pinot is digging in a corner where she seems to remember burying a tennis ball some months ago; when she finally nuzzles it from the ground, the ball resembles a large wet truffle, misshapen and subsumed with the very spirit of earth. To Pearl's eye, it's impossible to imagine the ball in its original incarnation; a fuzz of yellowness whizzing in bright sunshine around the Southdowns Sports Club to a cry of *deuce!* But that was where Pinot had pinched the ball from, right outside the courts, bouncing full and long into their path. Before she could react, Pinot had snatched it and raced away, burying it later that day in the allotment. To Pinot, this smutty ovoid ground-soaked trophy holds the same joy as it did when the sun was shining over Lewes all those months ago.

Axel is stamping his feet against the cold, wrapped in his padded red lumberjacket. 'I mean, seriously, Pearl, what can really grow like this? There's no sun.'

'Winter can slay: broccoli, Brussels sprouts, kale, parsnips, rocket, winter glut is the future. Careful, snail right there.'

'Sorry, little snail. But come on, like you'll get hardly zero crop, right?'

'Nah, enough for me to live on, maybe you as well, if you stick around?'

'Well it's true that I like Lewes and you're pretty fun. But living for the whole of winter off a bunch of weeds, are you actually kidding me right now?'

'Valid, but these are not weeds, all this stuff is packed full of real honesty, compare it to the half-dead stuff you find in the supermarket – this is real superfood.'

Axel flexes his best Superman pose and Pearl gives him a hug.

'Superfood for your real-life Superman.'

Pearl nuzzles into the warmth of his strong embrace.

'I needed that, you're the OG.'

'What is the OG?'

'Original Gangster. Appreciate you. And your hug. Anything to take my mind off that poor old guy drowning in red wine.'

Axel nods and steps back with a crunch on the snail. Pearl's face falls as Axel hops around wiping shell from his shoe on the frosty grass.

'Av, for helvede, so sorry, little snail!'

30

Across England, vineyards are spreading in a green tide of glowing life. With more than a thousand of them from Cornwall to Yorkshire, Essex to Herefordshire, this is a burgeoning corner of the wine world where the grapes thrive on the coolness of the climate and the wines are known for their freshness. Famed for sparkling wine in particular, Sussex is emerging as an epicentre for world-class bubbly with wineries such as Breaky Bottom, Hoffmann & Rathbone and Sugrue South Downs all popping corks on bottles to make the wine world fizz with approval. While Barclay admires the dazzling thrills of these bottles, he's beguiled by England's whites, rosés and reds too. Fragrant Bacchus is a white wine that he always associates with the word *scintillating*, its scented aromas reminding him of early summer elderflower sweeping through the hedgerows and the flavours as arresting as exploding gooseberries. For reds, aside from Dandelion Hill, his favourite Pinot Noir is Danbury Ridge, and at this precise moment he's holding a bottle in his arms, cradling it like a puppy, his eyes brimming with admiration as he dances it gently around the Bottle Bank. On the counter his latest jigsaw of Birling Gap is half finished, as is the bottle of Westwell Pelegrim fizz, which is perched jauntily in an ice bucket next to a line-up of eleven other open bottles of English wine.

'Another glass of Pelegrim for this old pilgrim please, Pearl.' Inspired by the wine, Barclay is crooning melodious gibberish over the sound of the record player crackling out the easy samba sounds of Jorge Ben's 'Tim Dom Dom'. 'And one for yourself, dive in, Pearl. Kent's finest is Westwell, such chiselled definition, each bubble a single grain of rice etched with the detail of a miniaturist carving the *Canterbury Tales*.'

Pearl refills Barclay's wine glass and grabs one for herself. In the Bottle Bank sparkling wine is only ever served in Zalto white wine glasses rather than flutes, at Barclay's insistence, to maximise the surface area and 'expand opportunities for the aromas to sing'. Barclay is in full flow today, celebrating the excellence of local wine with all the flair and gusto of Pavarotti at an all-day karaoke buffet. Pearl is more scrupulously evaluating the open bottles, trying to decide which ones to stock in the shop based on what customers might actually want to buy. She hands him a glass. 'Barclay, I totally rate English wine, thing is, we're here to sell it, not sip it. Let's hit up what we can shift instead of what we can drink, OK?'

'Spoilsport.'

'Whatever. We can't keep multiples of the same wine, it'll confuse the customers.'

'Dearest Pearl, we should stock sixty bottles of Bacchus if they all meet the exacting standards of my tastebuds; the same grape they may be, but different wines they most certainly are.'

'But who's going to buy that stuff, Barclay?'

Barclay is waltzing around the shop with his bottle of Danbury Ridge, a glazed look of ecstasy creeping over his brow.

'Barclay! You haven't even opened that one yet and your face is as soppy as Teddy over an Emperor Moth, I can't believe I even know what that is, I've been in this place way too long . . .'

'Danbury Ridge Pinot Noir, Pearl, is England's riposte to Grand Cru Burgundy. From the admirability of Essex some of the finest Pinot in the entire world has sprung from our very own shores and I'm building up to tasting this latest vintage as a judge might preamble passing sentence by manifesting a sense of brooding authority.'

'OK, how much wine have you actually drunk today?'

'Incalculable.' He drains his glass of Pelegrim weaving merrily towards the counter, stepping over Pinot chewing on her favourite hollow red rubber dog chew filled with peanut butter. The record has come to an end and there's a loud crackle as Pearl lifts the needle to place it back in its sleeve and into the rack.

'Time for a vibe change . . .' she murmurs, scanning the records as Barclay makes several attempts to land the corkscrew in the bottle of Danbury Ridge. Pearl pulls out *Luar* by Gilberto Gil and drops the needle on her favourite track from the album, 'Palco', just as Barclay triumphantly plucks the cork from the bottle.

'Thing is, Pearl, music and wine are emphatically and identically splendid. One is liquid fun, the other, aural ecstasy. And both inevitably lead to dancing.'

He is wiggling behind the counter with a broad grin, and despite her eye roll, Pearl can't help but admire Barclay's zeal as she takes the bottle and pours the Pinot into a fresh Zalto Burgundy glass. Her focus is instantly drawn by the aromas.

'Fire, this is serious. Love that complexity.'

'In half an hour this pamphlet of aromas will expand into a novel worthy of Dickens himself. Let us decant.' Barclay's pouring into the decanter is surprisingly accurate for his state of jollity. He grabs Pearl's glass and tips the wine into the decanter before repouring her a glass and one for himself.

'That's delicious.' Pearl is enthralled as she re-engages with the wine.

'You see! Decanting fast-forward's wine's hidden secrets that everyone thinks only time will tell. And we have no time left but to taste!' Barclay takes a dainty sip, rolls the wine around his palate and is suffused with memory, immediacy and unfolding enchantment. His eyes are closed, rolled back into his thoughts as he engages with the silken delicacy of the wine's texture, the finesse of the structure and the flavours which unfurl like pennants from an armada of delirious party ships. 'When tasting wine,' he whispers, 'one must give oneself away to the moment, it is surrender, embrace, unity and clarity.'

'OMG that's so tasty,' says Pearl.

Barclay's eyes pop open. 'Correct! But consider the counterfactual. When faced with a wine that let's say is less than palatable, what would be the appropriate tasting note to proffer to a winemaker?'

'Sorry mate, your wine's slack?'

'Slack is one tack. But in the wine trade we have a secret code. The word which signifies a cry for help, dear Pearl, is *interesting*.'

'"Interesting"?'

'If you ever hear someone say "interesting" in a wine tasting, it's guaranteed to mean that they are in a vinous pickle and, for whatever reason, unable to speak freely. Guaranteed.' Barclay necks his glass like it's the end of a pint. 'Should really make some notes, have you seen my telephone?'

Teddy comes in with a mixed case of six bottles, which he places gently on the counter. 'More English wines like you asked for, Barclay. Your phone's by the jigsaw.'

'Thank you, dear Teddy. Now, can somebody please explain why my telephone seems to have almost zero battery?'

'When did you last charge it?' asks Pearl.

'An hour ago.'

'It's down to seven per cent. That's weird.'

'Give it here,' says Teddy, taking the phone and holding it up to Barclay's face to unlock it with facial recognition. Barclay's face is a little flushed and his expression is a cross between a gleeful kitten and a dozing sloth. The facial recognition fails and Teddy asks Barclay to relax his face.

'Second time lucky, OK, let's see what your usage is. Settings . . . You're not really using anything except notes and emails, Barclay.'

'This is true.'

'So why's it losing charge so quickly? Hang on, what's this, Huntpeep?'

'And what, pray, is a Huntpeep?'

'Please tell me it's not porn,' winces Pearl.

'Nope. Hundred per cent spyware. Why is there spyware on your phone, Barclay?' Teddy and Pearl both turn to look at Barclay whose facial expression looks like he's trying to remember what colour his own eyes are. He pauses.

'Spy Wear. Is that a clothing brand?'

'No, Barclay, someone is hacking your phone.'

'Dear me, why would anybody want to do that? Sometimes I wish life was as easy as Pinot.' He gazes down at the dog in a moment of melancholy as Pinot looks back at him with eager eyes.

Maurice Le Brocq is pacing up and down the hall at Greenacres while Mrs McRae is dutifully following, matching his pace as he changes direction, pen and notebook in hand. Each time Le Brocq strides past the roaring fire in the hearth, the light flashes across his cheek as though a red glow is burning his spirit from within. 'What we need is a like-minded gathering to preserve our values, PLU, Mrs McRae, People Like Us.'

'The League of Rural Affairs, sir?'

'Precisely, Mrs McRae. A summit, LORA for short. Actually, scrub that, it sounds like a meeting with a long-lost niece. And we don't want that at our summit, do we?'

'Do you have a niece, sir?'

'Thankfully not. Now who to invite? The Suttons, Edgar and Enid Mason, Thomas Peller, Lady Harrison, Reg Castle, what was the name of that elderly couple over in Plumpton?'

'The Websters?'

'Yes, get them along, they might be good for a donation. We'll need your finest sausage rolls, pints of piping hot tea and remember to switch the lights on in the driveway so that we can all admire their cars.'

Mrs McRae nods and continues making notes while following Maurice Le Brocq down the hall towards the drawing room. One of the hallways lights flickers off as they pass beneath. As Le Brocq tilts his head upward peering open-mouthed with disdain at the errant light fitting, Mrs McRae flinches at his eerily lit vampiric silhouette.

31

Mike Delves is hunched over Harold's desk. A jar labelled DEB'S PICKLES is open beside him containing pickled onions the size of apples. Delves sets down his mug of black coffee and reaches for a pickle, which he crunches at deafening volume in the direction of Harold who is sitting across from him. The disdain on Harold's face erupts as a flinch of tension which Delves mistakes for trapped wind.

'Got Gaviscon if you need?' says Delves.

'If I need? Eat enough of those, Mike, and your innards will be a fishing net.'

'I'm used to the spice. Matured.'

'Those have been on the shelf since I moved back here,' says Harold. Delves looks at the jar, impressed.

'Well, they're good. Whoever Debs is, she knows how to pickle. Right, I'm in.'

'What's the legality of hacking into Flint's phone like this?'

'Harry. Son. I'm all the legality you need. OK. So, he likes Jimmy Cliff. "Come Into My Life"?'

'That's a song, isn't it?'

'He listened to it on loop yesterday.'

'So?'

'More than sixty times.'

'Sixty?'

'Three hours. Same song.'

'What the hell's the matter with the man?'

'Let's have a look in his notes.' Delves scans the monitor, his face reacting as though someone's just asked him to eat a handful of cat litter. He starts to read aloud. '"Liquid Kitchen. Dime Bar Dandies. Jazz Harvest. The Horny Vhineoceros. Jelly Tornado".'

'What is that? Some sort of code?'

'Says here . . . "new names for the Bottle Bank".'

'But those aren't even names. Why would anyone buy a wine from a shop called Jelly Tornado? Must have been pissed out of his mind when he wrote it.'

'Hang on, this is interesting. Calendar . . .'

'Anything about Dad?'

'No, it's completely blank. Never been used.'

'How does he know what he's supposed to be doing every day?'

'Guess he makes it up. Right . . . emails.'

'I'd be amazed if he even knows how to use email. I mean, the man's a total bloody shambles. What Dad ever saw in him . . .'

'OK, this is surprisingly organised, wine deliveries, wines samples, visits . . . visits, let's have a look in there. Nothing about this place.'

'I'm not surprised, Dad hated email almost as much as he hated other people.' Delves reads from the monitor. 'OK . . . notes . . . "Long deft brightness with some . . . underpinning of . . . crème fraiche . . . almond creaminess. Utterly seamless classy style. An . . . elision of excellence".'

'What the hell's he on about?' Delves looks back at the monitor.

'Chardonnay.'

'Well, that tells us nothing.'

'He writes like a perv. Don't like him,' growls Delves. The computer screen flickers as the link severs, the app disappears and the home screen shows a screensaver of Harold's old army squad.

'Solid lot,' says Delves, pointing at the squad.

'They were. What happened to the link?'

'Something his end, best guess, he deleted it.'

'Bugger.'

'Don't sweat it, Harry, he's old school, my kind of work. I'll find what he's hiding.'

'What's your plan?'

'Time to step things up a notch; get our prime suspect to play star witness.'

'Extract a confession?'

'Now you're talking. Force if necessary.'

'The last thing I need is any blowback.'

'Leave it to me.' Delves fishes out another pickle and crunches into it.

A little later on, Teddy is hunched over the Bottle Bank's ancient CCTV monitor, hard at work in the shop. 'Bullseye, check this out, plain sight, no shame, what a piece of work.'

'What d'you find?' asks Pearl, rounding the counter with Barclay. All three of them stare at the repeating footage of Mike Delves picking up Barclay's phone from the counter and tampering with it.

'Installing spyware, got to be. That's what he's doing,' says Teddy. Minty descends the stairs from her flat and crosses over to join the three of them behind the counter.

'What is who doing?' Minty takes a look at the monitor. 'Is that man stealing Barclay's phone?'

'Not stealing, Minty, hacking,' says Teddy.

'Mike Delves, rather an unsavoury type,' adds Barclay.

'Delves reckons Barclay had something to do with Victor Crawshaw, you know, how he died,' says Pearl. Minty is visibly shocked and shakes her head.

'What could possibly have given him such a cruel notion?'

'I have no idea, Minty, but this Delves character certainly means business,' Barclay says with deep seriousness.

'He's well sketchy,' adds Pearl, following Teddy's gaze out through the shop window. Mike Delves is standing, immobile and expressionless, watching them from across the street. Delves turns after a moment and walks very slowly down Priory Street.

'What is it with that guy?' asks Teddy.

'A question that I think requires resolving sooner rather than later my dear Teddy. Have you any deliveries scheduled?'

Teddy checks the record book on top of the counter. 'Nothing until tomorrow.'

'In that case, it is time for a nature ramble.'

'What, now?'

'Now, Teddy. Pearl, keep comms open; Minty, we may require revival by ginger cake.'

'I'll have it ready,' says Minty with a friendly salute.

Exiting the shop, Teddy and Barclay begin walking at pace away from the Bottle Bank with an air that suggests trying to rush without arousing suspicion, which, to every other passer-by, singles them out as behaving with weird intensity. Teddy is wearing his blue cagoule, Barclay his oversized herringbone overcoat.

'Keep walking,' says Barclay as he glances into the reflection of a house's front window and spots Mike Delves following them at a distance. 'Say nothing, Teddy, but it appears that Mr Delves has already decided to join us on this foray.'

'He's following us?'

Barclay nods.

'What d'you think he wants?'

'Well it certainly isn't information on day-flying moths, Teddy. Left here.'

They turn and walk under a railway bridge towards the wetlands of Lewes Brooks where they make a great show of pointing at various gulls, rabbits and waders, leading Delves in a steady circuit around the perimeter of the lake. For a moment, Delves disappears. Thinking they've shaken his tail, Teddy passes Barclay a pair of binoculars from his rucksack. Barclay scans the reserve in a wide circle; for a moment his mind turns to Lord Nelson at Trafalgar – he hopes that Nelson had a fortifying glass of something delectable before his last fatal battle and wonders what it would have tasted like.

'Any sign?' asks Teddy. Barclay concentrates as he renews his search for Delves.

'Not of our friend Mr Delves. But there's a marvellous kingfisher darting over there, just dipping over the surface . . . Aha. Mr Delves appears to be taking a comfort break behind the poplars near the rugby ground. Time, I think, we turned the tables. Teddy, let us take the shortcut to Lewes. Onward, while we have him at a disadvantage.'

As they head back, Mike Delves, after finishing his personal business, resumes following them, this time at a greater distance. As he increases his pace, Barclay and Teddy speed up and pass under the railway arch. Barclay gives Teddy a nudge and together they dart off, climbing the embankment and hiding behind a large holly bush. Teddy winces. 'Shush!' says Barclay. Teddy has managed to become entangled in a thicket and is doing his best to ignore the sharp prickles through his rustling cagoule. Below them, Delves exits the tunnel puffing after the brief exertion of jogging. He is peering left and right before making off for the centre of town. 'The hunter becomes the hunted,' murmurs Barclay.

'Ouch!' winces Teddy as he stumbles out of the holly bush while stiffly pulling a leaf from his armpit.

★

Barclay and Teddy are carefully tracking Delves through the streets of Lewes, using the narrow local twittens and lanes to take shortcuts and stay out of sight. Delves leads them to Friar's Walk car park where he meets Harold Crawshaw in a silver mud-splattered short-wheelbase Land Rover Defender. Watching from a window on the first floor of the Premier Inn overlooking the car park, Barclay turns to Teddy. 'Mike Delves and Harold Crawshaw? This is indeed a peculiar pairing.'

Delves and Crawshaw drive away while Barclay and Teddy make their way downstairs. While Teddy is thanking Elsie Sharpe behind the reception for letting them in, Barclay dials Tabitha on his phone. 'Tabitha, it's Barclay. Quick question, I wonder, are you aware of an acquaintance of Harold's by the name of Mike or Michael Delves? Yes, that's him. They were together in the army? I see. And . . .' He cups the phone and nods to Teddy. 'Delves is staying at Dandelion Hill. Hang on . . . Yes Tabitha I'm still here. And you wouldn't know why he might have an interest in yours truly by any chance? Well, that's very flattering but I can't imagine for a second that it's true. No, he popped into the shop and made himself known in a way that wasn't overtly friendly, I just wondered what the connection might be? Thanks so much, Tabitha. Will do.'

He hangs up the call while leading Teddy back towards the Bottle Bank. 'Seems Mr Delves is staying with Harold. Poor Tabitha is blissfully unaware of whatever skulduggery he and Harold are plotting. One thing's for certain; the scent of this particular pairing is as arresting as it is unnerving, we must proceed with caution, dear Teddy. But first, I think we've earned ourselves a glass of devilishly decent wine.'

On opening the door to the shop, they find Minty and Pearl tucking into slices of sticky ginger cake at the counter. With her mouth full, Pearl attempts to enquire after their mission, but the sound she makes is one of many vowels and very little sense. Teddy jumps right in.

'Delves tailed me and Barclay before we gave him the slip, then we saw him with Harold Crawshaw and Barclay reckons they're putting him in the frame for Mr Crawshaw's death.'

Minty looks from face to face.

Pearl takes a breath. 'If they think he was done in, we need to find out what they know, and fast.'

'There is only one way out of this for you, Barclay: prove once and for all how Victor Crawshaw died to clear your name,' declares Minty.

'Yeah,' say Pearl and Teddy in unison, turning to Barclay who considers them all for a moment.

'You're right, of course, Minty. Only the truth can set me free. It's just where to begin . . . Hmm, with wine, I think.' He starts unpacking a case of wine on the counter and placing the bottles among his Hot Bottle range on the shelf behind, writing tasting notes for each one.

'Barclay, Minty's right, you don't have a choice,' urges Teddy.

But Barclay is ploughing on with his handwriting. 'These Greek wines never cease to enthral me. Such a range of local grape varieties that simply taste of no other, youthful wine-making with a collegiate stratum of fresh talent across the country's industry and climates ranging from whitewashed sea-bleached islands to the very peak of Mount Olympus. England aside, do you know that Greece is my favourite country for wine production? And these pristine wines are going to soar in popularity when our customers get beyond the idea that all Greek wine is merely retsina.'

Teddy and Pearl both exchange a glance while taking another look at the images of Delves meddling with Barclay's phone on the CCTV screen.

'Can't believe the nerve of this guy. We've got to take him down.'

'That's a fact, Barclay. We're not going to let him come for you, no way,' says Pearl.

Barclay is touched as Minty and Teddy both nod; with an exhalation and a sense of resignation, he stops scribbling and reaches for the fridge. 'In that case, this calls for an extra special glass. Since the first seed of my plan is a nod to the Trojan Horse, it seems only appropriate to open this bottle of sweet Greek Monemvasia-Malvasia made by the delightful Tsimbidi family. Who's with me?'

Minty, Teddy and Pearl all pick up wine glasses and join them together as Barclay gives a broad smile and uncorks it with a pop before pouring out a glass liberally for each of his friends. 'A caramel dance floor for the sleekest sultanas in the world – and flavours that last an aeon once you're sipped it, always the hallmark of a truly great wine. Perfect for the inception of this mission, which I accept, by the way. To clear my name, the Bottle Bank is going to battle!'

'To battle!' they all cry as four glasses are raised as one.

32

Teddy, Pearl and Pinot are driving through horizontal rain that feels as though it's being emptied by the bucket onto the windshield of the Bottle Bank van. With Teddy at the wheel, Pearl turns to Barclay who is curled up in the back of the van hiding beneath a rug.

'You OK, boss?'

'Pearl, behave normally, I'm not here!'

'Chill, Barclay, we're not even there yet. So the plan is, we'll do a little peeping . . .'

'While I scour the winery for clues, yes, I am aware of my plan.'

'If that Delves dude rolls back to the store, Minty can handle it, right?'

'Minty? Absolutely. She's harder than a volcanic rhino. Proceed as planned.'

'Proceed as planned,' mocks Pearl. She turns to Teddy and whispers, 'The boss is definitely shook.'

'Yeah, well, I'd probably be a bit spooked if some ex-army thug started threatening me and asking questions about my dead friend,' whispers Teddy.

'OK, when you say it like that, it is a bit messed up.'

'Totally. This calls for stealth mode,' says Teddy.

'You do realise I can hear you both?' says Barclay. Teddy and Pearl bite their lips.

Pearl starts fiddling with the stereo which suddenly blasts

at top volume filling the van with the chorus of Iron Maiden's 'Can I Play With Madness'. The van careers left and right on the old lane leading up into the Downs with the sound rattling from within and Pearl's hands jabbing at the stereo trying to switch it off. Teddy leans over and slams a button, shutting off the sound.

He stares at her for a second. 'Really?'

'My bad!' she replies. 'Didn't figure you'd be jamming to heavy metal.'

'Not mine, it's an Iron Maiden CD, been stuck in there forever, I only ever use the Bluetooth. Sorry, Barclay!'

'Quite alright, my hearing will doubtless return within a month.'

'That's a legit relic. How we going to get it out of there?'

'Just leave the CD for now and let's hope you haven't just broadcast our approach to everyone up at Dandelion Hill.'

'Just delivering fireworks, right?'

'Right but if they know we're coming, how are we going to stake out what they're up to? Just stick to the plan.'

'Not my bad your stereo's stuck in the Stone Age with that crusty rock.'

'My stereo? This is Barclay's van, I just drive it.'

'"I just drive it,"' mocks Pearl, mimicking Teddy's voice.

'Again, I can still hear you both,' says Barclay from the back.

They both sink into silence as the van pulls up at the entrance to Dandelion Hill. Without speaking, Pearl and Teddy open the back. Pinot jumps out.

'Coast's clear,' says Teddy.

'The codeword?' hisses Barclay from under the rug.

Pearl looks blankly at Teddy and shrugs. Teddy strives to remember before whispering, 'I forgot the codeword.'

'The codeword is *Trojan*,' sighs Barclay.

'Right, *Trojan*.'

'Are you saying *Trojan* or just copying me?' whispers Barclay.

'No, I'm definitely saying *Trojan*. All clear. We'll do our sweep,' says Teddy, pulling a single firework out of the van and heading towards the barn with Pearl.

'This really all you've got?' asks Pearl.

'What can I say, I'm an efficient delivery driver. The next consignment arrives in a couple of days, this is all that's left to bring up here.'

'I could have brought it on my bike.'

'Oh yes, in this weather, a lovely outing.'

Teddy pulls the firework away from Pearl and picks up his pace towards the barn. They reach the entrance and he shelters from the rain. 'OK, let's get this over with. Wait, won't it look weird if we're snooping about without any fireworks to deliver?'

'Firework to deliver,' corrects Pearl pointing at Teddy's hand where the single paltry firework is going limp in the rain. 'You're right, though, snoop first, then we drop the firework. Barclay said Harold Crawshaw's office is round the back of the bungalow, can you put Pinot on the lead?'

Pearl hands Teddy the lead and moves off leaving him with the dog. 'Thanks,' he says with a healthy streak of sarcasm. The lights in the main house are off but there's a single light in the bungalow glowing through the rain. Teddy drops down like a secret serviceman and moves quickly after Pearl toward the bungalow. He keeps Pinot close to him while keeping lookout at a corner of the building. Pearl crouches carefully, taking up position beneath the window with the light on.

Inside, Harold Crawshaw is at the computer researching the rate of decomposition for corpses for his natural burial site. Pearl gently pokes her head up and is horrified at what he's reading. Mike Delves is stretched out on a chair next to Harold eating from an open jar of cornichons. Teddy spots that Pearl's face is struck with terror.

'What can you see?' he whispers. Pearl doesn't hear him. He tries again with a louder whisper. '*Pssst.* Pearl! What is it?'

Pearl turns her face to him and draws a single finger over her throat with a deadpan expression that unnerves Teddy who mimes the same single finger over the throat back to her. Pearl repeats it. Teddy beckons her over. 'What does that mean?'

'What this?' Pearl draws her finger across her throat again. 'You mean the universal sign for murder? I'm sorry, Teddy, was I not being clear enough?'

'I know that means murder, who's the murderer?'

'Both those freaks. Harold's searching facts on body decay while the other dude's snacking on pickles like it's normal.'

'Why's he eating pickles?'

'I don't think the pickles are the headline here, Sherlock. Like, wake up! They're planning to off Barclay! Now let's ditch that firework and bounce.'

Together they dash back over to the barn where Teddy pauses.

'OK, let's do this on three—'

Pearl kicks the door in before he has time to even count to one. Teddy tosses the firework inside then grabs her seeing Mike Delves approaching at speed from the bungalow brandishing a cricket bat. 'Time to go,' he says, dragging her back towards the van.

Mike Delves is shouting after them. 'Next time you try eavesdropping you'll be doing it without any ears, you come prowling up here again, I'll take all four of yours and wear them as a necklace!'

Pinot barks at Delves from the van as they leap in. Teddy and Pearl slam the doors shut and pull away as Delves stands and watches them go, hands on hips, immune to the deluge of rain which tumbles to the blaring sound of Iron Maiden.

'Bollocks!' calls out Teddy above the music.

'What?' asks Pearl.

'We forgot Barclay!'

They peer into the back of the van. The rug is there but Barclay Flint is nowhere to be seen.

33

Crouching at the entrance to the winery, Barclay can hear the sound of Iron Maiden fading into the distance as the Bottle Bank van revs away. Mike Delves' shouting reaches Barclay's ears. All alone, he gulps and steps inside. The winery is dim as a crypt, eerie and echoing with the sound of slow, steady dripping from somewhere in the distance. It feels cold to Barclay, and he pulls up the collar of his Daks overcoat and proceeds with stealth. As he pads deeper among the vats he replays Victor's last words in his mind, *We wunt be druv.* Victor was as stubborn as concrete, determined to nurture his precious harvest into wine; what was it that night that made him remain in the winery? How did he meet his end? As he passes the tank where Victor's body was found, Barclay pauses and tiptoes up the gantry steps to peer in. Each footfall seems as loud as a hammer on an anvil, and around him the winery is creaking and moaning, an old building with secrets to spill.

He can hear the wind picking up as it runs over the roof. Slowly, he peers down into the tank where Victor was found, trepidation hitting his stomach like a football full of nails. The tank is completely empty and it's pristine and polished. Hard to believe this is the place where Victor Crawshaw died. Barclay stares down for inspiration; no clue, not a single shred of evidence presents itself. He sniffs delicately. But beyond cleanliness, no distinctive scent is revealed. He suddenly whispers 'Victor' and the sound starts rolling around inside the tank like a pebble in a cave.

As the echo of his own voice flows back up to him, Barclay is struck by a thought and finds the pocket stone Victor gave him on the night he died. Terroir, he reflects, *the word that holds everything about a wine's origin in two subtle syllables. Motive is the terroir of murder.* Barclay begins mind-mapping everything about Victor's death, just like tracing wine back to a vineyard, logging everything that makes it unique and therefore traceable to its point of origin. In exactly the same way he would be able to identify a Cabernet Sauvignon from Coonawarra in Australia in a single sniff by the distinctive blackcurrant and eucalyptus aromas, he realises that his wine skills are the key to deciphering the conundrum of Victor's demise.

Climbing back down the gantry steps to the winery floor, Barclay follows the path Victor took into the darkness that night.

Outside the winery, Mike Delves is standing silently, listening. Slowly, he takes a step towards the winery door and, gripping his cricket bat tightly, slips inside.

In the dimmest corner at the back of the winery Barclay discovers a doorway that he doesn't recall ever seeing before. As he opens the old metal door, it scrapes on the stone floor. Entering the winery, Mike Delves stops dead at the sound. Barclay takes out his phone to light his way and drops his pocket stone in the darkness. With a silent huff, he tries to use his phone but the battery is dead. He gropes for his little black pebble but it has been swallowed by the dark. He is about to begin pom-pomming to cheer himself as he descends the small stone staircase beyond the metal doorway, but catches himself at the last minute and turns his mind to the job in hand: motive.

There are many things that impact the wine produced by a specific vineyard. The aspect of a slope, which could be sunny or shaded. The character of the soil, the age of the vines, even local traditions of farming and blending. Whether there's an ocean, lake or river nearby will moderate the climate and contribute to the wine's final character. Is the vineyard sheltered by mountains or exposed to harsh winds?

Memories of Victor's lonely last words break over Barclay's brow in the same way he contemplates a wine served blind. In a heartbeat a draught chills him rigid at the bottom of the stairs. To kill, it strikes him that motives are myriad: revenge, greed, hatred, love, to protect a secret or keep a loved one safe. But Barclay can't help thinking of Victor's last few ominous sentences, that perhaps he was snared by a dark thought and slipped into an abyss of his own choosing. For now, the evidence eludes him.

His spirits sagging, Barclay turns right into a small circular room where what he sees convinces him Victor Crawshaw's end was neither suicide nor accidental.

Stealthy as a tiger, Mike Delves reaches the door at the top of the stone stairs.

The circular cellar is around eight feet in diameter and dimly lit by a small grate in the ceiling. As Barclay's eyes become acclimatised to the near darkness, he is horrified by what he sees. The stone floor is scraped with interlocking circular patterns, somewhat in nature like a crop circle, and to his eyes, not far off a pentangle. It looks as though they have been made with a metal edge of some kind. On the walls, barely perceptible in the dark, a long dusty dark purple robe with a hood is hanging, almost the same colour as the damp brickwork. Barclay's thoughts are blustering into a squall of terror. Is this a place of ritual? Of sacrifices? Dark magic? *By the beard of Bacchus, what was Victor up to in here?* A small black and white framed photo hanging on the wall unnerves him further; seven men are standing in matching dark robes, all holding their hoods. In the centre, sombre and staring, stands a younger Victor Crawshaw. Behind Barclay, a small black pebble tumbles down the staircase and rolls to a stop at the entrance to the room. Barclay's blood freezes.

Mike Delves silently curses as his foot kicks the pebble down the dark stairs. He wishes he'd brought a torch or anything to illuminate this dank cellar. He advances very slowly to the entrance to the circular room and raises his cricket bat like a club. On a mental count of three, he lunges forward and steps into the cellar. But the cellar is empty.

34

Tabitha and Harold are walking the perimeter of the vineyard at Dandelion Hill. The leaves on the vines at this sheltered spot are turning golden with a few splotches of red, as though an Impressionist painter has daubed a few russet splashes just to keep things interesting. A solitary skylark is doing its best to keep the dreams of warmer days alive with a song that falls like glitter from the clouds. Treading over molehills, Tabitha in her broad hat and Harold tucked into his old Barbour are fringing the edge of a small copse where, deep in conversation, they both miss the sight of the UK's smallest bird, a goldcrest, as it flits up into the trees.

'And just how long is Mike planning to stay?' asks Tabitha.

'Not sure, good to have him around, old army stories are shared more easily than medals.'

'I understand, but what is he doing? Is he here on holiday? Are you employing him on the burial ground? Tell me.'

'Oh, Mike's just here helping with a project, doing some digging.'

'I see. And does digging refer to your burial ground or Barclay Flint?'

'What makes you say that?'

'He called me. Seems to think that Mike's been pursuing him, said he wasn't *overtly friendly* in the Bottle Bank.'

'You know Mike, he's just gruff.'

Tabitha stops walking and turns to face Harold. 'Harold. Be honest. Have you asked Mike Delves to do anything to Barclay Flint which might make matters uncomfortable?'

'All I've asked is that Mike look into what happened to Dad. And since Barclay was the last person to see him alive, yes, Mike is looking into a few leads.'

'For God's sake, Hal, when will you get it into your head that Dad had a terrible accident?'

'We don't know that.'

'The police do. The coroner couldn't have been clearer, the death was accidental.'

'But what if he was pushed? What if someone wanted Dad out of the way?'

'What if Dad wanted himself out of the way? Hasn't it occurred to you that he might have chosen to end his own life and all the digging in the world isn't going to bring him back?'

'That's preposterous. What on earth would make Dad suicidal?'

Harold starts walking back toward his bungalow. Tabitha hurries along beside him.

'He was miserable, Hal, utterly miserable, for years. He was more interested in ducks than either of us; ducks, insect numbers, weeds to feed the bees, in his head, his whole world was under attack. Why can't you leave him in peace, to rest, if not for him then for me?'

'Flint's evasiveness is all the evidence I need that he's trying to give us the slip on something.'

'Barclay's just scared, that's all.'

'Scared. Really? Mike and I have spent too long watching bad people in plain sight manipulating the world to their ends. Flint's behaviour is off, Tabs – and no wonder he's scared. He knows we're on to him. He hadn't been up to see Dad for ages, then suddenly, bang! The night he comes round, Dad goes missing. Come on, Tabitha, join the dots.'

'No, you join the dots, Harold. Dad's dead, OK. He's gone. And we will never know what happened that night. But if you keep raking up muck, none of us will be able to rest and move on. Stop being so selfish and imagine for just one second that you're not the only one going through this.'

They arrive at Harold's bungalow and he heads inside. As he does so he stares at Tabitha.

'Please?' she asks.

Harold turns away in silence and closes the door on his sister.

In the small circular cellar beneath the winery, Mike Delves can just about make out what looks like a photograph on the wall. He steps inside the room poking into the darkness with his cricket bat. He moves in a circle around the walls, searching, jabbing his bat at the wall, ready to strike with the speed of a viper and the strength of a bull. In the darkness behind him the barely perceptible shape of a shadow moves from beside the doorway to the stairwell, gingerly moving out of sight as it stoops to pick something up. Barclay Flint, wearing the long dark robe from the wall, is clutching his pocket stone and praying to Bacchus the god of wine for good fortune as he blends into the darkness while climbing the stairs back up to the winery.

Mike Delves is feeling his way around the room with increasing urgency. Meanwhile as Barclay tiptoes through the metal doorway at the top of the stairs his robe snags on the handle, dragging the door with a sharp grinding moan; after a split second he breaks into a run, flailing his way towards the winery door, peering through the two eyeholes in his hood, glimpsing the tanks, vats and barrels as he picks up speed like a tugboat down a flume.

Delves is accelerating up the stairs and as he reaches the top he sees a cloaked figure leaving through the winery door. He can hear an engine approaching outside. Barclay dashes down the winery steps pulling his hood back from his face. The Bottle Bank van screeches in a handbrake skid, clattering into the entrance to the vineyard as Delves hurtles from the winery. The back doors of the van fling open and Pearl reaches for Barclay.

'Boss! Grab my hand!' As the van starts pulling away she's desperately hauling him aboard. 'Teddy! Go!'

Mike Delves is gaining in pursuit. As Teddy floors the van, Pearl heaves Barclay inside and Delves is quickly left behind.

Hurling his cricket bat after the van, Delves slows to a halt, breathing heavily as he watches the van disappear round the corner of the lane.

35

The atmosphere in the Bottle Bank is tense. Pearl and Teddy are at either end of the counter, Barclay between them still wearing the robe, a cross between a referee at a boxing match and a vicar at the world's worst wedding.

'We're screwed!' exclaims Pearl, nervously biting her fingernails.

'We're not screwed,' says Teddy.

'They want him dead!' insists Pearl, pointing at Barclay.

'Impossible, the only person who's ever wished me anywhere near that level of harm was that winemaker in Bandol who bet I couldn't drink his entire stock of rosé in a single afternoon. Codswallop.'

'Pearl does have a point there,' continues Teddy. 'We saw Harold Crawshaw researching how fast a body decomposes in a shallow grave.'

'And that Delves dude is a maniac,' continues Pearl.

'He threatened to slice off our ears,' explains Teddy.

'Yeah and wear them as a necklace,' shrieks Pearl, eliciting a bark of concern from Pinot.

'Wearing ears as a necklace?' asks Barclay.

'She's a hundred per cent correct, he said we'd not be able to listen next time we came prowling around because he'd cut off our ears and wear them as a necklace.'

'But how would that even work? They'd look far too big dangling around the midriff. Medallions made of human flesh? I've never heard such fiddle-faddle.'

Pearl takes a hard look at Barclay. 'For real, Delves and Crawshaw are deadly, Barclay.'

Barclay takes a sip from his glass of white. 'It's true that Delves pursued me with the alacrity of a wolf. And this robe may have saved the day but it casts a sinister light on the death of old Crawshaw. I found a room of terrible darkness. Well, a cellar, really. At first I thought the floor was marked with the runes of an evil ritual, but on further reflection they may well have been the marks left by rolling barrels on their edges. But that still doesn't explain the robe.'

'Fancy dress?' asks Teddy.

'Very drole. In the darkness, I could just make out a photograph of Victor in his younger years, a group of seven, all wearing robes like this one.'

'Secret society?' suggests Teddy. Barclay shrugs.

'Alas, with the age of the photograph, I fear they are long gone and unavailable to ask.'

'So how do we figure out who they are?' muses Pearl. Barclay smiles.

'An underground cult in Sussex? If only we knew someone whose finger is on the pulse of the local seniors . . . Minty!'

Minty emerges from the back of the shop carrying some freshly baked ginger biscuits. 'Alright, I'm on my way, my darling, no need for shouting now.'

'Minty, it seems Harold Crawshaw and Mike Delves are involved in some murderous pact against me.'

'Never!'

'Well it's possible they just want to frame me for murder. Either way, it's a bit of a pickle, so to speak. And we need to find out if Victor Crawshaw was ever involved in occult practices: you know, robes, rituals, secret societies, that type of thing.'

'I know just the place to look.'

'Ah yes?'

'The library.'

Teddy's face falls. 'Minty, the library doesn't really keep those kinds of records. If you can help Barclay tap into any local gossip . . .'

'I never gossip!' insists Minty heading to the shop door.

'Sorry, local intel, then I can triangulate that with an online trawl of Delves' profile, see what that digs up.'

Minty waves as she heads into the street beneath the tinkling doorbell of the shop.

'Marvellous,' beams Barclay. 'Meanwhile I shall deduce how this weird wide web is woven together. Like a glass of wine served blind, I will identify the roots of the conundrum and together we shall discover once and for all what really happened to Victor Crawshaw that dreadful night in the winery.' Barclay gestures for his empty glass to be refilled when Pearl gently places her hand over his and puts the bottle down.

'Barclay! How about you spill the tea on what went down at the winery the last time you saw Crawshaw? Like, what did you guys chat about? Was he acting odd?'

'Victor was melancholy, certainly. He was disillusioned with his children, delighted by the surge in insect life across the meadows over the past several years from letting them grow fallow; let me see, he talked about red-tailed bumblebees, numbers are plummeting apparently due to a lack of forage, I think he said meadows were ninety-five per cent down since World War Two which is playing havoc with insects and therefore bird life and the whole food chain, which he insisted is coming to bite us all on the backside if we don't change our attitude towards the "nidgets", as he called them. We need regeneration, resilience. The simplest equation is the most powerful: life depends on life.'

'Sure but, like, was there any other tea besides the bees?' asks Pearl. Barclay shakes his head.

'Oh, except one thing. I did mention it to the police but it seemed so triflingly hypothetical that I barely paid it any mind.'

'And what was that, though?' asks Pearl.

'Well, old man Crawshaw said that if he could have his time again he'd cut his children out of the will and leave the whole vineyard to me.' Pearl and Teddy stare at Barclay. Teddy breaks the silence.

'He'd leave the whole place . . . to you . . .'

'I rather thought he was joking.'

'Unreal. Do his kids know?' asks Pearl.

'Shouldn't think so, I only told the police.'

'Yeah, his kids totally know,' says Pearl nodding, 'so like, that totally makes sense why Harold Crawshaw thinks you were involved in his dad's death.'

'But I haven't inherited the farm, I was never going to inherit the farm, it was mere conjecture, two old friends over a glass of youthful Pinot Noir.'

'That's not how Harold sees it. He ten out of ten thinks you want to get that farm,' adds Teddy.

'Oh, bum,' says Barclay. 'In that case I'm definitely going to need a snack. Who's for a bagel topped with toothsome butter and a lavish dollop of houmous? Ooh, and a glass of Meursault on the side? I'd say we all rather need a sip of something dandy.'

Teddy and Pearl roll their eyes and take a synchronised breath as Axel dashes into the shop with a tinkle of the bell over the door. He's holding a copy of the *Sussex Express* aloft like the Olympic torch. 'Pearl, we have been made famous! Check out this page at the front, we are all over it like soy sauce on sushi.'

'Give it here,' Pearl says grabbing the paper and opening the article. The headline reads 'Lewes Traffic Halted by Climate Activists'.

Axel is buzzing. 'This is so cool, finally we get people talking about the real issue. Pearl, this is so great. Hi guys, by the way.'

Barclay greets Axel and Teddy clears his throat with a grind which makes a curious sound like butterbeans clogging up a coffee grinder.

Pearl's face falls as she starts to read. 'They're acting like the whole town is trashing us, they just dropped a truth bomb full of lies.'

'What lies, what do you mean?' asks Axel.

'Says here we were being "yobby".'

'What is *yobby*?'

'Like . . .' Pearl demonstrates, pulling a face and making loutish gestures.

'What the hell is that? They are accusing us of dance crime?'

'No, *yobby* means badly behaved, aggressive,' says Teddy.

'But she looked like an angry hip-hop artist.'

'They are defo not accusing us of being dance criminals, Axel. This is such a clown move.'

Barclay is leaning over and reading. 'Oh, I don't know, it isn't all bad. Free wine seems entirely reasonable to me.'

'Reasonable!' Axel and Pearl utter simultaneously.

'It's true the piece is on the stern side but look, Pearl, the fact is you did bring the traffic of Lewes to a halt, and indeed you are "passionate climate protesters" as described on this very page and it is to your credit that this newspaper even deemed your tale worthy of the ink to spread the word. This is what I believe is described in common parlance as a *platform*. Congratulations to you both, you've made a splash.'

'But it's all crap!' insists Pearl.

'Crap is in the eye of the beholder. Have a glass of wine, your work is done, the good people of Lewes are now more aware than previously about your concerns for the climate emergency. Let the dust settle and meantime let me introduce you to the pleasures of Meursault. I have no doubt dear Victor would approve. Chardonnay of course, from Burgundy in France, legend has it the Romans named the vineyard after a tiny stream which they called Mouse Jump, Muris Saltus in Latin, hence Meursault in French. And in English we simply call it scrumptious.'

'My days, boss, is there anything about wine you don't know?'

'Here's to jumping mice,' suggests Barclay as he raises his glass. He gives Pinot a discreet peanut from his pocket. 'Yes, don't you worry, I love you the most,' he reassures the dog. 'Want to chew on a bone, I've got a lovely one here for you from Frank Richards the butcher.'

Barclay tosses the marrow bone in the air and Pinot leaps, meeting it at gravity's apex before taking it back to her bed and giving it a thoroughly good gnaw. The silence is broken by Pearl's, Teddy's and Axel's phones all buzzing at once with alerts.

'What on earth do these infernal telephones want now?'

'They're just alerts buzzing, Barclay, let's see what's up . . .' Pearl's face is shocked as she picks up the message. 'My vids have gone viral!'

'I shall be requiring inoculation,' Barclay intones, genuinely concerned.

'She means our social media stuff, Barclay,' corrects Teddy.

'Oh, my days, Teddy, more than one million hits!'

'Hits? As in the hit parade? Are we talking songs?' asks Barclay.

'Views, Barclay, views, number of views.'

'More than a million people have watched Pearl's videos, Barclay, the ones I shot on the allotment.'

'But they were ghastly.'

'Nah, iconic says a million others,' says Pearl shaking her head.

Axel stares at his phone. 'Pearl, I cannot believe I am seeing these numbers, this is so crazy!' he enthuses.

Teddy muscles in next to Pearl. 'Yes, Axel, and I only uploaded it last night, maximum points to me!'

Pearl shoves Teddy to one side and shares Axel's delight. 'This is our moment, babe, we can make another big splash off the back of this,' she says.

'Yes, I totally love the splashing,' Axel agrees. 'What is the next plan?'

'Planning is essential,' calls Barclay as he goes to choose some vinyl to play on the counter's record player. Teddy looks at Pearl. Pinot stares at Barclay. Axel smiles as he sees an idea cross Pearl's face. She grins.

'Flash mob yoga.'

36

Lewes High Street is empty. The war memorial on the junction of School Hill and Market Street stands proudly on the brow of the hill. A winged bronze statue of Victory atop a globe faces eastwards over the fields of Flanders, a laurel wreath held aloft. Down the slope, save for a couple of buggies pushed by puffing parents, the scene is tranquil with the distant Downs rising all around, green guardians keeping a watchful eye over any restive behaviour. A cream and red double-decker bus, the number 28 bound for Brighton, is slowly pulling up the hill, gears grinding and engine rumbling in multiple deep tones. Today, Barclay is crossing the Cliffe High Street down the hill, taking Pinot for a walk, tunefully humming The Beatles' 'Magical Mystery Tour' as he goes.

Overhead, flocks of rooks and seagulls are tussling for supremacy over the skies while at the top of St Nicholas Lane a face pops out to check if the coast is clear. Pearl Finch dressed in matching green running shorts and a strappy tank top swiftly emerges. She is barefoot carrying a yoga mat and aglow with the air of an elf about to execute a carefully planned heist. Axel joins her, marching with purpose in comfortable red and white robes shouldering a portable stereo with his yoga mat. From the alleys and twittens around about, one by one, yoga practitioners of all ages, shapes and sizes emerge barefoot and jovial with an air of determination and revolution, yoga mats in hand.

From above, it looks as though the Lewes war memorial is a mysterious yoga magnet inexorably drawing several hundred people in colourful motley clothing. Pearl waves the 28 bus to a standstill as Axel places his stereo on the war memorial and starts playing 'Portrait of Linda In Three Colors, All Black' by Sonny Sharrock as loudly as his speakers can crank. A couple of homemade banners unfurl across the scene saying STOP THE TRAFFIC. From all sides of the high steet yoga practitioners are blurring into a spontaneous barefoot throng. There's a pair of identical twins in matching crop tops and flare pants. Five octogenarians in an array of faded vintage joggers. A builder carrying his hard hat with his fluorescent hi-vis over his heavy-duty workwear. A group of awkward teenagers following along for the ride, taking excited selfies in the crowd. Elsie Sharpe and her gang from Priory Bonfire Society blend into the yoga scene wearing their matching navy-and-white diamond check jumpers. And there at the very back of the throng is Teddy Olsen, squeezed head to toe into an ill-fitting unitard. Teddy has never done yoga before and he's nodding nervously at the building fellowship of slow-moving strength, anxious for a friendly glance of welcome from anyone at all.

With a single loud peep on a whistle, Pearl rolls out her yoga mat at the top of High Street beneath Winged Victory. To the west of its base, a bronze statue of Liberty is seated holding a blazing torch. To the east sits Peace with a dove on her shoulder. The statues are serene in the face of the murmuring crowd of some two hundred people all unrolling yoga mats and settling in to follow Pearl's lead. She nervously exchanges glances with Axel and whispers, 'For real, I never thought this many would show up!'

'My mind is blowing up right now!' he replies, wide-eyed and shaking with joy.

Pearl begins leading the group in a sequence of Surya Namaskar sun salutations. Above, the rooks and seagulls settle their differences and land on roofs on either side of the high street in a temporary truce. The top deck of the stationary 28 bus is full of peering faces, some curious, others filming on their phones and one youthful, exasperated suit repeatedly checking his watch, horribly late for work. Pedestrians are starting to gather on the pavements, children pointing delightedly at the mass of bodies moving beautifully in approximate synchronicity. A few colourful jumpers from various bonfire societies dot the scene. Like a cranky cog in an otherwise synchronous watch, Teddy, towards the back, is doing his best to keep up with the moves and, to make sure Pearl notices him, is waving and pointing at his own face whenever she turns his way. Traffic is building up with a rising tide of sharp horn parps, and alongside the bus a sleek black Range Rover is revving its engine and edgily tooting its horn. Inside, at the wheel, Mrs McRae is getting flustered.

'Hit it again, Mrs McRae,' says Maurice Le Brocq from the rear seats.

'But Mr Le Brocq there's nowhere to move, it's wall-to-wall yoga, sir.'

'They have no right to block the king's highway, blast the horn!'

Mrs McRae hesitates and Le Brocq's bony hand shoots over the central armrest and prods at the horn, just out of reach, in a jerky Morse code of loud hooting. In front, Teddy Olsen gestures for Le Brocq to calm down. The sneer of disdain that breaks across Le Brocq's face is as empty and cold as the vacuum of deep space itself.

The carefully clipped nails on Le Brocq's right hand are reaching closer to the horn on the steering wheel when Minty Jarvis appears at the end of the car's bonnet, dancing with the fluidity and grace of a spring tide in full flood. Mrs McRae stifles a laugh while Maurice Le Brocq yanks himself forward, apoplectic at being pulled back by his own seatbelt. 'This is intolerable, release me!'

His complaining voice can be heard faintly outside the car by the gathering crowd of pedestrians and observers who are abandoning their vehicles and gathering to witness the yoga practitioners moving as one.

Monica Reeves of the *Sussex Express*, once again dressed in far too many layers, is bustling through the crowd, videoing on her mobile phone. Her commentary over the footage is breathless.

'Monica Reeves reporting on Lewes High Street from what seems a mob of yogis bringing the streets to a standstill, as you can see there are signs reading "stop the traffic" and . . .'

She zooms in on Pearl and Axel leading the demonstration:

'And some familiar faces appear to be leading this protest, Lewes once again brought to a standstill by Pearl Finch and Axel Nissen, the same climate protesters who bunged the centre with their recent yarn-bomb stunt that paralysed this proud market town.'

The sound of car horns in the distance is building as Monica switches to photo mode and takes as many snaps as she can of the closing moments of the serene yoga faces all glowing with the same calm focus from youthful power to ancient steadfastness. As Pearl blows her whistle once more, the crowd good-naturedly begins rolling up their yoga mats and dispersing back into the ancient lanes leading off the high street. Teddy Olsen cannot resist taking a bow with Minty in the direction of Le Brocq's shiny black Range Rover. The response is a single loud blast of the horn, which makes them giggle with glee. Axel swipes his stereo, and just as a couple of police officers are trotting onto the scene he grabs Pearl by the hand, kisses her and leads her into the crowd. To the south side of the high street, Monica Reeves spots Barclay Flint with Pinot, the black and white collie dog, on a lead, slowly making their way up the hill. She makes a beeline and whips out her camera, filming.

'Barclay Flint isn't it, owner of the Bottle Bank?'

'Indeed, lovely day for it.'

'Are you part of this protest, Mr Flint? Monica Reeves, *Sussex Express*, is this your doing?'

'Heavens, no, I'm merely a humble vintner wending his way through the day, isn't that right, Pinot?'

'This your dog?'

'No, no, this is Pinot, Pearl's dog who is . . . well she was situated just over there.'

'Pearl Finch? The instigator of the climate protest on Priory Street last week? How do you respond to the people of Lewes who have twice been brought to a standstill by your employee, Mr Flint?'

'What Pearl does in her own time, be it lunch break, day off or holiday, is a question for Pearl rather than Pinot and I, isn't that right, Pinot?'

'Is there a wine you'd recommend pairing with the bitterness many people will be feeling from this inconvenience?'

'Wine is about joy, Monica. For this time of the year a hearty red with a gentle jot of spice is the perfect antidote to terminal gloom; hard to beat wrapping oneself in the merry red robe of a Fitou from sunny southern France, it makes one's very spirit feel like plump dough rising in the warmest corner of heaven's own bakery.'

'Thank you, Mr Flint.'

'And a very good day to you, Monica. Come along, Pinot.'

And just like that, the 28 bus rumbles back to life, narrowly missed by a shiny black Range Rover setting off a little too briskly as the traffic begins flowing once again past the Lewes war memorial. The rooks and seagulls rejoin their battle for the skies over the high street but the statue of Victory remains silent, memories of the fallen trailing in the rising wind around her wings.

37

Minty's flat is warm and cosy. The smell of freshly brewed coffee hangs in the air and the distinctive sound of David Bowie's voice from her old CD player perched on the sideboard is brightening the mood. On the sofa, still dressed in his unitard that's squeezing his body like a sausage in cling-film, Teddy is hunched over his laptop balancing a plate of ginger cake on his knee. Minty is peering out of the window. 'Those poor pigeons, so hungry, people shoving them out the way, if there was only one left on the whole planet people would cherish it as the most beautiful bird, that purple and green glow around its neck, exotic as a sugar bird.'

'What's a sugar bird?' asks Teddy.

'I don't remember the name, you'd have to look it up. Antiguan sugar bird.'

Teddy types into his search engine. 'Bananaquit?'

'Bananaquit! That's it! My mum told me those yellow sugar birds were so nosey they'd come right into the house. Always looking for treats.'

'Sounds like Barclay.'

'Ha! They must be related, amazing what you can find on these computers. Got a photograph?'

'I'll find one in a sec, this is interesting, he doesn't have an Instagram account.'

'Well of course Barclay doesn't have an Instagram account, he can barely switch on his phone.'

'Not Barclay, Delves. But he does have a Facebook profile. Hang on.'

'What does it say? The only word about in Lewes is that Delves is always alone, unless Harold Crawshaw is about.'

'Well that tallies with what I'm seeing here. Check it out, he's quite the loner.' Teddy turns the laptop to show Minty.

'Just photos of himself.'

'Exactly, on an oil rig here, is that a mineshaft? And this looks like, not sure, somewhere deep in winter, Scotland maybe?'

'It could be Alaska for all I know. Are you saying this man has no friends at all?'

'I mean from his photos it's all heavy work in remote locations. Just him. The odd comment, men mainly, not much to go on, just a handful of likes and the odd single word. Hang on, what's this about a regiment . . .'

'Is that him in the uniform?'

'Yeah, says Kosovo here, he looks young, there's a tag. Yep, that's him. And bingo, Harold Crawshaw standing right next to him. Bingo! They were in the army together. We still need to find out about those robes of Crawshaw's, too.'

'I'll go back to the library.'

'Minty, I'm not sure . . .'

'Libraries are the best places to look, Teddy. Just you keep working on how Barclay's going to prove his innocence to a couple of bloodthirsty soldiers.' Minty gathers her coat and heads for the door.

'Well, I've started using AI for that and so far none of the answers are looking great. These are going to be tough nuts to convince. Barclay needs one hundred per cent hard evidence, an iron-clad timeline of what happened to Victor Crawshaw. He's got to be on his A game.'

★

Downstairs in the Bottle Bank, Barclay is lying on the floor, rolling around with Pinot licking his face, a small empty wine glass rolling on its side beside his flushed pink face.

'Can you taste Port? Can you? It's on my cheek . . . No, not vintage Port, Pinot, guess again . . . Tawny Port, quite right!'

Barclay gets to his feet and tosses Pinot a treat from the jar before pouring himself another glass of Quinta do Noval Colheita Tawny Port. 'This is a special one, Pinot, comes from the year 2000 and I've been squirrelling it away for a special occasion.'

Minty steps around Barclay and Pinot as she leaves.

'End of the bottle, alas. What a wine, Pinot. Tastes like sultanas burnished by the centre of the sun and served chilled with a salted almond it'll send your mind into orbit. Good dog. Since we have finished this particular bottle, it's time for a gear change, perhaps a bottle of deep red Hermitage, a black olive ordained by a liquorice priest . . .'

Barclay's phone is ringing and he struggles to find it under all the loose invoices, receipts, notes and books that are piled on the counter around his jigsaw station. Finally, he spots it perched on the shelf behind the counter and presses it to his ear. It continues to ring. He peers at it, jabs the screen, and a voice comes on speaker: Tabitha Crawshaw.

'Barclay, I have a proposal for you.'

38

Minty Jarvis is in the Old Library, a tiny second-hand bookshop down a narrow twitten in Lewes. Surrounded by books, she's sitting with a toothless eighty-year-old man with a white wispy beard and a senior woman dressed in robes, her long grey hair plaited either side of her neck.

'And when was this occurring?'

'Seventies, by my reckoning,' says the man.

'There was that runagate, can't place his name, always with Crawshaw, he was. Them robes was their bonfire costumes,' adds the woman.

'Seven of them, there were. Gummuts, the lot of them, all worked with vines in some regard or other, like a secret society . . .'

'. . . Secret society of drinkers was what it was. Come recent times, they all died off, reckon Crawshaw was the last of 'em.'

'And there's no way they were a cult?' presses Minty.

'Cult? Nah. No more than drinking in old Crawshaw's cellar awhile. That lot were always too steaming to march on Bonfire, let alone get up to strangeness,' says the woman with plaits.

'Butter-my-wig if it isn't so,' agrees the man.

Minty sits back in her chair and takes a bite of cake. She sends a text to Barclay: 'Crawshaw's robe was part of a group of bonfire marchers, no sinister cult, says my network.'

★

Pearl is sitting inside the Abyss Brewery with a pint of Super Pale. Music washes over the fermentation tanks along with the colourful lights from a revolving display as the DJ builds the laid-back mood. The crowd is youthful, colourful and, aside from a few bona fide beer nerds dialled in on their focused tasting group, the mood has the enticing energy of the first drink after the working day is done. From across the brewery Axel makes his way towards Pearl carrying his small knapsack and wrapped up in his waterproofs and hiking gear. They exchange a fond kiss.

'Hey stranger, didn't know what to get you. Share my pint?' asks Pearl.

'You know I am so thirsty, actually, after the flash mob I hiked to Mount Caburn to get fresh with my spirit, so beautiful, let me get a water first, you want something?'

'No, all good. Crisps though! Salt and vinegar,' calls Pearl after him. She watches his lean physique slide through the crowd, she'd almost forgotten how well put together Axel is. She opens her phone to check her messages. There's one from Teddy which reads mysteriously, 'Have to tell you something, sorry for being weird.' Axel sets down his water and a pint. 'I forgot your crisps, *fanden*!' he curses, turning back to the bar.

'It can wait till the next round. Tell me about your walk.'

'So many skylarks, they were singing like it is still summertime, even in all this grey with the wind and those moody rain clouds. They were singing to me the whole way back here, like they were leading the way, my spirit is a skylark.'

'Lit.'

'Yeah, so that kind of brings me to some news. It may be all crap but I heard it so I figured to tell you was the best plan.'

'Heard what?'

'I heard about who Priory Bonfire Society is going to be burning on November 5th this year.'

'Juicy. Spill it, who's the effigy?'

'OK, but like I said it might be complete crap so please, take this with a pinch of pepper.'

'Salt, you take it with a pinch of salt.'

'You may need both because to me this sounds a little weird and also a little bit scary.'

'What did you hear?'

'Priory Bonfire, they are going to be burning you, Pearl Finch.'

Pearl sits back with a frown.

'What? Why would anyone burn an effigy of me?'

'If you think about it, all your protests you told me about with the hay, the paint and the petrol pumps, then the yarn-bombing, our yoga flash mob, from what I heard you got a reputation already around town for pissing people off with demos. You're an activist. They really hate you.'

'Who told you?'

'I cannot say but it is definitely your name that was said, Pearl Finch is going to be blown up like a human explosion on Bonfire Night.'

'Alright, shush, keep it down, we don't need the whole of Lewes knowing.'

'Well, everyone's going to know this soon enough. See? It is a scary thing, right?'

'I guess. But also, badge of honour. Anyway, like you said it could be total crap,' says Pearl, taking a large sip from her pint. The flavour seems to be getting more bitter as she swallows it.

Axel shifts nervously in his seat and tentatively raises his glass. 'Cheers, I guess.'

Suddenly, Pearl feels as though everyone in the bar is furtively gawping at her. Spooked, she spills her pint over Axel's lap, sending him leaping into the air. With apologies tumbling out, Pearl does her best to mop up the spillage with beer mats while Axel darts to the gents to get cleaned up. 'This ain't how I saw today going,' she says to herself as she looks around, embarrassed. Is she imagining it or is everyone in the bar glancing furtively at her? For the first time in her life, Pearl Finch feels utterly alone.

39

Next day, surrounded by open cardboard boxes and wooden cases of wine, Teddy is stocking the shelves in the Bottle Bank before the shop opens its doors for business. The silver morning light is crystallising across the dewy glass between the street and the shop display, which has been augmented to feature a large model bonfire with a papier mâché Guy Fawkes perched on top. The bell over the door tinkles as Pearl comes in with Pinot. The two of them are sticking close together; it seems to Teddy that Pinot is comforting Pearl by keeping her body close against Pearl's leg. Pearl's eyes are red.

Teddy puts down the bottles of wine he's holding. 'Hey, Pearl, everything OK?'

'Dunno, Teddy, do I look OK?'

'To be honest you look sad. One hundred per cent sad.'

'Might be because I'm bummed. Priory are gonna burn me as an effigy.'

'Ah.'

'And I just got a message from Axel saying he's flown back to Copenhagen.'

'Yes!' says Teddy with a little too much enthusiasm.

'What do you mean, yes?'

'I mean, well, not yes, just, I thought he didn't approve of flying?'

'Apparently he hates being here more than he hates being on a plane.'

'Well, why's he gone?'

'Maybe he's completely freaked out that a twenty-five-foot-high effigy of the person he's been seeing is about to be burned in the streets of their home town.'

'Ah . . .'

'That's the second time you've said "ah", Teddy. Come on, spill the tea.'

'Yes, the effigy thing, I've actually been trying to tell you about that.'

'Not been doing a very good job, then, have you?'

'Well, truth is . . . I saw it in the barn up at Dandelion Hill. I saw it a while ago and it scared the pants off me. I've been trying to find a way to say something but it all just seemed so nuts.'

'That so? I tell you what's nuts, Teddy. What's nuts is you not telling me!'

'I was trying to protect you!'

'By telling Axel?'

Teddy swallows hard. 'I may have hinted at it, yes. But just to get his advice, it's been driving me mad, Pearl, making me feel like my whole head is going to just fall off . . .' But Pearl is turning on her heel, already leading Pinot back outside. 'Pearl!'

'I quit!' she shouts, with a slam of the door.

From his flat above the shop, Barclay flourishes down the stairs: 'Good morning, dear Teddy, I must say Minty's news of Victor Crawshaw not belonging to a sinister cult of robe-wearing devil-worshippers has primed me with the roots of a FIRST-CLASS MOOD – capital letters.'

'Wish I could say the same, Barclay.'

'Oh?'

'Pearl's just quit.'

'Quit? Quit? Quit what?'

'The job, Barclay, this place. Priory are burning an effigy of her on Bonfire Night, I stupidly told Axel, and he's done a runner back to Sweden.'

'Denmark.'

'Wherever, he's totally freaked out.'

'The burning of effigies is one of the stranger elements of Lewes life. But she can't possibly quit over that. In any case, what would we do without her?'

'Hopefully she'll come back when she's cooled off. I should never have told Axel.'

'And you chose not to share this information with Pearl directly because . . .?'

'I wanted to shield her; thought Axel might help find a way to stop it.'

'I see. And instead, he . . .'

'Took fright and legged it.'

'Not the ideal outcome.'

'Far from it.'

Pearl and Pinot are curled up on a bench on Priory Street. Pearl is mournfully munching on a Danish pastry. She neatly tears off a small corner and offers it to Pinot, who gently licks it into her mouth. 'It's so sus, Pinot. One minute he's Mr Funtime then first sign of problems he's back to Copenhagen with barely enough time for "seeya".' Pinot looks up, hopeful for another nibble. 'You get it. Good dog. It sucks that I miss him. And I get it, seeing someone in a different country whose effigy is about to be blown up, for sure, it could freak you out. On the other hand, my protests must have actually landed or, y'know, or they wouldn't be dragging a big statue of me through the streets to burn now, would they? You'd think he'd want to at least make me feel validated, right, Pinot?'

Barclay and Teddy approach the bench and sit either side of Pearl and Pinot.

'Mind if we join you?' asks Teddy.

'Yeah, well, Teddy. I don't know, got any more tea to spill?'

'Pearl, I'm really sorry for telling Axel about the stupid effigy. I was going crazy, I just felt like my brain had caught fire and the only way of putting it out was to just say something to someone and I know that should have been you, I know that, Pearl. I just didn't know how to tell you.'

'And?'

'And? Um, and . . . Oh yes, I'm sorry?'

'No, you're going to buy me pastries for a week,' corrects Pearl, holding up the end of hers before munching it, watched closely by Pinot.

'Oh, absolutely, no sweat, every day for two weeks is fine by me. I am really sorry, Pearl. I'll talk to the Priory lot, I'm going to get that effigy changed.'

'Oh, just drop it. You know how they are. If you stir the pot it'll make it ten times worse, they'll just make my brows look wild or give me horns or something.'

'We shall face this dramatic scenario as one,' says Barclay with a hint of pride. He holds up his hand for a high five. Teddy looks at him, unsure of what he's doing. Pearl considers his strange posture for a moment before reaching and obliging him with a high five. 'Thank you, Pearl. My first and last ever high fiver.'

'You ever got roasted as an effigy, Barclay?' asks Pearl.

He shakes his head. 'The closest I ever came was in the early two thousands when the Bottle Bank ran out of rosé during a late summer heatwave.'

'Was it like a ten out of ten certainty you were going to be blown up that year?' asks Teddy.

'Well, the story goes that Coombe, or was it Cleve? Well, one of the societies started fashioning my likeness into an effigy, but as soon as my flow of pink plonk resumed their anger was assuaged and they pivoted to burn, I think it was Saddam Hussein instead. If memory serves, they converted the bottle of pink wine I was riding into a Tomahawk missile. A detonation of deliciousness, you might say. Speaking of which, I may have had a breakthrough on the Crawshaw case. Tabitha has asked me to finish making her late father's wines.'

'What?' gasps Teddy.

'Stay away from that place, Barclay, Harold and Delves are total psychos!' adds Pearl.

Barclay gets up from the bench with a smile. 'The trail to Crawshaw's death is still warm, and I'll not rest until I've found the source of the sizzle.'

40

Barclay slams down the lid on a stainless steel tank of fermenting Chardonnay in the winery at Dandelion Hill. 'While I am a wine merchant rather than winemaker, Tabitha, with the assistance of your late father's notes, there's a distinct chance of creating wines that are worthy of the gods themselves.'

Tabitha surveys Barclay as he slowly climbs back down from the gantry to ground level. He's wearing a deep mauve Derry flecked Donegal tweed suit with neon orange buttons on the jacket and cuffs, and a pair of well-worn richly polished oxblood leather brogue Derby boots made by Loake, the distinguished British shoemakers founded in Kettering in 1880 and always favoured by his late father. If only Barclay wore the same size shoe as his father, he would have inherited a splendid collection of treasured pairs, but since he didn't, the thrift shops of Lewes had won the day after his late father's passing. From time to time Barclay likes to dream of all those pairs of shoes scattered to the world, adventuring with their new owners: sitting in the fine restaurants of Edinburgh, striding past Cardiff Castle or enjoying a night on the tiles in Belfast. Barclay's own shoes are currently walking next to Tabitha's wellingtons back into the house towards Victor's old office. As they enter the room together, it seems to Barclay as rambling and chaotic as when Victor was alive.

'It's a mess, I'm afraid,' Tabitha grimaces.

'It is a cascade of consciousness, thoughts surfing these pages to the realm of possibilities; do you know where his last notebook is to be found?'

'Right here on his desk, it's where he left it.' Tabitha hands a large red hardback notebook to Barclay, who sits down to open and read it. 'Would you like a cup of tea, Barclay?'

'Don't suppose there's any chance of a glass of wine? Anything cold that's either pink or white would more than adequately lubricate my mental valves.'

'I'll see what I can rustle up.'

Alone, Barclay riffles through the book to the final page. He murmurs as he reads aloud: 'Runner Duck fruit poppling, wild ferment, temperature holding twenty-one degrees, sugar levels dropping steady. Safe.' Picking up a pen, Barclay begins doodling absently across the page as he thinks aloud. 'So why, dear Victor, did you open the lid of that fateful Pinot Noir?' His eyes roam back and forth across the line 'Do not open' heavily underlined in Victor's sloping scrawl.

Barclay's musings are burst by the shadow of an intruder cast across the desk. Looking up, he sees Harold Crawshaw reddening as he stands across from him looming over the desk.

'Put that down.'

'Put what down?'

'That book. You have no right to be reading my father's notes.'

'My dear Harold . . .'

'Don't "my dear Harold" me, your presence in this house is deeply inappropriate.'

'But I'm here at your sister's invitation.'

'Invitation? What invitation?'

'Tabitha asked me to finish making your father's last wines.'

'You're not even a winemaker!'

It seems to Barclay that Harold is about to explode with unpleasantness rather like a geyser erupting with raw mince. Harold's teeth clench and his fists roll tightly as he flies out of the doorway. 'Tabitha! Tabitha!' From down the hall, Barclay can hear the row escalating from shouting match to crashing plates as someone hurls something. He turns back to his work and takes out his own notebook, which he starts to carefully annotate with the élan of an invitation to a calligrapher's wedding. As the crashing and shouting increases, he becomes calmer. He sets aside Victor's notebook and carries his own down the hall, gliding through the kitchen where Harold and Tabitha are screaming at one another, utterly absorbed in their fight.

Barclay moves between them and they seem entirely oblivious of his passing, the ghost of a wine saint whispering his way through a brawl in hell's rowdiest kitchen. He calmly steps around Queen Elizabeth the ginger cat, who is asking to be let out, and makes his way out the front door. While the cat trots elegantly away towards the vineyards, Barclay climbs the steps to the winery where he flicks on the lights and closes his eyes, sifting through the memories of his last night with Victor. In his pocket he squeezes the small black stone Victor gave him. The distant memory of accordion music playing in the barrel hall. Victor shuffling into the darkness. 'I wunt be druv . . .' He asks himself over and over again what could possibly have occurred with the fermentation for him to open that Runner Duck tank? And then it hits him. 'Victor never opened the tank,' he murmurs. As Barclay blinks in thought, the valves in his mind are blown apart by the realisation that his friend was so stubborn that nothing on earth could ever make him change his mind about anything. 'I wunt be druv . . .' *But if Victor Crawshaw never opened that tank of Pinot Noir . . . who did?*

A hand grabs his shoulder and he lets out a shout. Spinning around, Mike Delves is leering mere inches from his face.

'Hullo, Flint.'

'You scared the heart out of me.'

'Here for a drink?'

'I'm making wine, well, finishing Victor's last batch.' Barclay is nervously eyeing possible escape routes.

'Oh, I see. Tabitha asked, did she?'

'How did you know?'

'Well it wasn't Harold, was it?'

'No, I suppose it wasn't. Are you . . . stopping me?'

'Now why would I do that? Don't mind if I watch?'

'Making wine is hardly a spectator sport but, since you're here, you could always lend a hand.'

Mike Delves sits down slowly on a chair and starts rolling up a cigarette. 'Or you could just smoke, that would also be "helpful". You do realise that smoking in a winery is tantamount to worshipping Zeus in the Vatican?'

'Want me to wait?'

'Or at least go outside.'

Slowly, Mike Delves moves a few feet to the doorway where he leans against the doorframe and lights up, ostentatiously blowing his smoke outside. Barclay's mood thickens as he turns back to the tank and slowly takes out his notebook. In it his hand moves with the slightest tremble as he writes 'Did Delves murder Victor?' before turning to smile at Mike Delves. Delves does not smile back.

41

Maurice Le Brocq is standing in front of a large unopened cardboard box in the library. His hollow expression of excitement is that of a sleep-deprived six-year-old on Christmas morning eagerly anticipating the contents of a centrepiece gift. Mrs McRae is standing by with a Stanley knife which she seems curiously adept at flourishing. Le Brocq gives her the nod and Mrs McRae slices across the top of it with the precision of a laser. Opening it up, she stands back as Le Brocq peers inside with the closest thing to glee his crack of a mouth can muster.

'As I thought, Mrs M! It's the League of Rural Affairs branded livery for our fundraiser. The government's plans to restrict gun ownership is a blight on us all and, make no mistake, the fightback begins here, in Sussex, at Greenacres. We shall never surrender!'

Mrs McRae lifts out one of the retractable standing banners and pulls it up to have a look. She makes a face and Le Brocq draws a pair of pince-nez spectacles from his waistcoat to balance on the end of his nose.

'Mrs McRae. Aside from "League of Rural Affairs", why are all these campaign banners written in Welsh?'

'How can you tell it's Welsh, sir?'

'Look down here, the letter *w* is apparently being used as a vowel.'

'Oh yes, and the double *l*s and double *f*s, I see it now. Shall I be sending them back, sir?'

'Unless we plan on rattling our tins in Llandudno, I think you better had.'

'Apologies, I must have ordered them in the wrong language, I'm all fingers and thumbs online, give me a pheasant to gut any day of the week and . . .' Mrs McRae notices Le Brocq's cold deadpan stare and quickly changes tack. 'I'll get them replaced right away, sir.'

Down in the valley Tabitha is clearing up the kitchen and leaves a bowl of food out for Queen Elizabeth. She brushes a small pile of broken crockery into the old dustpan before straightening her clothes in the small mirror that hangs near the door to the hall. Taking a long look at her reflection, she wonders how it all came to this. Yelling with her younger brother like a couple of rudderless teenagers. The memories of sunny evenings when they were children playing on Brighton beach seem an awfully long way away. It was a golden time when her parents were happy and she would play for hours with Harold, pretending that the stones were planets piled into galaxies leading out towards the giant *neverness* of the ocean beyond. Was it a black hole? The edge of space? They never discussed the finer details of their game, only that if you ever fell into the great wash, you were 'out'. Tabitha notices that her reflection is streaming with tears and she dabs her eyes, composing herself as Queen Elizabeth nuzzles around her legs with a muted purr. Drawing her shoulders back, she resolutely moves to the front door, which she opens with a large inhalation of fresh air.

Advancing towards Harold's bungalow, she spots Mike Delves leaning in the winery's open doorway stubbing out his roll-up on a small pile of cigarette ends gathered around his feet. He nods at her as she passes by, trying not to catch his eye.

★

Inside the winery, Barclay is crouched behind a row of barrels holding his phone close to his face on a video call with Minty and Teddy. The image is glitching a little and while Barclay is doing his best to comprehend the position of the camera, his generously svelte eyebrows are all that Teddy and Minty are able to see.

'Barclay, try holding the phone a little further from your face,' suggests Teddy, 'and speak up, would you, we can hardly hear you this end.'

'I'm doing my best, Teddy, by deploying a row of sturdy barriques to keep the fiendish gaze of Delves at bay, it's as though he's managed to eject his eyeballs from his face like a couple of heat-seeking limpets, to stick to my every move.' Barclay's hushed tones rustle and echo around the winery, but not loudly enough to draw the attention of Delves, who's still guarding the door while opening a pouch of gherkins. 'What's the latest intel?'

'Not good, Barclay,' says Minty, 'from what Teddy's been finding online, there's plenty of co-workers who certainly don't want to be working with Mike Delves ever again.'

'Why not?' asks Barclay.

Teddy grabs the phone. 'Thing is, Barclay, he's lethal, security work, a bit of time as a private detective and his hobbies read like a compilation of solitary preparations for combat, there's weight training, judo, archery . . .'

'Archery?'

'Well, he did it once for certain, I found a photo with a bow and arrow and a bunch of dead animals at his feet. To be fair, he does look much younger.'

'Tell him about the AI assessment, Teddy,' suggests Minty.

'Oh lord, what does the robot overlord have to say about him, then?' asks Barclay.

'Based on all our research, I asked for a threat assessment

founded on the profile Minty and I have built up. The report is a ten out of ten code red, Barclay.'

'Is that what the computer said, "code red"?'

'No, it just said that based on the profile we delivered, his psychology suggests he's capable of violence.'

'But as of right now, there's no hard evidence that Delves means me any actual harm.'

'Barclay, he threatened to cut off Pearl and my ears,' says Teddy, 'and you're currently hiding from him behind a barrel of wine.'

'Good point, yes.'

'And we know from our research that he moves from job to job, what was that status update he left, ah, yes, here it is, "born to fight",' adds Teddy.

'Well, I haven't seen anything like that yet.'

'Come off it, you saw how he was in the shop with you and how he chased you out of that winery, his temper's on a hair trigger, Barclay.'

'You tread carefully now, the man's more dangerous than we thought,' says Minty.

'I shall, thank you both – now back to work, Teddy – those shelves won't just stock themselves.'

Barclay hangs up the call while attempting to spring to his feet, but his legs won't play ball and he has to hoist himself up by gripping the edge of a barrel with both hands. He finds himself face to face with Mike Delves, who is staring dispassionately. 'Lost something?'

'No, I was just taking the weight off the old pins for a minute, letting my mind cogitate, you know. Compiling tasting notes. I write them on my telephone. Here's one: "the wine is pristine as the reflection of seaside sunlight, it comes from the coast of Galicia in Spain, the sort of thing a mermaid would sip for breakfast, a citrus wonderland . . ."'

Delves leans slowly in, his face millimetres from Barclay's. 'You're weird, Flint. But that won't save you.' He pokes Barclay in the chest causing Barclay to take a couple of steps back, which he uses as momentum to spin and accelerate away from Delves and out of the winery. Delves tears into searching around the spot where Barclay's been crouching with the relentlessness of a crow devouring roadkill.

42

A damp vole pauses beneath a vine searching left and right to check that the coast is clear. A ginger cat is usually on the prowl and this vole is not in the mood to be a meal. Scampering off, the sound of distant shouting rolls like elongated percussion across the vineyard. Harold's head is poking out of the entrance to his bungalow like a tiny tortoise head from a giant carapace. His face is contorting in a fierce gale of rage. Tabitha, facing him, is remonstrating, her arms swaying and tumbling like a conductor guiding a runaway orchestra into a siding of calmer sonority.

'Of all the people, Tabs, that man is beyond the pale, I won't have him going through Dad's stuff.'

'I understand you're vexed, I do, but Barclay is the only person who can make sense of Dad's notes and keep all that wine from spoiling. We can at least make some money out of it.'

'Keep him out of the office, there's no reason for him to be in there.'

'Well, one of us has to clear it all out. What's the point hanging onto all that rubbish?'

'Rubbish? That's our father's life in there.'

'I don't see you lifting a finger to help.'

'I don't want to go in there.'

'Then that's settled, Barclay and I will clear out Dad's office.' Tabitha turns and heads back towards the main farmhouse leaving Harold's trail of invective in her wake.

Somewhere in the vineyard, a vole enters the safety of its burrow and curls up next to a breathing knot of warm, furry bodies.

Barclay's fingers are deftly running over the old notebooks on top of the late Victor Crawshaw's desk. Dating back several decades, they are a maze of doodles, sums, suggestions and half-considered projects. Among the scribbles, Barclay is tracking down the wines made in each year and the techniques that Victor followed. Reflecting on the step change from conventional farm with herbicides and pesticides to the most regenerative vineyard in the country, he feels a stirring sense of inspiration. He really must tap into Pearl's determination for her ongoing ecological projects with more commitment and support.

Victor's notes had become more deeply concerned with butterfly counts, rising diversity of beetle species and sowing cover crops in recent years. With copious references in particular to viper's bugloss, it seems that he was experimenting with which wild flower most benefitted the widest number of pollinators – in the case of viper's bugloss, the notes claim that its pollen produces three times the protein of sunflower hearts and the boost to local bumblebee numbers is recorded as 'spectacular'. His lists, unlike his handwriting, are meticulous when recording the growing number of species. Victor's notes also reveal that the more insect life flourishes on his vineyard, the more reptiles, mammals and birds thrive. He writes about slow worms, skylarks and voles, and as their numbers go up so wine production goes down, mainly because Victor's attention became unswervingly focused on one rather than the other.

Barclay can't help but conclude that because Dandelion Hill is imbued with such powerful biodiversity, it is now a shrine to vitality, perfectly charged to create plentiful wines of life-giving joy. And to lose all that just at the time when Victor's last vintage is fermenting seems as tragic as it is poetic. Barclay's heart dips for an instant before bobbing back up at the thought of a snack.

Tabitha steps into the office carrying an armful of large paper bags and a glass of white wine, which she hands to Barclay.

'Right, Barclay, time to toss out the rubbish, we can burn it up in the top field. This is for you . . .'

'Thank you, Tabitha. Delicious! *Aaaah*, as pure as pears rolled in gold. I've been reading your father's notes on regenerative viticulture. Utterly inspiring.' As Barclay piles the notebooks safely on one side of the desk, one topples off and he spots a discarded bunch of winery filter pads hidden under the desk. 'Hello, what's this?'

Picking the pads up, he examines the faint red wine staining and gives it a sniff of curiosity before Tabitha reaches out and tosses them into the open paper bag. As she does so, the subtle aroma wreathes Barclay's nose with a scent whose identity he does not immediately recognise. His brain is suddenly a grand miasma. He vanishes from his own thoughts and is no longer able to locate himself. He is lost to words; his whole being is momentarily enthralled to this unusual, unrecognisable and altogether minuscule scent, which drifts and eludes identification like a microscopic butterfly riding a coquettish breeze. Coming to himself, he loses the scent in a blink and his brow performs a little wave of discombobulation. He logs the dainty whiff as a riddle to unravel and silently sets his mental Rolodex of odours to work. He hands over a sheaf of ancient receipts and faded wine labels for burning.

Tabitha empties the wastepaper basket into the bag. 'You alright, Barclay?'

'Daydreaming, trying to make sense of all this,' Barclay gestures around the room.

'Dad's life was a bit chaotic at the end.'

'Except his annotations on insects. It seems everything he was planting on the farm in the latter years of his life was to secure the future for as many species as he could.'

'Oh, he was obsessed. It wasn't healthy, though, biodiversity is all well and good, but at the near total exclusion of his own family? Ask Harold. It was intolerable, making us both feel utterly invisible.'

'How's he ghosting me like this?' Pearl is furiously prodding at her phone in the Bottle Bank as Teddy steps into the shop carrying a small paper bag while munching on a cinnamon bun.

Pearl's appearance is unusually immaculate: her hair is tied up and she's wearing a smart green top and flowing trousers with a pair of shoes that look like shiny weapons.

'Who's ghosting you?' Teddy says, chewing on his bun.

'Who d'you think? Axel,' says Pearl as she catches sight of Teddy's cinnamon bun as if to say 'Where's mine?'

'As promised, here you go.' He tosses the paper bag to Pearl, who catches it easily with one hand. 'This is so good, feels like I'm being baked from the inside, in a good way,' says Teddy.

Pearl takes a sceptical bite from her pastry before realising how delicious it is and tucking in with gusto. 'OK, that is mighty tasty. Where from?'

'New Danish place on the high street.'

Pearl shrugs. 'Guess if I can't actually be with my Danish squeeze, may as well munch myself to death on their pastries.'

'Cracking way to go. Although being shrunk to face an Elephant Hawk Moth in combat would also be pretty cool.'

'You want the last thing you remember to be fighting a moth?'

'You're right, that's wrong. Better to tame it and ride across the dawn skies, we'd be closer than Han and Chewie.'

'Who are they?'

'*Star Wars* – Han Solo and Chewbacca.'

'These are just sounds you're making, Teddy.'

'Pinot understands me, don't you?' At the sound of her name, Pinot jumps up and gives Teddy a nuzzle.

For the first time, Pearl starts wondering why Axel couldn't be a little more like Teddy before quickly shaking it off like the spray from a cold shower.

'You OK?' asks Teddy.

'I'm chill,' replies Pearl, emphatically shoving the rest of the large cinnamon bun into her mouth. Struggling to get her words around the bite, she tries to add, 'Completely chill', which comes out as 'Kompeepee pill'.

Teddy pulls a quizzical face and gives Pinot a warm hug while Pearl stares at him struck by a curiously warm sense of horror.

43

There are more lights on than usual at Greenacres as the afternoon starts fading into shadows. The windows usually look like missing teeth in the grin of an old skull, but with the lights inside flickering and the distant sound of voices, it feels like an early festive gathering. Five cars are parked outside in a regiment of polished steel, illuminated by the floodlights on the driveway. There's Le Brocq's dark Range Rover proudly on display flanked by a white Mercedes GLS, a bronze metallic Bentley Bentayga, a silver Porsche Cayenne and an old yellow Fiat Panda from the 1980s which, in scale, looks like a matchbox parked next to a line of butter dishes. Inside in the library, the line-up of smart dresses and tweed jackets are guffawing over canapés and warm red wine.

'I haven't been offered a vol-au-vent since 1982,' says a woman's voice.

'*Shhh!* Cynthia, you don't want to upset him, you know how thin-skinned old LB can be,' hisses a man's voice, 'let's at least hear about his mysterious big plan.'

Outside in the hall, Maurice Le Brocq is wearing a stiff narrow dinner jacket with a pinched clip-on bow tie and a pair of black patent leather shoes. Mrs McRae notices that the shine from his shoes is a flash of incongruity against the flatness of the decor at Greenacres, which hasn't been refreshed since the house was built. She really must persuade Mr Le Brocq to spruce the place up a bit.

'How's my dickie bow?'

'Smart, sir.'

'And they've all had wine?'

'For twenty-five minutes precisely, sir, as you requested.'

'First glass should be trickling into their veins right about now. Time for me to make myself known.'

Le Brocq sweeps into the library; his gait reminds Mrs McRae of a grasshopper balancing awkwardly on stilts. She follows him, diligently closing the door behind them. As Le Brocq scans the room his eyes glide over the well-turned-out assembly, and the suits, ties, dresses and jewellery, various banners and pamphlets for the League of Rural Affairs placed variously around cause him a moment of pride until his mood is disrupted by a younger man with unkempt hair wearing a polo shirt. 'Mrs McRae, who is that young man?'

'The Websters' boy, you remember Eric? They're away in Antigua so he's come on their behalf.'

'He has, has he?' says Le Brocq, moving towards the young man; *even the most discerning fly will still be drawn to filth*, he thinks to himself. 'Eric, how good of you to come,' he says without cracking a smile.

'Hi, yeah, Mum and Dad are overseas so I'm flying the flag for the Websters,' says Eric, pretending to wave a small imaginary flag.

'Yours is the, er, yellow vehicle?'

'Yeah, love that car, Mum's old Panda. Been driving it my whole life, amazingly never conked out, always a first time, though, maybe the old girl will get stuck tonight and I'll have to leave her on your drive! Imagine that.' Eric pats Le Brocq on the shoulder, eliciting the merest sneer.

'Yes, I am imagining that.' Le Brocq, discombobulated, looks around the room and gently taps his wine glass stem with his signet ring.

With no response from the guests, Eric grabs a fork and bashes it against his glass. 'Folks, attention over here, thanks, guys, Mr Le B wants to say a few words.'

Le Brocq smiles thinly. 'Thank you, Eric. My friends, fellow members of the League of Rural Affairs, we are here tonight united as one voice of the countryside across this great county of East Sussex. The legislative threat to our way of life is based on misinformation and, as we are well aware, fails to promote our keen environmental interests, our dedication to boosting the local economy and the social importance of our gatherings, such as we are engaged in tonight. And what a pleasure that is.'

Le Brocq's eyes meet Eric's for the briefest moment and he represses a sudden urge to hurl his wine glass at the young man's lustrous hair. 'The time for words has passed. Action is required. Funds must be sought, not only to protect shooting as a historic pillar of our community but to expand it into many more pillars.'

A polite ripple of applause circles the room while Eric stares wistfully out of the window, wishing his Fiat Panda could fly him to Antigua to be with his parents. *They're probably sipping Piña Coladas on the beach*, he reflects silently.

Noticing Eric gazing through the window at his car, Le Brocq can't resist adding: 'And by appearances, some might be in more urgent need of funds than others.'

Eric zones back in to find the room chortling at him and manages to raise a good-natured smile. Behind his back, his hands stretch before flexing into balls of singular disquiet.

Le Brocq steps towards an easel and flips over a map of Greenacres subsuming Dandelion Hill into its environs. 'And while charity starts at home, so does business. With the recent passing of my neighbour Victor Crawshaw' – a name which he utters as though it is coated in hot sand – 'the opportunity presents itself to acquire the farm next door and finally put it to some better use by converting it into Greenacres' very own shooting lodge. Soon, my friends, we shall be toasting the first residential shoot on my expanded estate. Mrs McRae, time to break out the salmon terrine.'

Teddy is sitting on a high stool in Minty's kitchen watching her stirring a light brown cake mixture. 'So when do you add the ginger?' he asks.

'Stem ginger syrup's already in this mixture and here, you can tip in the dry mix from that bowl, that's where we get the lovely kick of that warming ground ginger working its magic. In it goes, thank you, my darling.'

'I haven't seen anyone make a cake in years.'

'Cake solves every problem and eases all troubled hearts.'

'Minty, the troubles of my heart might need a cake the size of Sussex.'

'Or just the magic ingredient.'

'Please don't say "love".'

'Why not?'

'Had a gutful of it with Axel and Pearl.'

'I thought that Axel scurried back to Denmark with his tail between his legs.'

'Don't think that was his tail, Minty . . .'

Minty playfully slaps Teddy's wrist. 'Now behave yourself. Tom wouldn't approve.'

'So are you two an item? Haven't seen him around lately.'

'Oh, just friends, friends you know, who adore spending the odd bit of time together.' Minty's face warms and she looks with tenderness over at Teddy. 'It's fine to like Pearl . . .' She shushes Teddy's attempted protest. 'It's fine, Teddy. Relax. Just be real and show her how much you have in common.'

'But everything I do just makes me seem even more invisible to her.'

'Wait for the right moment and focus on what you both love.'

'Pinot?'

'Nature.'

'Aha. But how will I know the right moment?'

'The right moment is always right now. Just ask her to go for a walk. Teddy, either the friendship is going to deepen naturally or, you never know, you may both hop on that little boat to the Island of Romance. Either way, you can't lose.'

'What if I get seasick?' jokes Teddy.

Minty laughs and tips her cake mix into a loaf tin lined with baking parchment. 'Happily, ginger is a well-known cure for that. And as you know . . .'

'I know I know, there's nothing that can't be solved with sticky ginger cake.'

'Fireworks for the soul.' Minty winks.

44

Victor's office is denuded. Aside from notebooks carefully piled on the desk next to his computer and a few books left on the shelf, it has the air of a vestry on a weekday. Quiet, calm, the atmosphere so soft it feels as though the air is doing its best impersonation of cotton wool. Barclay is standing, taking it all in. The life of his friend is now over. His last wines are all that's left to finish, which Barclay vows he will watch over with the vigilance of a chef cooking a perpetual soufflé. And do his best to lobby for the preservation of the vineyards. In the meantime, his mind is distracted by theories of Mike Delves' dark deeds in the winery. Tabitha is picking up the last two binbags.

'Tabitha, once the wedding business is up and running as the colossal success I've no doubt it deserves to be, what precisely is the plan for the vineyard?'

'Oh, I haven't really given it much thought. Sell the fruit to a contract winery? I'm not sure we want all the hassle of making wine any more.'

'But with the aid of your father's notebooks, it would be my pleasure to help take the hassle out for you!'

'You're so sweet, Barclay. Let the dust settle and see how we all feel.'

Tabitha carries two binbags out of the office followed by Queen Elizabeth the ginger cat. Barclay turns one last time to survey the room. He glances at the computer on the desk together with Victor's notebooks. Approaching the computer, he wonders if it might reveal any clues. Sitting down with a huff, he stares at it before prodding the keyboard. He presses one of the buttons on the monitor. Nothing happens. Checking the computer is plugged in, Barclay is baffled by how to switch it on. He pom-poms to himself briefly before picking up Victor's notebooks and making a note on a scrap of paper: 'Ask Teddy how to switch on a computer'. He tucks the paper into one of the notebooks and rises to his feet with a sound of surprising effort. Flicking off the lights, Barclay exits with Victor's notebooks, dipping his head under the narrow doorway.

Outside, Tabitha is carrying the bin bags round behind the barn to where a plume of smoke is rising into the air. Barclay muses that the flotsam of Victor Crawshaw's life is rising to be dispersed as atoms and recycled piece by piece having tumbled silently back to earth to take up residence in the soil. From there, the remnants of the old winemaker's things will transform into plants and trees, insects and reptiles, mammals and birds, to flow out from Dandelion Hill and across Sussex as his relics become one with the county where he once lived. Barclay and Victor loved describing wine as 'liquid places', and as Barclay watches the smoke fill the sky, he reflects on the timeless composition of wine: the decades and centuries of soil evolution that contribute to the detail in every glass; the secrets shared by those who dare to drink more deeply.

His phone buzzes in his pocket with an incoming text – Pearl asking him to share a photo of her effigy in the barn. With a sigh, Barclay pads over to the barn, opens the door and snaps the effigy, then tries to text it to Pearl. As he exits the barn finally managing to press the 'send' button, he fails to see Delves and Harold blocking his way. Delves gives him a shove, causing him to drop his phone.

'Ahoy! Careful there!' calls out Barclay.

'Or what?' asks Delves. Barclay faces them and instantly realises they mean business.

'Now look, chaps. I know you've got the hump—'

Harold cuts him off with a shove. 'Save it, Flint. We know you want the farm and you'll never get it.'

'Look, that conversation was merely your father caught up in the moment, I assure you . . .'

'Your wriggling words won't help you now. No Tabitha here to save you. This is my farm, my place, my rules. Rewilding is what Dad wanted and that's exactly what I intend to continue with my natural burial ground – and the vineyard can go to hell.'

'Flint here could fill the first spot.' Delves stares at Barclay.

'Steady there,' urges Barclay, panic rising.

'Oh, I think Mike and I are very steady, don't you, Mike? In fact, I could see you here as a permanent resident, Flint. One wrong move and you'll be part of this place forever, I'm ripping out all the vines for more graves to dig, the trees will spring up, the cash will flow and the winery, once I've gutted it, will make a very nice little venue for mourners, maybe a cafe, don't you think, Mike?'

Delves nods silently as Barclay stands his ground.

'If you think for one second that your father's legacy of these vines, planted before you were born, can be destroyed without a fight, you'd best take a long deep breath.' Barclay steps forward to face Harold. 'This is a heritage vineyard, Harold, one of the oldest in England. Just take a moment to think about what you're saying.'

Harold yanks Victor's notebooks out of Barclay's hands with a leer.

'If I'm to finish making your father's wines, Harold, those notes are indispensable. Think, man.'

'I'd rather burn them than give them to you.'

Harold nods to Mike whose fist hammers into Barclay's brow quicker than a spark. Barclay falls to the ground with a groan.

'If you show up here again, Barclay, the only thinking you'll be doing is about the plot you'll be buried in. Understand?'

Harold kicks Barclay in the stomach, receiving an encouraging pat on the shoulder from Delves as the two of them walk away. Alone, Barclay is sprawled on the ground. The scent of the earth is familiar to him as he slowly starts to process what's happening. He loves a ploughed field, the scent of so much life and often thinks of it as endless aromatic poetry. At this moment, it brings him a sense of comfort that numbs the pain he is feeling in his stomach and his head. Dishevelled, disoriented and unsteady, Barclay picks up his phone as he slowly gets to his feet and makes his way towards the Duke. Wiping mud from his cheek as he catches a glimpse of his reflection, he slowly opens the door and heaves himself into the driver's seat. Carefully turning the key in the ignition, 'Wonderful World, Beautiful People' by Jimmy Cliff erupts from the stereo as he pulls away from Dandelion Hill, perhaps for the very last time.

45

Pinot bounds along the chalk path trailing up through the South Downs to the gentle peak of Blackcap. Her paws feel the soft, springy moisture as the damp of autumn slowly soaks into the earth. Pinot measures this walk by the feelings of the seasons. In spring, her pace is inspired by the cowslips playfully erupting over the hills in a small fanfare of joyful exuberance. Summertime brings the heady scent of crawling marjoram, which she loves to roll in. Autumn delivers a flush of field mushrooms along with dainty, colourful Amethyst Deceivers and ludicrous Puffballs whose dynamic exhalations of spores always keep her on her toes. The gales of winter herald a frosty bite beneath her pads, with the stillness of the ground held in calm coolness, a final surrender before the grace of new growth begins moving with the magic of spring's first summoning. Pinot's delight in this downland walk is bringing a keenness to her gait as she explores every aroma, as though cordially greeting her sisters and brothers. Behind her, Teddy is puffing his way steadily up the hill while Pearl is striding a couple of steps ahead, their breath misting in a mutual trail as their faces glow from the exertion of the hike. Teddy is dressed in his anorak, wet-weather gear and ergonomic rucksack. Pearl is effortlessly windswept, the mood of her clothing pitched somewhere between 'combat' and 'festival'. As they follow the woodland path over the crest of the Downs and through the open valley towards the woods of Ashcombe Bottom, the auburn leaves are blazing before them just as Teddy notices the last swallow peeling south towards the English Channel in search of warmer climes.

'Won't see another for six months,' he says, 'first one back's always the biggest lift for me after the long dark of winter.'

Pearl's phone buzzes. She shows Teddy the image Barclay sent of the effigy in the barn at Dandelion Hill. 'Oh my days! Teddy, how do you even think for one single millisecond that statue looks even a smidge like me?' she shouts.

'Eh? Well, it does kind of look like you, doesn't it? I mean, it was dark! I just saw the face, same hair colour. It's totally you.'

'Did you seriously miss the Tudor lace collar and the old-time fifteen hundreds look on this woman?'

'Maybe they've dressed you up?'

'And those seventeen martyrs roasting at her feet?'

'They look like disco lights.'

'Teddy, there is no way that I look anything like Queen Mary I.'

'Mary I? *Aah!* Yes, I suppose now you say it . . . Look, I can ten out of ten identify a moth from miles away, but a giant effigy of someone I actually care about – I admit, I stuffed it up like one hundred and ten per cent – and I got Axel all spooked so he ran off to Denmark. Pearl I'll ring him, let me call him . . .'

'Please don't hit up Axel. What'll you say? Tell him I look like some ancient Tudor mass murderer? Yeah, that's going to make him sprint right back to me.'

'Depends if he's into history . . .'

'He's not weird, Teddy.'

'History isn't weird.'

'You're weird!' exclaims Pearl, stopping dead in her tracks. There's an awkward pause as they face one another. 'Why are you such a noob?'

'I guess I just like being a noob.'

Pearl is disarmed by this reply and looks over Teddy's shoulder at the most beautiful display of autumn leaves either side of the path leading down the valley. 'Wow. Those trees are ancient! Hey, this could be mad on my socials.'

'What's the angle?'

'If we show how it all hums, get across how fragile the ecosystem is, as well as the energy of how it's intertwined.'

'One hundred per cent. From growing your food you could show how you're drawing on the lessons of what happens out here in the ecosystem, almost like learning from nature.'

'Out here and in here.' Pearl points to her heart.

'Love that, love that a lot, pinnacle stuff, Pearl. Hey, have you seen Pinot?'

'She's just up ahead. Pinot?'

Deep in the scrub, Pinot can hear the familiar voices of Pearl and Teddy calling out her name. Her ear is cocked and she'll dart back to them in a second, just as soon as she's finished staring at the large toad gently crawling in the leaf litter in front of her on the forest floor. With a whistle from Pearl, she zips back through the trees leaving the toad noticing the flowing air in her wake.

'Good girl,' calls Pearl as she welcomes the dog back with an affectionate tickle behind her ears. 'Thought you'd ghosted us. What d'you find?'

'Let's stick a GoPro on her collar and watch Pinotcam!' suggests Teddy.

'A lot of it would be her catching some Zs in the Bottle Bank.' Pearl laughs as she mimics one of Barclay's musical shuffles.

Teddy points and chuckles in appreciation. 'Ha, Barclay's wiggly dance,' he says doing his version of Barclay dancing.

Pearl is hit by an idea. 'Wait up! Let's totally make Bottle Bank pop on my feed too. Goal: only pour bottles from eco-friendly vineyards. Let's convince Barclay we're only selling wines that love nature as much as we do!'

'Brilliant, all with lighter bottles, low carbon footprints, full marks, top score, Pearl, that's a stroke of actual genius. Winner!'

As the three of them stroll deeper into the woodland, Pinot lets out a yelp of excitement and starts running around Teddy and Pearl in a display of affectionate delight. From the undergrowth, the toad in the leaf litter watches them pass before digging into the soil ready for hibernation. Teddy plays Pearl 'I'm Not There' by Flyte on his phone as they stroll deeper into the woods, disappearing into the foliage, their voices fading between the branches as they move further out of sight.

'Here, check this out, love this song.'

'What is this, Teddy? Major sad energy.'

'No, it's apex, listen to his voice, what mark do you give it?'

'Out of ten?'

'Yeah.'

'I don't do that, Teddy.'

'Yeah, I don't really do that either.'

'Teddy, you do it non-stop. It's chill.'

'I don't do it all the time, do I?'

'Yup, you do.'

'OK, well then, I don't know, I've never thought about it, I guess ten out of ten for the voice, ten for the song and also full marks to the band, they're called Flyte.'

‘They sound like falling.’

‘They do not. They’re excellent, you should come see them play live with me, properly superb . . . hang on. Are we lost?’

46

Barclay's eyes are a little hazier and less twinkly than usual. He is peering at himself in his little shaving mirror. The bathroom of his flat above the Bottle Bank is cramped at the best of times, but today it feels to Barclay as though the walls are caving in. His head is throbbing from the blow of Delves' stony fist and his stomach feels as though a cricket ball is lodged in his gall bladder. Dabbing the bump on his forehead with cotton wool, a kaleidoscope of sounds is being shaped by the pain. With each dab, a new syllable is born, each as inventive, curious and musical as the last. Were it not for the aches in his body, Barclay would have found the noises he is making altogether comical. But not today.

The mood circling inside Barclay's mind reminds him of watching a motorcycle performing the wall of death at the Brighton fair when he was a youngster. It is buzzing with hot energy, roaring in upward spirals into every atom of his thoughts. He closes his eyes for a moment and conjures the flavour of a cool glass of his favourite Wild Ferment Greek Assyrtiko made by the inestimable Gaia winery on Santorini. But the pleasure of it slips from his mental grasp, and instead of the complex svelte refreshment of a comforting memory, he instead feels the strike of Delves' fist once again roaring into his temple. What could Delves' hands possibly be made of to impact with such succinct brutality onto both his body and mind? He can still smell the earth against his nose: a hint of funky cocoa, coffee grounds, the faint echo of roasted nuts. But this thought too is shattered by the memory of Harold Crawshaw booting him in the belly, a feeling so invasive that his involuntary shudder raises a single tear at the corner of his right eye. He immediately dabs it away with a flourish. Barclay's stomach is a cauldron of spells, the place where his entire lexicon of insights about flavour has ended up after being logged, processed and categorised in the library of his feelings. His stomach is the seat of his understanding, the place where his thoughts ferment and his instincts rule supreme. To feel them so wretchedly upset is causing him to wonder what on earth he will sip to set things right.

'Jing Wuyi tea,' he murmurs, turning his face away from the mirror and wrapping himself in his paisley dressing gown before tottering gingerly towards the door of his flat. Opening it onto the landing, he sees Minty with her back to him while she's locking up, dressed in her large coat, a bag of bird seed poking out of her left pocket.

'Morning, Minty,' whispers Barclay hoarsely. 'Off for a hot date with the pigeons?'

'Tom will be joining me so it'll be a crowded date . . . Barclay, what on earth has happened to your face?' asks Minty as she turns around, shocked to see the large bump on the side of Barclay's forehead.

'Mike Delves decided he didn't like my head.' As he takes a step, he clutches his stomach with a wince.

'He didn't like your stomach much either by the look of it,' says Minty advancing with an arm around Barclay and helping him down the stairs.

'That was Harold's foot which does an unimpeachable impersonation of a cannonball hurtling into the timbers of—*ouch!*'

'You rest your voice, my dear. We'll get you down these stairs and then have a look at you.'

'What's left of me.'

Minty helps Barclay across the shop floor and onto the stool behind the counter where his slump is partially ameliorated by the distraction of his unfinished jigsaw of the Seven Sisters white cliffs at Birling Gap.

'Something to drink?'

'Please, Minty, that would be most kind. I'd like a cup of Wuyi tea, please, the only restorative potion I know capable of warming my very spirit to the core. I doubt it will be the full "lizard on a sun lounger" effect, but I hope it will be enough to remind my system that all the goodness of this world can be found in a single sip.'

'I'll get that for you – and while I do you'd best be calling the police, Barclay, can't have ruffians like that doling out pain like it's a no-middle-riddle.'

'What on earth is a "no-middle-riddle", Minty?'

'Just something my friend Sandra used to say, I guess it's a thing that just makes no sense.'

'Well, I fear calling the police would be a no-middle-riddle in this case. I'm sure Harold and his henchman would cook up some tale of trespassing or some such.'

'Barclay, these are dark deeds by bad men. What if they were the ones that bumped off Victor Crawshaw?'

'Delves is certainly capable of violence, but there's no hard evidence.'

'Well, what is it that they always say: "follow the money".'

'Minty, do you truly believe a thug like Delves is motivated by money?'

'Greed, Barclay, is a disease.'

Barclay looks up at Minty. He is suddenly very still with an expression of deep thought on his face.

‘Trapped wind?’ asks Minty.

‘Not this time, no, Minty, although I am going to need something more potent than tea,’ says Barclay, struck once again by the curious aroma of the filter pads he encountered in Victor Crawshaw’s office. Its identity once again eludes him. Reaching for a bottle of red Seyssuel Sotanum 2020 from his array of Hot Bottles and uncorking it with the flourish of a conductor’s baton, he inhales deeply before taking a considered sip.

‘Fragrance, spice and depth. Three winemakers working as one on an ancient Roman vineyard, centuries of intimacy between land and hand all wreathed into one unified wine. I have a grave intuition that the conundrum of Victor Crawshaw’s death hinges on the identity of a single lost scent.’

47

A cold spell is hanging like wet laundry over the Downs. Spiders' webs are alight with fading silvery frostiness and the sky is shuttered by a steel ceiling of high bright cloud. Even the birds are hunkered down today, their song curtailed to the odd mournful cry, as though autumn is entering the final phase of its audit before the terminal bankruptcy of winter is at last declared. In the bungalow, Harold's finger traces over the page in Victor's old notebook which reads 'Do not open'. Barclay Flint has drawn a large goofy doodle of Pinot the Border collie across the page.

Irritably snapping the book shut, Harold exits the bungalow, picking up the rest of the notebooks as he goes. A billowing plume of blue smoke is thrusting upwards from the large central chimney of Greenacres. Down the valley, pale threads of white fume are drifting from the rickety chimneys of Dandelion Hill, held in suspension by a moment of calm, isolated in the valley from the subtle breeze that's uncoiling further up the Downs.

At the kitchen table in the farmhouse, Tabitha is surrounded by brochures and paperwork, her laptop jostling a half-finished cup of cold tea while Queen Elizabeth is steadily purring perched at the other end of the table, watching with the air of a restaurant manager overseeing the start of lunchtime service. Peering through a pair of vampish red cat-eye spectacles, Tabitha is typing into a spreadsheet when Harold steps through the door, tightly bound in his beaten old Barbour jacket. He dumps his father's notebooks on the table, sending the cat leaping to make herself scarce, looms a moment in the light and then hangs up his coat with a cough before loudly filling the kettle and dumping it down on the dark green Aga with a clang.

'Looks like a ruddy betting shop in here, Tabs. What's the big gamble?'

Tabitha chooses not to respond to her brother's jibe and continues attending to her sums.

'Anyone home? Tabitha? What is all this?'

Harold flexes his words like a butcher rolling minced meat into raw patties. He grabs a biscuit from the cupboard and stands over Tabitha with the menace of a lighthouse fitted with a giant magnet luring all ships helplessly onto the rocks. Munching his biscuit with force and dropping a small avalanche of crumbs onto the table, he finally manages to pique Tabitha's attention.

'For heaven's sake use a plate, Hal,' she says before looking up and continuing, 'and no, this is not some silly project, these sums show exactly what this farm could be with just a little bit of dedication and elbow grease.'

'I see, weddings again, is it?'

'Yes it jolly well is weddings. Look, if we're even catering for half the year, the barn still clears enough money to return the farm to profit by year five – three if we're lucky.'

'And how are we paying for the renovations?'

'I will borrow the money.'

'Borrow? On what deposit? And who's ever going to want to get married in a place made famous by a dead winemaker found bobbing around in a vat of Pinot Noir.'

'Stop it.'

'Stop what? It's true. The vineyards are a tangle of overgrown mess, there are insects crawling out of every furrow in the fields and crack in the buildings, animals are everywhere, the only person who'd ever want to get married here is Bear ruddy Grylls.'

'That's not true. It's picturesque. People can be happy here; I just want to make people happy, Harold, what's so very wrong with that?'

'If you really want to make people happy, Tabitha, tell them they can book in for the double: marriage in the tumble-down barn and then a few decades later I'll bury them on the hill.'

'How can you be so beastly?'

'How can you be so naive?'

Tabitha shoves her paperwork across the table and rises to her feet, shunting towards Harold. She advances as her voice rises. 'You think you've got all the answers, don't you? You've never had anything but coldness and arrogance with a face that's lined with an essay of life's little disappointments. I won't stand for it this time, this is my project, Harold, my dream, and it will take a damn sight more than you and your bullet-headed friend with his jars of pickled horrors to get in my way. You go and play at digging holes on the hillside and leave the real money-making to the only grown-up left in this family.'

Harold struggles to find his words and gives an unsettled laugh which further incenses Tabitha.

'You think this is funny? My weddings will bring events, maybe even a festival, but oh no, in funny little Harold's mind this is all just some silly idea that his big sister's concocting, for what? For fun? You think it's fun having to fight for every penny that this farm can deliver? Well let me tell you, Harold, I'm taking this farm into the future and if you get in my way, you'll find out what fighting really means.' Tabitha's eyes are burning as she stares into Harold's face.

From across the kitchen, Queen Elizabeth arches her back, feeling the tension and hissing at Harold before letting out a low, slow growl.

Delves is sitting with one foot on a stool in the living room of Harold's bungalow cleaning his clasp knife when Harold storms in.

'She's a piece of work, my sister, she never listens, always thinks she's right, she's just like Dad and a damn sight worse.'

'Happy families again?'

'She's losing it, Mike. I need you to set her straight, this whole wedding venue idea is pie in the damn sky, the barn would cost a fortune to renovate, she's throwing bad money after . . . Well, it's not as though there's any money to throw anywhere.'

'What do you want me to do?'

'You'll think of something.'

'Old-school?'

'Not that far, but get her to see things my way. Fast.'

Delves snaps the clasp knife shut and pockets it. His face is as stern as an ice-breaking ship as he sets the pickles aside and gets up. 'I'll do it my way. You'd best go for a walk.'

48

Barclay's hand trembles with anticipation. He is holding the final piece of his jigsaw of the Seven Sisters white cliffs between his left thumb and forefinger. A half-finished glass of Sotanum red wine is abandoned on the counter. With his right hand Barclay is swirling a frosty *copa* of Fino sherry and, raising it to his round nose, takes a deeply considered inhalation in a bid to find the original of the lost scent. While many would describe this experience as 'nosing' or 'sniffing', Barclay's mind becomes a mist of all the aromas unleashed from his glass. There is simply nothing else but aroma – Barclay's entire being is given over to interpreting every clue wrapped in the mystery of invisible fragrance. The scent of this particular Fino sherry – which has been matured in cask for longer than usual – has a woody fragrance that, to Barclay, feels as though a mushroom and a green olive are eloping to a beach of lightly salted almonds. While he's thinking of nothing else but that heady seaside scene, his left hand is held in stasis, the last piece of the jigsaw poignantly balancing over its corresponding gap. He cannot identify the curious aroma that he detected for a nanosecond emanating from the filter pads in Victor Crawshaw's office. Sniffing this glass, there is nothing in his memory banks to correspond with it, and every time he tries to lock onto its identity, like the most frivolous butterfly, it flits away just beyond the reach of his mental net. Rather like trying to ignore the itch of a mosquito bite, the more Barclay attempts to let it rest, the greater his urgency to know its origin. And with such an elusive and microscopic dimension to it, it somehow looms all the larger with every passing moment until Barclay can stand it no longer.

Setting aside the last piece of his jigsaw, he is suddenly a windmill of gyrations, his arms plucking bottle after bottle of wine from the shelves of the Bottle Bank. With the precision of a robotic librarian, he spins around the shop choosing a wide range from France, Chile, South Africa, Italy, Japan, Canada, India, England, Spain, New Zealand, Austria and more. Malbec, Grüner Veltliner, Zweigelt, Pinot Gris, Gamay, Syrah, Viognier, Cabernet Franc; the names of grape varieties rise and fall in his mind and he catches each one like a surfer, propelled ever onwards by the momentum of his mind. From young wines to mature, he is uncorking and unscrewing now, the counter a field of bottles all popped up to be harvested at once. With the grace of a fencer drawing a foil, his corkscrew is a flurry of speeding splendour, corks and screw caps hurled over his shoulder as he zeroes in on his prey. Grasping his tasting glass, he takes a moment to survey the line-up of vinous rogues he has assembled to identify in search of the lost scent. Barclay's instincts are inflamed, his feelings stretching out like solar flares and, deep inside his core, he wonders whether the case of Victor Crawshaw's death hinges on the aroma of this invisible clue.

He begins to nose the wines. The first is a youthful Zinfandel from the United States, all burly blueberries and cloves, a galaxy away from the detail of the nano-scent he's tracking. Next, he pours a Pinotage from South Africa, so smoky it's as though the grapes have inhaled a barbecue. And while he immediately wants to find a merguez sausage to pair with the wine, his obsession with the hunt drives him on. He's grabbing a Beaujolais Cru now from France, a silky light Gamay with the grace of a thousand red cherries falling from the dreams of a buddha, but although it has delicacy, the profile of the scent is too fresh for the darker, savoury streak in the aroma he's after. The Viognier is a dead-end and while he's captivated by the Pinot Gris and resolves to visit Alsace for a platter of fine charcuterie as soon as he is able, the lost scent is no closer to being found.

He pauses for a moment to consider his prey. Something dark, musty almost, a hint of copper, perhaps; but as soon as he lands near its identity, the memory flits and fades once again, the dying spark of the last matchstick in the box. He turns his gaze to a mature Gran Reserva Rioja. With its rust-coloured tint as he pours the wine which is more than a decade old, Barclay immediately recognises the colour of maturity. As a red wine spends time in barrels and bottles, it takes on a savoury dimension and steps into the realms of cigar boxes, dust on a summery night, umami richness, that curious deliciousness that rings like a bell carved from roast meats. As the wine glass rises to his nostrils, a series of connections leap from the surface of the wine as the molecules of scent spiral up from the swirling glass towards Barclay's nose. Almost before the aroma has connected with his mind, Barclay's thoughts suddenly bloom like a billion meadows into the singular memory of the filter pads' aroma in Victor's office.

He has found the lost scent. One word rises up from the roots of the wine, through the liquid's ten-year evolution in deep, quiet cellars and up into the clear space of Barclay Flint's considerable mind palace: *sanguinous.* He drops the glass onto the counter, red wine washing over the jigsaw like a tsunami of blood crashing up against the white cliffs.

Descending the stairs from her flat, Minty rushes over, her hand reaching across to right the glass. 'Barclay! Barclay, come around now! What's come over you?' She gently caresses Barclay's cheek, his eyes tight closed. 'Barclay Flint, come back now,' she whispers and his eyes flutter open.

'Minty. It's terrible.'

'The wine?'

'No, not the Rioja. Something wrong, foul and pestilent, Minty.'

'What the heck are you talking about, my dear?'

'Victor Crawshaw never opened that tank of Pinot Noir, I read it in his notes, he'd pledged to leave it to its own devices, never to intervene, Victor was as stubborn as iron, "I wunt be druv," he said – and nothing would ever stand between him and his ways with his wine.'

'Are you saying he was . . .?'

'Yes. Victor Crawshaw was murdered, Minty.'

'That is a very big word to be using, Barclay.'

'Large it may be, but this nose never lies,' Barclay replies, gathering his charcoal Daks coat and racing for the door. 'Hold the fort, there's no time to lose,' he says, tossing a bunch of keys to Minty as he hurries out.

Minty is left holding the keys and she surveys the mess. Carefully, she picks up the last piece of the jigsaw and inserts it into the remaining gap over the wine-stained white cliffs of the Seven Sisters. Looking around, she rummages under the counter and pulls out a half-finished bottle of Hermitage 40-Year-Old Grande Champagne Cognac with a hand-tied label in Barclay's writing underlined with IN CASE OF EMERGENCY. Minty thinks for a moment before plucking out the cork and pouring herself a large measure, which she drinks with relish. 'Light to the darkest corner,' she whispers in admiration of its potent deliciousness as she recognises a sensation in her heart she's never felt before: she fears for Barclay's life.

DI Alpert's face is one of concern mixed with consideration and a lacing of disbelief. Barclay Flint, a little breathless after hurrying across town, is sitting opposite her in a meeting room at the police station. To Barclay, it looks and feels like a bunker with all the mod cons of a 1980s youth hostel. DC Keane bursts in, dishevelled.

'Did I miss much? I was absolutely bursting. Blimey, sweet relief.' As he attempts to straighten his perpetually ruffled clothing and checks that the fly on his trousers is secure, Alpert and Barclay both take a moment to survey him. 'What? Something on my chin? Egg bap . . .' He rubs his chin before realising from Alpert's glare that he's oversharing.

'Something on your brain, more like,' says Alpert turning back to Barclay. 'Mr Flint, I appreciate you coming in and, look, it's a theory, a bold one, certainly, but with nothing more than your sense of smell, I just don't have enough to reopen the case.'

'What's not enough?' asks Keane.

'His hunch.'

'You must listen, this nose never lies and the lost scent is the identity of the aroma on which this whole case hinges. I'm telling you, Victor Crawshaw was murdered.'

'What if his hunch is right? Most of the time, you know, in the movies, there's a hunch and, *bam!* Case closed,' says Keane.

'If only this were a movie, Detective Constable Keane.'

'Right, but all's I'm saying is—'

Barclay leaps to his feet and nearly overbalances. 'There's no time for this. While I fully understand your predicament, DI Alpert, and thank you DC Keane for adding credence to my underthoughts . . .' Before Keane can ask what 'underthoughts' are, Alpert waves him down with a discreet gesture of her left hand. 'I will deliver concrete evidence and share it by sundown. Or at least, as soon as I possibly can. Barclay Flint is on the case.'

Keane claps his hands together. 'Love it. Hunches, man, you go on and get some, Mr Flint.'

'Or: please do nothing to endanger yourself or indeed procure evidence under false pretences. Makes my job a right mess,' says Nuria Alpert, smiling at Barclay as he awkwardly and hurriedly navigates his way around Keane to reach the door.

At the doorway, Barclay turns to face them both with a nervous smile. 'Wine crime. It's officially a thing.' With a curt nod, he closes the door behind him.

'"It's officially a thing",' repeats Alpert with a quizzical shrug.

'Boss, what if his hunch is right? We've got to follow him, got to see where the trail goes.'

'All we have to do is be professional and if Mr Flint finds anything we can go on, then, Oscar, you strange young man, we'll take a look. We can't be wasting police time on a smell.'

'What about sniffer dogs?'

'Flint's not a dog. Now cool it, Oscar. If he comes up with anything substantial, believe me, we'll be all in.'

'All in, yesssss.' Oscar holds up his hand for a high five which Alpert ignores as she picks up her paper coffee cup and strolls out of the door.

49

Tabitha slaps Mike Delves hard on the face. He doesn't blink. She readies to strike again but his cold shark eyes persuade her that it's a bad idea. She purses her lips and takes a deep breath through her nostrils. 'How dare you come into my house and threaten me. You are no longer welcome here, Delves. Now get out of my house. Leave.'

'Your house? Half's your brother's. Any move away from that and our next chat won't be so friendly.' He slowly turns and sits down at Victor Crawshaw's desk with the slow purposeful momentum of a boulder rolling to a halt at the bottom of a valley.

Tabitha glances left and right, fuming as her eyes search the room for comfort which does not come. She draws herself tall and dashes out in search of her brother, her whole body alive with fury.

Once Tabitha has departed, Mike Delves places his feet on the desk, bare but for the computer. He opens the drawers of the desk one by one; nothing. The office is empty now, the books, ornaments and stationery all gone. The only things remaining are a collection of pebbles in a jar on the coffee table, all gathered from the different vineyards that Victor once visited. Some people measure their days by the money that they earn, others by the respect of their peers, kind deeds or time spent with loved ones in special places. Victor's life is measured in forgotten stones. For a second, Delves wonders if it's a jar of pickles before dismissing it and turning his attention to the computer, which he flicks on and begins searching. He starts dragging old files to the trash when he comes across Victor's wildlife cam and flicks it on. The first video is nothing much, a couple of moths flickering at night. The next is a badger shuffling past. The third video is of runner ducks blocking the view of the camera, peering down the lens and giving it the occasional peck. As the ducks finally part a little, Mike Delves' eyes widen and he takes his feet down from the desk to replay the footage: in the background, partially obscured by runner ducks, someone is dragging Victor Crawshaw's body on a tarpaulin from the house to the winery.

50

Barclay is driving the Duke as fast as the old Buick engine will allow. He has always adored the swaying of his late father's car, which always feels as though he's driving a sofa, sedately wafting through the lanes of Sussex. Today, however, the engine is surging and Barclay taps the steering wheel, urging the vehicle onwards, his right foot pumping on the accelerator as he swerves and careens through the outskirts of Lewes, narrowly avoiding a cyclist, frightening a sausage dog as he mounts the pavement at the mini-roundabout in front of the Swan. Flooring the car, Jimmy Cliff's 'Give and Take' is booming from the stereo. Pigeons fly up from the street, seagulls arch overhead and the world is left in the wake of Barclay, the Duke and Jimmy Cliff combining as one force focused on arriving at Dandelion Hill as quickly as possible.

Mike Delves is trying to send the footage of Victor Crawshaw's body being dragged to the winery to his battered phone and struggling to make the tech work. His heavy, weathered hands are prodding it, but it keeps glitching. Cursing, he resorts to filming the computer screen with his phone. Saving the video, he tries dialling Harold but the battered screen is too faulty to operate. Grinding his teeth, he thinks for a second before saying 'Siri call Harry' to which the phone replies 'Calling Harry Crawshaw, mobile'. The call rings out without reply. 'Siri call Harry' repeats

Delves. The second call goes straight to answerphone: 'Hello this is Harold Crawshaw, I'm not able to take this call, leave a message.'

'Harry, sending you footage, watch it, call me back, double in.' Leaping to his feet, Delves dashes through the house, across the vineyard and charges into Harold's bungalow, calling his name. With no reply, Delves finds his dented metal lock box and, taking a key from a chain around his neck, unlocks it. The Glock 17 pistol inside is matt, dark and impeccably kept. He grabs it and tucks it into the back of his belt before heading back to the front door, checking the coast is clear and stealthily exiting the building, crouching low.

Dusk is gathering as Barclay flicks on the headlights of the Duke and golden beams sway across the hills as the Rover plunges and rises over the tide of hillocks that sweep up towards the peak of the Downs and Dandelion Hill beyond. The engine rises and falls as the car weaves up and over the winding lane.

From high above at the edge of a spinney fringed with gorse, Harold Crawshaw steps out and spots the car. 'Flint,' he murmurs with fierce disdain as he picks up his pace cross-country back towards the vineyard. In his pocket, unseen, another missed call from Mike Delves is flashing on the screen of his phone.

51

While Barclay Flint is racing to Dandelion Hill, Maurice Le Brocq is proudly marshalling his League of Rural Affairs stand on Cliffe High Street in Lewes. Various faces from his drinks party are flanking him on either side behind a table stacked with pamphlets, leaflets and posters. Sipping from hip flasks and passing around a thermos, the mood is one of levity despite the fading afternoon light and plunging temperature. Two volunteers are out front navigating the steady flow of pedestrians, shaking donation buckets marked with the League's livery. Le Brocq is puffed up with pride, the skin of his face tightly drawn against the frosty air, and from a distance it almost looks as though he could be smiling. The high street is also dotted with various rival bonfire societies in their colourful woolly guernseys raising money for Bonfire Night on November 5th. Good-natured banter fills the air as Eric Webster passes by wearing a faded camel-coloured duffel coat, folding a twenty-pound note into a donation bucket for Coombe Bonfire Boys in their orange guernseys with violet lightning bolts. Their motto, *Floreat Aeternum* (Flourish Forever), is written on the banner they are standing around, and after a few friendly words are exchanged Le Brocq recognises Eric and hails him towards their stand.

'Ah, young Eric, will you be making a donation to our little cause? Unless your funds are all tied up in repairs on that colourful car of yours? I'm pulling your leg; seriously, all donations no matter how large or indeed, small, are welcome.' Le Brocq rattles a bucket at Eric who smiles good-naturedly.

'Maybe later,' he says, strolling away to join some friends who are lighting sparklers with a loud burst of uproarious laughter.

Le Brocq calls after him, 'We'll be here if you change your mind, we'll always be here, devoted to preserving the values of the English countryside, maintaining its beauty for all to delight in. As long as nobody trespasses, of course.'

The Bonfire Boys from Coombe take an interest and move in closer. In spite of their name, Bonfire Boys are made up of men, women and children, and in this case it's a group of three young women who are keen to pry further into the dealings of Maurice le Brocq and his merry band of fundraisers.

'So, what're you all raising funds for?' asks one.

'Well, we're about more than just shooting, we believe in the values of the Great British countryside, creating jobs, looking after the environment and—'

'Killing animals?' suggests another of the Coombe group.

'Well, it's not altogether that simple,' suggests Le Brocq.

'Eric says it is. He says you love blasting pheasants out of the sky,' says the third woman, who is wearing a Coombe guernsey with a red handkerchief tied around her neck.

'Eric is mistaken, he's very young and perhaps not as experienced in the ways of the countryside as some of us.'

'You know he's a tech millionaire.'

'A tech, what's a tech?'

'He's a wizard on the Web. Made more than a million in the last year. It's him what's supporting his parents.'

'I think that's a little far-fetched, his parents are—'

'Retired.'

'But he drives that appalling car.'

'Hates being flashy, loves to give his wealth back to people who really need it.'

'A millionaire?'

'Billionaire by Christmas. Seeya.'

The three Coombe women depart and join Eric and his friends as Le Brocq stares after them, aghast. Eric gives him a little wave as he and his friends disappear into the night.

52

The Duke skids to a halt overshooting the lane and ramming into a row of vines at Dandelion Hill. Barclay wrestles with his seatbelt, which he manages to wrench free, and tumbles from the open door. He pauses for a moment, peering left and right, judging whether his entrance has drawn a welcoming committee from unfriendly eyes. Checking that he is still alone, he listens for any sign of life before picking himself up. He sees the winery lights are on and makes his way stealthily across the yard before tiptoeing warily inside. He presses his body against the wall and slides into the barrel hall, peering from side to side. He picks up the scent of a red wine nearing the end of its fermentation and cannot help but feel distracted and subsumed by its promise, a kaleidoscope of complex fruitiness. Shaking it off, he ducks down and scrambles beneath the fermentation tanks from where he hears a low hissing sound.

As though his nose is receiving a slap, he recoils from an invisibly adversarial blanket of gas. Grabbing a paisley handkerchief from his top pocket, he holds it clamped over his face as he advances towards its origin. His distended reflection haunts him as he passes through the narrow gaps between looming stainless steel fermentation tanks that tower above him.

The sound of escaping gas is getting louder as Barclay approaches a walk-in cool room whose door is ajar. He carefully opens it. Mike Delves' lifeless body slumps out with several argon gas canisters opened on the floor beside him. Barclay drops his handkerchief and drags Delves out of the cool room before sealing the door to prevent any more gas from escaping. He cradles the man in his arms and gently pats his face.

'Delves! Delves! Wake up. By the beard of Bacchus, Delves, Delves!'

As Barclay leans over he feels the faintest breath just as a pistol tumbles from Delves' trousers. The Glock 17 seems weightier than the entire world to Barclay as he stares at it resting on the winery's damp grey concrete floor.

Barclay grabs his phone and dials the Bottle Bank. 'Pearl? I'm at the winery, listen—'

But before he can finish his sentence Harold Crawshaw is standing over the fallen pistol, his face fixed in stone. 'Hang up the phone, Barclay,' he says calmly, picking up the Glock 17 with the coolness of a former soldier.

Thinking on his feet, Barclay pointedly says 'interesting' into his phone with the delivery of a theatrical magician just as he ends the call. Looking up at Harold, his face falls.

Suddenly fearing for his life, Barclay begins to feel a surge of dread rising from his stomach to his throat and realises that, unlike indigestion, this feeling is continuing to rise right to the very peak of his scalp.

53

Detective Constable Keane is wearing a large pair of headphones, blissfully zoning out to the sound of 'Archangel' by Beck. A wash of gentle trance-like electronic sounds bathes his mind. Off duty, he is wearing a boxy oversized jumper with a faded tropical island motif and a black scarf tightly wound around his neck. His chunky black slip-on shoes are well polished and his wide-fit trousers hoisted high beneath his jumper. He is feeling supremely relaxed while scanning the French section of wines in the Bottle Bank. To Oscar, glossing over the unfamiliar words on all the French labels presents a welcome challenge to his detecting skills. Using his phone to research and pronounce the more challenging place names such as Gigondas – Jig-On-Dass – he is becoming surprisingly gripped by deciphering the facts behind a deep, rich Tavel rosé that's just caught his eye. *Main grape . . . Grenache . . . Why's it so dark?* he considers silently as he reads about the appellation of Tavel on his smartphone using wine-searcher.com. He reads the text to himself: 'Tavel is an appellation named after a local town north-west of Avignon . . . Wines mainly from Grenache, Syrah and Clairette whatever that is . . . ah, it's a grape. And the good ones can improve with age. Far out.' Zoned into his music and research, he is blissfully unaware that Teddy, Pearl and Minty are roaring around the Bottle Bank grabbing coats in a whirlwind while dashing at speed out of the door.

'You're sure?' asks Teddy.

'The way Barclay said "interesting" was sus for real, he already told me "interesting"'s the code word for trouble,' says Pearl.

Teddy claps Oscar on the shoulder and he raises his headphones, tucking them around his neck. 'DC Keane?'

'Yeah, I'm just learning about rosé from Tavel, how come it's so dark compared to all the others?'

Teddy thrusts the keys to the Bottle Bank into his hands. 'Barclay's in trouble.'

'Nah, it's all cool, I don't mind the rosé being dark . . .'

'No, Barclay is in deep trouble in real life – call the police.'

'But . . . I'm the police.'

'I know! Lock up the shop and follow us.'

'Where?'

'Dandelion Hill, call for back-up, Barclay needs us.'

'Us?'

'Just call it in, will you!'

Teddy dashes out of the shop with Pinot and leaps into the Bottle Bank delivery van beside Pearl with Minty at the wheel. The engine screams as Minty floors the accelerator in neutral before jolting away into the night. Oscar Keane shoves the bottle of Tavel rosé back on the shelf and heads towards the door, dialling Nuria as he locks up the shop behind him. 'Boss? New intel, it's all kicking off at Dandelion Hill.'

Barclay is cradling Mike Delves' limp unconscious body in his arms. Looking down at him, Barclay can't help but notice how peaceful he looks, his pink skin weathered and blotchy and yet somehow serene in its stillness. Harold is pointing the pistol at Barclay and slowly moving towards him with the menace of a truck rolling towards a harvest mouse. Barclay's breathing quickens as his pulse rises and his pupils dilate.

'Harold, whatever has passed between us, this man needs urgent assistance. I can only imagine what this looks like and I assure you in spite of our history I mean him no harm, I have nothing to do with his predicament, I found him in this condition, I never laid a finger on him, you've got to believe me. Call an ambulance, Harold.'

But Harold Crawshaw is in no mood to bandy words. His mind is focused on justice and tonight, he tells himself, he is hell-bent on getting it even if it means bending the law to avenge his late father and settle the score once and for all.

Barclay continues, his alarm deepening with every one of Harold's heavy advancing footsteps. 'Your father, Harold, your father, his death was no mere accident, it pains me that it took me so long to piece together the chain of events as it pains me to tell you now that your poor dear father was, he was murdered, Harold. I had nothing to do with it, or this unfolding tragedy. Yet, I believe I know precisely who's behind this duo of terrible deeds.'

Harold stares at Barclay dispassionately, gripping the pistol, his eyes burnished with stinging grief.

The rutted track leading towards Dandelion Hill is quiet. Save for a snuffling badger calmy crossing the lane before exploring the side of hedgerow in the rain, not a creature is moving. The rising sound of an engine can be heard in the distance; it catches the badger's attention and prompts a hurried exit through the hedgerow. Headlights flood the muddy scene as Minty Jarvis crouches over the wheel of the Bottle Bank delivery van, which is lurching and bouncing its way at speed towards the vineyard. Teddy and Pearl are clutching one another and hanging onto the dashboard and door handles to stay upright.

'Minty, let me take the wheel!' shouts Pearl.

'No time, darling, Barclay's in a scrape and we've got to shift.'

'Fine, but let's get there in one piece, OK, Minty?' pleads Teddy.

'Teddy Olsen, I've been driving for a whole lifetime before you were even born.' The van takes a muddy skid and Teddy tumbles onto Pearl in a heap.

'Driving what, bumper cars?' asks Pearl.

The van swerves again and Teddy knocks into the stereo, which starts blasting out Iron Maiden's 'Bring Your Daughter to the Slaughter', giving Minty such a fright that she ploughs off the road and into a field, the van swerving and nearly toppling as it spins in muddy circles. Pearl grabs the wheel in the chaos and manages to wrestle it under control. 'Pump the brakes!' she shouts, and Minty jams her foot down. The van slides helplessly towards the tower of rectangular hay bales which looms ever closer in the headlights.

Teddy, Pearl and Minty all brace themselves as the van slides to a halt a mere inches from the tower of rectangular hay bales. They breathe a sigh, then Teddy smacks the stereo until it switches off. 'That was way too close,' he says, exhaling a sigh of relief. After the briefest pause the van starts sliding downhill into the hay bales, which start slowly toppling and bouncing off the bonnet like giant Lego bricks thumping from the sky. Pinot leaps from the back of the van onto Pearl's lap and barks in defiance at each hay bale as it lands. Pearl, Teddy and Minty are wincing in sync with every bale.

As the last bale cracks the windshield and bounces away, Minty takes a sideways glance at Pearl. 'I think better you drive, darling.'

54

Harold's fingers are gripping the pistol so tightly that it feels like their tips are ready to burst. He adjusts his grip, splaying the pads of his fingers against the handle, his fingernails plumping under the pressure. Above him, cobwebs ripple obliviously from the ceiling, dimly lit by the winery's industrial light bulb a little distance away.

Barclay stares up at Harold. His mind is in freefall. As Harold stares at him, Barclay's stomach flinches with the memory of the kick he took to the guts. The internal bruising is still tender and a timely reminder to Barclay of the current mortal predicament he finds himself in. He is at once grateful that he can still feel things and terrified that if Harold shoots at him, his ability to feel anything at all will come to an abrupt halt.

Barclay's toes are flexing and he can feel the heaviness of Delves lying unresponsive in his arms. Several thoughts are winding around one another in his mind and he tries to settle the chatter into one seamless emotion of calm analysis. He instantly regrets this as his momentary mood of defiance peels away and fear parachutes from high in his mind down to every molecule in his body. Barclay notices the muzzle of the gun that's pointed at him: a blank portal, a place of monastic silence and zen-like symmetry. If Harold pulls the trigger, he imagines the bullet flying from the chamber, and calculates that before he's even registered the sound of the gunshot, his lifeless body will be slumping next to Delves on the cold concrete winery floor.

He can't help but think of the bullet's origin as he would do with a bottle of wine. Where was the metal for the bullet mined? In which country were the components melded together? Who made the gunpowder? What language was spoken in the place where it was made? Which countries did it pass through on its journey before being loaded into this gun? How was it packaged? What was it shipped alongside? How was it delivered to the merchant before it came to settle inside the gun pointing at him right now? And what would be the fate of the next bullet in the chamber?

Life is connections, molecules are always in movement, we are what we see and we see what we are, Barclay hears emanating from within his mind as his spirit begins to rally. 'Set down the gun, Harold, and let's get this man some help.'

Harold's stare is immovable and unnerving.

Then the door of the winery clatters open. Tabitha bursts in and, with an instant glance of horror, surmises the dreadfulness of the situation and rushes towards them both. 'Harold, no! Don't harm him! Barclay, what on earth's going on?' As she steps closer she sees Delves' lifeless body and lets out a terrified shriek, her trembling fingers half covering her open mouth.

'Tabitha, stay back,' urges Barclay, gently laying Delves' body down and pulling himself up to his feet. 'Harold . . . please lower the gun.'

Harold ignores him and does not lower the pistol; indeed, it seems to Barclay, he is curiously aloof, almost as though frozen from the inside out.

'Harold, come on, let's talk this out, set aside the pistol,' urges Barclay.

Tabitha rushes forward and throws her arms around Barclay, sobbing into his lapels.

Harold watches, unmoved. 'Step aside, Barclay.' Harold motions with the gun and Barclay gently takes a pace away from Tabitha whose tears are still running down her cheeks. Harold's gun is trained on Barclay as he clears his throat and struggles to speak. 'Tabitha . . . Tabitha, Dad's death was no accident.' Harold's gaze falls on Tabitha and she stares back, aghast.

'Suicide?' Her whole body is trembling.

'I told you I wouldn't rest until I found out what happened to Dad, didn't I? And now, I have,' says Harold with the ghost of a smile passing his lips. Horrified, Tabitha follows Harold's gaze to Barclay and she begins to sob.

'Monster! You killed Dad? Barclay!' Tabitha starts hitting Barclay and falls to her knees in a crumpled heap while Barclay is doing his best to avoid her blows. Barclay begins protesting his innocence with a flotilla of desperate sounds, but this is swept aside by the storm of her rising anger. Summoning a look that's dripping with despair, Tabitha points at him as she rages: 'How could you? My poor daddy. You were his friend . . .' She slumps to the ground, convulsed with tears.

Harold tightens his grip on the gun and prepares to shoot.

55

Pearl turns the key in the ignition but the Bottle Bank van's engine whines and grinds, refusing to rev back into life. She bashes the steering wheel in a mixture of defiance and despair. 'Dammit, we're totally stuck!'

Teddy and Minty peer back at her like two nervous dormice.

'So, Teddy, maybe get out and push?' suggests Pearl.

'Yes, Teddy, step out and push,' echoes Minty.

'Righto, I get it, message received,' says Teddy, hopping out and heading around the back of the van.

There's a rumble of thunder from across the Downs as it starts raining harder, as though the night is wringing out its darkest laundry on a cosmic washing line far above. He whacks the back of the van, signalling for Pearl to give the engine another try, and leans in with his shoulder, ready to push. The engine gives a cough, the back wheels start spinning in the mud, and then it promptly dies. Pearl whacks the steering wheel in frustration. There is a gentle knock at her window. Teddy is standing there, covered from head to toe in mud from the wheel spin. Pearl winds down her window. The rain is pelting over Teddy's muddy face.

'Jeez, did you fall over?' Teddy shakes his head. 'Are you saying this is my bad?' Teddy nods. 'How could this be my bad? I was just starting the engine, it's not my problem if you don't know where to stand.'

'I was trying to push.'

'Teddy, get inside, you'll catch your death,' suggests Minty.

Pearl tries the engine, but it doesn't even turn over. 'This is not happening,' she moans.

'I'm soaking!' wails Teddy. Pinot barks at them both from the back of the van to get their attention.

Minty turns to Teddy and Pearl. 'Good girl, Pinot. Barclay needs us. She's right, come on, out we get.'

'Damn right, on foot,' says Pearl, galvanised and leaping out of the van followed by Minty and the dog. She gets out her phone and uses the torch. 'Is the lane back that way?'

The three of them peer into the rain across the muddy field in the dark, realising they have completely lost their bearings. Teddy has a rummage in his pocket before pulling out a compass. Minty and Pearl look at him quizzically.

'What? I'm not a caveman. Who leaves home without a compass? Right, if we bear south-east, we should triangulate with the lane, er, yes, this way.'

Led by Teddy's compass, Pearl's torch and Pinot's wagging tail, Minty follows them into the darkness of the deep Sussex night. Pearl offers her her hand across the squelchy field and, after mud has soaked deep into their socks, they find themselves back on the lane heading down towards the vineyard. Teddy is just able to make out a light coming from the winery and points with pride.

'You slayed!' says Pearl, throwing an arm around Teddy who is equally startled and elated, torn between memorising the moment and wondering whether to throw his arm around Pearl, which causes him to freeze with an odd grin.

Before he can shake off his curious expression, the four of them are shocked by a single loud crack: the unmistakable sound of a gunshot slices through the night from the winery at Dandelion Hill.

56

Maurice Le Brocq is lying in a bath crowned with a ludicrous amount of foam. The free-standing bath is rather older and smaller than it ought to be, standing on a raised blood-red carpeted platform in the middle of a rather large and draughty bathroom. The room is wood-panelled and painted in a shade of navy so dark that it closely resembles the apex of the night sky, which clashes with the rather odd carpet, which is threadbare in places and smells of wet wool. There's a small nook of a fireplace in which a low-burning log is already falling to embers and the draught from the chimney is playing with the ash trailing into the grate. From somewhere beneath the foam, Le Brocq plucks a large loofah from the bath rack and holds it up like a shotgun, aiming left and right before he begins scrubbing his back expressionlessly.

On the wall hangs a large dingy portrait of him. It's far too big for the room, with an ornate fading gold frame, and in it Le Brocq is standing in full tweeds with a shotgun broken over his arm and a fallen cohort of pheasants strewn at his feet. Mrs McRae has always thought there's something oddly Tudor about the mood of this image, almost as though in its commissioning Le Brocq is attempting to channel his inner Henry VIII as the confident master of all he surveys. Whenever Mrs McRae sees the portrait, she is always of the opinion that Le Brocq's complexion and the way the paint has bumped over the canvas look regrettably like sausage meat. And not the smooth russet of a fairground hot dog, but rather the pallid innards of a burst Cumberland. Le Brocq has never noticed this; in fact, whenever he sees his favourite painting, he can't help but hum the tune to 'Rule Britannia', which is precisely what he is doing right now.

The moment is shattered by the unmistakable sound of a gunshot coming from down the valley at Dandelion Hill. For a split second Le Brocq is taut as a switchblade before standing perfectly upright, the foam clinging to his naked bottom like spittle from a thumb. 'Mrs McRae!' he bellows. The sound of approaching footsteps gathering pace reaches the other side of the bathroom door from where Mrs McRae asks how she might be of service. 'In precisely seven minutes I shall require full wet-weather gear in readiness to depart: mackintosh, gumboots and my twelve bore.'

'Of course, Mr Le Brocq.'

As Mrs McRae's footsteps recede at speed and Le Brocq steps out of the bath into his long black towelling robe, a tightness pulls across his lips as though an unseen hand is pinching the skin at the back of his head. Is he in pain? Or could this be excitement?

As Mrs McRae places a pair of wellingtons at the door and starts assembling various items of clothing for Mr Le Brocq that are appropriate to the wild weather outside, she swears that she can hear the distant sound of a police siren rising up the lane.

57

A breath of smoke lingers from the muzzle of the pistol in Harold's hand. His eyes are wild with the roiling of pent-up fury, a tsunami of fire defiantly blazing everything in its path. He is holding the pistol above his head and there is a bullet hole in the winery roof where it has passed through, leaving a small circle of infinite darkness. Tabitha is slumped staring up at Harold through reddened eyes, a barely detectable twitch crosses her lips.

Harold turns to Barclay who raises his hands in surrender. 'Put them down, Barclay. How did my father die?'

After a long pause, Barclay lowers his hands and faces Tabitha and Harold with a deeply considered look of sombre focus. 'I am deeply sorrowful to share that your father was murdered.'

'Enough, call the police, Hal, he's done in Delves and it's as clear as day he wanted Dad gone to get his paws on the vineyard,' insists Tabitha.

'Be quiet, Tabitha. Let him speak,' interjects Harold. He nods to Barclay to continue.

'In your father's office, while clearing out his various tides of gubbins and detritus, I came across a bunch of filter pads. The kind that's used for clarifying wine. It occurred to me in the moment that the staining on the top pad was unusual, that it must have been from a spillage or some such. However, there was an unfamiliar scent that, try as I might, I simply could not fathom. It returned to my thoughts day after day and no matter which scent trail I pursued in my lexicon of aromas, I was unable to grasp or glean its origin. And the more I thought of the scent and the colour traced across those filter pads like a faded pathway on a map to nowhere, the less it seemed to me that its origin was traceable.'

'What happened to the pad?' asks Harold.

'Alas, the pad was rubbished and burned too rapidly for further analysis, but this nose never lies and, together with the faded colour, the rustiness of its lost scent haunted my waking hours; a nasal apparition hell-bent on rattling my spirit from my toes to my temples. Metallic. Musty. Flat. And that colour, lifeless yet oddly full of life. When the promiscuity of my thoughts finally settled into a more meditative humour, I sought an answer in every bottle of wine I could open. It was an old Rioja that provided the answer. The lost scent was sanguinous. It was blood.'

'Was it Dad's?' asks Harold.

Barclay solemnly shakes his head. 'There were no wounds found anywhere on your father's body. No. Those two parallel stains came . . . from your palms, Tabitha.'

'Mine? What on earth gives you that idea?'

'Oh, but this is not an idea; no, this, I am deeply saddened to say, is a fact. You forced the wad of filter pads over your father's mouth and nose, choking him in his office until he was unable to breathe and lost consciousness; your own fingernails dug into your palms with such force that blood was drawn. Isn't that right?'

'Absolutely not. There's not a shred of evidence—' begins Tabitha, but Barclay is quick to jump in.

'I left your father in that winery alive as I am. Before turning in, he decided, as was his daily habit, to fill in his notes from the winery that day. But that day, unlike all the other days, they were left unfinished.'

'This is preposterous!' exclaims Tabitha.

'You recall the day I visited the vineyard and found you clearing brambles? I loaned you a pair of driving gloves. Alongside the scrapes from the thorns, I noticed those lesions on your hands, fading but as unmistakable to me as the pink capsule on a bottle of Vieux Château Certan. As with wine, much can be discerned by sight. In this case, the faded cuts from your fingernails the night you suffocated your father into unconsciousness and dumped him in a tank of his own wine to drown.'

'Have you been drinking, Barclay?' sneers Tabitha.

'Let him finish,' says Harold with firmness.

'Surely you don't believe him, Harold? The idea that I would harm Dad is beyond ludicrous. How dare you accept our hospitality only to cook up these poisonous lies against us. From where I'm standing, you meant the same fate for Delves as you did for our father. Pot, kettle, black. Harold, call the police.'

'Yes, the police,' says Harold distantly, still covering Barclay with his pistol.

'Your theory is just that, Barclay. A theory. And you know what I think? I think you killed Dad, always wanting the life of old Victor Crawshaw for yourself, up here on the vineyard. You're the murderer. You. And you're going to pay for it with a very long stretch in prison. Harold, call the police.'

58

The rain is streaming over Teddy's brow and running in rivulets across his mud-soaked body like an involuntary recipe for midnight gravy. Through the deluge, Pinot is romping ahead into the darkness and yapping her way back again, excited at the prospect of such an adventurous walk after nightfall and enthused by such a range of damp, fresh downland scents. Pearl keeps calling the dog back as she gives Minty time to pause and catch her breath. The three of them struggling on towards the faint light of Dandelion Hill's winery resemble castaways in a swamp as the sky's tide continues to surge down on them with the relentlessness of a jilted lover. Teddy and Pearl are both using the torches from their smartphones to guide the way, yet their radiance seems frailer than two candles lost in a waterfall. Exchanging glances, Pearl silently rallies Teddy who responds with a committed nod of assent.

Pinot darts ahead, urging them on with an upbeat bark, disappearing around the corner of the lane past the great swaying beech at the driveway of Greenacres and on down the rutted lane that leads to Dandelion Hill. She picks up the scent of someone familiar and dear to her: Barclay Flint.

Inside the winery, Tabitha is sneering at Barclay. 'Your little theory is just the oafish ramblings of a washed-up drunk. Call the police, Harold!'

'Yes, I will call the police, Tabitha. And I think they'd be most interested to see this footage.' Harold holds up his smartphone and plays the runner duck video filmed spontaneously by Victor's motion-triggered camera. As the film runs on, the runner ducks move aside and a stooped silhouetted figure can be seen heaving and dragging Victor's lifeless body from the house into the winery.

'Is that Dad? Who's that with him? Oh my God, Harold, what is this?'

Harold stares at Tabitha as the footage becomes clearer: in a split second the face of the person dragging Victor Crawshaw's body looks towards the camera where the image freeze-frames. The faintest tear wells in Harold's right eye as he turns the pistol from Barclay onto his own sister. 'It's you, Tabitha.'

Barclay's face changes to concern mixed with relief.

'Now wait a minute, Hal. That's one of those fakes. It's obviously a deepfake, AI from the internet, that's never me – Flint and his cronies must have put this together, you believe me, I would never hurt Dad, just as you would never hurt me. Isn't that right? That's right, isn't it?'

Harold takes a deep breath and purses his lips with a sense of sorrowful resolve. He stiffens and takes a step towards Tabitha.

Before he can speak, Tabitha launches herself at her brother with a terrifying shriek that passes through Barclay's heart like an icicle slicing through mist. Scrabbling to grab Harold's phone, Tabitha's fists fly into Harold's face while he's attempting to repel his sister's ferocious onslaught. Locked in a tussle of tremendous force, a sudden shot rings out, bringing Tabitha and Harold into a shocked embrace. Their eyes meet, Tabitha's brimming with tears while Harold's expression is crystallised with deep disbelief. Tabitha clings to her brother, her knees giving way. Harold falters. At the doorway, Pinot rushes in with a bark with Pearl in hot pursuit followed by Teddy with his smartphone's torch on full beam.

'Stay back!' calls Barclay.

Teddy starts surreptitiously filming with his smartphone as Pearl calls Pinot back and Minty jostles in behind them.

'It's alright now, Barclay, we're here . . .' begins Minty, puffing and blowing with exertion before she takes in the scene and her eyes widen. 'Dear heavens . . .'

Pearl and Teddy exchange startled looks, Barclay gestures for them to stay put and stay calm. Harold shoves Tabitha away and stumbles backwards, a dark stain expanding like a deathly rosette from beneath his shirt. Tabitha is clutching the gun and looks down at her hands and back to Harold, who appears utterly stunned. Tabitha's face hardens and she raises the gun, preparing to fire at Harold for a second time.

Barclay leaps forwards. 'Tabitha don't,' he blurts as Harold staggers backwards and falls into his arms. Gently lowering Harold's fading form next to Mike Delves, Barclay notices that Harold's eyes are swiftly glazing over and his complexion is paler than Camembert. 'Breathe, breathe, Harold,' he calls as Harold's hand falls from clutching the wound at his chest.

With a gasping groan, Harold Crawshaw exhales for the final time.

A profound silence engulfs the winery that seems to emanate from within the walls themselves, a cushion muffling the horror of the moment. Barclay's shocked face is staring down at Harold's lifeless appearance and, much as he is whispering his name, he knows that Harold is dead.

He looks up, aghast. 'He's gone,' he says quietly to Tabitha, who responds by pointing the gun with menace towards him.

'All you had to do was leave my family alone, Flint,' she murmurs as she wipes away a tear and stands over him. 'Get up.'

'Delves needs help, Tabitha.' Barclay gestures to Mike Delves whose breathing is desperately shallow.

'Up!' shouts Tabitha, thrusting the gun into Barclay's temple.

59

Maurice Le Brocq grabs his shotgun and with practised ease loads two cartridges into the chambers. He barely needs to look at the gun, such is the fluidity of his gunmanship as he strides across the wide hall at Greenacres. Faded portraits of distant relatives stare down at him from the walls with an air of judgement and expectancy. Le Brocq's blood is up, piqued by the sound of the gunshot which disturbed his bathtime; he is stimulated and keen, ready to pinpoint the source of the sound. Mrs McRae hands him his waterproofs before standing back as he dons his kit in silence. She notices that he smells of Badedas bubble bath, which is in stark contrast to the stern focus of his mood. She nods at him as he straps on his final gear before opening the hall door to the porch where his wellingtons await.

'Would you like me to come with you, sir?' asks Mrs McRae.

'Best you stay here, Mrs McRae. Who knows what hullabaloo awaits down the valley. Have a hot drink standing by for my return.'

'Bovril, sir?'

'I'll leave the details to you,' says Le Brocq, pulling his green tweed sixpence cap down over his brow. 'Perhaps a crumpet?'

'Aye, I'll be ready, sir. Best of luck.'

With a curt nod, Le Brocq opens Greenacres' front door

revealing a swirling storm of chaotic rain flustering down over the dark Sussex night. He strides out into it, blustered side to side and holding down his cap as he advances through the rising gale. Le Brocq ploughs down the driveway towards the old beech whose branches are being flung in all directions by the howling downpour. Glancing left and right into the darkness, he is in full hunting mode as the light of the porch closes behind him in the distance and Mrs McRae disappears behind the old oak doorway. His mind starts racing with what to expect. A firearm discharged accidentally, nocturnal hunting or even a break-in; whatever caused that shot to ring out, Maurice Le Brocq vows to restore order to this quiet corner of the Sussex countryside – and most importantly, have the culprit answer for the unforgivable disturbance of his weekly bath.

Le Brocq can't help but momentarily dream of Dandelion Hill as his hunting lodge bathed in the golden sunlight of a perfect summer's day. For a split second as he walks, he sees the lane, aglow beneath a perfect blue sky, lined with beaters, gundogs and cheering local children waving League of Rural Affairs pennants as he strides along preparing to take ownership of Dandelion Hill. For some reason, in his imagination everyone is dressed in Victorian-era country attire; there's a hairy farmer and his wife proudly holding a pig on a lead next to a bucolic shepherdess and shepherd standing with a bouffon pink sheep on a powder blue ribbon. In his fantasy, Le Brocq is strolling down the lane carrying an elephant gun with colourful bunting rippling overhead and the sound of a marching brass band behind him as he waves to well-wishers like a dictator at a military parade. A group of milkmaids rush out to offer him a large fruitcake with candles, which he politely waves away. Behind him, Mrs McRae is dressed in the attire of a military attaché, Toby the Labrador obediently padding beside her. For some reason, the dog is wearing a monocle and black leather boots.

Le Brocq's daydreaming is shattered by a large raindrop splatting on the end of his nose. Picking up his pace onto the lane, the squall is corkscrewing down from the sky. From the distant darkness a police siren is rising and faint blue flashing lights are flickering on the horizon. From behind Le Brocq roars the sound of a car engine as a mud-spattered navy Skoda Yeti four-by-four overtakes him before bumping to a stop and blocking his way. DC Oscar Keane, in civilian clothing, leaps out of the passenger seat and approaches Le Brocq through the sheeting rain.

'Evening, Mr Le Brocq, shotgun's gonna have to go.'

'Nonsense, I have my licence.'

'Sir, police business, time to head home.'

'You're not even in uniform.'

'Please, sir, step back.'

'Where's your identification?'

DI Nuria Alpert flings open the driver's door and stands over the car flashing her ID.

'We've already met, Mr Le Brocq, but to refresh your memory, I'm Detective Inspector Nuria Alpert, this is DC Keane. And we'll be taking that gun, sir. Unless you were just deciding to turn around and make your way home?' Nuria stares hard at Le Brocq, who bridles visibly.

'You'll never take my gun,' he says quietly.

Nuria nods to Oscar who grabs Le Brocq's shotgun and tosses it in the boot of the Yeti.

'Home, sir. Now!' says Nuria as she motions for Oscar to get back in the car.

Le Brocq is speechless as the Yeti wheel-spins a light spattering of mud across his body before careering down the lane towards Dandelion Hill. Rooted to the spot, he fumes, a raging incandescence beginning to steam lightly in the rain as he stares after them. One word rises in his mind: *vengeance.*

60

Barclay is getting to his feet and finding his balance, his nervous stomach somersaulting because of Harold's lifeless body at his feet. He is also deeply concerned for the fate of Mike Delves, who looks to be nearing his last breath on the floor of the winery next to Harold. He can't help but turn his gaze towards Delves, and feels a growing frustration at being unable to give the life-saving assistance that's required by a person on the brink of death. Tabitha's eyes are wild and frenzied as she focuses between Barclay to her right and the Bottle Bank gang to her left. She swings the pistol between them, causing Teddy to cower each time it sweeps in his direction. Pearl and Minty stand defiantly while Pinot sits obediently, unsure if this is a game and wondering whether there might be a tasty treat in Barclay's pocket.

Tabitha's mind is racing with a catalogue of thoughts, each one spiking the next one with heightened urgency. With throbbing desperation and cold panic rising in her heart, she ushers Barclay towards the winery door with the pistol.

'Go, over by the others. All of you, move!'

'Tabitha, let's talk this through, stay calm—'

'*Shush!* I'm not being told what to do. I'm sick of it, you hear? This time it's my story, my version, my truth. I found you here, you murdered Delves, took my brother's life and then escaping to the barn, a tragic accident, a fire started, no witnesses, only me, free, no more of other people's ideas infecting me, the endless voices all the time, what happened to my voice? Where's my voice, Barclay?'

'I hear you, Tabitha, don't do this . . .'

'Over there, all of you. If any of you try anything, I'll shoot this windbag stone dead.'

Slowly, Barclay starts moving towards Pearl, Minty and Teddy. Tabitha follows him close behind, pointing the pistol into the soft flesh of his back.

The rain is pelting down on the winery roof, drumming out a rising torrent of chaotic noise. A few holes are letting droplets fall in small puddles on the concrete floor and Barclay spots his walking reflection in one that's disturbed with each new drip. Seeing the droplets, he is struck by an idea. He catches Pearl's eye as she's giving Pinot a reassuring tickle behind the ear.

Pearl whispers to Minty and Teddy to get ready. Barclay slowly leads Tabitha past the fermentation tanks towards his friends and then, with a wizardly flourish, he spins and flings open the large door to one of the tanks, sending a torrent of red wine cascading into Tabitha who loses her footing in the crimson deluge and slips to the floor.

Before Barclay can rally and run, Tabitha twists and aims the gun at the Bottle Bank gang, catching Teddy in her sights. She fires, the bullet passing close by Barclay and heading directly for Teddy's forehead. Pearl leaps in front of him, shoving him back and taking the bullet square in the shoulder.

In a blink Tabitha is back on her feet, a fearsome sight covered in red wine flashing the Glock pistol wildly around. Minty supports Pearl, who is reeling from the pain in her left shoulder, while Teddy gets to his feet, horrified that Pearl's been wounded. Tabitha shrieks at them to move and Barclay helps them support Pearl through the winery door and out into the wild wet night.

At gunpoint, Tabitha marches the Bottle Bank crew across the yard towards the barn.

'Keep moving!' she orders.

From the vineyard, Alpert and Keane's flashlights flick on and Tabitha freezes momentarily, caught in the glare.

'Drop your weapon, we have you surrounded,' calls out DI Alpert.

Oscar Keane looks across at Alpert and mouths, 'Do we?' She shakes her head at him exasperatedly and repeats her command. Police sirens are approaching and blue headlights are flashing at the end of the lane as their back-up begins to arrive. Tabitha thinks for a moment before responding to DI Alpert's instructions by opening fire and grabbing Barclay as her hostage.

'Into the barn, Flint!' screams Tabitha.

Teddy and Minty make a dash towards the vines while supporting Pearl whose face is racked with pain from her shoulder wound. Pinot starts jumping up at them all, concerned that this is not a game she has fully understood how to play.

61

Tom Hurst is sitting on a soft red sofa reading a book on the architecture of Brighton Pavilion in the comfort of his clean modern flat on St Nicholas Lane. The decorations on the walls are from his various travels around the world. A painted tiger mask from Bhutan, a decorated gourd from Indonesia, a striped woven Chilean poncho and various framed photographs of sunrises in exotic corners of the globe. The mood of Tom's home is the sort of ordered domesticity which he hopes invokes the scent of freshly baked bread. Marking the page in his book, he hops to his feet and makes his way to the kitchenette where his tray of dinner is already partially assembled. A tomato salad with salt, pepper and dressing, which he further garnishes with a pork chop hot from the oven. Setting his orange oven gloves aside, he fetches a bottle of non-alcoholic Harvey's Old Ale from the fridge, opens it and carefully puts it on the tray before carrying the tray back to the living room and placing it on his little table. Fastening his napkin around his neck, he is preparing to tuck into his dinner when he picks up the remote control and flickers the telly to life. *Ocean* with David Attenborough begins. Tom picks up his knife and fork. Before he can cut into his pork chop his mobile phone starts ringing from the sofa. Patiently, Tom sets aside his napkin, pauses the TV and amiably makes his way to his telephone.

'Minty! How lovely to hear from you.'

On the other end of the line comes the deafening sound of police sirens amid raised voices and Teddy's voice shouting, 'Where's the ambulance?!'

Tom recoils. 'Minty?' he says. His relief at hearing Minty on the other end of the line is palpable.

'I'm here, Tom, there's been a terrible to-do, I'm at Dandelion Hill, Pearl's been shot . . .'

'Shot? Shot how? An accident?'

'Not an accident, no, it's terrible, Tom, poor Barclay's being held as a hostage in the barn.'

'I'm on my way, Minty.'

'No, dear, you mustn't come, it's too dangerous, the police are here now and I just wanted to say something to you: I'm falling in love with you, so there it is and I just want you to know.' Minty waits as the rain pelts down on her for Tom's response on the other end of the line, but the phone is silent. 'Tom? Can you hear me?'

At home, Tom's eyes are welling and his smile quivers. He briefly punches the air before clearing his throat, his voice wavering. 'I'm the same, Minty. From the first moment we met.'

'This is wonderful news, my dear, now I've got to help Pearl, but just in case anything happens, for the first time in my life I've found something that's even better than ginger cake. And that something is you!'

'Everything's going to be alright, Minty, just be careful, will you?' replies Tom. But Minty is gone, the line is dead.

An ambulance with sirens blaring is drawing to a halt outside the farmhouse at Dandelion Hill, sending flashing lights revolving from the farmhouse to the barn. With further police vehicles arriving, Minty hangs up her call to Tom and helps assist Pearl towards the ambulance. The crew immediately begin attending Pearl with Pinot close by her side and they throw red blankets around Minty and Teddy. DI Alpert is briefing an armed officer beside the vineyard while a cordon of further personnel is fanning out around the barn. From the vineyard, DC Keane is watching the entrance closely for any sign of movement.

Inside the barn the effigy of Mary I is eerily lit by the oblique flashing blue lights of police cars which penetrate some of the old gaps in the walls. The large cache of fireworks at the other end of the ancient building is piled up in the darkness. The roof is pin-holed with tiny gaps and the storm outside is doing its best to get in through the draughty walls and across the uneven old stone floor. Tabitha is holding Barclay at gunpoint, the Glock pointed at his head as she moves him behind the giant effigy, which, it strikes Barclay, does bear a passing resemblance to Pearl.

'I can almost see why Teddy thought it looked like our Pearl, don't you agree?' asks Barclay, trying to mask his fear with a genial dose of charm.

'Nonsense, anyone can see that it's Mary I. Now be quiet,' replies Tabitha peering up at the effigy.

Seizing his chance, Barclay rolls out of her grip and dives for cover towards the fireworks as she fires a shot in his direction. Outside, the police officers duck for cover while DI Nuria Alpert is unmoved by the sound of the gunshot. Fixing her jaw with stern resolve, she begins advancing towards the rickety old barn. Oscar Keane spots Alpert moving and follows her, grabbing a taser from an officer he passes. Inside the barn, hiding behind the large pile of fireworks, Barclay notices there are also a couple of jerrycans of petrol ready for the bonfire on November 5th and realises he may have chosen the most dangerous place to hide in the entire history of concealment.

'Tabitha, may I suggest not shooting at the massive pile of fireworks, I for one am rather keen not to do my impression of a human Catherine wheel this evening.'

'Die, Flint,' comes her chilling reply.

62

Detective Constable Keane is backing up Detective Inspector Alpert as she moves stealthily towards the barn door. Her regular gym routine has kept her in excellent trim and her movements are as fluid and sly as a covert puma. Keane, on the other hand, is cursing as he trips over a large boulder and crashes to the ground, tearing down the twiggy branches of an old vine as he grabs it and fails to keep his balance, spilling the taser into the night. An armed officer clutching an MP5 carbine is following Alpert at speed. Keane picks himself up and pursues, dishevelled and limping from his fall. On arrival at the barn, the armed officer kicks in the door and Alpert dashes inside, taking cover behind a wooden pillar. Tabitha fires a shot towards the doorway which thumps into the wall just beyond Alpert. As the armed officer returns fire from the doorway, Tabitha dives inside the effigy of Mary I for cover. Inside, the effigy is cramped and smells of fresh paint and newly sawn wood. She can see through a couple of holes, which afford her a curtailed view of the barn. She peers left to right and can only make out the armed officer peering out from the doorway, while Nuria Alpert is tucked behind the pillar in the darkness at the other end of the barn.

Barclay is cowering behind the fireworks just as DC Keane arrives at the doorway crouching beneath the armed officer.

'Mr Flint . . .' hisses Oscar in a hoarse whisper.

Barclay is curled up in a ball imagining a cool glass of Provençal rosé on the terrace of a wine bar in southern France. He can see the dewy condensation on the cold bottle of Domaine Tempier Bandol rosé which he is happily hallucinating in a southern French idyll of dappled sunlight. He can even hear the distant sound of a jazz violin playing 'La Mer' on the maritime breeze which is suddenly pierced with the harsh whisper of DC Keane again calling his name.

He emerges from his reverie slowly peering through half-closed eyes at Keane across the barn. Keane beckons and whispers, pointing to the armed officer: 'When she shoots, run to me, OK?'

Barclay is a hot mess of deep breathing and finds himself unable to move or respond to Keane, who is gesticulating forcefully at him to get ready to run to safety. Deep in his pocket, his warm hand grasps the black stone given to him by Victor Crawshaw on the night he died. *Miracles start small*, he remembers Victor telling him as he clutches the round pebble and, hearing a faraway bark from Pinot, he rallies. Seizing command of his mind once more, he prepares to risk his life in exchange for the freedom that waits beyond the barn door.

63

Tabitha is peering out from the effigy, her pistol at the ready. She spots Barclay's generous frame momentarily shift behind the fireworks like a seal rolling over on a rocky beach, as he turns himself towards the doorway. She aims her gun but hesitates as he ducks down from view. In frustration, she bashes her pistol against the structure of the statue.

'Barclay, why did you have to spoil everything? It was bad enough Harold making that Delves poke around. Action had to be taken. That night in the winery, I was there, Flint, I heard what Dad said about leaving the farm to you. He'd have done it, Barclay. Oh, believe you me, he would have gone through with it. Cutting me out of the inheritance was the final straw. Plundering my birthright, running the whole place into the ground, enough, he had to be stopped. He was finished anyway, a washed-up old soak with more love for wildlife than his own flesh and blood. If I hadn't killed him he'd have died of drink soon enough, he wanted to go, can't you see he was so unhappy, I was helping him, the winemaker making himself into wine . . .'

Tabitha lets off a wild shot, DI Alpert nods to Keane as the armed officer opens fire at the effigy. Under the cover of the assault, Keane screams to Barclay to run for the doorway, and clutching his pocket stone for bravery, Barclay rises and picks up momentum as Alpert darts out from behind her pillar. She moves with the speed of a cheetah, grabbing his hand and moving towards the doorway. With a bloodcurdling scream, Tabitha takes one last shot at the armed officer. It flies wide towards a dark green jerrycan filled with petrol. The bullet spins as it hurtles through the air, glinting with the blue flashing lights cast through the gaps in the barn wall by the police vehicles outside. The armed officer pulls Oscar Keane out of the building as Barclay catches Tabitha's eye peering from the effigy and for a split second locks with her gaze. The bullet hits the jerrycan, and it ignites in a shower of flame. As the first of the fireworks begin to pop and ignite, Barclay dives headlong out of the barn door behind Alpert.

Outside, Teddy and Minty look up from nursing Pearl with the ambulance crew to see the inside of the barn glowing. From the driver's cabin of the ambulance, the radio is playing the chorus of Jeff Buckley's 'Lilac Wine', which can be heard faintly beneath the rising crackle of explosions. The police cordon is lit up as flames rush up the walls, climbing towards the deluge of rain crashing down from above. It feels as though the world itself is taking a long deep breath before the entire barn blows sky high in a spectacular display of crimson, magenta, blue, orange and gold. In a glittering display that erupts across the entire night sky as far as Lewes, Brighton, Uckfield and Seaford, the whole cache of Priory Bonfire Society's fireworks for their display on November 5th explodes. Barclay is thrown to the ground by the blast as Tabitha and her dreams to transform the barn into a wedding venue are blown in an instant to ashes.

64

The fireworks over Dandelion Hill thunder for what seems an aeon to Barclay as he considers the colours festooning the sky and slowly gets to his feet peering upwards with DI Alpert and DC Keane by his side. The cacophony of percussive crackles and rhythmic explosions subsume the entire valley in a rising echoing onslaught of cascading eruptions. Brocades, chrysanthemums, crossettes, comets, spinners, palms, peonies, willows, tails, strobes and all manner of fireworks are colliding with one another, illuminating the Sussex sky, while on the valley floor below the barn is engulfed by flames. The vineyards of Dandelion Hill glimmer on their trellises, damp wood and dull metal picking up the reflection of the whistles and screaming eruptions above. In Lewes, lights flick on across the streets as the local population is awoken from its slumbers. Rooks take to the skies from their nests and dogs are barking across town. Elsie Sharpe rolls out of bed and peers open-mouthed up out of her skylight at the fireworks, recognising in a horrified instant that the display is coming from her bonfire society's stash at Dandelion Hill. The sound of her startled expletives are tastefully muffled by the vast coating of explosions.

With one last resounding boom the valley returns to silence, illuminated by the blazing barn, and Barclay Flint begins piecing together the world he once knew which has just been splintered apart by the largest explosion he's ever encountered. And considering he's a Lewesian, the UK's spiritual home of incendiary displays, this is, he reflects, *strong mustard.* Grabbing Alpert and Keane, he leads them directly into the winery.

'Delves might still be alive. When Tabitha found out he was onto her, she tried to suffocate him with argon gas, poor fellow was at death's door, I hope we're not too late . . .'

As Barclay disappears into the winery with Alpert and Keane, Maurice Le Brocq barges down the lane and up towards the ambulance parked at the edge of the police cordon. His face is as inclement as the weather as he marches straight up to a uniformed officer who is urgently calling in the fire brigade.

'What the devil's going on here? Unlicensed fireworks display, it's not even November 5th, I trust you'll be locking up the perpetrators, some of us in this valley are law-abiding citizens trying to uphold the old values of countryside ways. This rabble . . . Are you even listening to me? The cheek of it!' The police officer is holding her phone to her ear and trying to block out Le Brocq's voice with a finger in her other ear while she communicates with the fire brigade. 'How dare you ignore me!'

Minty Jarvis rises from her seat at the back of the ambulance and throws aside her red blanket. She marches across the vineyard, reaches down and picks up the taser lost by Oscar Keane. 'Mister Le Brocq. If you have a complaint to make, let me tell you, go and make it to yourself in the nearest mirror, and while you're looking, try to find the humanity which you lost along the way. There's been murder here tonight, you know, we'll not be hearing about your countryside ways, we'll be healing as best we can and letting these brave people get on with their jobs. Now get out of my sight before I set Pinot here on you.'

Pinot obliges with a low growl and a curl of her lip.

'She is vicious,' says Teddy, before catching a look from Minty and backtracking. 'Not you, Minty, the dog. The dog's vicious.'

Minty turns from Teddy and gives Le Brocq a cold hard stare. She brandishes the taser. Le Brocq's mouth opens and closes like a beached mudskipper, and before he can even muster a response she turns on her heel, handing the taser to Teddy, and climbs back into the ambulance to travel with Pearl to hospital as the paramedic team continues to stabilise her. Le Brocq taps a foot while Teddy and Pinot stare him down and a second ambulance pulls past him up the lane. With as much dignity as he's able to summon up, he holds his head high and makes a swift exit back in the direction of Greenacres, swallowed by the night, muttering as he steps alone into the darkness.

From the winery, Nuria Alpert and Oscar Keane follow Mike Delves as he is stretchered down the steps. He's wearing a transparent oxygen mask, which mists with the faintest breath as he's carried down the yard. A path is cleared as a second ambulance arrives on scene to deliver him straight to hospital. Barclay Flint follows to see Delves lifted into the ambulance with marked tenderness and care. Alpert and Keane turn and face him.

'Got to hand it to you, you had it bang on,' says Nuria, a little out of breath.

'Yeah, we was off the pace. That daughter, what a piece of work,' says Oscar.

'I only wish we'd acted sooner, Barclay,' adds Nuria. Barclay nods amiably with a conciliatory raise of his eyebrows. 'When did you start to suspect she was the killer?' she asks.

Barclay purses his lips and thinks for a moment. 'To me, wine has always presented the tantalising challenge of solving a liquid puzzle. It is so tempting, when presented with a glass, to sniff it, taste it and pronounce judgement on the impressions that it yields. But looking at a wine can reveal its true soul. A red wine with a purple perimeter lapping the edge of the bowl will always be youthful and fruity, full of vim. A rusty hue to reds indicates maturity, savoury flavours and uniquely delicate complexity. The size of the bubbles in your fizz are the footprint of its eminence – the smaller the bubbles, the higher the quality. White wines . . . I could go on, but in answer to your question, it was the cat that first piqued my suspicion.'

'What cat?' asks Oscar.

'Queen Elizabeth, the ginger cat. I first noticed her in the winery the night when Victor disappeared. And every time I saw her after that, she was always close to Tabitha. Just as the scent of a struck match in a wine's aroma always reveals the presence of sulphur compounds, I began drawing a connection between Tabitha and the fate of her father: the lesions on her hands, the filter pads – finally, the footage from the wildlife camera which nearly cost poor Mike Delves his life when he confronted her with it. But it was the cat, at least initially, that stirred my searching. Almost as though she knew something that none of us were prepared to consider even believing. Crime, it seems, is as obliquely nuanced with hidden clues as the wonderful world of wine. And that's the world I intend to return to.'

Nuria shakes her head, impressed. 'I'm almost regretting that I'm teetotal.'

'Still doing your tasting this week?' asks Oscar. And before Nuria can castigate him for an inappropriate question, Barclay claps his hands on Oscar's shoulders.

'My dear chap, that is the whole point. Wine, like life, flows on regardless. And I look forward very much to seeing you downstream for a glass of liquid splendour. And Nuria, I should be delighted, if you ever feel inclined to visit, to show you my burgeoning range of non-alcoholic libations – they are, without question, the new frontier of flavour, with the most inventive and curious profiles, a veritable rainbow of ecstatic wonder.'

'Ha! Maybe, maybe, Barclay Flint, you might just tempt me. We'll be needing you for a debrief at the station. How about you bring a bottle?' calls out Nuria.

Barclay takes his leave with a wave of assent as he approaches Teddy, mud-spattered, dishevelled and shaken. Pinot scuffles up to Barclay with an affectionate whimper and nuzzles into his hand. Teddy hugs Barclay, who fondly embraces the Bottle Bank delivery driver. 'It's alright, Teddy. You're a thoroughly excellent chap.'

'You're not so bad yourself, boss. Pint of Best?'

'Pint of Best,' nods Barclay.

65

The Bottle Bank gleams with the gentle glow of soft lighting caressing its treasury of wine bottles. It's late in Lewes and the streets are empty; the town has returned to slumbering after the explosions earlier on. Not even the rooks are calling, nor the seagulls. The sky is beginning to dry out but the pavements are still bright with the wash of the storm, which is starting to pass away out to sea. Across town, the war memorial keeps a silent vigil over the high street, Harvey's Brewery stands guard like a fortress beside the banks of the River Ouse, and a couple of pigeons are huddling under the eaves of the old bus station, cooing quietly. Barclay Flint is making his way steadily along Priory Street, his gait that of a weary bear returning to its chosen place of hibernation after an arduous trek up the side of a rugged mountain. Beside him, Teddy Olsen is walking stiffly.

As they reach the door of the Bottle Bank, Teddy turns to Barclay. 'Key?'

'Ah, key,' replies Barclay patting his pockets. 'Yes, key,' he repeats, finding nothing but his pocket stone.

'I gave mine to that Constable Keane,' says Teddy. Barclay continues searching his pockets when Teddy notices he is holding a bunch of keys. 'Barclay. What are those in your hand?'

'The keys to the Duke,' replies Barclay.

'And . . .?'

'Teddy, my dear chap, you're quite right, these are also the keys to the Bottle Bank. Perhaps I ought to rechristen it the Haven of Lost Liquors?'

'Just get the door open, Barclay. I could murder a drink.' Teddy bridles at his unthinking use of the word *murder* but Barclay lays a reassuring hand on his arm.

'It's quite alright, Teddy. With the events of this evening I, too, have built up a thirst that could win first prize in a parch contest against the Gobi, Atacama and Sahara deserts all combined.'

With a flourish of his keys, the tinkling door to the shop swings wide open and the two friends heave themselves over the threshold. The familiar scent of wooden crates and open bottles of wine fill both their hearts with comfort and Barclay's footfall lightens to a dancing delight as he approaches the Hot Bottle line-up behind the counter. He surveys it with the pride of a parent reunited with an army of lost children. 'Since the pubs are shut, what takes your fancy, Teddy? Cold white? Comforting red? Suave rosé? Or perhaps the glittering mood boost of a bottle of English fizz?'

'Actually, Barclay, I rather fancy this one,' says Teddy plucking an unmarked bottle of white wine from his jacket. '"Lychees on a pogo stick". Lifted it from the winery before we left.'

Barclay's face flushes with unbridled admiration. 'Teddy, my dear boy, from desperate thunder comes the lightning of inspiration. I shall fetch a chiller jacket and two glasses.'

The bell to the shop door tinkles as Minty helps Pearl over the threshold with Tom.

'Better make that three more,' says Pearl with a weak smile, her arm in a sling.

'Pearl! Shouldn't you be in hospital?' asks Teddy.

'Nah, bullet only winged me, just a graze.'

'She's a brave one,' says Minty proudly.

'You all are,' adds Tom.

Barclay and Teddy move towards the others who all embrace in a deeply felt group hug. Pinot rubs at their legs until Pearl winces with her shoulder being squeezed a little too tightly.

'Alright, break it up,' she says, patting her friends on the back. Teddy cracks open the bottle of Pogo Stick and Barclay fetches his chilling device to wrap around the bottle. Pearl's phone is buzzing; Teddy helps her to lift it from her jacket pocket. Axel's face pops up on the screen calling from Denmark. Pearl answers the video call, 'Hullo, stranger.'

'Hey, Pearl this is me, Axel, I am a little high right now so it's OK to call, right? I mean so late? Maybe it is early? What even is the time?'

'Gone midnight.'

'OK, so if I calculate the question then here in Denmark it must be at least one o' clock in the morning. Man, where did this evening go? I am having too much fun. How's life in lovely Lewes going? Still crazy times or what?' Axel laughs a little too wildly.

'I mean, the usual, I guess. Explosions, sketchy stuff and a bit of wine. Tonight's been wild, though. You'd never believe what just happened.'

'Let me try to guess. It will be a wild goose chase of a guess, but maybe somehow there was a protest that took over the whole town, like so much confetti fired from a confetti cannon that it made a solid rainbow?'

'Yeah, not quite. Look, I'll fill you in but I'm with my mates just now. Call you back?'

'Of course, you can call me any time, you know, I am really so high right now, is my name even Axel? What does "Axel" even mean? Maybe my name is just "Name"? Does that make sense to you?'

'OK, Name, peace out.' With Axel still wittering down the line about his elusive identity, Pearl hangs up. 'Wrong number,' she jokes. The pop of a cork accompanies the gang's gentle ripple of laughter and Barclay pours out a glass for his four friends.

'My dear friends. Through travails untold, to rejoin our camaraderie here in the heart of all things, where this adventure began, let us toast its ending, to Lychees On a Pogo Stick.'

'Lychees On a Pogo Stick,' say Pearl, Teddy, Minty and Tom in assent.

With a large swig, Barclay drains his glass. 'By Jupiter that revives the senses. Good old Victor. A stirring for the spirit, a joy for the tastebuds and a cleansing of the mind.' Pouring himself a second glass, he drains that too. 'I can't hold back, I mustn't, it calls to me, the scent of splendour, élan, *joie de vivre*, the cuckoo of infinite deliciousness . . .'

'Hang on, why a cuckoo, Barclay?' asks Teddy.

'Smuggled unbidden into the nest of my entire being. All that I am is wine and all that wine is . . .'

'Here we go,' says Pearl. Minty taps her glass with a long purple polished fingernail and summons the group to order. 'Before Barclay slips away into his colourful words, I have something to say. More accurately, three questions I would like to ask. And they are all for you, Tom.'

'For me?' he says, his curiosity and delight are equal gentle forces behind the kindness in his eyes. 'I'd better take a sip of Dutch courage!'

'First question. Tom, would you like to continue being my dance partner?'

'Yes I would.'

'And would you like to keep feeding the pigeons whenever we can afford the bird food?'

'Of course!'

'And would you also be my husband?'

'Would I?'

'Well, would you? There's either a yes or a no coming my way, so which one is it to be, then, Tom?'

All eyes are on Tom. Even Pinot looks up at him adoringly. If Pinot's sentiment could be put into language it would be: *surely this guy must have a treat in his pocket if the rest of them are suddenly so interested in him?*

Tom looks down at his shoes and then up and deeply into Minty's eyes. 'Minty. This is my heart's desire.'

With a fond embrace, they kiss and the others cheer and applaud as Barclay empties the last of the Pogo Stick into his glass and rushes to the fridge. 'Celebrations and salutations to this auspicious and happy union. Let us toast with a glass of England's finest bubbly, made by my old friend Peter Hall, a wine of such grace and purity that it would make the moon turn pink with delight should it ever be poured into one of its lucky craters. I give you the English wine of worldwide wonder with the most memorable name of all: Breaky Bottom!'

With a reciprocal cry of 'Breaky Bottom' the five friends raise their glasses and, outside, the windows of the Bottle Bank begin gently misting up with the sudden surge of palpable warmth from within.

66

The front page of the *Sussex Express* is emblazoned with the headline: 'Wine Crime Solved'. Hailing Barclay and his Bottle Bank cohorts as heroes, the papers are delivered to Newhaven and Uckfield, Hailsham and Crowborough, and the story is rolling across the county of the amateur wine sleuth who solved the case of the murdered winemaker. Across the breakfast tables of East Sussex, Barclay Flint is the talk of the moment. On a television set in Tom Hurst's flat, he and Minty are tuned in to the local news on his soft red sofa, each nursing a cup of warm ginger tea. Barclay is in his element as the interviewer asks him, 'Would it be fair to say that the Bottle Bank is the most highly prized asset in Lewes?'

'I wouldn't go that far. Lewes is blessed with a treasury of talent. Who hasn't tasted a pint of Harvey's Best and felt a sense of instant nirvana? I myself would count my friends among the greatest prizes of all, but you know what's most valuable about this indomitable town of ours? Independence. No campaign is too small, no cause too minor. The spirit of Tom Paine, proud Lewesian and Founding Father of America, is alive and well. Together we look to the future and, from this tragic tale, my wishes are simply for a return to the days of wonderful wine and beautiful ideas.'

Showing clips from Teddy's footage of the night at Dandelion Hill, the news continues as Minty and Tom share a gentle kiss and a cuddle.

'Love you,' he says.

'And I love you too. And our new home together. Needs a bit of cheering up, mind you,' says Minty as she peers at the decor of the flat.

A few miles away the sea is lapping up the shingle shore of Brighton beach, hissing and rumbling as it sucks and shoves the pebbles in a never-ending reshuffle. The colours of the shingle are a myriad of pale fudge, grey flint, bony white and russet, all weaving their way into one another under the late autumnal light. It is a clear day and the swell reflects the open sky in flowing breaths along the shore and out into the deep. Just a few paces inland, the city is thrumming with movement, commuters rushing, seagulls on the wing and shops opening their doors to the day. The General Hospital's regimented facade is a mournful shade of cement grey facing the English Channel.

From a high window inside, Mike Delves is peering out over the seaside streets towards the sea, shading his eyes from the light reflecting back from the water. In navy pyjamas and a pale old towelling bathrobe, he pads over to a low chair and takes a seat. Pulling out a pair of glasses, he's slowly casting his eye over the *Sussex Express* story.

Mike reads slowly aloud: 'In a shocking turn of events, local wine merchant Barclay Flint has uncovered the truth behind the grizzly death of winemaker Victor Crawshaw. It has come to light that Tabitha Crawshaw is responsible for her father's murder. Authorities have confirmed that she suffocated Victor before callously disposing of his body in a fermenting tank of Pinot Noir at the family vineyard. The investigation has also unearthed a second chilling revelation: Tabitha is also believed to have been behind the death of her brother, Harold

Crawshaw. In a further dramatic twist, a third murder attempt – targeting houseguest Mike Delves – was narrowly prevented thanks to the quick thinking of Flint himself. The details are still unfolding but this case has shocked the community, leaving many struggling to comprehend the events that have shaken the close-knit town of Lewes to its core. According to witnesses, Tabitha Crawshaw died in a barn fire at Dandelion Hill which set off a store of fireworks in a torrid display seen from Peacehaven to Uckfield . . .'

As he lowers the newspaper he sees Barclay Flint standing in the doorway of his hospital room with a bottle of wine in one hand and a jar of jumbo pickled gherkins in the other.

'I presumed you'd prefer these to a bunch of flowers,' says Barclay with a gentle smile.

'Got that right,' says Delves as Barclay slowly walks in.

'How's the recovery?'

'Fine. Headaches, bit dizzy, out tomorrow.'

'That's good. Look, I'm sorry—'

'Barclay, I was off the pace. And my bad thumping your noggin. No lasting damage?'

'None at all.'

'And thanks. If you hadn't found me . . .'

'You're entirely welcome, Mike.'

'Harold, though . . .'

'Yes, a terrible end. Seems Tabitha had the knack of evading all those closest to her in plain sight. Quite the chameleon.'

'Until I saw that video of her lugging the body, I'd never have believed it.'

'So many clues and yet she snuck by all of us. I wish I'd acted sooner . . .'

'And I should have saved Harry. Never left my oppo behind. Ever.'

'He was trying to save you. And me for that matter.'

'My old mucker's gone.' Mike looks up at Barclay, his eyes a couple of lost pools.

'You are a brave soldier, Mike.'

'Not a brag rag to show for it.'

'Well, I see your bravery. What's next, when you're released from this palace?'

'Not a scooby.'

They sit in an awkward silence for a moment. Mike Delves opens the jar of pickles and offers one to Barclay, who declines. Barclay stares longingly at the bottle of Jayden Ong Yellingbo Syrah which he's brought along, but Mike shows no sign of opening it. The room is sparse, pale and cool. There's a plastic jug of water and an oxygen mask but no real items of comfort. Barclay wishes he'd brought Mike a jigsaw to tackle, but then second-guesses that Mike may not actually be into jigsaws as much as he is. While battling internally over whether Mike could be lured to the joy of the game by the correct subject, perhaps a World War Two gun emplacement or the Charge of the Light Brigade, Mike's phone rings, yoking Barclay's drifting mind back to the hospital room.

'Delves. Yes. I remember, hullo, Mister Le Brocq. I see. That so? How long? I'll stop by. Right. And you.' Mike hangs up the phone. 'Might be staying local. Le Brocq's after a gamekeeper. Seeing as I'm at a loose end, sounds a plan.'

'Up at Greenacres?'

'That's the one.'

'Working for Le Brocq?'

'Yeah, that's the man.'

'And you get on well?'

'He likes guns, I like guns.'

'Well, Mike, that's great news.'

'Something at least. Harry, hard one to take, he was nails. Hard as.'

'It will become less painful with time. Embrace this fresh start, Mike. I'll be down in Lewes whenever you need . . . wine, I suppose.'

'Sell any pickles?'

'We do not, not yet, no.'

'Stock up, mate – got yourself a local customer now.'

As Mike Delves bites into a gherkin, Barclay can't help but smile and begins wondering how to make the crunchiest pickles in the world.

67

A few weeks later autumn and winter are locked in a duet of progressively cooling harmony. Late in the afternoon on November 5th Lewes is eerily calm and potent with tension. The odd banger reverberates off the castle walls as the bonfire societies make their final preparations before proudly marching down the high street in their extraordinary costumes with burning torches held aloft. At this precise moment, anyone walking through the streets feels as though the town is taking a deep breath before plunging headlong into the mayhem of flame. In just a few hours, as darkness veils the town, fireworks and thronging crowds will begin cheering and jeering the effigies as they're carted down the high street to meet their fate in the purging blaze of each society's giant bonfire site. Some of the fires tower into the air, taller than houses; Barclay is always mesmerised by how they keep upright rather than tumbling over the crowds in a destructive inferno of calamitous horror. Elsie Sharpe is darting past the war memorial wearing her navy-and-white diamond check guernsey with a red neckerchief around her neck. She's carrying a bundle of torches down St Nicholas Lane with the air of a furtive burglar returning stolen goods after a sudden change of heart.

She picks up her pace as she passes a small black sign intricately calligraphed in gold with the name A. M. SOLICITORS hanging over a neat oak doorway. An elderly gentleman with long flowing grey hair is locking up the front door with an elegant bunch of keys on a large oval ring. It would look like a jailor's ring of keys were it not for the prime condition of the metalwork and the elegance of the gentleman's stout winter garb. He meets the world with a Dickensian sense of élan; grey mutton chops, a flowing black suit with the air of academic robes, a brown leather documents folder and black polished shoes with neat golden side buckles. As he sets off after Elsie Sharpe in the direction of Southover, the elderly gentleman's heels click rhythmically down the hill, his metal heel protectors ringing out on the tarmac with every step.

Elsie disappears into the maze of Lewesian twittens and the senior gentleman in his striking garb makes quick progress across the railway bridge, rooks cawing and swooping overhead. With impressive speed, he arrives in no time at all outside the glimmering window of the Bottle Bank. The door tinkles open and he steps inside, clearing his throat. He finds himself surrounded by a world of wine bottles and pauses a moment to take it all in. Barclay is behind the counter, slouched over his new jigsaw of Lewes Castle.

'Mr Barclay Flint?' enquires the gentleman, his voice a tremolo singsong somewhere between a clarinet and a recorder.

'Greetings. Yes, indeed, I am he and he is me. At your service. May I assist you in plucking the finest wines available to humanity from my shelf into your glass?'

'Most kind, but I am here on a matter of some delicacy. My name is Avery Moss.'

'Moss? The solicitor? Mr Moss, I confess I have been meaning to return your telephone calls, my apologies, you must think me the rudest person since Rudolph the Rude, high prince of rudery.'

'Not in the least, Mister Flint. I understand only too well that these past days have been, to say the least, extraordinary for you and your staff. Now, then, my purpose, if you don't mind . . .'

Avery approaches the counter with the clipped formality of a general approaching the seat of a captain in a mess hall to deliver immediate instructions for battle. Opposite Barclay, he lays his document folder adjacent to the jigsaw and plucks out a sheaf of closely bound documents and an ivory envelope in thick laid vellum addressed to Barclay. The calligraphy is so immaculate that it would not have surprised Barclay to learn that it had been written by the ghost of Leonardo da Vinci using ink dipped from the mythical Well of Exactitude. 'Here is a letter for your kind attention, Mr Flint. Thought we'd lost it for a while, but here it is, safe and sound.'

Barclay takes the envelope and sniffs it, instantly analysing the aromas in his mind. *No perfume, sealed the old-fashioned way with moistened glue rather than a peel off and stick . . .* He notices Avery Moss is staring at him. 'Old habit, this nose never lies,' he explains, patting it with his forefinger.

Carefully opening the envelope he is holding in his thumb and forefinger with the delicate powerful flourish of a vet removing an eyelash from a hippo, Barclay lifts out the letter. With great ceremony and respect for the sheer weight of the paper, he unfurls the carefully folded handwritten document and begins to read. At first, his face remains, as it always is, softly good-natured with a few subtle creases and folds that gently roll with the movements of his rippling brow. But suddenly his face hardens and he rereads a certain passage over and over again, blinking in surprise. His eyes rise to meet Avery's. 'Sole beneficiary?' he says.

'Sole beneficiary,' nods Avery Moss with practised solemnity.

'Of Dandelion Hill?'

'The vineyard, farm, land and property associated with its title and deeds. All yours, as per the wishes of my client, the late Mr Victor Crawshaw, in the event of his children passing away without heirs of their own. I shall leave a copy of the will and various documents for you to digest and sign in your own time. I should also add that the substantial life insurance policy taken out by the late Mr Crawshaw has also been approved.'

'Substantial?'

'Indeed, most substantial. More than double the outstanding mortgage on the property, in point of fact. The policy had all but been forgotten in my files, but there we are, the details are all in these papers. My congratulations, Mr Flint. According to this last will and testament, you are now sole proprietor of Dandelion Hill as well as a rather ample nest egg. Enjoy the fireworks, good day.'

Avery folds up his documents case and before Barclay can process what has just happened, let alone offer a glass of something special to mark the occasion, the elderly solicitor's heels are clicking away beneath the tinkling doorway of the Bottle Bank and he is sweeping away into the falling Lewesian night.

Barclay flumps into a chair as Minty huffs down the stairs and into the shop. His eyes are rapidly glazing over, as though his very spirit is escaping through a vent in his mind. Minty approaches the counter and rests both hands while peering over at Barclay.

'Hmm. Pearl!' she calls out.

Pearl hurries from the storeroom followed by Teddy wearing his Priory guernsey and munching on a slice of hot sourdough toast thickly layered with melted butter and cold houmous from the fridge.

'Oh, jeez, has the boss had a stroke?' asks Pearl rushing over and holding Barclay's eyes open. 'Barclay? Barclay! Teddy, get the sherry.'

Teddy tosses his toast down on the counter and plucks a cold bottle of Corrales Fino from the fridge. He rapidly plucks out the cork and pours a large measure into a white wine glass. Handing it to Pearl, she wafts it under Barclay's nose like smelling salts. Pinot wanders in, her paws tapping on the wooden floor, and peers up at Teddy's toast which is precariously balancing over the edge of the counter.

'Easy, Barclay, easy, you hearing me? It's Pearl. You in there, boss?'

Barclay's eyes steadily return to focus and he peers good-naturedly at Pearl. 'You're here too! How nice.'

Teddy picks up the letter and looks up at Pearl and Minty.

'Holy moley. Er, high score alert, if this is correct, the boss just inherited Dandelion Hill.'

Pearl and Minty both swivel their gaze to lock onto Teddy. Pearl snatches the letter and reads before handing it to Minty.

Minty's face breaks out into a lively grin. 'Barclay! Victor left you his beautiful vineyard!'

'And the farm,' says Pearl.

Teddy's mouth is open as they wait for Barclay to respond. Barclay slowly rises to his feet and drains the glass of sherry.

'Invigorating as the ocean, refreshing as the Arctic. Excellent.'

As he bangs his glass back down on the counter, the impact dislodges Teddy's toast which falls into Pinot's mouth. Unseen, she scurries to her bed to feast on her toasty boon. Outside the shop, a loud rumbling is heard as the Priory Bonfire Society begin parading down the street dragging burning tar barrels with bangers flying in all directions. As the marchers parade past in blue-and-white diamond check guernseys to the beat of their drummers, Barclay picks up the bottle of sherry and pours a round for his friends.

'Tonight, we mourn Victor as we celebrate his generosity. Let the tragic events at Dandelion Hill plant the seeds of hope in our hearts to share in one another's fortunes – and misfortunes – with alacrity and vim. Tomorrow, and for the rest of our lives, let us devote ourselves to one single purpose, my friends: the joy of wine.'

'The joy of wine!' cry the others as they raise their glasses in a toast just as an extraordinarily loud banger shakes the windows as it detonates outside the door. The high street procession is just beginning. Above Lewes Castle the sky is glowing red with the smoke and fire of the procession carving its way through the town accompanied by a cacophony of jubilant marching music. Toddlers wearing ear defenders dressed in bonfire guernseys are carried on the shoulders of their parents. For this one night of the year the cafe workers, bank tellers, record shop owners, baristas, hairdressers, florists, publicans, musicians, influencers and dancers stride the streets of Lewes in time to the beat of marshal drumming.

Teddy leads Pearl, Minty and Barclay out across town to join the festivities, tucking Pinot safely in bed to sleep through the night. As they thread their way into the crowd and move steadily up towards the high street, they hear the cheers erupting as the first effigy of the night is slowly carted down. Squeezing to the front of the crowd opposite the law courts, Barclay can just about make out the shape of it through the haze of smoke coming down with the parade. Coombe Bonfire Society are marching in their orange knitted jumpers with violet lightning bolts, dancing and moving to the drumming of their parade leaders. The parade is a rampage of runaway noises, the crackle of rookies peppering the air and the crowds either side of the high street jostling for a glimpse of the first effigy of the night.

In the thick of the parade is young Eric Webster carrying a burning torch alongside his bonfire buddies as the giant effigy finally hoves into view. As it comes closer, the group in the parade leading the effigy can be seen all dressed up for shooting in the countryside. They are carrying a load of League of Rural Affairs signs and livery.

Teddy screws up his eyes. 'Are those banners all in Welsh?'

Pearl and Minty catch Barclay's astonished face as he recognises the massive statue of Maurice Le Brocq, dressed in country tweeds and bent forward under a League of Rural Affairs banner. He is wearing an expression of stunned surprise while being blasted from behind by a pheasant wielding a cannon. As the Coombe parade passes, the Priory parade passes by and Teddy runs to join them, waving goodbye to his friends. Elsie Sharpe greets him like a long-lost brother and Teddy picks up a burning torch, joining the ranks of marchers down the high street. Behind them, dragging slowly and roundly jeered by the crowd, is a newly built giant effigy of Mary I. Minty and Barclay exchange glances as they peer at Pearl, who seems completely oblivious to the striking similarity the effigy bears to her own likeness.

'Almost certainly a coincidence,' winks Barclay to Minty.

Above the town, the first firework blasts in celebratory defiance, igniting the night; the castle ramparts are reverberating beneath a halo of smoke and the memories of centuries are roused for a moment from the slumbering silent brickwork of this ancient Sussex town.

68

A few days later Barclay is surveying the ashen remains of the old barn up at Dandelion Hill. It stands in ruins, the walls, around waist height, charred and blackened after the explosion and fire. The old stone floor is scorched and a family of voles have already set up camp in one of the cracks in the floor.

He peers around the vineyard. The vines are bound to their trellises ready to be pruned in a few months, after which their twig-like demeanour will burst forth once more into lush green vegetation. Barclay spots a pair of runner ducks moving dutifully through a row of vines. *The snail police*, he says to himself. With a few shrubs and trees already growing among the vines, he resolves to plant more in a bid to diversify and strengthen the ecosystem. If he's going to continue making wine at Dandelion Hill, he pledges to honour the memory of Victor Crawshaw in his methods. A wildflower haven for insects, mixed farming and every unique wine he makes to be named after someone dear to him. Perhaps he'll call his first wine 'Victor'. Either way, he resolves to use more of the old Sussex words in his vocabulary and rehearses saying *boffle* repeatedly with a different nuance each time as he continues poking around the vineyard with the wind whiffling gently over his new realm.

Up on the hillside next to a small oak marking Victor's grave are two further saplings where Harold and the remains of Tabitha are laid to rest. Barclay can't help but reflect on the tragic irony of Harold's burial plot coming to fruition with his own close family. The vineyard stretches out beneath Dandelion Hill bathed in golden winter light as the frost begins knitting its fine weave of silver brocade over the branches and trellises. The runner ducks are further off now as they continue foraging through the vineyard. Queen Elizabeth approaches Barclay and weaves around his legs, purring intently.

'Queen Elizabeth. How lovely. Shall we begin?'

Followed by the cat, Barclay weaves towards the Duke which is parked outside the farmhouse. Opening the boot, he carries his first box of possessions inside. The house is strangely bare, stripped of the previous inhabitants and freshly painted in bright colours and warm tones. With plush new carpets and a fire already burning in the hearth, Barclay's wine fridge stands in pride of place in the kitchen with his personal cellar all being kept at the correct temperature in a regiment of perfect preservation. On the table, neatly piled, are Victor Crawshaw's old notebooks. Barclay gives them an affectionate pat as he strolls out through the farm door.

Striding inquisitively over to one of the large old sheds, he prises open the door. Inside, it is empty except for a few grass clippings piled next to an old lawnmower in the corner and a old can of oil. Taking a deep breath, Barclay is struck by an idea and gently hops into the Duke, reversing steadily into the shed. Queen Elizabeth hops onto the passenger seat, purring and nuzzling her way onto his lap.

'Welcome to the Dukedom,' he says, giving her a stroke, which produces a friendly *miaow* as she stands up and nuzzles his cheeks with her whiskers. 'We wunt be druv,' he whispers.

Down in Lewes, Minty is setting up her new nest at Tom's place while Teddy Olsen is moving into her former flat above the Bottle Bank. The walls he's already decorated with numerous framed photographs of his favourite moths: an Emperor Moth with its striking eye-patterned wings to ward off predators; a large brown Privet Hawk Moth with pink and black banded hindwings; a Scarlet Tiger Moth with its glossy black and red markings with yellow and white dots; and the show-stopping Elephant Hawk-moth with its tropical olive green and bright pink display of wild colour. He opens his front door to find Pearl emerging from Barclay's old flat opposite. Pinot bounds over and gives him a lick.

'How's the new gaff?' asks Pearl.

'Ten out of ten. Yours?'

'Getting there. Not sure what's Barclay's been up to but the whole place smells like essence of petunia.'

'Sure that's not just you?'

'Very funny. All set?' asks Pearl.

'One hundred per cent ready,' replies Teddy as they make their way downstairs to the Bottle Bank. The shop is its usual twinkly self, decorated with a joyfully colourful selection of twinkling Christmas lights and endless tinsel. Teddy unlocks the door and surveys the scene out in the street. 'All quiet,' he says. Behind the counter next to Barclay's selection of Hot Bottles is a newly curated selection of Pearl's Cool Bottles and across the shelves round green labels indicate the provenance and environmental credentials of each wine carefully written in Pearl's handwriting. The doorbell tinkles and Pearl looks up, ready to greet the first customer of the day.

'Welcome to the Bottle Bank,' she grins.

Epilogue

The memories of winter are long dissolved into the gorgeous green endless shades of summer. Across the Downs, the skylarks are rioting in the sky with a cavalcade of exuberant song, butterflies meander through the tall grass and returning swallows are dipping over the dew ponds. A gentle breeze with the warmth of the land tucked into its breath is teasing life out from the quietest corners of the land. Lewes is murmuring with the jollity of day-trippers visiting for antiques, sightseeing and sunny pub gardens. The seagulls arch over the town while the rooks settle down to their nesting and every bonfire guernsey is neatly folded away at the bottom of a drawer, November 5th's explosive antics a bold memory locked into the stones and bones of this curious town with its wealthy hoard of secrets and ghosts.

Greenacres is covered with lavish ivy creeping up its walls, and deep inside his shaded drawing room, Maurice Le Brocq is waiting impatiently for the shooting season to begin again. Agitatedly, he is drawing up a list of ways to turf Barclay Flint off the property at Dandelion Hill and claim it once and for all for himself:

1. *Buy Flint out.*
2. *Weaponise wine against him.*
3. *Deploy Delves.*

He is underlining Delves multiple times with such force that his pen is scratching through the paper when a large bumblebee dozily knocks into the window. The sound distracts Le Brocq and he is suddenly struck by an idea. His face begins clenching with intrigue as a sly plot starts tightening the knot of his mind.

Outdoors, Mrs McRae is busying herself in her favourite place of the summertime, the vegetable garden. A small keen-eyed robin is keeping her company, perching on her garden fork whenever she takes a rest. She pours herself a glass of homemade elderflower cordial from an iced glass jug and decides to name the robin Leo after her great-uncle and the happy memories she treasures from her days growing up in Ullapool. Mrs McRae smiles as a large bumblebee buzzes right past her and makes its way sonorously down the valley.

The bumblebee wends its way past the old beech tree towards Dandelion Hill from where Barclay Flint, dressed in a rust-coloured linen suit with a yellow floral shirt, is admiring the view. He stares out over the wildflower meadow sown by Victor Crawshaw the previous autumn. It is happily blooming in a kaleidoscope of colour with bumblebees and butterflies feeding and merrily pollinating their way around every flower. Barclay reflects that the seed scattered by Victor Crawshaw on Maurice Le Brocq's land is a fitting tribute to his affection for the nidgets. Barclay turns back to the ruins of the old barn decorated with bouquets of wildflowers. He revels in the riot of cow parsley fringing the vineyards, which, he muses, are *blooming in a display so fecund as to make the world feel as festive as a bridal boutique.* As Barclay rounds the corner of the barn, the wedding guests are settling into their seats and Tom, suited in his favourite fuchsia tracksuit, is standing nervously in front of them with Pinot by his side wearing two rings on a green ribbon around her neck. Barclay makes his way to the front and stands in the middle with a wink to Tom. 'All set?' he asks.

'Can't wait,' replies Tom with a glimmering smile as he checks the orange rose in his buttonhole. Barclay gives the nod to Teddy who presses 'play' on his stereo which begins playing The Beatles' 'Here, There and Everywhere' as Minty Jarvis emerges at the other end of the barn's open ruins accompanied by Pearl. Minty is dressed in a fabulous dark purple ball gown with a smile so wide it reaches across the whole valley. As Minty glows, Pearl too is resplendent in a sparkling golden jumpsuit of such delight that she resonates perfectly with the bride's dazzling aura. Behind them, innumerable runner ducks are waddling up the aisle as the assembled guests dab tears and inhale with outright joy.

As Barclay begins the ceremony, he succinctly celebrates the blossoming of love from his little lavish world of wine and supervises their vows with the warm sincerity of a summertime Santa. The rings are retrieved from Pinot's ribbon collar and exchanged with fidelity. At the close Minty and Tom exchange a kiss, marking the beginning of the festivities with an erupting cheer from friends and family. With champagne flutes tinkling, English Pét-Nat frothing and glimmering in fizzy spirals, finger food of the finest order is being served on silver platters and the guests are awash with sheer delight.

Barclay taps the stem of his glass and calls the assembly to order as a flying insect buzzes a little too closely to his open mouth. He pulls out his speech written on cue cards before discarding it on the table. Pearl and Teddy share a silent moment of anxious apprehension. Barclay takes a deep breath.

'My dear friends. I shall speak from the heart. The fragrance of adoration is sighing over my cheeks. I have just narrowly avoided becoming a mausoleum for a fly and love rules the day, two great causes for celebration. Minty and Tom, we are all enthralled by your commitment to be bound to one another's days and the delight you have unleashed upon us will fringe our hearts forever with glittering delight. May the tragic events of last year finally settle into the peace of this altogether magical place. This little corner of Sussex is emblematic as a place where life's endless repurposing is laid bare for us all: a place reminding us that our bodies are but seeds to be planted back into nature; a joyful wedding bringing two lives together as one; and, more widely, a haven for wildlife and indeed equal rights for all beings, from trees to mushrooms' microscopic filaments. Three worthy legacies to furnish the happy future of Dandelion Hill, rejuvenation, love and togetherness, forged into this fresh moment where we dedicate ourselves to the enduring tenderness between Minty and Tom. Now, the greatest treat of all is, of course, opening and sharing a bottle of wine. English wine at that. And Dandelion Hill to be specific. But even the greatness of wine can feel diminished, somewhat empty, without the crucial additional ingredient of good company and great cheer – which today are happily flowing like tributaries into a charging torrent of unstoppable glee. And so, my dear friends, as one, as we raise our glasses to Minty and Tom's special bond, let our toast today be a simple one: to love!'

The assembly rises to their feet with glasses raised 'to love'. And with that begins Minty and Tom's first dance with Teddy pressing 'play' on his stereo. As Arrow's 'Hot-Hot-Hot' begins belting out across the scene, Teddy is peering around for a glimpse of Pearl; in her glittering jumpsuit, she is beginning to dance. With an exhalation and a gentle smile, Teddy's face relaxes for the first time in months and he slowly walks towards the gathering circle of well-wishers. In the centre, Minty and Tom begin their exuberant frolicking, with Barclay the first to break ranks and join their dancing with a cacophony of joyful laughter. One by one, every spirit gathered at Dandelion Hill joins in the merry twirl of bodies surrounded by vineyards teeming with life.

Rising over this bucolic idyll, skylarks, seagulls and swallows proliferate while myriad insects flourish through the colourful meadows below. This splendid Sussex day broadens into an infinitely golden moment and a joyful spell is cast over the green scoops and chalk pits of England's South Downs.

Acknowledgements

Thanks to www.sussexhistory.co.uk for the free online *Dictionary of the Sussex Dialect* originally published by Farncombe & Co. of Lewes *circa* 1875.

With thanks to Rachel Mills, Jade Chandler, Jocasta Hamilton, Will Smith, Ellie James, Dave Lamb, Amanda Ross, Nick Ostler, James Wood, Tom Parker-Bowles, Toby Huckerby, Sarah Thomas, Caroline Westmore, Hilary Hammond, Carrie Hutchison, Sarah Arratoon, Alex Haywood, Alice Herbert, Charlie Tonks, Kyla Dean, Megan Schaffer, Natasha Weninger-Kong, Dominic Smith, Sinead White, Claudine Sagoe, Lucy Scholes, Sara Mahon, Amanda Jones, Laurence Cole, Peter Hall, Tamra Kelly-Washington, and every winemaker in the world, especially those who appear in this book.

To my family with thanks for their support throughout, Sophie, Ruby and Lily, you all have perpetual access to the wine cellar of my heart.

List of Wines

Domaine Georges Vernay, Coteau de Vernon Condrieu
Château Grand-Puy-Lacoste 2016
English Pét-Nat
Sadie Family Wines, Palladius
Hatzidakis Assyrtiko de Mylos 'Vieilles Vignes' 2017, Santorini
Neudorf 'Home Block' Moutere Chardonnay
Hoffmann & Rathbone Blanc de Blancs
English Bacchus
Austrian Grüner Veltliner
Alain Graillot Crozes-Hermitage Rouge 2023
Château Pichon-Baron 2009
Tio Pepe Fino 'En Rama'
Contino Gran Reserva Rioja 2011
Bodegas Hidalgo, 'Pastrana' Pasada Manzanilla, Single Vineyard
Soalheiro Alvarinho (Classico)
Domaine Jean-Marc Burgaud, Morgon 'Côte du Py'
Danbury Ridge Pinot Noir
Westwell Pelegrim NV
Monemvasia Winery, Monemvasia-Malvasia, Vin Liastos
Quinta Do Noval Colheita Tawny Port
Gaia Wild Ferment Greek Assyrtiko, Santorini
Seyssuel Sotanum 2020, Collines Rhodaniennes, Les Vins de Vienne
Hermitage 40-year-old Grande Champagne Cognac
Vieux Château Certan

Domaine Tempier Bandol Rosé
Breaky Bottom, Sussex
Jayden Ong, One Block Syrah 'Yellingbo'
Fino Vina Corrales

